Death Of The Master Builder

Love, Envy, and the Struggle to Raise the Greatest Cathedral of the Italian Renaissance

By Mark E. Fisher

Extraordinary Tales

Publishing

Death Of The Master Builder By Mark E. Fisher

Extraordinary Tales Publishing
P.O. Box 6196
Rochester, MN 55903

First Extraordinary Tales edition May 2021

Print Book ISBN: 978-1-950235-10-0
EBook ISBN: 978-1-950235-09-4

Cover art by Jenny Q at Historical Fiction Book Covers
Interior Design by BookNook.biz

Available in print from your local bookstore or from Amazon.

For more information about this and the author's other books visit:
MarkFisherAuthor.com

Library of Congress Cataloging-in-Publication Data:
Fisher, Mark E.
Death Of The Master Buildcer / Mark E. Fisher 1st ed.

Printed in the United States of America

CONTENTS

Cast Of Characters (By Order Of Appearance) vii

Prologue ~ July 1456 xi

Part I ~ The Masters of Their Trades 1

 Chapter 1 ~ The Lord Of Colpena ~ March 1469 3

 Chapter 2 ~ The Proposition 14

 Chapter 3 ~ The Architect ~ April 1469 24

 Chapter 4 ~ Jacopo Passero 33

 Chapter 5 ~ The Tower 37

 Chapter 6 ~ The Site 44

 Chapter 7 ~ Plans 48

 Chapter 8 ~ A Florentine Wedding ~ June 1469 53

 Chapter 9 ~ The Signoria 62

 Chapter 10 ~ A Surprise Visit ~ July 1469 66

 Chapter 11 ~ The Building Committee 71

 Chapter 12 ~ The Contract 78

 Chapter 13 ~ The Florentine Stone Master ~ August 1469 81

 Chapter 14 ~ The Debtor 87

 Chapter 15 ~ The Roman Carpenter 90

 Chapter 16 ~ Carrara 97

 Chapter 17 ~ The Final Master ~ September 1469 105

 Chapter 18 ~ Amadeo's Grand Welcome 109

 Chapter 19 ~ Aldo's Plan ~ November 1469 113

Part II ~ La Cattedrale del Figlio sul Mare 119

 Chapter 20 ~ The Ceremony ~ April 1470 121

 Chapter 21 ~ Side Trips ~ August 1470 128

 Chapter 22 ~ A Night Of Misfortune ~ June 1472 136

 Chapter 23 ~ The Reception ~ August 1472 145

 Chapter 24 ~ Troubling News ~ July 1475 150

 Chapter 25 ~ A Difference Of Opinion ~ December 1475 156

 Chapter 26 ~ A Disastrous Affair ~ April 1476 163

Chapter 27 ~ For The Least Of These   169
Chapter 28 ~ The Scultori ~ June 1476   174
Chapter 29 ~ Murder In Florence ~ April 1478   179
Chapter 30 ~ Progress ~ August 1478   189
Chapter 31 ~ Account Troubles ~ November 1478   193
Chapter 32 ~ The Dwarves ~ December 1478   199
Chapter 33 ~ A Season Of Discontent ~ March 1479   204
Chapter 34 ~ Simona ~ November 1479   212
Chapter 35 ~ The Ox-Hoist ~ November 1480   219
Chapter 36 ~ The Civil Dungeon   222
Chapter 37 ~ A Bad Vintage ~ January 1482   224
Chapter 38 ~ Ferata's Relics ~ June 1482   231
Chapter 39 ~ The Voyage ~ October 1482   236
Chapter 40 ~ Recovery ~ November 1482   241
Chapter 41 ~ Charges ~ April 1486   245
Chapter 42 ~ In The Palazzo Of Il Magnifico ~ June 1489   250
Chapter 43 ~ Of Marble And Glass   256
Chapter 44 ~ Savonarola   261
Chapter 45 ~ The Beggar   265
Chapter 46 ~ A Summer Evening ~ August 1491   273
Chapter 47 ~ The End Of An Ally ~ May 1492   279
Chapter 48 ~ The Attack ~ November 1494   283
Chapter 49 ~ Censured ~ June 1495   293
Chapter 50 ~ Michelangelo Buonarroti ~ April-December 1497   299
Chapter 51 ~ The Dome Ceremony ~ October 1506   304
Chapter 52 ~ The Fortunes Of Luck ~ October 1508   308
Chapter 53 ~ Friends And Lovers ~ April 1509   315

Part III ~ The Death Of The Master Builder   321
Chapter 54 ~ A Belated Revenge ~ October 1512   323
Chapter 55 ~ Consequences ~ November 1512   330
Chapter 56 ~ Downfall ~ March 1513   334
Chapter 57 ~ The Courtesan ~ April 1513   338
Chapter 58 ~ The Final Frescoes   343
Chapter 59 ~ Aldo's Decision ~ July 1513   348

Chapter 60 ~ Pretrial Maneuvers ~ September 1513   353
Chapter 61 ~ The Inquisition   359
Chapter 62 ~ The Dedication Ceremony   365
Chapter 63 ~ Last Visitors   369
Chapter 64 ~ The Events In The Piazza   374

Epilogue ~ June 1521   383
Author's Notes   387
Mark's Books   393
Glossary   395

CAST OF CHARACTERS

(BY ORDER OF APPEARANCE)

- Amadeo Puccini—Young architect and apprentice.
- Leon Battista Alberti*—Painter, author, philosopher, and architect. The quintessential Renaissance man.
- Dario Rossi—Gonfaloniere and leader of Colpena's Signoria, wealthiest man in the city, and majority owner of the Rossi Bank and Rossi Shipping and Transport.
- Delfina Costa—Wife of Arturo Costa, a spice merchant in trouble for his gambling debts.
- Grazziano Delucci—Dario's snide, middle-aged servant.
- Aldo Rossi—Dario's cousin and part owner of the Rossi bank and shipping company.
- Jacopo Passero—Dario's hired tough who'll do anything for money.
- Emilio Gonzaga—Overweight Spanish cardinal whose brother married into Italian nobility, securing him a cardinalate in Tuscany.
- Rinaldi Ferata—Bishop newly assigned to Colpena whose duomo is being constructed; a member of the building committee.
- Simona Mancini—Beautiful, nineteen-year-old daughter of Callisto Mancini.
- Callisto Mancini—A member of Colpena's Signoria whose country estate Amadeo stops at.
- Luigi—Prison tower guard.
- Skender—Thirteen-year-old Rumanian slave boy given to Amadeo by Dario as a houseboy and cook.
- Lorenzo de' Medici*—Wealthy, unofficial ruler of Florence; patron of sculptors, artists, and poets.
- Enzio Borroni—Wealthy member of Colpena's Signoria and Dario's archrival.
- Rocco Marino—Member of Colpena's Signoria from whom Dario bought Acque Salutari, the spa with the alum mine.

- Fabiano Trentino—Beak-nosed Fabiano sits on the Signoria and becomes treasurer of the building committee.
- Basilio Bramante—Half-brother of Donato Bramante* of Urbino, he's the architect of a years-long project to bring water up from beneath the city. Chief rival to and critic of Amadeo's plans to build the duomo.
- Vittorio Rivera—Master stonecutter and lodge master for the duomo.
- Umberto Sabbatini—Tall speaker for Vittorio; the man who explains Vittorio's and Amadeo's plans to the workers.
- Bonifacio—A baker whose debts to the Rossi Bank land him in debtors' prison.
- Bernardo Pugliesi—A former shipbuilder and carpenter skilled at making lifting machines whom Amadeo tries to convince to become his master carpenter.
- Damiano De Luca—Master mason, often difficult to work with.
- Tiziana Lombardo—Slim, black-haired beauty; daughter of Nicola Lombardo in Carrara.
- Nicola Lombardo—A quarrymaster with rights to cut bardiglio marble in the mountains above Carrara.
- Letizia Udinesi—Dario's out-of-wedlock daughter whom he calls his niece.
- Savina Udinesi—Former prostitute and Letizia's mother with whom Dario does not get along.
- Baldassare Fanucci—A condottiere that Dario hires to bring his mercenary army to protect Colpena.
- Elnora Rossi—Aldo's wife.
- Desideria Rossi—Aldo's thirteen-year-old daughter.
- Marcello Esposito—A wool merchant and member of Colpena's Signoria.
- Michelangelo Buonarroti*—Master Florentine sculptor and fresco painter.
- Piero de' Medici*—Lorenzo's father and patron of the arts.
- Piero de' Medici*—Lorenzo's disagreeable son of the same name as Lorenzo's father.
- Gervasio Fontana—Amadeo's first Florentine glass master.

- Elmo Siciliano—Amadeo's second Florentine glass master.
- Savonarola*—Fiery preacher who rails against the hedonism and corruption endemic in the Italian leadership and the Church.
- Bettino Scutari—Dario's emissary, ambassador, and spy in Florence.
- Maria—Skender's young wife.
- Cleto Violante—Merchant sea captain who turns to piracy.
- Rifat Basara—Arabian spice trader, seller of religious relics.
- Ulisse Rua—Cardinal Gonzaga's Grand Inquisitor.
- Raul—Head guard of the civil dungeon.
- Paolo—Dario's second manservant

* Indicates an historical figure.

PROLOGUE

~ JULY 1456 ~

Since well before dawn, the young man's sandals had clopped the thirty-five miles of dusty road all the way from his father's leather shop in San Gimignano to Florence. The Tuscan heat rolled in waves over the green hills, and sweat poured off his forehead, drenching even his tunic. But today was the first day of Amadeo Puccini's new life, and even the swelter wouldn't deter him from his goal.

When the path topped a hill, the city spread out below. Dominating the skyline, the dome of Santa Maria del Fiore rose regal and majestic above a sea of red-roofed houses. Amadeo had never been this far from home, and his first view of Brunelleschi's celebrated masterwork nearly stopped his breath. Surely this was the tallest, grandest structure in all the world. As he drank in the sight, he slipped the pack from his sweat-soaked back and entered a tall cypress's shade.

An oxcart burdened with dung creaked up the path. "Please, signore"—Amadeo stepped from the shadows—"how might one find the church of Santa Maria Novella?"

The driver, a gray-haired elder draped in a ripped, dirty tunic, waved back the way he'd come. "Cross the Ponte Vecchio, go straight, then turn left at the Piazza Duomo and baptistery." He snapped a whip, the ox snorted and lashed its tail, and the cart trundled on.

Amadeo grabbed his pack and started down the slope. What would his new master be like? He'd heard so much about Leon Battista Alberti. Painter, author, philosopher, architect—the man's talents seemed endless. After Amadeo had sent his letter with samples of his work, he'd rejoiced at the unexpected reply. For months, he'd looked forward to this meeting. But now that the moment approached, his heart hammered inside his chest. What if the great man didn't like his new apprentice?

At the Ponte Vecchio, he held his nose and hurried across. Butchers occupied the bridge, souring the air with slaughterhouse smells. Evening was already falling. Preparing for home, the workers hurled buckets full of the day's accumulated offal and blood into the River Arno.

Across the bridge, architectural wonders lined the way, but he couldn't stop. He needed to find his new master before the man left the church.

When the street opened into the Piazza Duomo, Florence's grand cathedral filled the square and part of the sky. The sight rooted Amadeo to the cobbles. Surely, here was the grandest, most beautiful building in all the world. Oh, to build a duomo like that! What glory the architects had brought their God! What he wouldn't give to someday design such a structure!

Transfixed, his eyes feasted on the sight so long he lost track of time. Around him, peasants hurried home, bearing nets of wood or leather goods or leading horses carrying unsold bags of wool or wheat.

A hundred paces distant, a crowd gathered around a tall man dressed in blue and red tights with a ruffled yellow waistcoat. Men were engaged in heated discussion around a tripod holding an easel. Curious, Amadeo sidled over.

"No one, signore, can do such a thing. Not even you." A brown-mustachioed man in a red tunic with a gold, tasseled belt waved his hands. "No one can render the baptistery with all its details onto a blank parchment in the time a man of good health can run from here to the Ponte Vecchio and back. I'll wager six florins on it."

Six florins! Amadeo could live for a month on six florins. These men must be nobles, all.

"I'll join my six with his," said a second man with long, black hair. By his expensive four-cornered hat and silk brocade, he, too, must be a noble.

The tall man shook a mane of curly, golden hair and smiled. "I'll take your wager, Alfonso. Yours, too, Biagio." He pointed at a lanky, black-haired youth in the crowd. "You, there. Can you run as fast as the wind?"

Startled, the lad said he could try.

"If you race to the bridge and back for us, it will profit you a florin."

His eyes eager, the lad bobbed his head.

Mustachioed Alfonso smiled. "And I'll give you two florins to return before our fanciful artist accomplishes his feat. Start on my signal."

Ready to run, the appointed racer crouched and faced the square.

With an impish grin, the blond-haired man—was there ever a kinder, more handsome face than this?—gripped his pencil.

Alfsono clapped his hands, the runner bolted, and the tall man's pencil flew over the parchment, sketching faster than any human hands had a right to draw.

The crowd watched, breathless, as the baptistery's outlines, its cupola, its many-faceted niches, windows, and different-colored bricks magically burst onto the canvas.

As time passed, men switched their glances from the drawing to the far end of the square.

Now the runner was in sight, his arms swinging, his legs sprinting, and the crowd cheered him on.

Moments before the youth arrived, the tall man threw down his pencil, raised his arms, and cried, "Finished!"

Amadeo gaped in wonder at the finished sketch. His gaze went back and forth, comparing the canvas with the baptistery, but he could find not a single missing detail.

After the crowd and the nobles did the same, people began shouting their judgment—the artist had won the bet. The people dispersed, and the runner collected his wages.

Biagio dropped six florins into a waiting palm. "I thought it was an empty boast, Alberti. Such skill I have never seen."

"Skill and practice, my friends. But now it's evening, and I long for wine and sustenance. Won't you signori join me for dinner?"

With regrets, both men cited previous engagements and, bowing, left.

"Alas," whispered Alberti to no one in particular, "I dine alone."

"Signore?" But Amadeo's voice was so weak he feared the man hadn't heard.

"Sì?" The older man turned to him with a puzzled look.

"Are you Leon Battista Alberti?"

"I am."

He swallowed. "My name is Amadeo Puccini, and I—"

"Amadeo Puccini!" A wide smile broke his face. "My new apprentice? The youth who sent me that wonderful painting of the San Gimigiano towers?"

"The very same."

"What fortune that on your first day we meet by chance. Surely, this is divine providence. Then, come! This evening, you and I will dine together. We will talk of art, architecture, and life. I will buy." Alberti wrapped an arm about Amadeo's shoulders and began leading him across the square. "The point of all art, Amadeo, is to bring out the beauty God placed in the world around us. Sì?"

Beaming, Amadeo could only nod. He was already liking his new master.

"You are surely a painter, young man, but what think you of architecture? For that is what you and I are charged with and why you are here—to finish the façade of Santa Maria Novella." They entered a narrow street already cooled by evening shadows. Couples walked hand in hand while merchants hurried home from the day's labors. "Have you seen it yet?"

"The church? No, signore, I just arrived."

"And a long walk it must have been. Right now, the front is nothing but a rectangle enclosing some arches with a square on top. An aesthetic eyesore if ever there was. All architecture must please the eye with beauty, grace, and symmetry. Do you not agree?"

Feeling foolish and bereft of words, Amadeo nodded again.

Ahead, swallows screamed and dove between buildings.

"Santa Maria Novella presents an architectural puzzle. But just as you filled your painting with life, with colorful people, horses, and trees—a lesser artist would have done only the towers, my friend, and that is why I agreed to take you on—just as you created beauty from what could have been a dead cityscape, so I am charged with eking beauty from a rectangle and a square. Perhaps massive scrolls on either side and a pediment on top?" Alberti stared down the street as if picturing what he'd just said. "We must imitate nature's beauty, my young friend, even in architecture. Every part of the whole must present harmony and symmetry. Have you seen the ruins in Rome?"

Amadeo shook his head.

"How old are you, by the way?"

"Thirteen."

"And you've only ever worked in your father's leather shop?"

"Sì."

"Yet you found time to draw, paint, and learn art. Have you done other paintings, then?"

"I have. But I'm leaning more toward architecture. I want to design buildings." He swallowed again. Dare he say it aloud—this new desire raging within him? "Even . . . churches."

"Churches, hey? Then thirteen is a good age to begin your education." Alberti dropped his arm from Amadeo's shoulder as they skirted a pile of horse dung. "The ancient Romans were masters of the building arts. Unfortunately, much of their expertise was lost. In Rome, their ruins lie everywhere, and one would do well to study their arches, columns, domes, and the great structures they left behind. The Coliseum is a wonder to behold."

Alberti stopped at an eatery with tables in the street. "My favorite trattoria." He spread his arms wide. "The spaghetti with garlic, olive oil, and Sicilian cheese is very good."

They sat, and after the proprietor brought wine, Alberti lifted his glass. "To your apprenticeship, Amadeo. To a long and successful career as an architect."

"Thank you, signore." He sipped the wine and set it down.

"But what, my young friend, is your life's goal?" Alberti's eyes narrowed, and he placed both palms on the table before him. "Is it just to learn a trade and make a few florins? Did you come to me just to follow your father's desires like so many others? Be honest."

Startled by the question, Amadeo sat back in his chair with lips pressed together. Before today, he'd always wanted to become only a common architect, designing and constructing houses or public buildings. But after seeing the cathedral, he knew that would never be enough. No, a fire had been lit within him—he could feel it smoldering even now. He took a deep breath. "My life's work must glorify God, signore. And to that end, I will devote all the talent and skill I possess. And someday"—his voice clear and strong, he caught Alberti's gaze—"someday, I'm going to build . . . the greatest duomo the world has ever seen."

Alberti frowned. "Very few among us—even the best—are ever chosen for such a grand task as building a duomo. Are you sure you haven't a lesser objective?"

"No, signore. That is what I want to do."

"I warn you: Such a work will consume a man. You might begin it in youth, but the task will steal from you all your waking hours, haunting your nights with sleeplessness. I've seen it happen to others—stealing their energy and youth, leaving them old and exhausted, their goal unmet. The duomo, my young friend, is a hard and unforgiving taskmaster. So I ask you again: Are you sure that's your life's goal?"

"Sì, signore. That's my goal. I've never been more certain of anything."

"It seems I've chosen my apprentice well." Alberti lifted his glass. "Then here's to your ambition and energy and to a goal so grandiose and lofty that only the greatest among us would ever dare proclaim it. Here's to Amadeo Puccini and a bright, illustrious future."

Smiling, Amadeo raised his glass and drank.

As the restaurateur lit torches to chase away the shadows, a warm glow filled Amadeo. But it wasn't the wine or the lingering heat from the cobbles or the company that swelled his soul with joy. It was the sure knowledge that tonight—for the first time in his life—he knew exactly why God had made him, and the task to which he would someday devote the rest of his life.

PART 1

~ The Masters of Their Trades ~

CHAPTER 1

~ THE LORD OF COLPENA ~

MARCH 1469

Naked but for a robe of exquisite silk draped about his slender frame, Dario Rossi slumped into a chair before a crackling fire and pondered the end of his existence.

"Flames, Dario Rossi," the mysterious monk had said. "I've seen you . . . in the flames."

Was it only last week that the wandering mendicant in rags had slipped from the shadows to deliver his cryptic warning? Surely, the man was deranged. But the honesty in his eyes, the calmness in his voice, the steadiness in his hands—all combined to burn an image of the Franciscan friar's judgment into Dario's brain, an image now resurrected in his hearth. He shuddered.

Behind him, Signora Delfina Costa rustled the bedsheets. Apparently, she'd been speaking. ". . . won't you?"

"Won't I—what?"

"Won't you now release the note you promised my husband?"

He swiveled around the side of the chair in time to glimpse her naked back, the golden sheen of her skin. She drew the gossamer *gamicia* over her shoulders.

If only she'd face him. If only he could glimpse once more those ample perfect breasts, that tight belly, those full round hips.

"Sì." He sighed. "On the stand by the wall."

Her bare feet padded across the marble. Picking up the parchment, she read.

She whirled toward him. "But this is only half." A furrow marred her delicate brows. "You promised to forgive the entire debt."

He waved a hand. "A baker's dozen, signora? One more afternoon? Here in my bed?"

"But you said twelve times." Her lips quivered. "Only . . . twelve."

Even shaking with fear, she was one of the most beautiful women he'd ever laid eyes upon, one of the best he'd ever bedded, and he had to lie with her once more. "What's another afternoon, my lady, after all we've had together?"

"Another . . . afternoon?" As if a puppeteer had cut the strings holding it up, her hand dropped. Her gaze lost focus, wandered to the fresco filling the palatial suite's north wall—*The Rape of the Virgins* by Sandro Botticelli. Lorenzo de' Medici had suggested the artist. The first work Dario had ever commissioned.

"Sì, just one. Then you'll have your note. I promise." What was ninety florins compared with twelve, now thirteen, afternoons with such a woman? If only she hadn't rebuffed his earlier advances. "But pray, do not tell your husband about our extra tryst. It would only upset him."

Arturo Costa was a mere spice merchant, a minor player in Colpena's affairs. After Dario had bought Costa's gambling debts and presented his proposition—the loan of his wife in exchange for the debt—Costa had closed his eyes, dropped his head like a man condemned, but finally nodded.

Dario would never understand such spineless creatures.

"One more afternoon, then." Slowly, she returned to the foot of the bed, pushed aside the lace curtain, and clutched her clothes to her breast. "And I won't tell him." She slid her lithe arms through a full-length gamurra and silently departed the room.

Why did Italian women have to cover so much of themselves with their gamurras?

Picking up the jewel-encrusted goblet on the stand beside him, he sipped his wine and stared again at the fire.

A fiery lump broke away and sizzled into the glowing coals. He knelt to the hearth, stuck his fingers toward the heat, and moved them as close as he dared. Not even a foot away and the pain was unbearable. Jerking his hand back, he stared at his palm. An eternity of that? How could anyone endure it?

He rose from his seat, stretched his striped calze over his legs, and pulled on his pointed leather shoes and ruffled blue waistcoat. Walking to the mirror as usual, he brushed aside his shoulder-length, jet-black locks, curled slightly inward, and smiled.

Most women quickly succumbed to his charms. Who wouldn't want to sleep with the richest, most powerful man in Colpena? What a shame he'd had to force the signora to his bed.

"What a handsome rogue you are." He smoothed his hair, twisted his red beret, and left the room.

"My lord, will you take supper before you go out?" White-haired Grazziano rose from his chair. "Or will you, as usual, take sustenance tonight in the bordello?"

"Trattoria, Grazziano. It's a trattoria." Dario glanced aside at his dour-faced, middle-aged servant.

"Of course." Grazziano bowed.

"Grazie for the thought, but I'll get something at the inn."

"May your exploits tonight be worthy of the gonfaloniere of Colpena. Perhaps you'll find a wife among tonight's conquests?"

Dario shook his head. The man was incorrigible. Why did servants nowadays feel compelled to be so irreverent to their betters? He'd heard the same complaint from other wealthy acquaintances. Was Grazziano worse than most? He didn't know. "I'll be back late. Don't wait up."

"You have the key." The servant bowed again. "I'll lock the front."

Dario spun away, his feet echoing down a great marble hallway lined with ancestral portraits. If he could pry just one new artist from the bottegas of Florence, he could start replacing these musty old paintings.

Bounding down the grand staircase, he crossed the cavernous atrium of the Rossi family palazzo and descended stone steps. Out in the street, a setting sun glinted off the Piazza dei Rossi's rain-wet cobbles. Overhead, swallows screamed and dove in crazy circles.

He turned right onto the Via delle Trombe, past the fire-ravaged Church of Santa Croce, where flames had gutted an entire block. Workers had again spent the day demolishing the structure.

Winding around the debris, he entered Via delle Rose and paused at the top of the old wall. Below lay Temestre Inferiore, the steep lower quarter, home of servants and lesser merchants.

Beyond, the Tyrrhenian Sea shone a deep azure. Today, six ships— including two slave galleys, two vessels from Pisa, and two ships belonging to Rossi Shipping and Transport, the company he owned with Cousin Aldo—were docked at the western wharf. From one vessel, a bell clanged.

Dario descended the first series of steps through the old wall onto Via Servi. As he passed, old men sitting on benches sipped their wine, nodded, and smiled. A baker gathered baskets with unsold panini and pulled an iron grate over his storefront. A saddler locked his wooden shutters. And a fishmonger brushed blood, gills, fins, and heads of salmon and flounder from a board into a bucket.

Beside the narrow *quintanas* between houses, his nose wrinkled at the piled refuse. Most of Colpena was orderly, well maintained, clean. But these quintanas in the lower quarter were a breeding ground for rats. Someday, he must bring the issue before the Signoria.

The Via Servi wound down and around until he walked beside the new wall leading to the western docks.

Fifty yards before the Allegra Taverna, a young woman approached, wearing high heels and a bright red gamurra reaching only to her knees. The garment revealed the tops of her breasts. "Signore, I beg an audience."

With such scandalous attire, she must be one of the street prostitutes here. He didn't remember ever having her.

"On a matter of personal, not professional, business," she added.

"Later." He waved her off.

"Please, signore." She tried to follow, but he slipped inside his favorite haunt and shut the door behind him.

Dozens of voices, all talking at once, whelmed up around him. The odor of spilt wine, fresh-baked bread, and pork roasting on a spit hung in the air. In one corner, a young man plucked the strings of a lyre. A blond friend accompanied him with bawdy lyrics, the music scarcely rising above the conversations.

"Welcome, signore." Mario, the corpulent, pock-faced innkeeper, rushed forward. "As usual, your room and Aldo await."

Dario nodded. Aldo had already spent the morning with Dario discussing business. But tonight, the two would meet as fellow revelers, far from petitioners, business, and Aldo's wife. Dario was looking forward to some hearty drinking, good company, and perhaps a romp upstairs with

Calandra or Bianca. Just like in the days before his father passed away and the weight of the gonfaloniere's responsibility fell upon him.

Crossing the main room, he tilted his head, acknowledging the patrons' smiles, nods, and raised glasses. He hoped none would approach, asking for yet another boon. How many men here had asked him for help? He didn't know. Enough so that many owed him favors. And loyalty. And support.

But tonight, his purse was closed. And with it, his benevolence.

Pushing through the oak door, he entered the tiled back room, its walls dressed with cheap tapestries, paintings, oriental beads, and gilt-edged mirrors—the innkeeper's attempt at pleasing the lord of Colpena.

"Dario!" Aldo rose, lifted a goblet high, and offered a mock bow. Tonight, Aldo's curly black hair and pink waistcoat with slashed sleeves gave him a roguish air. Too often, he was dour-faced, focused only on business. "The richest man in Colpena, soon to become even more so."

"What do you mean?"

"Wait till you hear what Jacopo has to tell us. He's back from Acque Salutari. And he carries grand news, indeed."

"Back so soon?"

"Sì. He should be here any minute."

Buxom, black-haired Calandra bore in a tray with a flagon of wine, three glasses, a loaf of bread, a wedge of Sicilian cheese, and two plates of spaghetti sprinkled with herbs, chopped prosciutto, and drizzled with olive oil. "Here you are, my lords, our best as always."

"Grazie, Calandra." He laid a hand on hers and squeezed. "Where's Bianca?"

"Has the night off." A smile raised her full lips, and she planted a kiss on his cheek. "I'll be upstairs if you need me." She winked and left the room.

Pulling a plate toward him and taking a fork from his pocket's silver cadenza, he stuck it in the pasta. After a few mouthfuls, he downed half his goblet in one draught.

Gaunt, thin-faced Jacopo burst through the door. He plopped down beside Dario and smacked the table with one hand. "My lord, your desire to purchase Acque Salutari was prescient."

Aldo faced Dario and grinned. "And I thought you wanted the property only for its spa and its orgies."

Waving his cousin away, Dario focused on Jacopo. "What about the assayers Rocco Marino sent? Did they find what they were looking for?"

"They did." A rare smile burned in oil-black eyes, lifting the slit that was his mouth. "The property has alum shale."

Dario almost dropped his glass. His lips parted, but no words came out. Alum!

"Do you realize what this means?" Aldo was smiling ear-to-ear. "We'll be rich thrice over. No, ten times over. Everyone in Europe is clamoring for alum."

A frown tightened Dario's mouth, pinching his forehead. "It's not ours yet." He fixed his gaze on Jacopo. "Did the Austrians tell Rocco about it? Does anyone else know?"

"No. When I arrived, one of them was preparing to leave for Colpena to tell him, but I gave them each a hundred florins for their silence. Just as you requested. They've given me two weeks before they tell him."

"How many Austrians?"

"Two brothers named Bergman. And another, name of Kuhn. They dug a shaft beside the spa's villa. It's alum, for certain. A big deposit they think. More than big. Two centuries ago, when they dug the villa's base, the builders scattered the stuff across the volcano's slopes. The fools didn't know what they had."

Dario pushed back from the table and gripped the top of his head.

After the Turks cut off the alum route to the east, and with the papal mine at Tolfa running out, whoever controlled Europe's alum trade would be masters of their own destiny. Without alum, the dyers couldn't fix their colors to the bright clothing all Europe now demanded.

The Rossi bank was breaking even. The shipping business was barely growing.

But now—to control a major source of alum!

Dario laid both hands on the table. "Return to Acque Salutari tomorrow. Give the Austrians whatever they want—seven hundred, a thousand, fifteen hundred florins. You know how to negotiate. Whatever they want. Tell them to cover up the hole and dig another, not as deep, in a place with no deposits. Then have them tell Rocco they found nothing. He was ready to sell until this rumor started circulating."

Jacopo narrowed his eyes. "But you also need to hear this. After seeing my—your—interest, the brothers pulled me aside and suggested a similar deal. They're willing. But Kuhn?" He opened his hands and shook his head. "At first, Kuhn wouldn't accept any money for a delay. He wanted to go to Rocco immediately. The brothers were eager for the money. They argued until he relented. But he has scruples. I fear he won't go any farther."

"Why did Rocco hire these Austrians in the first place?"

"Better than anyone, they know the alum extraction process and how to make it saleable. They have a small operation in Innsbruck. But not much of a deposit there."

"Tell them if they go along, if we get the property, they'll get exclusive rights for the extraction."

"That will work for the Bergmans. But for Kuhn? I fear not."

Dario stared across the room. He knew what he must do next, but he hated situations like this. Again, he thought of the monk's warning. And of what Lorenzo would say—Lorenzo the philosopher and sometime moralizer.

But to control the only source of alum for all Europe?

Grimacing, he turned to his cousin. "What kind of men are we, Aldo?"

Aldo's head jerked back an inch. "What do you mean?"

"Are we creatures of God? Do we know right from wrong?" That was something Lorenzo would say. "Or are we simply animals, just grubbing for our next meal?"

"That's a stupid question. What's the matter with you?"

"Can you think of any way out of this?"

Aldo frowned. "No."

Dario rubbed his forehead and faced Jacopo. "So, no matter what agreement we make with the Bergmans, Kuhn will go to Rocco?"

"Sì."

Slamming a fist on the table, Dario swore. He turned to the man who'd do whatever he asked. No hesitation. No questions. "Then make whatever arrangements you can with the brothers. If Kuhn won't go along, if he leaves for Colpena to tell Rocco, well . . . follow him." He pointed at the blade strapped to Jacopo's hip. "You know what to do."

Jacopo pursed his lips and stared at the table. He grabbed a goblet, filled it, and drank. He nodded. Then he left.

Aldo's frown deepened. "If Rocco weren't on the Signoria, this business would be easier."

"Sì. And he nearly always votes with Enzio Borroni against us. But think of it this way." Dario grinned. "This is sweet revenge, is it not?"

Aldo returned the grin.

For the remainder of the evening, the two drank, took turns going upstairs with Calandra, and basked in the promise of a Colpena—not to mention their bank and shipping company—nearly as rich as sister-city Florence to the north.

HOLDING A TORCH, DARIO STAGGERED late out of the inn. He'd drunk too much wine, but it was a special occasion. After Aldo had left an hour earlier, Dario had joined the noisy commoners and merchants in the main room, buying drinks for all. Good fortune had flown from Heaven this day and landed on the Rossis, and he felt like sharing. It was the perfect end to a splendid afternoon. As he tottered into the night, he raised his flame high to chase away the shadows.

Only ten steps from the taverna, the whore with the scandalous red gamurra stood from adjacent steps. "Please, signore? An audience?"

"It's late. Tomorrow." He tried to walk faster but found himself weaving.

She followed close by his side. "My husband died. He was Agapito Donini, a wheelwright."

As he turned a corner, the torchlight caught a rat scampering into a hole in the bricks. Donini . . . had he heard that name recently?

"My son tries to continue the business." She hurried to walk beside him. "But we've no money for wood or iron or rent. For six months, the bank has frozen my husband's account. To keep us going, I am reduced"—she spread a hand down her breasts to her hips—"to selling this."

"Not now. Come to the palazzo tomorrow. Ask my man Grazziano for an audience." He increased the pace. Somehow, he didn't trip over his own feet.

"I have. He won't let me in."

He stopped and closed his eyes, tight, to clear them. Then his glance swept over her. Certainly, she was attractive, possibly worthy of his time.

She smiled, seeming to acknowledge the unspoken compliment.

From somewhere up the hill, a dog barked. While the city slept, sound—and the schemes of men—could travel far.

"What bank?"

"The Rossi Bank, my lord."

"Why won't we release the funds?"

"They say Enzio Borroni has a lien."

Borroni! He and Rocco Marino objected to most of what Dario put forth to the Signoria. He scratched the back of his neck. Vaguely, he remembered the case. Borroni claimed the wheelwright owed him fifty—or was it sixty?—florins. Only yesterday, Dario ordered that Borroni's claim be denied. If he remembered correctly, the funds would be released to her tomorrow.

"I will give you anything"—her tongue wet a corner of her mouth, traced a circle around full lips—"anything you want, my lord."

He smiled. "Grazziano will let you in. Come before noon. He'll send you directly to my apartment. And do bathe."

"Thank you, my lord." She bowed low. "You will not regret our time together."

He grunted an acknowledgment. Nothing like a morning romp before lunch. But now he must ensure her funds were not released for a few days—enough time to sample her wares. In six months, she'd apparently learned her trade well.

Somehow, he made the steep climb to the wall gate, then veered left onto Via delle Rose. Stumbling into the Piazza dei Rossi, he found it deserted. Most of the torches lining the square had burned out. Ahead waited the steps leading to his palazzo. The wine was still swimming in his head, when—

"I know you, Dario Rossi." A man clad in a black cape stepped from the shadows.

The monk! Dario stumbled back a pace. He'd come again.

The man threw off his hood. A gaunt face under a mop of blond hair. An angelic face marred by a thin scar across the right temple. Too pleasant for the face of a grim accuser. Nevertheless, Dario feared it.

"I know all that you've done," said the monk. "And your sins have risen like a shroud from a funeral pyre, a putrid stench reaching even to the angels in Heaven."

Sweat beaded on his forehead. His heart raced. Who was this man? Why was he here?

"When God revealed you to me, I was working in the abbey's vineyard." The monk spoke calmly, softly, as to a child. "I've walked fifty miles from Salvia to get here. Even with this—" He banged a cane on a bulging sandal wrapping the lump of a foot.

This time, Dario noticed the foot, twice as big as his left. He'd limped fifty miles on that? Just to see him? "What do you want? Why have you come again?"

"You haven't listened. I saw your future, Dario Rossi."

"W–what do you mean?" His chest constricting, he gasped for breath. "What did you see?"

"Your naked body. Screaming. Writhing in flames. Twisting in the lake of eternal fire."

"N–no . . . no." He backed away, dropped the torch. Even sizzling on the wet cobbles, the flame burned on, refused to go out.

"Writhing, Dario Rossi. Squirming and turning in endless fire."

"*No.*" After bounding up the stairs, he fumbled his key into the lock. It wouldn't turn. Shaking fingers wrenched it until it turned. He smashed open the massive palazzo doors, then crashed them shut.

From outside, the monk's muffled warning droned on. All he heard was a single word—*flames.*

His back slammed against cold bronze. Spreading out his arms, he pushed as if his body forming a cross could stay the monk's judgment.

"No!" he shouted, and his scream recoiled off the tiled marble floor, ricocheted off the wall sculptures, wound through the crystal of the high chandelier, and echoed back from the shadowed ceiling.

And the image that bounced and reverberated through the corridors of his mind was of a man twisting, twirling, plunging down the shaft of a bottomless fiery pit.

CHAPTER 2

~ THE PROPOSITION ~

When morning's light glared through a crack in the curtains and the cicadas began buzzing outside, Dario still sat on the reception room sofa. His clothes of the night before reeked of woodsmoke, spilt wine, and sweat. Up on the wall, the black piercing eyes of some distant relative bored down at him from her portrait. How long had he watched that woman, her pert torso emerging from her ancient full-length *houppelande*, her short arms grasped tightly to her bulky frame? Even from across the centuries, he was certain those eyes held accusation. Rebuke. Even disgust.

For the thousandth time, he laid his head on the couch, shut his eyes, and tried to sleep. But as soon as his head hit the rock-hard pillow, his eyelids popped open, and the monk's words echoed again through his brain—

Writhing, Dario Rossi. Twisting and turning in endless fire.

He jerked himself upright, breathing fast.

Surely, he was cursed. He knew all too well who he was. No question about that.

For a time, he might give up the women, the drinking, the gambling, even the orgies. In the past, he'd abstained from those. But only for a time. Always, he went back. Were they not simply woven into the fabric of daily life, as ingrained within him as eating? Like the sun rising in the morning and setting at night? Like grapes greening the vines in spring, ripening red in the fall? How could anyone fight such a thing?

Then there was the business and the deeds it demanded. Such as the affair with Jacopo and the alum mine. The opportunity was impossible to give up. Sure, the man Kuhn might be killed—if he was foolish and didn't listen to reason. But he had a chance to keep his life, didn't he? It was up to him. And if he rejected the offer—well, afterward, Dario could always go to confession. He'd done it before.

He squirmed on the sofa, twisted to find a more comfortable position.

How many sins would a confession cover? Was there a limit? Did the magnitude of the offense matter?

And most important of all—would the priest keep silent?

His head throbbed. All night, the same thoughts had raced through his head, over and over. And then, as always, the monk's words came roaring back. Ending with a single promise—

Flames.

The door creaked inward. Grazziano crossed the room to the curtains and jerked them aside. Opening one tall window a crack, he let in the cicadas' buzzing drone. When he turned to leave, he saw Dario on the high-backed couch and started. "Oh, signore, I'm sorry. I didn't see you there."

"It's all right." An imp inside his head awoke and decided to beat a hammer against his temples, trying to pound his eyes out of their sockets. Stray locks stuck out from his head at all angles, obscuring his vision.

"You look terrible. Did you sleep last night?"

He shook his head.

"If the *populo minuto* only knew how much our gonfaloniere suffered, working so hard and so late in the bordellos on their behalf."

Dario sighed. Certainly, the man was solicitous, competent, always catering to his every whim. But along with that came such a biting sarcasm Dario sometimes wondered why he kept the man. Had it only been six years since his father, Orsino Rossi, had died and bequeathed him the servant? But no, he could never let Grazziano go. Help like his was difficult to replace. And besides, Grazziano knew too much.

"Would you like breakfast? Some bread? A boiled egg?"

"Sì, and—"

The front door's knocker began rapping. Dario motioned Grazziano to see who it was. It was far too early for the usual retinue to start gathering in the back office to discuss the day's business. More petitioners? Grazziano would get rid of them.

He stood and walked to the end table where waited a half-empty wine decanter and a glass. He rarely drank before lunch, but this morning was different. Pouring a full glass, he lifted it to parched lips, downed it in one gulp.

"My lord," said Grazziano behind him, "you have visitors."

"Who?"

"A young woman of the night, scantily clad. She claims you invited her here. But as I was letting her into the foyer, Cardinal Emilio Gonzaga and a young man in bishop's robes climbed the steps. All are now standing in the hall. Together. Perhaps I should let the churchmen have a go at her?"

"Grazziano, you know better." He frowned. Why would Gonzaga show up today, of all days? And naturally, he came at the exact moment as the whore. "Tell the woman I'll see her tomorrow."

"Should I tell the priests you're unavailable?"

"No." He hadn't shaved. His clothes were a mess. And his head was a melon about to pop. But he stood, smoothed his hair, and told his servant to admit them.

DARIO'S FEET ECHOED ACROSS THE marbled floor as he met a grossly overweight man in a bulky red cassock—Cardinal Emilio Gonzaga. Gold and silver rings wrapped every finger. Hanging below heavy jowls were the links of a gold necklace weighed down by an enormous ruby encircled with sparkling diamonds.

Beside Gonzaga stood a much younger, slimmer man in green bishop's robes. But when Dario saw the bishop, he gasped. Wasn't this the very monk who'd visited him last night? The same pale angelic face below a mop of blond hair? Same thin scar across the right temple? Same blue eyes, hinting of sincerity?

What kind of cosmic joke was this? His heart thumped wildly.

Then his glance fell to the man's feet. No clubfoot. And no cane. He breathed easier and whirled away. The resemblance—uncanny—but just a coincidence. He tried to compose himself and again faced his visitors.

"Are you well?" Gonzaga's eyes scanned Dario with concern. "Have we caught you at an inopportune time, my lord?"

"No, I'm fine." Dario wiped a hand through his hair and straightened his posture. "For a moment, I was taken aback. Your companion . . . I thought he was someone else."

Gonzaga narrowed his eyes and nodded. The cardinal placed a hand on the newcomer's shoulders. "Then may I introduce to you Bishop Rinaldi Ferata?"

Dario took the bishop's offered hand and wondered again why they hadn't made an appointment. "To what do I owe a visit from such illustrious persons so early in the morning?"

"It's nearly midmorning, signore." Gonzaga cleared his throat. "We have much to discuss. Of matters most grave. Can we sit?"

"Certainly." Dario motioned them to two chairs facing the couch by the open window. Sitting opposite the men, he winced as the bright morning sun burned holes in his head. The cicadas prompted the imp inside his brain to take up his skull-bashing mallet again.

"Are you certain we shouldn't come another time, signore?"

Dario waved off the suggestion. He rubbed his temples to ease the pain. Then he faced the younger man. "Bishop Ferata, I'm unfamiliar with your bishopric. Where do you serve?"

Gonzaga leaned his considerable bulk toward Dario. "That's what we came to talk with you about. The Holy Father wants to place Rinaldi here, Dario, in Colpena."

"In my city?"

"Sì, signore."

Dario sat back on the chair. A bishopric in Colpena? What a stroke of luck.

"Colpena has risen in importance and wealth," said the cardinal. "Your wine, wheat, and cloth exports are growing. The number of souls here now rivals Pisa. All thanks to your thriving ports."

"I'm glad the Holy See has noticed." Colpena's two ports were its trading lifeline to Majorca, Menorca, Flanders, and London—a pale shadow compared to Venice, sì, but still vibrant and, with a bit of luck, growing.

"Not to mention that you have a friend in Piero de' Medici and in his son, Lorenzo." Gonzaga shifted in his seat, and the chair groaned. "Yet two problems prevent us from moving on the Holy Father's proposal. Serious problems. Both of grave concern to the Holy See."

"Problems, cardinal?"

"Sì. The first"—Gonzaga again cleared his throat and sat back in his chair—"ah, there is simply no delicate way to say this. The first is that, since taking control from your father, you have accumulated a list of sins that is . . . well . . . astonishing. As evidenced by the tart who preceded us up the steps."

Dario stared at the man, his heart thumping, the imp inside his brain striking his skull even faster. "We all have sins, your grace." Who hadn't heard of the whores this very cardinal had entertained, of the sumptuous feasts he threw, and of the bribes he'd accepted? Not to mention his fondness for expensive jewelry.

"Ah, but none like yours, my lord. I'm speaking not only of the usury you engage in but the unpardonable act of murder."

Dario's face drained of blood. Every banker faced the charge of usury, did he not? For how could any bank survive without being repaid more than was lent? He played many games to disguise it, but in the end, the Church's definition of usury was so slippery, they could easily slap such a charge against him.

More concerning was the charge of murder. What did the cardinal know? Dario tried to run down the list of the men who'd stood in his way, who'd subsequently met their demise. It could have been anyone. Unless it was—

"Twice now, you asked for a priest to come your quarters to hear your confession. In both cases, these servants of the Church left your palazzo shaken, deeply troubled, and refusing to go back. And in both cases, the men soon died unnatural deaths." Bending further forward, Gonzaga fixed Dario with a stare to freeze a fountain.

"Everything points to murder, Rossi. But no one can prove a thing. Only you know the truth."

His head was about to burst. His hands sought the arms of the chair and squeezed.

With impeccable timing, Grazziano knocked loudly and entered. He bore in a tray of boiled eggs, bread, butter, and cheese and a pitcher of water and glasses. These he placed on the end table that he moved closer to the three men. "Pardon the interruption, signori, but I thought you might like a midmorning repast."

"Thank you, Grazziano." Dario bit off half an egg, chewed, and swallowed. Then he downed a glass of water.

After the servant left, Gonzaga faced him again. "We didn't come here to formally accuse you of anything. But the rumors of others killed in like manner have come before the Church. It seems, Dario Rossi, that your sins gather before you like flames around a condemned heretic."

Again, that word—*flames.* He sucked in breath.

"If it's true you had a hand in their deaths, well—one would be hard-pressed to find a confession or an indulgence great enough to keep you from the lake of eternal fire."

He wanted to run from the room, to get on a horse and ride far out into the country. Anything to escape yet another judgment of eternal damnation. For the truth of it was—he was guilty of everything the cardinal said.

"Yet there is one thing a man in your position could do. One act of repentance of such great import and charity that it would—with the pope's blessing—absolve even you."

"What?" Dario squirmed to the edge of the sofa. "What is it? Tell me." He begged like a man trapped in a burning building with no escape while Gonzaga offered to pull down the walls.

"It is for this reason I am here, signore." Now the young bishop with the angelic face spoke. "Last year, your only church burned down. You are without a place of worship. Thus, the Holy Father has agreed to place my bishopric, here, in Colpena. And, of course, a bishop must have a cathedral from which to minister."

"A *duomo*?"

"Sì, signore." The bishop was smiling. "A duomo which you, yourself, with your own wealth, would solely fund. And with you offering such a grand act of repentance and devotion to the Church, the Holy Father himself is willing to grant you total absolution from all your sins—past, present, and future. But, besides agreeing to wholly fund this venture, there is one final requirement. For this indulgence to be effective, your act of charity in funding the duomo must equal or exceed the magnitude of the evils you have committed."

"Meaning what?"

"Meaning this duomo must be a truly great cathedral on a grand scale. And to build on such crowded land as yours will not only take great skill, but the one who builds it must also meet the highest of moral standards. Our builder must be a truly righteous man."

Dario sat back against the sofa, his head whirling. Total absolution? A complete pardon for every sin he'd ever committed—yesterday, today, and tomorrow? This was a gift from God himself. Yet one thing troubled him. "What would such a venture cost?"

The green-robed bishop looked from his superior to Dario. "We have an initial figure, given us by Fra Bevignate who's currently building the cathedral in Perugia. It's only a guess. It's not a small sum."

"What is it?"

"Mind you, it's only an initial estimate. And, of course, it all depends on the final design. The expenditure in future years could be less."

"And . . . ?"

Ferata's voice lowered. "In the first year, signore—thirty . . . thousand . . . florins."

Dario gasped. In a good year, the bank only brought in forty thousand. Such a venture would suck the business dry like a chef squeezing juice from a lemon.

"And, of course," continued the cardinal, "this is the work of a lifetime. Whatever builder we select must not only be righteous but also young enough to complete the work before both he—and you—pass on."

"Thirty thousand florins," Dario whispered to the woman in the portrait. He stood and ambled across the marble. "A truly great sum."

"It is, indeed, a great sum." Cardinal Gonzaga opened his hands in apology. "Unfortunately, right now, the Church cannot afford to participate in the funding."

Dario shot him a glance. Of course not. Naturally. The church must pay for jewelry; concubines; sumptuous quarters with servants, including slave women; and legendary feasts for the cardinals. And was not the papal palace itself filled with luxurious robes, nearly bursting with gold and precious gems? Did not the pope himself recently purchase one thousand ermine furs to cover his pillows and bed? Furs that Dario's shipping company had imported from the frozen north.

He paced the room's edge. If the sale of Acque Salutari went through, the subsequent alum trade would triple, possibly quadruple, his income. Or more. That deal was now more important than ever.

"Should we give you time to think about the project?" asked Gonzaga. "We don't expect an answer today. And, of course, you will receive the indulgence in writing, signed by His Holiness. We—"

"Sì!"

"Sì?" The cardinal's mouth opened in surprise. "You mean you accept our proposal?"

"I do. In its entirety."

The cardinal beamed. The bishop's smile nearly broke his face. Both men exchanged excited glances. "Good," said Gonzaga. "Let's shake on it." With effort, he pushed himself from the chair, reached a hand across the space, and shook Dario's. Rinaldi Ferata also offered his palm.

"Then the next matter is the choice of a master builder, our *capomaestro*." Gonzaga's ponderous form slumped back into the chair. It creaked under the weight, its legs wobbling dangerously, then stilled. "As I said, because of the nature of this indulgence, the builder must not only be skilled in what he does but also be a true man of God. Not given to heavy drinking. Someone who doesn't frequent brothels. Who isn't heavily indebted."

"The obvious first choice," said Ferata, "would be Basilio Bramante."

"Perhaps." Gonzaga waved a hand in dismissal. "But he's still working on your water project, is he not?"

"Sì, and he's difficult to work with." Dario frowned. "And after ten years, we still have no water. I would rather see him finish what he started." Under his father's reign, the Council of Thirty had given Basilio, the half-brother of Donato Bramante of Urbino, the commission to bring water from the spring at the hill's base to giant cisterns at the city's summit.

Water had always been a problem for Colpena, and Bramante's ingenious proposal to carve a reservoir under the bowels of the hill and build a chain pump to bring it up to the surface had won the bid. But seven years after he'd started, the workers were still digging, and the oxcarts were still hauling water every day from the lower springs. Fortunately, the Wool Guild and the Council of Thirty were paying for it.

"I agree." Ferata nodded. "I would prefer someone else."

"What about Luciano Laurana?" Hands clasped, the bishop braced his elbows on his knees. "I hear his work is excellent."

"Laurana is unavailable. He's building the palace for Duke Federico III in Urbino."

"Is not the greatest builder of renown, Leon Battista Alberti?" Dario raised his eyebrows.

"The man is skilled, I'll say that." Gonzaga gave another dismissing wave. "But he's a hedonist. His lifestyle is anathema to the Church. Back in Barcelona, we would never have tolerated him. Besides, he, too, is occupied, working on the basilica of Sant'Andrea in Mantua."

"What about Alberti's former assistant, Amadeo Puccini?" questioned Dario. "After Adolfo de Tocci died, Puccini finished the Church of San Ambrose, also in Florence. I've seen it, and the building is a masterwork."

"Sì, the church is beautiful and built in record time. Puccini is certainly a builder of exceptional skill. So says Alberti himself. The man is only twenty-seven. And righteous. I'll give him that. But the rumors about his views on the Virgin Mother trouble me."

"In what way?" Ferata frowned.

"They say he doesn't pray to her. He reserves prayer for Christ, alone."

The bishop gasped. "B–but we wish to name the duomo for her."

"Exactly."

"How big a problem is this?" Why did they look so concerned? Dario couldn't see an issue.

"I . . . I don't know." Gonzaga examined the marble at his feet. "He's the only one available. But I'm sure he can be persuaded. What do you think, Rinaldi?"

"Surely, in the end, he'll relent. And if, despite these rumors, we can dedicate and name the duomo for the Virgin . . . I will accept the choice."

A smile crept across Gonzaga's lips. He slapped a hand on one knee. "Then it's decided. Bishop Ferata, you will leave at once to find him and present our request. I've made inquiries, and even though I have reservations, I knew it would come down to him. After San

Ambrose, he returned to Colpena but recently left for the country east of here. I'm told he often retreats to the countryside to pray and get closer to God."

"But will he accept the commission?" asked Dario.

"He must." Rings clattered as Gonzaga clasped one hand around the other. "He's the only available candidate."

CHAPTER 3

~ THE ARCHITECT ~

APRIL 1469

Amadeo Puccini paused on the hilltop. Sparrows chirped from the olive trees behind him. Sweat drenched his back under his knapsack. For the first day of April, it was already warm. He wiped his brow and breathed deeply the hot breath of lavender, bougainvillea, and blue iris. Truly, here was a land untainted by city smells and corruption.

Ahead on the Tuscan countryside, the curving dirt road lined with pillars of cypress pressed against the hills like a lover. To the left, row upon row of vines, with new leaf greening in the sun, marched around the rise. On the distant hillock perched a nobleman's columned villa. Just below to the right, sunlight glistened off a stream filling a pool.

He bounded down the hill, occasionally planting his walking stick. For the last hour, he hadn't seen anyone. Looking both ways to ensure he was still alone, he left the road, waded through tall grass, and stopped at the pool's edge. He dropped the stick, doffed his clothes and pack, and descended into the water, cool and bracing against bare skin. The pool was only chest deep. He sank to his neck and sighed.

What king, with all his wealth, could compete with the luxury of God's cool, clean water on a hot afternoon?

Thank you, Lord, for your goodness, your provision for a weary traveler.

From the bank behind came a woman's giggling. He whirled, sloshing water.

"Signore," said a slim, blonde-haired beauty carrying a basket of blue irises. "I believe I've caught you in a compromising position." She was about twenty years old. Her eyes carried an impish gleam.

Feeling the fool, Amadeo opened his mouth, but no words came out. Had she watched him wade naked into the stream?

The woman set down her basket and picked up his white tights and black waistcoat. Wrinkling her nose, she examined them with a critical eye. "In need of washing, I'd say."

"They are, indeed, signorina. As was I."

She laughed and laid his clothes carefully where she found them. Then she spied a heavy volume sticking out from a corner of his pack. Pulling it out, she leafed through its pages. "What manner of traveler carries such a ponderous tome?" She squinted at him. "And with all these drawings."

"An architect, my lady."

"Ah, so a great builder you must be?"

"Only a fair one. And now a wet one."

Smiling, she shoved the parchments back. "And how do you propose to dry yourself when you exit the stream, Signore Architect?"

Despite the cool water, he felt his face getting hot. "The sun, I guess. I thought I was alone."

"Don't mind me. I'm just picking flowers for my father's table. You may dry yourself at any time." But she made no move to depart.

"And who is the lady having such fun at a weary traveler's expense?"

Her smile curving her high cheeks, she blinked and gave him a mock curtsy. "Simona Mancini, at your service. This stream and all the lands of this valley belong to my father, Signore Callisto Mancini."

"My lady Mancini"—Amadeo inclined his head—"if you would be so kind as to give me some privacy, I will leave this stream, dry myself, and depart your father's lands."

Still smiling, she folded her arms and shook her head.

"My lady, *per favore*! This is not seemly."

"Very well. I will wait for you on the road. When you are dry, I will escort you to our villa."

"Thank you, but that's not necessary."

"Ah, but it is. A young architect like yourself, wandering alone through Tuscany—why, beyond this valley are bandits. You must come to our villa and stay the night."

"Really, signorina. I can manage on my own."

She picked up her basket and ran through the grass, her yellow dress billowing around her.

When he was certain she'd gone, he splashed from the stream, keeping watch in case she returned. Without waiting to dry, he pulled his clothes back on. White calze on his legs, black cioppa over his chest, and a black four-cornered beret on his head. Simple clothes for a simple servant of God. Grabbing his pack, he pushed through the grass to the road, where Signorina Mancini waited with her impish grin.

She curtseyed again, and he bowed.

"And what, if I may ask, is the name of the architect who stands before me with wet clothes sticking to his back?"

"Amadeo Puccini, signorina. But the sun will dry me quickly."

"Well, Amadeo Puccini, you will please follow me. I will not take no for an answer." She began striding down the road toward the villa.

Mancini. The name seemed familiar. In what connection had he heard it? But she was already fifty feet ahead of him.

He raced to catch up.

When they left the road, their feet crunched over a graveled lane. A quarter-mile up the hill loomed the villa, built as a traditional rectangle. Its white marble columns bespoke of ancient Rome and the distant past. Two uniformed men with spears stood guard outside the entry, and as Amadeo and Simona approached, one disappeared inside. A moment later, the guard reemerged accompanying a tall gray-haired man, slight of build, with sun-weathered skin and twinkling eyes.

"Welcome, signore, to my villa." The man wore a white, ankle-length Roman toga, the first Amadeo had ever seen on a living person. "I see my daughter has waylaid yet another traveler, and—"

"He's an architect, father." Simona tilted her head toward Amadeo. "Traveling alone, going east."

"An architect? Then you will, of course, stay for supper, take a room for the night."

"Thank you, my lord." Amadeo accepted the man's hand and bowed. "But I would not presume to—"

"Bah!" Callisto waved away the objection. "I do enjoy my time away from Colpena. Though we have the sea air, the city is noisy and demanding. Here in the country, a man can live a clean, wholesome life, free of seductions and obligations. But we get so few visitors here. Per favore, what is your name?"

He gave it.

"Amadeo Puccini? The very same who just finished Florence's Church of San Ambrose?"

"I am he."

"I've walked under its arched roof, seen its pilasters, gargoyles, its apse with its carved angels, demons, and Apostles so real I thought they would speak to me. I still remember your fresco of John the Baptist. Signore, your work is without equal."

"You exaggerate. I only finished what was started before me."

"I excuse your modesty. But why are you traveling alone, going east?"

"For the very reason you mentioned—to free myself of the city. And to get close to God."

"A noble goal. But on foot?"

"Sì. After my work was done, I rented a room in Colpena. But no sooner had I done so than I needed to get away. This is my second day out. Last night, I camped in the fields under the stars. I plan to find an inn near a quiet meadow or hilltop where I can meditate and renew my devotion to the Lord."

Disapproval scrunching his face, Callisto pointed to the sack at Amadeo's waist. "Is that a money bag?"

"Sì."

"But you must not go farther east. Please, signore, stay the night with us. About ten miles over the rise, bandits have been active."

"When you see our garden and its small chapel"—Simona's eyes were alight—"you will fall in love with it."

Amadeo smiled and bowed once more. "You are both too kind. I will stay the night."

Hours later, Amadeo left the guest bedroom in a clean giornea provided by his host. He followed Simona through the colonnaded garden to the triclinium where half a dozen couches surrounded a long table. In the far corner, a marble faun spouted water from his mouth into a basin.

Servants brought them roasted capons, spiced ham, herbed eggs with onions and cheese, leeks cooked in olive oil, beans, sweet figs, oranges, and pine nuts. All washed down with a fruity red wine.

"From my own vines." Callisto swirled his glass.

"A good vintage, indeed." Amadeo set down his empty glass. "And a feast fit for a lord."

"Pardon my toga." Callisto flicked the cloth at his waist. "And making you recline as you ate. Our ancient customs and history intrigue me."

"As they do me. This villa is remarkably well preserved. You must have done well for yourself."

"We call the place Fair Fields."

"May I ask, is there a Signora Mancini?"

Callisto frowned and examined his plate. "My wife passed away two years ago. Consumption."

"I–I'm sorry."

Callisto waved a hand. "We are—all of us—temporal beings. One day you and I and everyone alive will follow her."

Amadeo nodded.

"Did you know my father is on the Signoria?" Sitting directly across from him, Simona beamed.

"Of course!" Amadeo slapped the table. "I should have remembered the name. Having me here—you do me too much honor."

"Bah!" Callisto gave another dismissing wave. "My spice-importing business has done well. My wealth, not my political aspirations, secured the position. Sometimes I wonder why I let them talk me into it."

"Enough talk." Simona rose from her seat. "It's time you come with me, Signore Puccini. I must show you the garden before we lose the light."

"Please call me Amadeo."

"Very well . . . Amadeo."

He looked to his host, who motioned them both away. "Go with her. She'll not be satisfied until you do."

At a slower pace than this afternoon's near race, she walked close by his side, leading him from the dining room into the colonnaded peristyllium. Only now did he realize this wasn't the garden she wanted to show him.

On the north side, the peristyllium's columns opened into a larger area beyond where servants had lit dozens of torches on the perimeter. Shady olive trees lined a tiled walkway and circled a fountain, where a nymph's mouth spouted and bubbled water into a pool. Tall cypress circled the enclosure and reached for the evening sky. Flower beds bursting with color bordered the crisscrossing paths. Stone benches hid in nooks under trellises of ivy and bougainvillea.

In the garden's center, Simona led him between fluted columns topped with capitals into a dome. Four benches faced a lone wall with a simple marble statue of Jesus on the cross. On an altar before the Savior, candle flames flickered inside glass globes.

"I come here often," she whispered as she sat on the front bench. "In all the villa, this is my favorite spot."

A cool breeze washed his face, bringing the smell of lavender and rosemary. He eased down beside her. "I can see why. It's peaceful. Wonderful."

"Please stay with us, signore." She turned her face to him. Gone were the earlier impish grin, the playful jesting. Before him now sat a more thoughtful, reverent, and—lonely?—woman.

He looked up at the sculpture. He'd left the city to find a place to meditate. Maybe he'd found it. But he wanted no romantic entanglements. Long ago, he'd made a vow of chastity. He faced her. "All right. I'll stay a few days. But I need quiet. Solitude. And time to think. Can you give that to me, Simona?"

She lowered her gaze to the floor as if thinking. But she nodded.

"Then I'll stay."

A smile curved her full lips. She jumped up, and before he could react, she planted a kiss on one cheek. Bounding down the path, she was gone.

On his fifth day at the villa, he sat at a shaded table Callisto had set up for him in the peristyllium's far corner. As sparrows warbled above, he glanced again at the letter from his father asking for money. Once more, the leather shop in San Gimignano was doing poorly, orders weren't coming in, and his brother, Antonio, was deep in debt.

He'd received the parchment before leaving Florence. Everyone in the family looked to him, the wealthy, respected builder, to keep them going. But he barely made enough to pay for his own meals, clothing, and rent. As an architect, he was expected—no, forced—to maintain a certain façade. One of these days, on his way to Florence, he would have to trek the ninety-some miles to San Gimignano. And he'd have to send more money soon.

Folding the note back into his pocket, he picked up his notebook. His pencil resumed the sketches he'd been working on—plans for the construction of a great building. But it was just a thought exercise, worthless scribblings to occupy the mind. Without a commission to put his ideas into practice, what good were they?

His time here had been peaceful, though at first Simona had difficulty leaving him alone. When he reminded her that she'd promised him solitude, she began spending mornings and most afternoons walking the fields or riding her spotted gelding or playing her lyre or pestering her father.

On the third day, Callisto had taken him for a walk beside the field where his sheep grazed. "I'm much impressed with you, Amadeo," he'd said. "You seem an intelligent, virtuous man with good prospects. Have you given thought to taking a wife? My Simona needs a good husband, someone to control her impulsiveness. I fear that without a husband, when we return to the city—well, some of her friends are . . . unbridled. And she seems taken with you."

Surprised by the suggestion, Amadeo had cleared his throat and groped for words. At length, he said, "Thank you, signore. I think someday she will make someone a wonderful wife. But that person cannot be me. I have taken a vow of chastity."

"I . . . see." Callisto had pursed his lips and stared off into the hills. "Well, if you ever decide to renounce your vow, please consider my Simona. I would welcome you into the family."

"Thank you, signore." He had bowed low.

Now on the fifth day, he was finally sloughing off the city's corruption. Though Callisto was on the Signoria, Amadeo now trusted him as a good man and possible future ally. What providence that God had led him to this place of peace and rejuvenation.

His pencil resumed sketching a cupola for an imaginary church.

On the garden's far side, his host was pruning flowers with a clippers.

Loud footsteps crunched over gravel, interrupting his concentration. Beyond cracks in the trellis, a servant led two men toward Callisto. One visitor wore a bishop's green robes. The commoner beside him bore a sword.

"Signore," said the servant to Callisto, "may I present these men of the Church?"

Callisto rose from his work and brushed dirt from his hands. "A bishop, signore?"

"Sì. I am Bishop Rinaldi Ferata, sent on a mission of some importance from the cardinal himself. This is my servant." He waved to the shorter man beside him. "For nearly a week, we've sought a certain Amadeo Puccini, an architect. Have you—?"

"I am he." Amadeo strode the tiled garden path toward them.

The thin-faced bishop rubbed his hands together and beamed. "Glad I am to have finally found you. We've searched every villa, village, and hut from Colpena to here."

"Why do you seek me, bishop?" Amadeo stopped before the two.

"I come on orders from Cardinal Emilio Gonzaga and the pope himself. Signore, we bring you the opportunity of a lifetime. The Church wishes to build a grand cathedral in Colpena. And we have selected *you* as the architect and capomaestro."

Callisto put hands on hips and grinned.

Like the first time he saw the seashore as a child, excitement started Amadeo's heart aflutter. To build a grand duomo—what an offering for God that could be! Such a project would be the work of a lifetime, consuming him, devouring every waking thought, becoming the center of his existence from the moment of the commission until the day of his death.

Yet with whom was he to work? Who was the *padrone* funding it, and was he worthy of the task? For whoever paid for such an enterprise would want a great deal of control in the matter. The builder would have to work closely with him. Amadeo fixed his glance on the green-robed bishop. "Will the people of Colpena fund it with contributions and indulgences? Or will the patron of this grand enterprise be the Church itself?"

No longer beaming, Ferata lowered his gaze and shuffled his feet on the graveled path. "No, signore. The sole padrone will be Signore Dario Rossi, the gonfaloniere of Colpena's Signoria. It is to be a grand indulgence for his sins. By order of Pope Paul II himself."

"Dario Rossi?" His stomach lurched. All the exuberance of moments ago crashed down around him.

"Sì, signore. And because of the nature of the sins involved, the duomo's design must be on a grand scale."

To build a great cathedral—that, precisely, was his life's goal. But how could he agree to work for a man such as Rossi? It would entirely negate whatever glory the work brought to God.

He whirled and stared across the garden. It had to be Rossi, didn't it? He'd heard the stories. Of all the men in Colpena, the patron had to be the one man with the worst reputation, a worshiper of hedonism if ever there was. And, if the rumors were true, also a murderer. Amadeo spun on his heels and faced them, his lips pursed, his jaw set.

"No, bishop. I cannot—I *will* not—spend a lifetime working for Dario Rossi."

The bishop's mouth opened, and he gasped. "B–but, signore, it is for God's glory! It is for—"

"My answer is final. I cannot build a duomo for such a man." While their eyes widened in disbelief, he stalked under the columns, along the path to the garden chapel.

There he slumped heavily onto cold stone. He'd just abandoned his penultimate desire and cast off his chance at the one goal he'd hoped would be his life's work. Dropping his head into his hands, he tried to still his racing heart.

A quiet moan escaped his lips.

CHAPTER 4

~ JACOPO PASSERO ~

Three days had passed since Jacopo Passero arrived at Acque Salutari. Three days since the Bergman brothers dropped their shovels, clanking over the rocks, and looked up to greet him with outstretched hands.

"Where's Kuhn?" he'd asked, noting the absence of their business partner.

"He lie in his room. His foot—very bad," Rudolf, the red-bearded brother built like a horse, had said.

"Cannot walk." Wolf wiped sweat from his brow. "Maybe tomorrow."

Jacopo cleared his throat. Their Italian was bad, but he understood. "I have a new deal for you. One I think you'll like. Can we go somewhere comfortable and talk?"

Rudolf glanced at Wolf and exchanged a few words in German. Then they took Jacopo down the slope to an isolated table at the empty resort where a waiter brought them each a mug of beer. This week, as it was most weeks, the hot springs was nearly deserted.

"Tell us, Jacopo, of this deal." Wolf grabbed his mug and downed half of it in one gulp.

"My master wants to buy this property. And he doesn't want Rocco Marino to know about the alum you've found."

"But, Herr Passero." Wolf threw back his long brown hair. "The alum we do find. We cannot keep this—how you say—to us only."

"My brother is right. This secret we cannot keep," said Rudolf. "We want to deal, but Herr Kuhn—he tell Marino."

"Not yet, though?"

"Nein. He cannot walk or ride. Bad injury."

"Then you and I can agree on a deal. Leave Kuhn to me." Jacopo proceeded to bargain. They settled on a price of one thousand florins for each brother—a great sum, sì, but so were the stakes. In return, they would bury the first hole, dig another where they would find no alum, and report the bad news to Rocco Marino. After Dario secured the land's purchase, they'd receive the sole franchise for the mining and manufacture of alum for as long as the ground produced.

As they shook hands, the Bergmans gave each other wide smiles. Why would they not like this arrangement? Money up front. And a guarantee of employment for as long as the mine held out.

"But, Herr Jacopo." Wolf held up a callused hand. "Nothing happen to Kuhn, ja?"

"No, signore. I'll present him with the same offer."

"But if he not agree, then what?"

"I will convince him."

"But if he go to Herr Marino . . . ?"

"Leave that to me. He won't."

The next day, Kuhn returned, limping, to the site. Jacopo took him aside and tried to reason with him, but Kuhn angrily waved him away, saying in broken Italian that Jacopo and his boss were dishonorable crooks. Stalking to the Bergman brothers, he said in German, "I am going to Colpena now." Jacopo understood most of what was said. "Herr Marino must know what we found."

The Bergmans tried to convince him otherwise, but Kuhn wouldn't hear of it. He gathered his things, found his horse, and rode off.

"Deal no good now." Wolf laid his hands on his hips and shook his head.

"No. I will go after him." Jacopo's horse was already saddled and waiting. "I'll change his mind. The deal is still good. You'll see."

Jacopo followed Kuhn at a distance, always keeping him in sight, but being careful that Kuhn didn't see his pursuer. As evening's shadows lengthened, the crickets' deafening chorus masked the clomp of his horse's hooves. But the man obviously didn't know the area, for he stopped in the orchard by the road only two miles from the next village. Did he not know bandits sometimes roamed the highways?

Jacopo tethered his horse out of sight under an apple tree. While he waited, his mare munched fruit from the ground.

As the darkness thickened, Kuhn lit a fire, ate bread from his pack, and lay down.

Another hour passed. Jacopo pulled out his twelve-inch, serrated blade with its deep blood gutter and crept through the tall grass.

When he neared the campsite, Kuhn's horse whinnied, stamped its foot.

Breathing heavily, Jacopo stopped. He didn't enjoy this part of being the Rossis' distant cousin. But Dario was counting on him. On a different job, he'd have taken Paolo and Naldo to help. But surely, he could take care of this Austrian—thin as a post with an injured foot—by himself. Besides, showing up at the Bergman brothers in force wasn't an option.

His plan was not to knife Kuhn, but to knock him out. Then take the blanket and suffocate him, make the death appear natural. It must not look like murder.

But the deed must be done, must it not? Jacopo needed Dario's largesse. And he feared to cross this gonfaloniere.

He gripped the knife so hard, his knuckles ached. How many times had he done such a deed?

Even *he* had heard the rumors about the Rossis. Rumors undergirded by a truth Jacopo himself had created.

Standing, he crept through the grass, placing his feet gently, silently, on the turf.

The horse neighed again.

Only ten feet away, Kuhn lay under a blanket beside the fire. The logs had burned to coals, shedding a dim light.

Jacopo's heart fluttered, for surely this was a dishonorable act—to murder someone in their bed in the dead of night. All for money. But was not money the fuel that fired business, that gave one the good life and opened all doors?

What the priests peddled was fantasy. Jacopo and Dario lived in the real world.

The irritating horse neighed once more.

Kuhn rolled toward him and opened his eyes.

No time for a natural death now. Jacopo raced the distance.

Kuhn jerked himself upright, fumbled in his pack for something.

Jacopo grabbed the other's hand and squeezed it so hard, the man cried out and dropped something—a knife? His own blade plunged deep into Kuhn's side and twisted. He struck again. And again. His hand came back warm, wet, and sticky.

Kuhn's limp form collapsed to the ground.

The horse whinnied and stomped. A bit of blanket, having fallen into the fire, began smoking. Jacopo pulled it out and rose from his work, breathing hard.

What a mess he'd made of this! Now he'd have to bury the body and the man's possessions. He'd have to free the horse somewhere east of here. And clean the blood off his clothes. No one must see him like this.

"But at least, Dario Rossi," he said to the night sky, "you'll have your alum mine."

CHAPTER 5

~ THE TOWER ~

Five days after their first visit, the bishop and his companion came again to Amadeo, restating the same question. Would he not relent and build Colpena's grand duomo?

But his answer hadn't changed.

A week after that, only two days ago, Bishop Rinaldi Ferata had returned, bearing a plea coupled with a warning—if Amadeo refused again, the decision would be out of his hands. The statement was vague, ominous, and the bishop seemed uncomfortable delivering it.

Still, Amadeo would not relent.

After the two men had gone and as he sat scratching out a drawing on a garden bench, Callisto had approached. "Amadeo, my friend, you should accept Dario's proposal. The people need this building. When a cathedral comes to a city, it gives the place a new, thriving center, a new reason for existence, and an increase in commerce. So do it for them. Do it also for God's glory."

"What you say is true. But the man who's paying for it is . . . unholy."

As the breeze curved his toga around his torso, Callisto frowned. "I'm his distant cousin, and I sit on the Signoria. So I know him well. I tell you truly, he has a stranglehold on the council. And who hasn't heard the rumors of murder? I've seen his machinations and watched him destroy many—too many—who've crossed him. Everyone knows he's licentious. But these days, who isn't? Yet the man has a good side."

"What?" Amadeo snorted.

"His friend, Lorenzo de' Medici in Florence, has convinced him to patronize the new breed of artists, of whom we have too few here in Colpena. He also gave money to help build the hospital, though I admit this was a bribe to secure votes in the Council of Thirty. But consider this—most of what he does, though it increases his wealth and power, also benefits the city."

"He's an unrepentant sinner who taints all he comes in contact with. You're asking me to work with him for the rest of my life." Amadeo shook his head. "I'd fear for my mortal soul."

"Are you not strong enough to resist his bad example?"

Callisto's question silenced him. Still, he remained unmoved, and Callisto left him alone, saying no more.

TWO DAYS LATER, IN MIDMORNING, as Amadeo sketched in a new notebook Callisto had given him, the rustling of leather, the creaking of armor, and the crunch of boots on gravel disturbed his peace. Six helmeted men armed with pikes approached. An angry, flustered Callisto followed.

"You must not do this." His face red, his hands gesturing, Callisto paced back and forth. "Is there no sanctity in a man's own villa?"

"I'm sorry, signore." Brass armor wrapped the stocky leader's chest. "But we have orders to arrest this man and return him to Colpena."

"On what charge?" Amadeo rose from the bench. Anger began burning his face, but even as it rose up, he tried to quell it.

"Failure to obey a summons from the gonfaloniere."

"Bah!" said Callisto. "The city guard can't arrest him for *that*. He was offered a position, not given a summons."

"I have my orders." The guard shrugged, his armor clanking. "From Dario Rossi himself."

At least they allowed him to gather his notes and possessions. As Simona watched with teary eyes, her hands covering her mouth, they shoved him in a closed carriage out front.

It trundled off down the dusty road. Soldiers rode in front and behind.

When the Mancini country refuge disappeared over a hillcrest, Amadeo realized his heart was racing. What price would he now pay for his principles? He'd heard the rumors of disappearances, murders, and the scores whose lives had been ruined because they'd crossed this gonfaloniere. And then there was this—Rossi was a man against whom no accusation of wrongdoing ever stuck.

ABOUT AN HOUR BEFORE SUNSET, the carriage rumbled through Colpena's northern gate, onto the cobbled Strada del Nord, and climbed the hill. At the narrow Piazza della Signoria, it stopped below the town hall doors. A heavyset guard with a stubbled chin marched Amadeo up long, echoing steps. They passed cramped, barred cells. One floor above that, at the tower's top, the guard ushered him into a larger room. Twelve feet in diameter, it was furnished with a bed and blankets, a table, chair, candles, a washbasin, and a chamber pot—perhaps the best accommodations the tower offered.

A cell, nonetheless.

Hugging his knapsack, he stood in his new quarters before the guard who introduced himself as Luigi.

"I am now to say"—Luigi winced as though in apology—"that you must think upon the offer you have received. The gonfaloniere will not release you until you agree to his request." Before Amadeo could respond, the iron door banged shut, the lock clicked, and the wind whistled through the open window.

He ran to the opening, grabbed the stone casement, and looked down. The square bustled with tiny ant-men and ant-women ending their day, sitting beside the fountain, or simply passing by. The drop was over seventy feet.

So this was how it would be? The gonfaloniere would keep him locked up until he relented? Well, he would not relent.

FOUR DAYS PASSED. THE GUARD brought him meals, emptied his chamber pot, and quietly, apologetically, repeated Dario Rossi's demand. Each time, Amadeo refused and requested to see the gonfaloniere in person.

Starting at six o'clock in the morning, the bell above his room would begin tolling. Six strikes shook the walls, pealing so loudly he had to cover his ears. Then each hour throughout the day, it announced the time until twelve o'clock in the evening after which it fell silent until morning.

The bell marked his time in the tower prison, reminding him of each hour Rossi had stolen from him.

On the fourth day, Bishop Ferata himself brought him his morning repast. "I'm truly sorry for this." The bishop set down a tray containing two boiled eggs, two slices of bread, a wedge of cheese, and butter and jam. "I just found out. I thought he meant to undertake some kind of legal action—not this."

"Yet this is what he did." Amadeo sat at his table and drank from a glass of water flavored with lemon. They provided him with far better food than most prisoners ever received.

"This morning, I wrote to Cardinal Gonzaga about the matter. But I know what he'll say. He'll not approve what Rossi has done. Yet he will do nothing to change the mind of this gonfaloniere." Ferata waved his hand over the cell. "You must understand—this is not the Church's doing."

"Yet here I am." Amadeo bit off part of an egg.

"But, signore, what would it hurt for you to build the duomo? Everyone involved believes you are best for the work. The Wool Guild, the Church, the Council of Thirty, even the Signoria—all want you for the task. As do I."

"Thank you, bishop." Unmoved, Amadeo spread butter and jam over the toast. "But Dario Rossi is unworthy to be the padrone of such a grand and holy work. His participation taints the project."

"I . . . know. But when he agreed to wholly fund the construction, did he not confess his sins? Was that not an admission of penance? The cost is truly extravagant. I hear it will take most of the Rossi Bank's income to fund it. Signore Rossi himself has said he must pay for the sins he's committed."

Amadeo stopped eating and looked up. "He has?"

Ferata hesitated, then nodded.

"Will he come here to me and admit as much? In person?"

The bishop's eyes brightened. "I will request that he do so."

THAT VERY AFTERNOON, WHEN LUIGI opened his cell door with a loud rattling of keys, Amadeo expected to see his persecutor standing behind him. Instead, the guard ordered him to follow.

They descended the narrow, winding tower staircase, emerging on the town hall's ground floor. Luigi then led him down an echoing hallway to a street-side chamber. Pushing open the door, he entered a small room crowded with three stuffed chairs, one against each wall.

The door clicked shut behind him.

"Please sit." Before him sat a man of nearly thirty, leaning his elbow on an armchair. "Let us talk."

Hair as black as night curled inward above his shoulders. Prominent dark eyebrows outlined intense black eyes. His nose curved slightly out at the tip. With a clean-shaven face, he presented the perfect picture of the handsome rogue.

But the intensity of his eyes! Something was going on behind those orbs that Amadeo could not grasp. Was it sadness? Weariness? Pain?

"You have imprisoned me without cause, signore." Only six feet separated them. "What gives you the right?"

With a sigh, Rossi lifted his chin from his hand. "The Church sent delegation after delegation to ask you to build my duomo for me. Yet you refused."

"Because I do not consider you a worthy patron for such a grand work. And it would not be *your* duomo."

Rossi narrowed his eyes. "Worthy or not, I need this duomo, architect."

"Why?"

Rossi's gaze unfocused and wandered to the wall beside them, to some painting of the haloed Virgin and child, dark and discolored by age. From an open window came the smell of manure and the sounds of a cart creaking along a narrow back lane. "I'll tell you the truth, Amadeo Puccini. I'm a doomed man."

His head jerking up in surprise, Amadeo gripped the chair's arms. "Doomed?"

"I know, Puccini, what I am. And one of those wandering priests, a Franciscan I believe, confronted me with a vision of my future."

Was Rossi serious? The man appeared afflicted by some inner turmoil. Amadeo leaned forward in his chair. "What future?"

"In the lake of eternal fire."

This man before him—this great wielder of power, this leader who controlled the lives of everyone in the city—appeared tortured, racked with guilt. This he had not expected. "And you think building a great cathedral will absolve you?"

"Sì. I have a guarantee from the pope himself."

Sitting back, Amadeo released his grip on the chair's arms. The man believed it with all his heart. Was this not what the bishop had said? That he was truly repentant and looking for absolution? But how could a man's works ever make him right with God if he himself was not a true child of Christ? Yet this was no time to debate theology.

"I will pay for everything you ask for." Rossi sat up straighter, his eyes suddenly alight, his hands gripping the armrests so his knuckles whitened. "You'll have complete control over the construction. For I know nothing of building a duomo. You'll receive a reasonable salary, a clothing allowance, the best quarters near the site, and as many workers as you need."

"I haven't agreed to anything yet."

"If you do not, architect, you will doom my soul to an eternity in the flames."

Was Amadeo now responsible for this man's soul? No, it couldn't be. Yet Rossi seemed truly repentant. Or at least, he believed building the duomo was his repentance. "I admit, gonfaloniere—you've given me reason to reexamine my refusal. But first, you must free me. I'll not agree to anything while a prisoner in your tower."

Rossi's eyes closed. He pressed fingers to his forehead and massaged it. "I've not had a good night's sleep since the monk's second visit." He opened pained eyes. "You see, Puccini, I am cursed to believe in the Christ and in God's eternal judgment. I am also cursed to do what I must do."

"Will you free me?"

Rossi looked into Amadeo's eyes. "What kind of man do you think I am?"

Startled by the question, Amadeo stammered. "I–I don't know what you mean."

"Am I a good man? Or am I something else?"

"Every man has some good within him, I suppose."

"You suppose." Rossi grimaced. "So you don't know whether there's any good in me or not?"

"I don't know you, Signore Rossi. Only what I've heard."

"I can only guess what you've heard. The tongues, they do wag, do they not?"

"Will you free me?"

"Sì, I will free you. I've already bought suitable quarters for you near the building site, a site that the bishop and cardinal have already chosen. Any architect charged with building my duomo must not live in the hovel you rented. I've also taken the liberty of moving your things there—but only two bags, signore? Really? What kind of life requires so few worldly goods?" Abruptly, he stood, opened the door, and held a muffled conversation with the guard. Turning back, he said, "The guard will lead you there. If you decline the task . . ." He opened his hands and shook his head.

"I promise I will consider it with the utmost seriousness."

Rossi only nodded. Haunted eyes found the floor. "Then go."

The guard led Amadeo through the hall and down the steps into a crowded palazzo.

He was free.

CHAPTER 6

~ THE SITE ~

As the guard led him from the bustling street into the quiet house, Amadeo gawked. These quarters were better than anything he was accustomed to. Only a block from the Piazza dei Sole, it occupied the first floor of a three-story building, with a bedroom, dining room, kitchen, sitting room that could become his study or workroom, and best of all, a patio inside a walled garden in back, accessible only by him. The upper-story tenants even had their own outside stairwell. The guard dropped the key in his hands and left.

Was he being bribed? Every master builder expected to receive lodging, clothing, and a significant salary. But usually, one stayed at an inn. This was better than most in his position ever received.

Amadeo poured wine from a bottle they'd left him and went into the garden. Sitting before a small table, he mulled Rossi's proposition. The man seemed truly repentant. Rossi believed that, by funding the duomo's construction, his sins would be forgiven.

Amadeo wasn't so sure. Yet, if Rossi believed it, what did it matter?

Then there was the project itself. For the better part of his adult life, creating such a work was all he'd ever dreamed of. To build a truly great cathedral—why, the very thought sent his heart racing.

His notebooks were full of sketches for arches, pilasters, façades, domes, stained-glass windows, statues, and frescoes. Ever since his apprenticeship to Leon Battista Alberti, he'd been designing a new kind of cathedral on parchment—a duomo based on symmetry, geometry, and classical Roman architecture. One with a massive central dome, like Brunelleschi's. And instead of the usual mishmash of styles, everything would be ordered. Hemispherical apses and niches. Semicircular arches, not pointed as in the past. And to support the great weight—stately columns, not bulky flying buttresses.

Rossi, for all his sins, was giving him a chance to bring all these ideas—and those of Alberti—together. It would fulfill a lifelong dream.

Intending to review his sketches, he pulled out the notebooks bulging in his knapsack when someone rapped on the front door. He rose, walked through his—that is, Rossi's—house, and opened the door. "Bishop Ferata, what are you doing here?"

"The gonfaloniere just gave me an important message." Ferata was breathing hard as if he'd been running. "I'm to escort you to the building site."

Amadeo's heart quickened. Rossi had said they'd already picked a site. In spite of his suspicion he was being manipulated, he nodded. "Lead the way."

THE END OF THE STREET opened onto the Piazza dei Sole. He'd walked the square many times. Peasant women now rushed past, bearing armloads of bread, wine, cheese, and foodstuffs for the night's meal. Merchants called to customers, and hawkers sold slices of panini from street-side stalls. Ferata pointed north to a small, aging palazzo belonging to a recently deceased member of the Signoria. The Church had purchased it for him and his eventual retinue.

On the square's eastern side began a few shops and buildings untouched by the fire. Farther west lay charred timbers and tumbled stones, where flames had devastated the old church and nearly an entire block. Before rains had damped the blaze, the city had emptied its largest cistern trying to put it out.

"The Church has purchased the burned-out section and all the remaining houses in this block." Ferata's wave encompassed the entire space. "It's the one thing we were prepared to do. The area west of the Piazza dei Sole is a hundred fifty yards wide. It extends two hundred yards to the lip of the old wall."

Whenever a duomo was built, it was always thus. People had to give up their homes, shops, sometimes even their livelihoods, to make way for the new city center. The fire had already done much of the demolition work.

"Of course, we're paying the remaining tenants for their properties. And Rossi will hire some of the displaced as laborers."

"Can we climb to the top floor of your palazzo for an overall view?"

"Sì. Follow me."

Ferata ushered him through empty rooms to a roof overlooking the Via san Cristo and the site. Amadeo gazed west at the block of homes, shops, and the ruined church. "They're piling rubble in the square?"

"The debris? Some of our newly hired laborers have already begun the demolition work. We will, of course, turn the bills over to Rossi."

"You already have a building committee?"

"Only two Signoria members and myself. The Signoria will choose the other two members tomorrow."

His gaze sweeping again over the area, Amadeo imagined the duomo that could soon rise from this spot. What a grand monument to God it could be!

If he had his way, it would be a work of art and architecture like nothing on earth—a holy structure where every niche, wall, and column would pay homage to the Creator of the world and his Son.

"Signore? Are you all right?"

Amadeo turned to the bishop, his face flushed, his heart beating faster. "I'm fine. Now let's inspect the area."

And so they did. At the far end of the designated building site, a group of forty young men wielded sledges, crowbars, and axes. They were dismantling the charred stone and wooden houses, brick by brick, board by board, carting off the debris in wheelbarrows.

"We're piling the bricks and the old Roman stones in the piazza." Ferata pointed in that direction. "We'll burn the wood."

When they reentered the Piazza dei Sole, Amadeo thanked the bishop and returned to his new home.

After the tour, he desired more than ever to build the cathedral. Yet, because of Rossi's involvement, he remained torn.

Nursing a glass of wine, he sat in his garden, gripped by an inner torment. It was late when he finally found his bed.

THE DREAM THAT DESCENDED UPON him was like nothing he'd ever experienced.

He was walking down the central aisle of an enormous cathedral. Slanting rays of light filled the space, but the light came not from the sun, but from the walls, the floor, the ceiling. The tiles at his feet glowed and pulsed with crimson, azure, yellow, jasper. The floor shone with all the symbols of Christendom—the fish, the cross, the priest's miter, the offering cup, the bread of Christ's body, the robe of Jesus, and on and on. They shone with such brilliance he feared to tread upon them.

On the walls, row upon row of angels, Apostles, and Old Testament figures came to life in frescoes and sculptures so well painted and carved, they seemed alive. The high, stained-glass windows told the Bible stories, glowed, and shot beams of colored light.

Far above on the ceiling, giant figures of Adam and Eve, Abraham, Moses, and Joshua were painted in glorious color, caught at various moments in their stories.

He glanced down the row of seats, their railings etched with intricate designs, their backs padded, awaiting congregants.

Ahead in the nave, a huge statue of Christ, wrought from pure white marble, seemed about to ascend to Heaven. Beyond it loomed great paintings of Christ at his birth, as he preached, and on his way to the cross.

Above, a massive dome sparkled with brilliant color and light.

He fell to his knees and cried out, "My Lord, is this what you've planned for me? Is this what I am to build?"

A being of light—an angel?—coalesced before the altar and floated across the floor. As Amadeo's heart pounded furiously, the gossamer creature took his hands, looked into his eyes, and nodded.

A sense of wonder, awe, and holiness such as he'd never experienced permeated every fiber of his being. So great was the happiness that gripped him, tears flowed down his cheeks. Sobs racked his body.

Then the angel vanished, and Amadeo was alone in the nave.

Here, in this duomo, was a vision of God's glory captured by the work of human hands.

Here was his life's work, laid out for him by the Creator.

Here was the answer he sought.

CHAPTER 7

~ PLANS ~

The next morning, ready to start and unwilling to wait for a summons, Amadeo walked the short distance to Rossi's palazzo and left a note with his man Grazziano, saying he'd made up his mind to work on the duomo. Grazziano agreed to bring the gonfaloniere's reply in person.

He waited. But no reply came.

Another day passed in an agonizing wait. Why didn't Rossi respond? The gonfaloniere had even imprisoned him to make him agree. So why the delay?

On the second morning, he was preparing to return to Rossi's house when a young messenger arrived at the door. "I was told to give you this." The boy handed him a piece of paper.

Amadeo opened it and read:

To Amadeo Puccini, Master Architect,

Happy I am that you have decided to be our capomaestro. But there has been an unwelcome development.

The final building committee has been chosen, and yesterday, we met. Against my wishes, one of the new members has insisted we follow a certain protocol inscribed in city statutes regarding the construction of all major public buildings.

Therefore, we must hold a competition for the building design. Only the one who presents the committee with a superior design will hold the title of capomaestro for Colpena's duomo.

The other candidate is Basilio Bramante, the half-brother of the illustrious Donato Bramante from Urbino. Though deeply involved as head of the unfinished city water project, Bramante is eager for the commission. He also has a champion on the committee.

It is now late April. The contestants have until the second week of July to present the committee with their plans.

This in no way changes your domicile in the Strada delle Campane. I am confident your design will prove the most worthy.

Signore Dario Rossi
Gonfaloniere of Colpena

Amadeo stared at the letter. So now, after all of Rossi's manipulations to convince him to become the architect, he must compete against another? Now, when the idea of building this great cathedral was pumping through his blood like floodwater down a river?

Basilio Bramante's brother was a respected architect, but what had Basilio himself ever done? For seven years, he'd worked on Colpena's water project, and still, it lay unfinished. Had the man ever constructed a building?

Well, if it was competition they wanted, they would get it. He'd design not just a grand cathedral, but perhaps the greatest cathedral the world has ever known. Now it would be bigger, taller, grander than any building yet conceived.

He nearly ran to his desk.

ITS WINGS BUZZING, A MOTH hovered above the parchment spread out over the garden table. Amadeo rubbed bleary eyes. With the back of his hand, he knocked the insect toward one of seven candles sputtering in their waist-high stands. Scraping his chair over the flagstones, he stood and glanced down at the night's work.

Over a month had passed since he'd started drawing and sketching, a month of furious, concentrated effort.

Tonight, he'd drawn details for the center of the duomo's façade—the door complex. Forty-foot-high bronze doors would lead into the nave. Surrounding the recessed doors were thirty arches, starting large, growing smaller, diminishing with each new layer. The effect would be like entering a heavenly tunnel.

Above the arches sat a unique addition—a mammoth stained-glass window in a starburst pattern. He planned to set the window inside a steel hub, using the same marble as the façade and with steel-reinforced arms.

He straightened his back and yawned.

Behind him, leather scraped on gravel. "Will my master be wanting breakfast?" came Skender's sleepy voice.

"Lad, have you been there all night?" He hadn't noticed his young servant curled up in the corner under the palms.

"Sì, signore."

"No, thank you. No breakfast." Somewhere outside the high garden walls, a dog barked. The sky was lightening. Once again, he'd worked through the night. "I think I'll sleep now."

Skender brushed aside tawny locks falling to his shoulders. The boy had arrived at Colpena's port at the age of seven on a slave galley from Rumania. Rossi had bought him and sent him to his palazzo's downstairs kitchen. Only days after Amadeo had begun work on his plans, the lord of Colpena bequeathed the slave, now thirteen, to the architect as house-boy and cook.

Amadeo tried to free the lad, but it was no use. Having lived half his life in Italy and not even knowing his own last name, Skender had nowhere else to go. Amadeo gave in to his plea and let him stay, but as a freeman with a salary of seven florins a year.

"Shall I take in your parchments, signore?"

Amadeo nodded, smiling at the short handsome youth, so eager to please, so happy to be in Amadeo's service.

Skender collected the parchments covered with lists of materials needed, detailed sketches of the outside columns, the dome, the interior supporting arches, and the campanile.

He'd finished it all in four weeks. Behind it were years of apprentice-ship to Alberti. Years of studying Alberti's designs, listening to Alberti's musings about building, and reading snatches of Alberti's grand unfinished treatise on architecture. Years of directing work on Florence's Church of San Ambrose. Years of visiting every duomo within a month's travel. Years of filling so many sketchbooks and notebooks that they lined an entire shelf behind the kitchen. These he'd taken from his parent's house in San Gimignano and brought here.

No, the sketches bulging in Skender's arms were more than the work of a few weeks. They were the pent-up ideas, experiences, and aspirations of a lifetime, bursting onto paper in a single furious month.

Amadeo blew out the candles.

Skender brought the precious parchments inside and laid them on the study table.

"Before I sleep, Skender, come and walk with me."

"As you wish, signore."

Amadeo rose, exited the house, and turned left onto the cobbled street. A short walk later, as the sun rose, they were looking out over what remained of the Piazza dei Sole.

The duomo was yet without an official capomaestro. Still, Amadeo had pleaded with Bishop Ferata to quintuple the number of *contadino* the Church employed to clear the site. Whoever won the contest, Amadeo had argued, would need the buildings cleared at a faster pace. Otherwise, construction couldn't start until next year. Ferata had agreed.

With three hundred and fifty men now employed, they were quickly removing the stones of the old church, demolishing the burned-out shops and warehouses, and even pulling up the flagstones of the Piazza dei Sole and gathering them in a pile.

With little room to spare on the hill, they'd need to construct the future Piazza del Duomo as soon as possible—but on the very location where the old church and the burned-out shops had stood. The workshop lodges would rise atop the new piazza.

"They've done much in a short time, signore."

"But there's so much more to do. Tomorrow—I mean, this afternoon—I'll start making the model."

"A model, signore?"

"I've finished the basic design. Now I must create something to present to the building committee. The sketches in my rooms—they'll never understand them. Such men have no concept of geometry. Or how two dimensions can illustrate three."

Skender's bewildered look stopped him. "And, lad, with making the model you can help."

The boy beamed.

"But now I think it's time for sleep."

"Signore?" A question twisted Skender's upturned face.

"Sì?"

"I am glad to be with you. You are a good master. I will serve you always."

Amadeo smiled, patted the boy's shoulder, and they returned to the apartment, he to his bed, and Skender to his mat on the kitchen floor.

He would now put all his energies into creating the most impressive model he could conceive. For only that would sway the building committee.

CHAPTER 8

~ A FLORENTINE WEDDING ~

JUNE 1469

As the horses in his entourage clattered across the bridge over the River Arno and entered the heart of Florence, Dario sighed with relief and anticipation. His long weeks of anguish had finally ended. Two architects were working on the duomo design. One of them would soon begin construction. Dario's absolution was guaranteed.

Not only that, but Jacopo had returned from his third trip to Acque Salutari. At first, the Bergman brothers were troubled by Kuhn's disappearance. But with gory anecdotes about travelers who'd met disasters at bandits' hands, Jacopo impressed upon the brothers the dangers of traveling the roads alone. As the weeks passed, they seemed to accept that their business partner had met with some unknown disaster. And, of course, Jacopo's payment of a thousand florins to each helped squash any lingering qualms.

Having successfully convinced Rocco Marino that the site contained no alum, the brothers left for Siena, there to await Dario's summons. Before a notary, Dario sealed the land purchase with Rocco for three thousand florins.

Expenses of clearing the land for the duomo were already arriving on his desk. Since Acque Salutari was now his, he had instructed the Bergmans to return to where they'd first dug and begin working on the mine. They needed the income as soon as possible.

But for the next seven days, he'd leave all that behind. This week, it would be like the years when he'd lived in the Palazzo Medici with Lorenzo before he became responsible for Colpena's welfare.

"Dario, look." Aldo pointed from atop his horse to the great dome of Santa Maria del Fiore rising majestically above the city, announcing that here, a new Rome, a new center of culture, had arisen.

"Sì, cousin. While we're here, we must take mass in that cathedral. And just think: someday, Colpena will have a duomo to rival Florence's."

"For the price you agreed to pay, I hope your architect can compete with Brunelleschi's dome."

"I have confidence in him."

Aldo twisted in the saddle, frowning. "I'm not happy about this. You've just cut my income by three-fourths. And without asking me."

"It was necessary. The alum mine will soon make up for what we spend on the cathedral."

His cousin threw a dismissing wave. "That could take months. Possibly a year. Meanwhile, we could go broke."

"The duomo will bring new life to Colpena. Every city with a cathedral sees an increase in trade and wealth. That will also pad our accounts."

"As you've said. But why couldn't the Church have helped with the expense? It's not too late to ask them for indulgences from the people."

Dario shrugged and faced away. He wouldn't argue his reasons with his cousin. "I needed to do it, Aldo. It's done."

His jaw tensing, Aldo stared at him, then jerked his horse away. He fell to the back of the line—behind two men and two women servants, plus four mercenaries they'd brought for protection.

Dario exhaled, low and deep. Let Aldo cool his anger with their hirelings before they met their host.

When they arrived at the Palazzo Medici, servants took their horses and ushered them through a wide patioed garden, where a fountain's nymph gurgled water into a basin. Lorenzo himself greeted them under the palms in the open-air foyer beyond.

"My friend, it's been too long." He crushed Dario in a hug, then regarded Aldo. "This must be your cousin. Welcome, both of you." He shook Aldo's hand.

"How's your father?" asked Dario.

"Not well. He's up in his room. I fear he may miss most of the ceremony."

"The gout is bad, is it?"

"Sì, my friend. A family curse, I'm afraid."

Gripping Lorenzo's shoulders, Dario looked long at this man whom he'd grown to love in the three years he lived here. With a strong chin, a protruding lower lip, and a broad, squashed nose, he was not particularly handsome. In spite of this and his clumsiness, he was tall and muscular and exuded a kind of primitive charm women found attractive. "When is the feast?"

"Three days hence. Enough time for you, your cousin, and perhaps Luigi Pulci to help a man enjoy his last bout of fun as a bachelor. Do you know Luigi?"

"No."

"A clever poet. And a diplomat I've used in the past. But this week, I throw obligation to the wind. This week is for feasting, revelry, and celebration."

"Where's the bride?"

"Staying with the Alessandris. Where else could we put a daughter of nobility but with other nobles?"

"How are the people taking this marriage?"

"You've heard the whispers, then? My father thinks to marry me into the Orsini nobility. But the common folk are not happy she's a foreigner from Rome. Every wealthy Florentine family wanted me to marry their daughter. So the pageant I put on last February and this feast"—he waved across the square—"I'm hoping it will mollify the lot of them."

Dario had badly wanted to attend the jousting in the Piazza Santa Croce in February, but events conspired to keep him away. Apparently, young men from every wealthy family in Florence had paraded into the square wearing so much ermine, velvet, and silk, it all but concealed the expensive armor beneath. The families bore their crests on pennants attached with silver or gold thread. Even the horses were bedecked with pounds of silk, handfuls of jewels.

The jousts went on all afternoon until a victor had emerged. It was Lorenzo, of course, and the battle was rigged. But the folk filling the stands in the square's center and in the balconies above cared not, for they'd been given a grand spectacle the likes of which no one had seen for centuries. Everyone had cheered wildly.

That, at least, was the report Dario had received.

"But evening approaches." Lorenzo's eyes were bright. "So let us forget the people and their demands. Let us celebrate."

Lorenzo's moods could swing quickly from deep thoughtfulness to wild abandon. In his presence, friends were always entertained, lurching from crazy antics, drinking, and whoring, to deep philosophical discussions, poetry, and a quiet somber moodiness. Today, Lorenzo was in high spirits.

LUIGI PULCI NEVER CAME, so the three of them walked the narrow lanes to one of Lorenzo's favorite haunts. They left a street crowded with talking, gesturing couples and bands of laughing young men. In a taverna's main first-floor room, they drank wine, laughed, and sang along with the other boisterous customers. One by one, they ascended the steps to the brothel upstairs, where young women eager to please such celebrity patrons satisfied their every delight.

Leaving the taverna late, the three weaved through the streets, laughing and sharing a last jug of wine. But as they rounded a corner down a narrow alley, Lorenzo's torch shone on a body lying flat on the cobbles. With a pale face, eyes staring straight up, and limbs unmoving—was it a corpse?

The bottle Dario carried slipped from his fingers, exploded on the stone. Shards of broken glass shot across the alley.

The others' laughter ceased.

Lorenzo dropped to his knees, laid a hand on the man's cheeks, then ripped it away. "He's dead." He stepped back, his gaze fixed on the corpse. "And I know him."

Dario stared. The man wore the clothes of a wealthy merchant. Brocade. Silk. A cravat sporting a large emerald. He must have died recently, as no thief had yet stripped him of valuables.

"He's Celino Vecoli. And he owns—he owned—a spice business." Lorenzo's voice lost all its gaiety. "I talked with him . . . only yesterday."

"What happened to him?" whispered Aldo.

Holding the torch high, Lorenzo knelt again, examined his left and right side, and then rose. "A natural death, I think. They said he had trouble with his heart. It must have happened just like that." Lorenzo snapped his fingers. "One moment we breathe, we eat, we drink, and we make love. The next—we're food for the worms."

Dario shuddered. He didn't like this new mood of Lorenzo's.

"We are poor creatures, are we not?" Lorenzo's brows furrowed. "Designed by our Creator to enjoy life. Driven to take pleasure at every opportunity, wherever and whenever we find it. We need it, we want it, and yet we are also cursed by it. For as much as we desire the touch and feel of flesh on flesh, the smell, the taste, the headiness of a good wine, and the indulgence of a good meal well flavored with spice, they are curses to us."

"But how can enjoying the pleasures of life be a curse?" An irritating whine heightened Aldo's voice.

"Say what you like, my friend, but you and I and everyone alive are struggling against damnation. All will end up like Celino. Stripped of life, what is he now?" Lorenzo waved a dismissing hand. "Just a bag of flesh. Soon, the worms will make dirt of him. And if he wallowed too much in delights, if he took unwarranted revenge on his fellow man, what awaits him, do you think?"

"Perhaps he paid the Church for absolution?" Dario thought of all the men he himself had sent to their deaths. "And right now, he's in Heaven."

"Bah! The Church. I wish they could grant absolution. If only they had the powers they claim. If only that was all there was to it. They forget they are only men. I don't know, Dario. I simply don't know. I fear we are wandering through life without a clue why we're here. Not really knowing how we should live. Or to whom we should turn."

"You're becoming morbid." Aldo frowned.

Lorenzo glanced at Aldo, withering away from the corpse. Then he faced Dario. "Perhaps the best of us presume to capture the essence of life in sculpture or paint or fine words. But even there, is our art not simply a futile attempt to understand what will always be beyond us—a vain effort to rise above this world through imitating, distorting, and exaggerating life, using form and structure, technique and color? Ah, but I fear it is so. I fear there is no understanding either of life or of death. Not in priests, not in art, not even in love. So what's left? Only revelry and sin, eh?" He shook his head. "Sì, Dario, I fear we are cursed."

"Enough of this." Aldo backed further away from the dead man. "Let's report this to someone and get out of here."

"Afraid of the truth, Aldo?" Lorenzo staggered as if drunk, then turned back to the corpse. "So am I, my friends. So am I."

At that moment, the town crier approached, saw the corpse, said he'd bring the constable, and left.

Only then did the group abandon the dead man to his fate.

THE NEXT TWO DAYS DARIO and Aldo spent in drunken celebration much like they had on the first night, only without Lorenzo and his morbid reflections on death. Despite his vow to abandon all responsibility, Lorenzo found himself increasingly occupied with wedding arrangements.

Dario marveled at the preparations as columns of carts from nearby towns rolled through the streets. Led by mules, the creaking wagons bore calves, caged geese and fowl, mounds of almonds, sugarplums, sweetmeats, iced fish from the sea, and trout from the rivers.

On the morning of the fourth day, Dario and Aldo joined half the city and followed Lorenzo's bride, Clarice Orsini, as she left the Alessandri palace. Wearing a white gown with glittering gold thread, she rode Lorenzo's white stallion, Falsamico. Trumpets and fifes played as thirty matrons from Florence's leading families, all bedecked in their best gowns, seemed to float beside her. At the steps of Palazzo Medici, she dismounted to a cheering throng. The Medici and Orsini crests adorned awnings above the palace windows. Colorful tapestries hung from the upper stories.

Then servants hauled a live olive tree from the square up through a second-story window. "It will be a fertile and abundant marriage," said a nearby woman twice Dario's age. She nodded approvingly at the symbolism.

What followed were three days of feasting, drinking, and dancing. Inside the palazzo, uniformed servants ladled ice water and wine from copper vessels while Donatello's bronze *David* stood guard on a pedestal above. Dario marveled at the statue, depicting a lithe, handsome, slightly built David standing naked in only his boots with one foot on Goliath's head. In another age, the artist would have been pilloried in the stocks over such an irreverent seductive pose for a biblical figure. But this was Florence, and they seemed to be entering a new, more enlightened age.

In another room, tables were heavy-laden with roasts, fish, sweetmeats, jellies, and sweetened pine nuts. Guests stood in line while servants filled crystal goblets and dished food onto silver plates. In the entrance garden, Clarice dined with fifty young women selected from the best and most beautiful of Florentine society.

Only the wealthy and important crowded the palazzo's interior. Outside on the Via Larga, the common folk ate, drank, and danced on a platform set up for that purpose. Servants streamed in a continuous line from the kitchens and cellars to the street to keep the masses fed and in wine.

Through the next three days, hundreds of musicians, servants, and entertainers catered to the crowd. Dario had never seen anything like it.

He vowed that, someday, he would put on a similar display in Colpena.

He partook of everything. But every evening, even though they'd feted all day, he and Aldo still staggered out to the bordellos. But without Lorenzo.

When servants began dismantling the stage and taking down the decorations and as guests began departing, Lorenzo pulled Dario aside. They strolled through a garden, where Lorenzo was collecting sculptures, both ancient and modern. "I fear my life is changing, Dario."

"As it ever is after one marries."

"More than that. My father is unwell. These last three days, he's only risen from his bed long enough to catch a few glances of the festivities. I fear he'll not be with us much longer."

"Ah, losing one's father is difficult."

"Difficult, sì, but neither is that the issue. Soon, I will have to take his place. And that, I fear, will change everything."

Dario looked long at his friend. "I've ruled in my father's stead for many years now, ever since I was twenty. It does change a person." Then he grinned. "But I still find time to enjoy life's pleasures."

Frowning, Lorenzo shook his head. "But where is your family? Where is the wife you need by your side to give you sons? Family is everything. And when you start a family, you must give up nights like we've had together this week––nights at the brothels and tavernas with the young women. When my father dies, that's what will change."

Dario's mouth opened. His friend was starting to sound like Grazziano. "For me, that kind of thing can wait. Without the pleasures of life—what's left?"

Lorenzo's frown morphed into a smile. "You must keep your family and city first, my friend. I include in that the support of these new ideas about art, philosophy, and poetry arising here. In Colpena, you need to seek the best that mankind can create and encourage it. Painters. Sculptors. Poets. Architects. After that, must come the more mundane—your business. Only last comes the satisfaction of one's personal desires. And, of course, one must put God in there somewhere. And that, I fear, is our eternal undoing. For only that which is dedicated to God will be of eternal value."

Dario frowned. Except for Lorenzo's passion for art, he was listening to the voices of Grazziano and his father. "Lorenzo, I'm not ready for the kind of sacrifice you're making with Clarice."

"Someday you must. Or what will come after you? Who will succeed you? Without sons, when you're gone, what will all your accomplishments amount to?"

Dario realized his mouth was hanging open. But he had no words with which to respond. He didn't want to think about this.

He and Aldo went out one more night. Much to his surprise, at the last minute, Lorenzo, who had just extolled the virtues of sobriety and purity, joined them. Dario had the sense that, despite all his host had said, Lorenzo was desperate to cling to his old life. And that last night became their wildest yet.

Lorenzo took them not just to a bordello, but to a certain palazzo where they engaged in a night of orgy. That night Lorenzo seemed driven to rebuke everything he'd said earlier. But as they walked home, spent and exhausted, their host was silent, dour-faced, sullen.

The next day, groggy and satiated after more than a week of heavy drinking, voracious women, and gluttonous feasting, Dario woke late.

A hand shook his shoulders. He opened heavy eyes to a messenger standing above him. As he rose and accepted the paper thrust into his hands, his personal imp took up the familiar mallet against the inside of his skull. He broke the wax seal. Bleary eyes read Jacopo's hasty scribbling:

"Return to Colpena at once. Rocco Marino is gathering the Signoria for a special meeting. He plans to accuse you of fraud and murder in the purchase of Acque Salutari."

Dario swore, crumpled the paper, and called for servants to prepare the horses.

CHAPTER 9

~ THE SIGNORIA ~

His feet echoing in the vast space, Dario entered last into the grand council chamber on the town hall's second floor. As he settled in the center chair, his glance swept the long table. Built to receive petitioners, all the seats were on one side. On the far right sat Enzio Borroni, with a scowling Rocco Marino beside him. On Dario's left sat Aldo Rossi, Fabiano Trentino, and Callisto Mancini. He could always count on those three to support him.

"Where is Marcello?" He looked to the empty chair on his right belonging to Marcello Esposito, a successful wool merchant and another member who usually voted with him.

"Meeting with customers in Pisa," said Fabiano.

Dario nodded. That would still leave him four votes against Borroni's two. He eyed his archrival, a thin man with a severe face, sunken cheeks, hooked nose, back-sloping forehead, and thinning gray hair. Today, Borroni wore his usual black tunic, hemmed in gold. "Why have you called this meeting, Enzio?"

"It is not I, gonfaloniere, who called it. As you well know, Signore Marino is the injured party here."

"Injured in what way?" Dario turned to the stout, middle-aged man beside Borroni. Blond hair. Round face. Tiny blue eyes.

Rocco Marino raised a pudgy finger, pointed it at Dario. "As you well know, we are meeting to resolve a matter of fraud. Before you purchased Acque Salutari, you connived to hide from me the fact that the land contained alum."

"Marino, did you not own the land for twenty years? And was that not enough time to know what it contained?"

Fabiano and Aldo laughed.

"I only recently hired assayers." Marino was red-faced.

"And as I understand it, signore, your assayers reported that no alum was present."

Tiny eyes narrowing further, Marino shook his head. "For some reason, they lied to me. They—"

Dario faced the others with a smile. "And how is it my problem if your hirelings don't tell you what you paid them to do?"

Now even Callisto chuckled.

"Because one of them was murdered on his way back to report his findings."

The chamber fell silent. Dario's smile vanished.

Now Aldo spoke. "Serious charges, Signore Marino. What proof have you?"

"To make the inspection, I hired three Austrians from Innsbruck, experts in assaying and alum production. One of them was murdered before he reached Colpena with his report that they'd found alum."

"Bandits, Marino." Dario waved a dismissing hand. "Happens all the time. Especially to a man traveling alone. And then, as I understand it, the other two reported they hadn't found alum." He reached for the document Aldo had prepared and shook it. "This testimony, signed by the two brothers and witnessed by a notary, says they reported not finding the mineral until after I bought the land." He passed it down the table for the others to read.

"They're liars!" His face reddening further as he read the paper, Marino glanced at Borroni with alarm.

Borroni produced a saddlebag from beneath his seat. He slapped it on the table. "The murdered man was named Kuhn. This is his saddlebag, found in the hills not far from here." After reaching inside, he pulled out a lump of rock and smacked it down. "This is alum from Acque Salutari."

"How do you know? The man could have brought a sample with him. That rock doesn't prove anything."

Marino's mouth opened and closed.

Then Enzio Borroni nodded to the uniformed sergeant-at-arms standing by the entrance. The guard opened the door and admitted a sun-browned farmer dressed in a humble brown tunic.

"Enter, signore." Borroni beckoned him in. "And tell us who you are."

"I am Adalberto Tocci." His quiet words barely rose above a whisper.

"Louder, please." Borroni raised a hand.

"I own an apple orchard in the hills above Scaldi. A small but productive grove. For generations, my family provides fruit to Colpena. My lords, Scaldi is ten miles from Colpena. We are a humble village. You must climb the ridge trail and—"

"Sì, signore, we know where Scaldi is. And we are grateful for your fruit. Now tell us, did you find this saddlebag in your orchard?"

"It was on my land, sì."

"Now tell us about the body you also found."

Tocci rubbed his hands together, looked at the floor, at Aldo, then back at the floor.

"Well, Signore Tocci"—Borroni's voice rose—"what about the body? You found a recently buried body, did you not?"

"I found a body, but as to how old it was, I–I do not know, signore."

Borroni's face paled. "You don't know? What do you mean, you don't know? Did you not find a recent hole that you dug up, wherein was laid the body of Signore Kuhn?"

"The body—it could have been new. Or it could have been old. I do not know. I am no expert. But very bad smell. Not good for the fruit. I burned it."

"But was the hole not recently dug?"

Tocci's face paled, and his voice became a whisper. "Perhaps not. I . . . don't know."

Rocco Marino stared at the farmer. He shook all over as he lifted a finger and pointed it at Aldo and Dario. "Y–you have done this. You have bribed this man."

Dario's gaze focused on the farmer, now staring at his own feet. "Did we bribe you, signore? Look at me and tell me if I or my cousin, Aldo, bribed you?"

The farmer raised his glance, and, shaking, he whispered something.

"Louder," said Borroni. "We can't hear you."

"N–no. Neither Signore Dario Rossi nor his cousin bribed me."

"This is an outrage. This witness has been compromised." Borroni's jaw muscles tightened, and his right eye twitched. He faced the rest of the Signoria. "Kuhn was on his way back to tell Rocco they'd found alum at Acque Salutari. He had a sample in his saddlebag. Someone killed him and buried the body. Then Rossi bought the land from Rocco, and—what do you know? It contained alum. Now the other two Austrians—who must have been in league with Rossi all along—are mining the site."

"Fraud!" shouted Marino. "*Murder.*"

"Bah!" said Aldo. "Bandits killed the man. The Bergmans later apologized to you and said they were mistaken in their original assessment. You're simply trying to frame my cousin."

Dario's glance swept from one member to another. "Is this even worthy of a vote? Raise your hands if you think we should vote."

Callisto and Fabiano exchanged worried glances but did nothing.

Then Dario dismissed the meeting.

Back at the palazzo, Dario slumped into a chair before Aldo and Jacopo in his sitting room. He tapped the bottom of his wine glass on the end table.

"Sloppy, Jacopo." Dario's gaze bored into him. "This must never happen again."

"How was I to know the farmer would dig up the body?"

"But you left the saddlebags in plain sight."

Jacopo shrugged. "It was dark. I didn't find them. I'd planned to make it look like a natural death, but things just didn't work out. I had to use my knife."

"At least the farmer agreed to be bribed." Aldo raised a glass to his lips. "Not by us, but by you, Jacopo."

"He said he wouldn't lie." Jacopo smiled. "If Rocco or Enzio had asked him the right questions, you would've had no defense. But with a little coaching, he agreed to answer only what you asked."

Dario stared at Jacopo. "This must never happen again."

"And yet"—a grin lifted one side of Jacopo's mouth—"you have your alum mine, do you not?"

CHAPTER 10

~ A SURPRISE VISIT ~

JULY 1469

Late in the afternoon, Amadeo threaded his way through the lower lanes crowded with women buying last-minute cheese, bread, herbs, and wine for dinner. He stepped around a line of creaking oxcarts hauling barrels of water from the lower springs to the huge cisterns atop the hill. Before he could finish painting the duomo model, he needed woad from a shop near the city wall to make more blue paint. Panting from the climb, he pushed open his front door.

Skender rose from the foyer where he had apparently been sleeping.

"Lad, why aren't you making supper? Are you ill?"

"No, but there's someone——" The noise of pots banging in the kitchen interrupted. He raised both hands in apology. "I couldn't stop her. She insisted."

"Who?"

"The signorina."

Simona Mancini stuck her head around the corner. An apron wrapped her tunic, and her hands held a pestle and mortar. When she saw Amadeo, a smile brightened her face. "Welcome home, signore. Forgive me, but I forbade your boy to cook for you tonight. This evening, it will be I who'll fix your supper."

"Fix m—my supper?" He had stammered, and now his mouth was hanging agape. Even with a smudge of flour on one cheek and a hint of perspiration on her forehead, she presented the picture of enticing young beauty. "But why . . . are you here?"

"Father had some business in the city for a few days, and I came back with him. Did you know he's on your building committee?"

"No, I—"

"Sì, and we are both so pleased you are competing for the commission. I'm sure you'll be chosen and become a great architect. And believe me, Father will be your best ally. So when I heard Dario Rossi had given you this house, I just had to come and make dinner."

"Well, thank you, signorina, but Skender—"

"Oh, I'm sure Skender is a wonderful cook, but you haven't tasted my ham and chicken ravioli. And sometimes a man just needs a woman to cook for him. Don't you agree, Skender?"

Skender shrugged, faced Amadeo, and arched his eyebrows.

"I've been frying the chicken with onions, eggs, parsley, and saffron. That goes into the chicken ravioli. The ham ravioli has pork, cheese, cloves, and ginger. I top it all with my Sicilian cheese sauce. And, of course, a good Tuscan wine must complement the meal. I've seen your garden, and on such a beautiful evening as this, we absolutely must eat there, don't you think?"

Amadeo smiled. "Signorina, we would both be pleased to sample your ravioli and all you've prepared and do so in the garden. Please carry on. Meanwhile, I'll be working in my office."

Simona gave him her impish grin, whirled, and rushed back into the kitchen.

Smashing the woad with water in a mortar and pestle, he created the bright blue color he sought. But the smells from the kitchen made concentration difficult. Skender's cooking was adequate, but he was no chef. When Simona finally announced her dinner ready, Amadeo covered his paint, washed his face and hands, and sat at the garden table with her.

Bowing and smiling, Skender excused himself and took his food to the kitchen.

Four fluttering candles illuminated a plate piled high with Simona's pasta.

"Will you say the prayer, Simona?" asked Amadeo.

A smile touched her lips, and she bowed her head. "Dear Lord, we thank you for Master Amadeo and the wonderful design he's creating for the duomo. Now bless this food in the name of the Holy Virgin and Jesus, the Son, amen."

When Amadeo's spoon finally lifted the pasta to his mouth, he thought he'd never tasted better ravioli. "It's truly delicious."

"Thank you, signore."

"But you are the daughter of a wealthy merchant. How did you learn to cook like this? Didn't your servants do all the cooking?"

"Sì, but I wanted to learn how and insisted they teach me."

Amadeo stifled a grin. "I'm sure you did. And it seems you learned well."

The softest pink highlighted her cheeks. "Do you have family somewhere, signore?"

"A father living in San Gimignano who runs a leather shop. With my brother, Antonio."

"Do you ever visit them?"

"Not often enough. It's a long trek."

"And your mother?"

"She died when I was very young. I never really knew her."

"And my mother died two years ago. I miss her very much."

"Sì, I remember. I'm sorry. It must be difficult losing someone so close to you."

She shrugged. "But I still have my father."

"Won't he miss you tonight?"

"Oh no. He's meeting some men in some palazzo down the hill, discussing business. Something about difficulties with ships from the east."

"The Venetian war with the Turks, no doubt. It's created a lot of problems for importers."

"But tonight I thank the Turks." She smiled. "Because they let me cook for you."

"Simona." He reached across the table and held one of her hands. "This was nice of you. Unexpected. And very nice."

She blushed again. "I so enjoyed your stay at the farm. And I was so distressed when they took you away in chains, as it were. But now you'll soon become the capomaestro in charge of building Colpena's first duomo. I'm sure of it. And I just had to see you again."

When Amadeo had finished eating, Skender took their dishes to the kitchen, again leaving them alone in the garden. Evening had fallen, cloying warmth hovered in the air, and candles lit their faces. The steady cooing of pigeons, some sitting atop the garden wall, joined the whine of the cicadas.

"Do you not feel alone sometimes, Amadeo?"

Taken aback by the question, he shook his head.

"I sometimes do. Sometimes, I feel like I'm only half a person, and somewhere out there"—she waved a hand toward the wall—"the other half of me is walking around. Someone else, someone nice, someone loving, who will make me whole."

"I can't say I've felt that way. I do have my work."

"I suppose men do. But for women, it's different. We need a man. And whether he knows it or not, a man needs a woman in his life. Why are you not married, Amadeo?"

Again, her directness and abrupt questions startled him. He'd never met anyone quite like her. "I–I—"

"Father told me about your vow of chastity. I understand your wanting to be close to God and all. But married couples can be close to God, too, don't you think?"

"Taking a wife would only interfere with my work."

"Oh, I've heard of many architects and artists with wives. And they do just fine."

"Let's not talk about such things tonight. You've made such a wonderful meal. I do thank you for that, and . . ."

"And what, Amadeo?"

"And you are simply lovely, Simona." Heat prickled across his neck, cheeks, and forehead. Why had he said that? Because she *was* beautiful, especially in the candlelight with wisps of her blonde hair in disarray after cooking.

She looked at her hands, now folded before her on the table. "Thank you," she whispered.

At that moment, Skender returned, announcing he'd finished cleaning.

"And now, Simona"—Amadeo rose from the table—"I must return to my work."

"So late?" Her eyes widened.

"He often works all night," said Skender.

"Then I'll leave the master architect to his work."

Amadeo escorted her to the front door, where he lifted her right hand to his lips and kissed it. "Thank you, again, for a wonderful evening."

She curtseyed and hurried off down the street.

He stood there as she merged with couples taking their evening stroll. She wanted marriage, didn't she? Marriage to him. But he wasn't ready to abandon his vow or take a wife. That would surely distract him from his work.

But if he ever did make such a decision, he could think of no better prospect than Simona Mancini.

CHAPTER 11

~ THE BUILDING COMMITTEE ~

His feet echoing across the marble, Dario entered the town hall's large antechamber and nodded to the other four men comprising the building committee—

Beak-nosed Fabiano Trentino, the group's official head. Dario didn't want the task.

Bishop Rinaldi Ferata in his green robes.

Black-garbed Enzio Borroni, who insisted on being included in all decisions related to the duomo. Dario could find no reason to keep him off.

Finally, Callisto Mancini, with a knowledge of building, an interest in the project, and a predictable reliability to vote his way.

"Welcome, signore," said Fabiano to Dario. "We await the architects and their proposals."

Acknowledging the welcome with a nod, Dario sat. He knew nothing of architecture, but his money funded the project. And someone had to counter Borroni's influence.

Bills for the demolition in the duomo's path were already coming in. The Church had greatly increased the number of workers contracted to tear down everything between Via Santa Croce and Via San Christo. Every week, they now expected him to pay a salary to three hundred and fifty men.

Some of the debris they burned, and a great funnel of smoke rose daily into the skies from the now-barren Piazza dei Sole.

Upon his return from Florence, Dario and Aldo had gone over accounts and were shocked by how much they'd already spent. The mine at Acque Salutari needed to begin production soon.

The sergeant-at-arms opened the far doors and entered. "My lords," came his deep baritone, "may I present the architects, Amadeo Puccini and Basilio Bramante."

In stepped Puccini, dressed in a brown tunic of finest cotton hemmed with gold. Side slits revealed a red giornea beneath. A star-bedecked white shoulder piece hung around his neck, and a red beret topped his head. Puccini bowed before the committee.

Dario smiled. Puccini was finally presenting himself as an architect should. Whenever he'd found the man in his study, a simple brown tunic, ragged from wear, always draped his form. But a man could put on an affectation of poverty as well as wealth. And that could be just as insincere. In Puccini's case, Dario feared the man was incapable of affectation. And strangely, that bothered him.

Today, at least, Dario was glad that in public his chosen builder was finally dressing and acting the part.

Following Puccini came Bramante. Short, stout, with close-cropped black hair and mustache, he strode into the room with exaggerated pomp. "My lords." He bowed low with a flourish of one arm.

"In the competition for the design of Colpena's duomo," said Fabiano, "I give the floor first to the head of our waterworks, Basilio Bramante. Signore, what is your entry in the competition?"

As if he'd already won, Bramante gave them a knowing smile. He motioned to the sergeant-at-arms who opened the door.

Two brown-smocked laborers bore in a painted model created from plaster of paris. Two by three feet wide and three feet high, it reminded Dario of cathedrals he'd seen in France and Germany.

With the two transepts required by the contest, it followed the traditional cross-shaped structure. But even to Dario's untrained eye, the façade appeared cluttered with pointed arches topped with jagged spires and slopes bristling with crenellations.

But therein also lay what beauty it possessed—in the effect of its many pointed arches and spires. From each side jutted ponderous flying buttresses.

"What will be its dimensions, architect?" asked Fabiano.

"One hundred sixty feet wide at the front. Two hundred eighty feet through the nave to the back of the chancel. The transepts are sixty feet deep. But the great spires!" He raised his hands. "They will rise three hundred feet, like two hands reaching in prayer for the heavens."

"A most impressive work." Smiling, Enzio Borroni walked around the model. "Most impressive, indeed."

"But does it fit in Tuscany?" asked Callisto.

Bramante scowled. "It does borrow from traditional designs, from the tried and true. But in the building of it, there will be no surprises. And it's a work of art, no?"

Dario also stood and circled the model. It was certainly well designed. But it seemed . . . busy, overburdened with spires, crenellations, jagged edges.

When the committee had finished their examination, Fabiano had the men move the model to the side. Then he turned to Puccini. "Signore, what do you have for us?"

The architect looked to the door and clapped his hands.

Three workmen and the young Skender, whom Puccini had foolishly freed, labored to bring in a wooden stretcher atop which sat a three-by-four-foot form draped in canvas. When they set it before the committee, Puccini thanked them and faced the five men who would oversee the construction.

The architect carefully removed the canvas, revealing his vision for the duomo.

Gasps issued from everyone present—from all except Bramante.

Dario knew little of architecture or building, but he knew a work of art when he saw it. And this was it.

The structure was the traditional cross Bishop Ferata insisted upon.

"The duomo must sit on the Piazza dei Sole now being torn up," said Puccini. "The duomo's chancel will face east as is traditional. That also allows us to leave the old church's foundations untouched. That should save time."

The model's façade sported three tall rows filled with semicircular arches between fluted columns. Each arch enclosed three rows of niches containing statues of saints, Apostles, and popes. On the top was a row of round, stained-glass windows—the clerestory. In the bottom center, an entryway with receding semicircular arches gave the illusion of a heavenly tunnel. Above the arch complex hovered a circular stained-glass window in a starburst pattern, far larger than the clerestory windows. A triangular pediment adorned with tracery topped the roof's entire length.

The sides and back were similar but graced with columns. In the center of the third story, two starburst windows let in light.

Dominating the duomo was a central egg-shaped dome similar to Brunelleschi's in Florence. A smaller cupola, its sides draped by a half-dozen supporting ribs, topped it. A columned loggia circled the cupola's base.

To the right of the duomo's façade towered a campanile. Columned arches led to an open interior through which the bells would resonate. Alternating white and black marble layered the tower's sides all the way to the top, where it ended in an open-sided cupola, enclosing not one, but three bells.

The overall effect was one of a regular, ordered, yet artistic structure.

"My lord, how long did it take you to create this model?" A tone of reverence muted Bishop Ferata's voice to a whisper.

"Four weeks. I hired a master woodworker to help me carve it. I painted it."

Even Borroni's mouth now hung agape.

"What will be the interior dimensions?" asked Callisto Mancini.

"To walk from the façade's entrance to the back of the chancel—five hundred and forty feet. From the east to the west transept—three hundred and sixty feet."

Bramante snickered his disbelief.

"Enormous," whispered Callisto. "What about the dome?"

"My plan is to duplicate Brunelleschi's feat at Santa Maria Del Fiore. The dome will be only slightly larger than Brunelleschi's—one hundred fifty feet in diameter, but with an apex ten feet higher, at two hundred ninety feet from the floor. Its final exterior height will be three hundred and sixty feet. The lantern atop the dome will add another eighty feet."

"And the duomo's façade?"

"The façade is two hundred forty feet across, as is the chancel in back. The façade's main door will be thirty feet wide, forty feet high. If built today, this would be the largest cathedral in the world."

"Is all this . . . possible?" Fabiano glanced at the others before facing Puccini again. "Can you actually do this?"

"I can, my lord," said Puccini. "If you give me the materials and the workers I need and do not interfere."

Fabiano addressed the two architects. "Do either of you have anything to say about each other's work?"

Puccini smiled at Bramante. "Your duomo is well designed, Bramante, but a bit ponderous and busy on the eye. Its artistry borrows from a routine, well-worn path. But I'm thinking it would be much happier in Saxony than in Tuscany."

Dario suppressed a grin.

Bramante placed hands on hips and narrowed his eyes at his competitor. "You have reached for the heavens, signore, and like the Tower of Babel, you will fail. How will your walls not cave from the stress? You have no buttresses."

"Columns, my friend. They'll take the weight. And much easier on the eye."

"Bah! And your dome." He huffed. "You dare to repeat Brunelleschi's genius by replicating his miracle dome and making it taller? What arrogance. You have neither the skill nor the experience. You'll never be able to complete this work. Its dimensions are simply beyond your ability." He faced the committee. "I submit to you not to waste your time with this fool of an architect. His walls will buckle, his dome will collapse, and you will have sunk your money into the vision of a buffoon."

Fabiano waved to Puccini, who responded. "I have spent years studying how Brunelleschi built his masterpiece. I've crawled inside his dome and spent weeks inspecting it. I know well the details of its construction. My sketchbooks burst with drawings of his machines. And I know how he solved his construction problems." He eyed each committee member. "In short, signori, I can build this duomo and its dome."

Bramante scowled and crossed his arms.

"Thank you, both," said Fabiano. "I am well pleased with your efforts." He glanced at the others. "If everyone has seen enough, the sergeant-at-arms will lead them out while we make our decision."

With everyone's agreement, the two architects were ushered into an adjoining room.

Alone again with the committee, Fabiano said to the others, "Do we need more discussion? Or should we simply vote?"

The consensus was for voting. Fabiano gave each man a white and a black bead. "White for Puccini," he said, "black for Bramante."

When the bowl reached him, Dario dropped his bead in the bowl and passed it along.

Fabiano counted and, smiling, looked up. "The vote is four to one. Puccini will be our capomaestro."

He motioned to the sergeant-at-arms who returned both men to the room. Then Fabiano said, "Let it be known that the committee has selected Amadeo Puccini as the master architect and builder of Colpena's cathedral. Basilio Bramante"—he turned to the dour-faced loser—"we thank you for your continued efforts on the water project and your participation in this contest. You are dismissed."

After a scowl at his rival, Bramante whirled to face the committee. "You have made a great mistake, signori." Then he stalked out.

"Congratulations, capomaestro." Fabiano leaned over the table and shook Puccini's hand, as did the others.

"Master builder," said Enzio Borroni, "though I did not vote for your design, I am impressed by its magnitude and artistry. Be assured that this committee will provide everything you need." He grinned and faced Dario. "Whatever you want, architect, just ask. Our generous patron has agreed to pay in full."

Dario suddenly realized why Borroni was smiling, what he was saying. Puccini's plans were so expansive, so ambitious, and the man so zealous for his work, to keep the project going would be like dropping an endless supply of gold coins down a well. Dario's sins would be absolved, sì, but in the process, it might ruin him.

Borroni would like nothing better.

Reaching a hand to brace himself on the table, Dario felt the blood drain from his face.

"I'm glad of that assurance," said Puccini. "And how will I receive monies to pay for the ongoing construction?"

Fabiano opened a hand in Dario's direction. "If the committee agrees, I will disburse what is needed directly to the architect from an account funded by the gonfaloniere."

The others nodded. Reluctantly, Dario agreed.

Servants began carrying both models away, and a smiling Puccini followed his out the door.

Dario rose with the others. The duomo would certainly be the grandest building in all Italy, perhaps in all the world.

But at what cost?

CHAPTER 12

~ THE CONTRACT ~

Before noon the next day, Amadeo ushered Dario Rossi, beak-nosed Fabiano Trentino, and Bishop Rinaldi Ferata into his new quarters. Behind them came a bald, rotund notary. Amadeo led them all into the former sitting room. Sliding chairs across the floor from the kitchen, he bade them sit at the table where he often worked.

"Signore," said Rossi to Amadeo and Fabiano, "we three have been charged by the building committee to set the contract terms."

Amadeo bowed in acknowledgment.

Rossi motioned to the notary who laid a sheaf of parchments on the table.

"This should be straightforward." The notary huffed as if each word were an effort. "The contract has the usual terms. No competing work on other projects. You are employed at the committee's pleasure until the duomo is complete or the Lord takes you away. And thanks to our generous padrone"—he nodded toward Rossi—"your salary will be two hundred florins per year. Plus suitable clothing for a man of your station. Plus lodging in this house. And the slave you have already received."

Amadeo nodded. "He's been freed. These are all generous terms. But will I have sole authority to make decisions on the project?"

"The usual agreement"—Ferata's eyebrows rose—"is that the Church will have oversight on all matters of theological importance. I will give you general guidelines for the interior's theme—what goes in the bays and so forth. The Church will also name and dedicate the duomo, and—"

"What will the duomo be named?"

Ferata glanced at Fabiano and cleared his throat. "The Cattedrale della Beata San Maria."

Amadeo took a deep breath. "You wish to dedicate yet another duomo to the Virgin? To 'The Blessed Virgin'?"

Swallowing, Ferata nodded.

Amadeo rose from his chair and turned his back on the group. He paced to the wall and stared at the tiled floor. He was on dangerous ground here, but he'd thought long about this. "May I ask how many cathedrals the Church has dedicated to Christ, the one to whom we all owe our salvation?" He whirled.

Ferata's jaw opened, closed, but no words came out.

Fabiano frowned and looked to Rossi.

"Well, bishop?" questioned Rossi. "How many?"

"Offhand, I can't think of one."

"Then why do we not dedicate this duomo to the Son of God instead of to his earthly mother?" Amadeo felt his face warming, but he kept on. "She already has Florence's grand duomo in her name, does she not? As well as many others."

"The cardinal has decided on the name." Ferata's face paled.

"I'm confused, bishop." He really wasn't, but he had to bring the man around to his point of view. "I have read the Bible, and I—"

Gasps from Fabiano, Ferata, and the notary.

Grinning as if he enjoyed the bishop's discomfiture, Rossi's gaze settled on Ferata.

"Sì," continued Amadeo, "I have my own New Testament and Psalms, copied by my own hand in Latin. I've studied it, and I do not find a book of Mary. I also do not find anyone—even Mary herself—asking us to worship her. So how is it, bishop, that we pray to the mother of Jesus and then dedicate building after building to her? Why do we not find one duomo—not even one—dedicated to the Son of God himself?"

Ferata blinked as if someone had just slapped him across the face. He shook his head back and forth. "You must not say such things, signore. It is heresy. It is forbidden."

"Heresy to follow the words of the Apostles? So you have no answer to my question? You will insist, against all reason, that this work—a work to which I should give my entire life—must be dedicated to the Virgin Mary?"

"Sì, signore. And it is not neg—"

"Stop!" Rossi raised a hand. "The man asks a good question. Why do we not dedicate the cathedral to the Son of God? I'm paying for it, am I not? I rather like the idea."

As Amadeo's glance fell with wonder and appreciation on his new patron, silence filled the room.

Ferata's jaw reopened. Again, he was bereft of words.

"Why not the Cattedrale del Figlio sul Mare?" Rossi was grinning.

" 'The Cathedral of the Son by the Sea'?" Amadeo smiled. "I like that. Sì, I do."

"No, my friends." Ferata found his voice. "We name our duomos after saints. Or the Virgin. The cardinal—he will not agree."

"I think he will, priest." Rossi waved a hand at the notary. "Put that name for the duomo in the contract——the Cattedrale del Figlio sul Mare. Let it be as I have said." He smiled in Amadeo's direction. "For my architect's sake. Don't you agree, Fabiano?"

The beak-nosed man closed his mouth, glanced at the pale-faced bishop, then back at Rossi. "As you wish, gonfaloniere. The building committee will go along with your request. Let the duomo be named the Cathedral of the Son by the Sea."

"And you, Rinaldi?" Rossi turned to Ferata. "Will you sign it that way?"

The bishop put his hands over his eyes and squeezed his temples. He again faced the lord of Colpena. "May the Holy Father and the cardinal forgive me. I will sign."

After everyone signed, the notary officially witnessed and sealed it.

Beaming, Rossi stood and grasped Amadeo's hands. "My friend, it appears we will have ourselves a cathedral."

"My lord, it will be the greatest cathedral the world has ever known."

CHAPTER 13

~ THE FLORENTINE STONE MASTER ~

AUGUST 1469

Amadeo woke with a pounding heart, a blanket soaked with sweat, and a driving need. The first foundation stone must be laid by next spring. This he knew. This monument to God, this lifetime work of sacrifice to the Creator, must reach that milestone before Easter. He didn't know how or why he knew this. He just knew it must.

After crossing to the nightstand, he poured water into a basin and splashed his face.

It was now early August. Much was left to do. In the last month after presenting the model to the building committee, he'd made drawing after drawing, with dimensions of every detail he could imagine:

The width and height of the walls.
The interior columns and the design of their capitals—Corinthian, all—and their bases.
The mammoth piers supporting the dome.
The bays along the nave's arcade.
The chapels in both transepts and behind the choir and sanctuary.
The arches on the ceilings.

What he'd designed was truly massive, greater than any duomo ever conceived. But he worried that, by the usual methods, he'd never finish on time. Something had to change. But would the masters he chose agree to what he had in mind?

The extra laborers had cleared the ground in astonishing time. Using shovels and a special iron bar the forgers had poured for him, the workers had scraped it flat. The site was nearly ready to build a new piazza from the old flagstones—but with stonecutters and masons he didn't yet have.

The contadini, the common laborers, he'd put to work with sledges to crush the rubble from the demolished houses. The resulting gravel they would use for the foundations and as a base for the new piazza.

With the duomo site exposed, Amadeo himself excavated an exploratory trench eight feet on a side. As luck—or providence—would have it, they hit bedrock after digging down only ten feet. An ideal depth.

With the site's eastern end scraped, leveled, and ready, he'd used stakes and ropes to mark off the foundations for the chancel, choir, and both transepts. Then the men began digging the foundation holes. Wheelbarrows hauled away the dirt.

Only yesterday, he and Ferata had stood at the far eastern end and gazed down the lengths of rope marking the future duomo.

"Even without the nave," Ferata had said, "what you've outlined is enormous. Are you sure you can do this?"

Amadeo had caught his breath. "I can, bishop. With God's help, I can."

That was yesterday. Too long had he focused on preparing the site.

The floors creaking, he stepped away from the washbasin and dressed. It was time to find a master stonecutter and masons.

"Get up, Skender," he called to the kitchen. "We're going on a trip."

As Amadeo, Skender, and two mercenaries provided by Rossi rode into Florence, their horses' hooves clopped through torch-lit streets.

"Tonight"—Amadeo twisted in the saddle—"we'll stay in the city. Tomorrow, we ride up to Settignano to find our stone master."

"Who is he?" asked Skender.

"Vittorio Rivera. He was lodge master for the renovation of the Church of San Matteo in Genoa. A few years ago, we became good friends when I stayed with him on my tour of churches and cathedrals. I greatly admire his work."

"He will join us?" Skender slapped away a buzzing fly.

"If he doesn't, our travels will take us farther yet." If necessary, he would venture to Germany, Sweden, or even Britain to find a good stone master and a team.

They found rooms at an *albergo* on the Via di Mezzo and woke early the next morning. No longer needing protection, only Amadeo and Skender rode up to the village of stonecutters, home to generations of *scalpellini*.

Already, the sun baked the path and rippled the air.

As the duomo's campanile bells pealed and echoed up the valley behind them, the hilltop view nearly stopped Amadeo's breath. On nearby slopes, cypress and palms surrounded stately columned villas. To his left, grapevines clung to the hills in ordered rows, interrupted by low stone walls. In the valley, all of Florence spread out before them, the dome of Santa Maria del Fiore rising majestically above red-tiled roofs. The tree-lined Arno wound through the town like a ribbon of shimmering silver. It was as if someone had painted the scene, putting every item exactly where it belonged. "If God ever blessed a land with an abundance of green and color and grace," he whispered, "it was Tuscany and Florence."

"Sì, signore."

He turned his mount and rode a single cobbled lane lined with small stone houses, where flowerpots hung from every window and stone benches fronted every house. When Amadeo paused to ask a young girl directions to Vittorio's, she began to turn away. But when he told her who he was, she smiled, bobbed her head up and down, and pointed to the end of the row.

Dismounting, he knocked on the wooden door—somehow they'd forgotten to fashion it, too, out of stone. A middle-aged black-haired woman wearing an apron opened it.

"Signora, I seek Vittorio Rivera."

"And who"—she was frowning—"may I say is asking?"

When he gave his name, recognition crossed her features, and she sighed. "It is ever thus, is it not? I have him for a few months, and then he's off again. Follow me."

She led him out the back into a lush garden where Vittorio sat with a plate of panini, cheese, and a glass of wine. The smells of wisteria and roses drifted on the air. When Vittorio saw Amadeo, he rose with a smile, hugged him, and pounded him on the back. "What brings the builder of San Ambrose so far from Colpena?"

"Business, my friend. And an offer of work."

Vittorio's eyes widened. He motioned for Amadeo to sit on the stone bench beside him. Skender found a seat opposite.

"Work, you say? What kind?"

"I have the commission to build a grand cathedral in Colpena, perhaps the grandest ever. I want you for my master stonecutter. And if the men will have it—and I'm sure they will—for my lodge master as well." Amadeo removed his backpack, reached inside, and spread an armful of drawings on the bench between them.

As he studied the plans, Vittorio's eyes glowed, and his breathing quickened. "Why, there is nothing like this—anywhere. And you have approval to build it? You have a padrone?"

"I do."

Vittorio clasped his hands and bowed his head. "This is an answer to prayer." He lowered his voice. "I've only been home three months, but already I'm going mad. I need a chisel in my hands and stone beneath me. Being apart from the stone—ah, my friend, I need it like other men need air to breathe, like a young man needs the young woman he loves. That is what the stone is to me. And my mind! I need men to direct and plans and drawings to focus my thoughts." He glanced quickly toward the house, then faced Amadeo, lowering his voice even further.

"Margherita is my wife. I love her, and she's my heart's desire. But when we are together more than three weeks"—he raised hands in the air, gripped the top of his head, and shook it—"sì, Amadeo, I will join your venture. I will pledge my life to the construction of this great duomo, my service to you and to God for whom this work will give great glory."

They stood, clasped hands, and again pounded each other on the back. Vittorio broke the news to his wife, who already suspected what was coming. Then she prepared a grand breakfast of boiled eggs, veal sausage, goat cheese, oranges, more panini, and a carafe of the local red wine.

"I must gather my crew." Vittorio gazed out over his garden. "Most of them are here in Settignano. A few are single, without families. Those have taken their pay and run off to the bordellos and tavernas. To complete your grand vision, I'll need every skilled scalpellino I can find."

"Grazie, Vittorio. You and I will work well together. But there is one change, a major one, that I wish to make to the normal method of construction." Amadeo sucked in air.

Vittorio cocked his head. "What?"

"I must finish this project within our lifetimes. What I have designed here is possibly greater than anything yet conceived. To hasten the work, I propose to hire *two* crews of workers. Two of stonecutters. Two of carpenters. Two of everything."

Vittorio's jaw gaped. He examined the ground. "And who would run these crews? Another stone master?"

"No. You would oversee both. We would start by having one crew build the north wall and the corners of the apse. The other would build the east wall and its corners."

"I . . . see." He rubbed his chin. "But you must understand: I have only done churches, my friend. Never anything as big as this."

"I've seen your work. I have confidence in you."

"But running two crews—this has never been done before. Where will I get the extra workers?"

"I leave that to you."

Vittorio stared off into his garden. "I could increase the number of apprentices. Over time, that would give us more workers. I might be able to convince some of Alberico's men to join us. Currently, they are out of work. Alberico won't be happy about it. But he's showing his age. Soon, he will have to relinquish his men to someone else anyway." Vittorio slapped a hand on a knee. "I'll do it. But who will be the master mason?"

"I had in mind Damiano De Luca."

"De Luca is skilled, to be sure. But I've heard he can be difficult to work with. Will he agree to your plan?"

"At the moment, he's the best available."

"Then that is who we must have." Vittorio's eyes remained alight with energy. "With your permission, I'd like Umberto Sabbatini for my speaker. He's available, and I've worked with him before."

"As you wish, master stonecutter." Amadeo bowed.

"You have set yourself a nearly impossible task—to complete such a work in one lifetime." Vittorio smiled. "But I will dedicate everything I have, all I am, to the effort."

Amadeo grasped his hands. "I thank you, Vittorio. With your help, we'll be well on our way."

CHAPTER 14

~ THE DEBTOR ~

Dario sat at his desk in the downstairs palazzo rooms reserved for business. Despite a hangover from the night before, he tried to concentrate on the shipping manifest going in and out of focus in his hands. Off in the corner, Aldo clicked beads across the spindles of his abacus and shuffled invoices. Behind Dario, three young accountants were busy clinking Venetian ducats, French francs, German marks, and Spanish reals onto piles. Someone else scratched a pen across a ledger. Facing the street entrance behind a high table, the clerk Manfredo was talking with a client.

Such were the offices of the Rossi Bank and the Rossi Shipping and Transport Company on a Tuesday.

"But the note is now due, Signore Bonifacio," said Manfredo for the third time. "And we've already extended it once."

Bonifacio, a middle-aged baker in a rumpled white tunic with a flour-dusted forehead, wiped a hand through blond hair and stared at the loan document. "I need more time. The business, she will pick up soon. I know it."

"How much time?"

"Three months."

"I–I don't know. I—"

"What's the trouble, Manfredo?" Having heard everything, Dario was already crossing the room.

"Last year, this man borrowed forty florins to start his bakery business. In April, the note was to be paid in full, but he paid only half. We've already extended the loan by three months."

"How much does he owe now?"

"After the extension . . . twenty-four florins."

Dario faced the baker. "Why haven't you paid your debt, signore?"

He opened his hands, and his face fell. "The customers—they are not coming. Macario across the street—he take my business. But now the duomo workers are here, and they need much bread. If I buy a bigger oven, I get a contract for the noon meal. Give me three more months, signore. Lend me another ten florins, and I make a good profit. You will see."

It happened all the time. They borrowed too much in the first place. They couldn't outsell their competition. And they couldn't manage their expenses. Then all they needed was more money, a little more time, and—poof! Everything would work itself out.

"So now you would have us lend you—what? Ten on top of twenty-four, making thirty-four. And next November, you'd have to pay back"—he wrote some numbers on the paper's margins—"thirty-six florins and some fiorinos?"

The baker swallowed but nodded.

Dario shook his head. "No, signore. We cannot do it."

"B–but it will mean bankruptcy."

"Better yours than mine. Pay what you owe today."

"I–I do not have it." Terror now twisted his face.

Dario stared at him. "If we sell your equipment today, how much is it worth?"

"M–my bowls, m–my spoons, flour, and ovens?"

"Sì."

"Maybe fifteen, sixteen florins." He waved his hands. "I don't know."

"But, signore," said Manfredo to Dario, "if we give him another extension, the workers do need bread, and—"

"Take a lesson, son. When a business deal goes bad, you cut your losses early. Don't compound your original error. Now go get the constable."

"No, gonfaloniere." Bonifacio's voice rose, and his hands shook as if palsied. "Not debtor's prison. Please."

"It only takes two of us on the Signoria to declare you in default." He called behind him. "Aldo, do you agree?"

Aldo barely raised his head from the abacus. "Whatever you say, Dario."

He faced the baker again. "I hereby sentence you to prison until you pay what you owe. We have your address. Manfredo will go to your home, confiscate what he can, and sell it. Whatever he receives will satisfy some of what you owe. You will stay in prison until you pay the rest. That's the law."

The man fell to his knees, sobbing. "P–please, signore. My wife. My two bambini. What will become of them?"

Dario shrugged. "You should have thought of that before you agreed to the loan." He motioned for Manfredo to leave.

The clerk nodded and ran out the door.

Tears running down his cheeks, the man stood and turned from the table. Sobbing quietly, he huddled unmoving in the entryway.

Dario returned to his desk and called over his shoulder for another accountant to take the counter.

Moments later, with the baker still frozen where he was, Manfredo arrived with the constable and a burly assistant. The two ushered the man from the building.

"Manfredo," said Dario, "take someone with you and collect what you can from his apartment, including his clothes. Sell it all in the market."

Manfredo nodded, grabbed one of the others, and hurried away.

When the room had quieted and Dario was again staring at the shipping manifest, the numbers once more swam before his eyes. Pushing back from the desk, he rose. "I'm going out early today."

"But it's barely noon." His cousin finally looked up.

"These numbers are giving me a headache. I'll work on them tomorrow." He walked out the door and turned right. In a few hours, a certain taverna in the Temestre Inferiore known for its primero was starting a new game. The bid for each round was only ten florins. Two nights ago, he'd lost fifty.

Today, surely, he could win it all back. And then some.

CHAPTER 15

~ THE ROMAN CARPENTER ~

Amadeo, Skender, and the two mercenaries returned from their trip to Florence and stayed the night in Colpena. With replenished supplies, the four men took off early for Rome, their horses' tails swishing, their hooves raising dust.

Rumor had it that the archbishop of Mainz was refurbishing his cathedral and wanted Bernardo Pugliesi for his master carpenter. But Amadeo's plan was to reach him first. A former shipbuilder, Pugliesi was renowned for his skill at making cranes, lifting equipment, scaffolds, platforms, arches, and the complicated web of beams that would support the roof.

This would be Amadeo's third trip to Rome in his lifetime. And as his group topped a rise and the seven hills appeared below, he again shook his head in disappointment. Seventy thousand souls now rattled around inside the ruins of what was once, in the time of the ancient Empire, home to nearly a million people.

As they entered the city's outskirts, dark abandoned buildings and lots filled with rubble appeared on all sides. Ancient columns, nearly hidden by tall grass, lay broken and toppled, testifying to a grandeur long past. Now they offered only grazing space for sheep, cows, and pigs.

When they rode farther, public women stepped from bordellos and street corners, calling out to the four.

Dark-skinned, black-haired beauties. Blue-eyed blondes. White-gowned women with belts. Women draped in colorful silks. Roman courtesans with monkeys and parakeets atop their shoulders. Women from every corner of the world—from Turkey, Germany, Spain, Greece, Egypt, and the Orient.

He'd heard the city now boasted seven thousand prostitutes. In this alone could Rome claim to be number one.

Garbage and debris littered the avenues. Why did they not employ contadini to sweep and wash the streets each night? Where the streets of Florence and Colpena were clean, the houses well maintained, their societies ordered, Rome seemed to embrace only disorder, decay, and decadence.

The Church only worsened the problem.

Income from all over Europe now flooded into the Church's coffers. Everyone knew someone who made a living selling their wares to the pope, the cardinals, the archbishops, and their entourages. Each day, these holiest men of Christendom bought copious amounts of tailored cloth, rare wines, imported Sicilian cheeses, loaves of bread, sides of beef, racks of lamb, fish on ice, sweet pastries, precious jewels, expensive furs, rich carpets, rolls of parchment, gold rings, and silver necklaces. And who hadn't seen the steady stream of courtesans being led in and out of the cardinals' and archbishops' dwellings?

Like other foreigners, the Florentines lived and mostly worked in a single section of the city. When Amadeo arrived at Pugliesi's modest house in the Florentine quarter, he was greeted warmly. Short, with beard and eyes as black as night and unkempt hair down to his shoulders, Pugliesi gave the appearance of a forest wild man. He listened intently to Amadeo's plans and studied the parchments. "Let us eat while I mull it over," he said. "We're having spaghetti, beefsteak, and wine."

After Pugliesi's plump wife served a dessert of custard and Amadeo swallowed his last bite, Pugliesi pushed back from the table and gripped his waist. "Who will be the master stonecutter on this project?"

"Vittorio Rivera."

"I've heard of the man. I think I can work with him." Pugliesi was silent a moment. "Sì, capomaestro. Your plans are masterful. Gladly will I help you build the greatest duomo on God's earth. I venture my men will join me. Such a guarantee of work comes along rarely in one's lifetime. But my crew is scattered. It will take some weeks to round them up."

"Master carpenter, with skills such as yours, you could work anywhere. But before you agree, there is one major change I want to make. Vittorio Rivera has already agreed to it. I'm hoping you will, too."

Pugliesi frowned. "What change?"

"This project is bigger than anything attempted. The padrone and my contract insist I complete it within our lifetimes. Thus, I want not one, but two teams of everything. Two of stonecutters. Two of carpenters. And so forth."

A scowl crossed the carpenter's face, and he narrowed his eyes. "But this is unheard of. I know my crew, and I work well with them. To add others, perhaps foreigners from another city—this would turn everything upside down. And I will not work in competition with another master carpenter."

"You would be the only master carpenter, Bernardo. All carpenters and foresters would be under your authority. I know it breaks tradition and the way we've always done things. But I need this change."

"I don't have these extra workers. Where am I to get them?"

"You could assign more apprentices. Eventually, it will enlarge your crew."

"Sì, I could do that. But that won't provide skilled carpenters for many years. Am I to steal from someone else's crew?"

"If you find men who are out of work, would they not be glad to join you?"

"They might. But no, signore. I will not break from tradition. We are a tightly knit group—we Florentines living here in Rome. We must work with whom we have always worked."

"Won't you think it over before giving me your final answer?"

"I will consult with a few of the men. That's all I can promise."

"Fair enough. For when you decide, I'll leave this." Amadeo pulled out his moneybag, counted out seventy gold florins, and placed them on the table. "This should be enough to get your men to the site. A down payment on their wages. But if you decide not to accept my offer, I trust you'll return it by letter of credit through the Rossi Bank office here in Rome. I need your final answer by month's end. Or I will have to look elsewhere for my master carpenter."

Pugliesi stared at the pile of gold. "You trust too much, signore. And you ask much."

"I do. But is not this project worth breaking a few traditions?"

"I don't know." Pugliesi shook his head.

"It's the offer of a lifetime, Bernardo."

"That, signore, I cannot disagree with."

That night, Amadeo stayed in Pugliesi's home. The next morning he ate a breakfast provided by his wife, but the master carpenter himself had already gone out.

He and Skender found their mercenaries in a nearby inn and trekked, not to Colpena, but to Bologna. In that city, he hired both a master forger and a master blacksmith who both said that with only half as many more apprentices and larger workshops they could keep up with the demands of servicing the other crews. When they gathered their men, they would follow.

AMADEO RETURNED HOME BY WAY of Siena. On the city's Il Campo, a huge bowl of a square slanting down toward the town hall, he found Damiano De Luca sitting cross-legged with a bottle of red wine, chewing hunks from a loaf of bread. Red-haired and burly, he was difficult to miss. Once, for the space of eighteen months, until the men had voted him out, De Luca had been lodge master for the Church of San Giovanni in Bologna.

Amadeo introduced himself, then said, "I understand you're currently without work."

"That I am." De Luca waved to a spot beside him on the vast, red-bricked piazza.

Amadeo sat, drew the detailed plans from his pack, and spread them on the stones. "This is the duomo I'd like your help in building."

De Luca studied the plans, his eyes and his smile seeming to grow larger.

When Amadeo also told him of his plan to double the number of men on each crew, De Luca nodded. "I have many apprentices eager to become companions. And I have many relatives with sons eager to be apprenticed but without work. This is not a problem, signore. Give me a week or so, and I will come with many men."

They shook hands, Amadeo gave him travel funds, and he departed for Colpena.

Except for the glassmakers, who wouldn't be needed for years, his workforce was nearly complete.

Now, more than ever, he needed his master carpenter. Without Pugliesi and his crew, they would have no workshops or lodges. They couldn't lift the stones from the docks or raise them to the walls. They'd have no scaffolding or platforms from which to work.

In short, they couldn't build anything.

The moment Amadeo entered his house in Colpena, Skender handed him a message delivered days ago by Rossi's servant, Grazziano. "I am not a king with a people's treasury," said the note, "and you are far exceeding the rate estimated for your first year's expenses. You must slow the hiring of additional men and equipment until the bank and our new mine at Acque Salutari bring in additional revenue."

Amadeo stared at the request, crumpled it, and threw it in the fire. The patron had already agreed to provide all necessary funds, had he not? At this stage, Amadeo felt a need to hurry, not slow, the pace. Somehow, the gonfaloniere would find the money.

After coming home from his trip, he started each morning with the hope that Pugliesi would ride in from Rome with his men. But each night, he went to bed disappointed.

On the tenth day back, the forger and blacksmith crews arrived with their tools from Bologna.

A few days later, Vittorio Rivera rode into Colpena with two wagons, twenty companions, and nearly twenty-five apprentices. From the wagons, they emptied countless iron chisels and large- and medium-sized hammers along with handsaws, axes, shovels, crowbars, drawing boards, buckets, a pair of dividers, and two wheelbarrows.

With Vittorio rode a thin man with a hooked nose, gray hair, and a pockmarked, clean-shaven face. After they dismounted, Vittorio said, "Capomaestro, this is Umberto Sabbatini of Pisa, my speaker."

The tall Sabbatini bowed. "I am honored, signore."

Amadeo shook his hand and welcomed him.

That afternoon, Vittorio rented a nearby ground-floor room in which they locked their tools. His men found lodging in nearby inns with Vittorio renting an apartment for himself.

As Amadeo watched the workers settle in, adding to his growing workforce, he felt his excitement building and a compulsion to begin. Now, if only Pugliesi would come.

That evening, he and his master stonecutter sat at a trattoria in the Piazzetta dei Fiore sipping glasses of wine, waiting for their supper. "When will our master carpenter arrive?" asked Vittorio. "We can do little without him."

"He has not yet agreed to run two crews."

"He is traditional. I'm not surprised."

"If he were going to refuse, I would have expected him to send a messenger. In two weeks, his month will be up."

"I would press him for a decision, my friend. If we had a carpenter, we could complete much work before winter."

"I plan to write him this evening."

"And tomorrow, may I suggest a tour of the local quarry at Montemerano?"

"On that, Vittorio, I have bad news. Last week, I visited Montemerano. The ancient Romans took from it all the building marble there is to take. On one side, plenty of limestone still remains, but it's soft. Good only for making lime. The masons can set up a kiln there."

"Then our best option for building stone is from Carrara. It sits on the coast, the travertine there is the best, and the expense of shipping by barge won't be excessive."

"Then tomorrow, we should sail to Carrara."

Vittorio nodded. "It means we'll have to send stonecutters to live permanently up north. Have you estimated how much stone we'll need?"

"Only for the chancel and transepts. I'll bring you the numbers I have."

"Good."

After they parted, Amadeo returned to his rooms and sat at his garden table with quill in hand. "My dearest Bernardo," he began.

It is with the greatest anticipation I await your decision. I have secured masters and teams for all the major tasks except carpentry.

But the growing numbers of men here in Colpena lack lodges and proper workshops for their trades. Everyone inquires when you will arrive. All look forward to the addition of your skills.

My heart aches to see the work begin, but without carpenters and foresters, we cannot start. I implore you. What is the meaning of life if not to spend it in service to the One who created Heaven and earth? And what better service for us than to build possibly the greatest duomo the world has ever seen?

Though you are my first choice for master carpenter, the mounting expense of lodging men who might otherwise live free in workshops and the delay in starting construction forces me to reiterate my deadline.

On the first of September, if I have not heard from you, I will sail north to Lyon to seek another master carpenter.

My dearest Bernardo, I plead with you. Will you not come at once to Colpena and join our efforts?

If you have decided against my offer, please respond by fast courier. Otherwise present yourself in Colpena at the earliest opportunity.

Yours in Christ,
Amadeo Puccini
Capomaestro della Cattedrale del Figlio sul Mare

He handed the letter to a courier with instructions to take it to Rome in the morning—as fast as his mount could carry him.

CHAPTER 16

~ CARRARA ~

The morning after Vittorio's arrival, Amadeo stood in the entryway of Fabiano's palazzo on the Via delle Rose and asked for money to secure contracts in Carrara. But when he told Fabiano how much was needed, the building committee's treasurer winced. "I pay the bills, sì, but it's Rossi who funds the account. It's becoming more and more difficult to squeeze the florins from him."

"But he agreed to do it, no?"

"He did. But as of this moment, I don't have everything you ask for. I can only give you a third."

"For now, that will do. But by the time I return, you must ensure he fulfills his obligations."

"He is the gonfaloniere and a powerful man." Fabiano raised his hands in entreaty. "What am I to do?"

Amadeo shrugged, took the bag of coins, and left.

Seagulls cried and circled at the western jetty where Vittorio already waited. From an owner only too happy for the fare, Amadeo hired a sleek, two-masted brigantine with a crew of twelve.

The voyage to Carrara's port of Luni took a day and a half, stopping at a wharf where treadwheel cranes creaked and moaned as they lifted huge marble blocks from the dock. The cranes were powered by men walking inside giant wheels. Lifting the heavy loads, they settled the stone in the beds of barges and cargo ships filled with sand. Water then flushed the sand through the scuppers so the craft bore only the marble's weight.

They hiked three miles from the port up to the village of Carrara, where they stayed the night at an albergo.

Early the next morning, the proprietor sent them to a stone hut on the town's outskirts. There, they met Tiziana, a fetching young woman with flowing black hair, who agreed to lead them on the long hike into the Apuan Alps to the Battaglino quarry.

"My father works the mountain there." With a jerk of her head, she threw her long black hair over her shoulders. "It has the bardiglio marble you look for. He give you what you need."

They followed her up a steep ravine. Halfway up the ascent, they scrambled out of the way. A dozen bare-chested men strained against creaking ropes tied around a massive rectangular block they were inching down the mountain. Rolling on logs thrown before it, the gray-and-white-streaked marble crunched and rumbled over the ground. The men cursed, sweated, and dug their feet into a path scattered with marble chips as they tried to keep their load from barreling down the slope.

"For a column?" Amadeo was sweating and breathing hard from the climb.

"Sì, signore," said Tiziana. "I think that one goes to France."

When they'd climbed perhaps a thousand feet, they arrived in a steep valley where different crews worked opposite slopes. After years of being quarried, both sides of the mountain were terraced. At his feet as far as he could see, gray chips and powder covered the ground. Cool thin air washed his wet cheeks.

"Father has the south face." She led them past two men working both ends of a six-foot saw, supported from above by ropes strung from a wooden tripod. They cut slowly back and forth into a large gray-blue block while a boy poured water and sprinkled sand into the cutting crack. The metal grated and ground against the marble.

A hundred and fifty feet up on the slopes, eight men worked the highest terrace with hammers, chisels, and crowbars.

"My father up there." She pointed. "We take the marble from the top."

Circumventing the terraces, she bounded up a steep path. As Amadeo sucked in breath and tried to keep up, he marveled that she seemed not the least bit winded.

Emerging behind the upper ledge, he watched men strike heavy mallets onto wooden stakes while others poured water onto the wood.

"The wood, she swells and splits the rock," said Tiziana. "This block is for later."

Amadeo nodded, having been at quarries before.

But when the men heard her voice, they stopped, whirled, put hands on their hips, and smiled.

"Tiziana!" The gruff voice came from a man whose marble-scarred, sun-browned face was as rough as the rock he worked. "Why have you come?" Scowling, he brushed marble dust from his pants and approached.

"These men are buyers, Father."

"Ah, well. Then go home. With you here, the men do not work. They feast their eyes on you instead."

She winked at the visitors and hurried toward the trail.

"Nicola Lombardo." He extended a hand. "This side of the mountain—my quarry."

Amadeo took the offered palm and received a crushing grip from fingers used to holding hammer, chisel, and stone, not flesh.

"You come to buy bardiglio, signori?"

"Sì." Amadeo examined his bruised fingers. "We need hard high-quality marble for building. As soon as you can send it."

The man's eyes lit up. "You sign contract today?"

"If the price is right."

Vittorio borrowed a chisel and hammer from one of the workers and faced the back wall. He chipped off a piece and held it up to the light. "Is it all as good as this?"

"Sì, signore. For building, sì? Not statuary?"

"Sì. But we'll need some white statuary marble later."

"Good. Then let us go down to my hut." He started down the path. "We do business."

After they descended to the bottom and while the workers were still sawing, a shout came from above. "Rock fall!"

The two men dropped their saw and ran. Nicola waved to Vittorio and Amadeo, and they, too, scrambled for higher ground.

High above, the men wiggled crowbars and pounded sledgehammers into wooden wedges in a final effort to free the piece they were working on. On the bottom slope, others pulled on long ropes attached to the same piece.

A massive block cracked away from the cliff. It thundered and bounced off the ledges, split along a fault, and the pieces rolled and tumbled to the bottom, causing a minor slide, finally grinding to a stop.

"Safe now." Nicola led them a hundred yards to a low wooden hut. Pulling two barrels from outside, he placed them before a table. While he claimed the lone stool, he motioned for them to take the barrel seats. Iron tools and an oil lamp hung from wall pegs. A low cot stretched across the corner.

"How much marble you want?" It seemed Nicola always came straight to the point, using as few words as possible.

"Signore Lombardo"—Amadeo focused on the quarryman—"we are building a great cathedral in Colpena. For many years, we will need much of your marble—perhaps all you have." He passed the quarrymaster a parchment on which he'd estimated the sizes and numbers of blocks needed for just the chancel and transepts. Vittorio had worked on the sheet and changed a few figures. "To reduce transport costs, we ask your men to dress the blocks using only their *subbia* chisels. We'll send some of our stonecutters here to live permanently and work beside yours. They'll cut the blocks to their proper sizes with their *scarpella* chisels based on templates from Vittorio, here. He is my master stonecutter."

"To avoid marring the blocks in transit," added Vittorio, "the rest of our crew will do the final rough filing and polishing steps in Colpena."

For the longest time, Nicola studied the paper with a grim expression. When he again faced the two men, suppressed excitement darkened his eyes. "Is much bardiglio you need, signori. You must rent quarry. Not pay by the piece. First, we finish small work already contracted. Maybe one month. Then we give all quarry to you."

"I understand." He didn't want to wait a month, but this was to be expected. "Then how much to rent your quarry and for the men to do the first step in dressing the blocks?"

Nicola's face grew serious, and he scratched his sculpted chin. "Maybe . . . each year . . . four thousand ducats."

Vittorio leaned over and whispered. "Too much. Pay no more than three thousand florins."

"No, signore." Amadeo folded his hands on the rough-hewn table and turned back to the quarryman. "I'll pay two thousand florins. Not ducats."

"Bah!" The man's calm demeanor vanished with the wave of an angry hand. "How long it take to saw a block of hard bardiglio, signore? You know? All day the men work—saw, saw, saw—and they cut four, five inches. One day's work." He threw a disgusted glance to the side. "How long to pry the rock from the mountain, hey? Pound the iron stakes, make a crack. Pound in the wooden wedges. Pour on water. Pound more wedges. Lean on crowbars. Over and over. All day for a week. And what comes? Hey? Maybe forty, sixty tons. And still, we have the mountain to go down. Your price—not enough."

"Two thousand five hundred."

"We live a hard life, signore. Each day, the mountain take from us. Little bit here. Little bit there. We grow old before our years. Last summer, my cousin—the mountain take him in a fall. He leave behind a wife, three bambini. Many mouths to feed with your florins, signore. Three thousand five hundred."

"Three thousand."

"Three thousand, two hundred. No less."

Amadeo looked to Vittorio, who nodded. So Amadeo reached across and shook Nicola's hand, grimacing again at the crushing grip.

"I go down with you now to notary in Carrara. We sign today?"

"Sì."

The angry façade of a moment ago transformed into a wide grin. "Good."

Thus, did they leave the quarry and descend to Carrara, where they signed a contract to rent the part of the mountain where Nicola Lombardo had the rights to mine. Amadeo dropped enough gold coins into his hands to cover half of the first year's payment.

The quarryman left smiling.

Late that afternoon, they arrived at the port of Luni, where they negotiated barge transport for everything Nicola and Vittorio's men would send them. But the barge price was per shipment, and Amadeo estimated that costs for yearly transport plus export taxes would be twice the price to quarry the stone. He consoled himself that shipment by land was often twelve times that by sea. After paying the barge owner for the first few shipments, he had barely enough gold left for passage home. Rossi had better come through with the promised funds soon.

That night, they returned to their room in Carrara.

As Amadeo ate the inn's ham ravioli and sipped the region's red wine, he said, "I've spent a lot of Rossi's money today. And this is only the beginning."

"But is it not said that the padrone Rossi has a bottomless well of funds?"

"That, Vittorio, is an exaggeration. From what I've seen, the deeper his hand digs into the well, the harder it is for him to bring it out again."

AFTER THEIR SHIP DOCKED AT Colpena's western port, Amadeo went first to the Piazza dei Sole, or what was left of it, hoping to see his master carpenter. But all that met him were the sounds of crowbars scraping against rock and the old paving stones crashing into wheelbarrows. Once again, he left the square disappointed.

"If he hasn't arrived next week," he said to Vittorio, "I will set sail for France to look for someone else."

"Sì. We need our carpenter now."

Shortly after Amadeo settled into his rooms, a boy sent by Rossi appeared at his door with a message. At precisely ten o'clock on the morrow, Amadeo was to appear at Rossi's palazzo.

ON THE FOLLOWING MORNING, THE servant Grazziano admitted Amadeo to the patron's study. Amadeo still didn't know what to expect.

Sitting around a long table with a sputtering candle was the entire building committee: Dario Rossi, Enzio Borroni, Callisto Mancini, Fabiano Trentino, and Bishop Rinaldi Ferata.

As he took a seat beside a smiling Callisto, his gaze was drawn to a portrait of Dario hanging above the man in the flesh—Dario Rossi draped in brass armor, left hand touching a sword at his belt, right foot resting on a tree stump, right arm crooked as if in victory, with a bronze helmet atop his head. But as far as Amadeo knew, Rossi had never led men in battle. Did he even know how to draw a sword?

"Ah, here is the great architect himself," said Fabiano with a tone of utter sincerity. "We are eager to hear about your trip to the quarries. And learn of your progress on the duomo."

Amadeo bowed. "Most certainly. What would you like to hear first?"

"Your progress on the duomo, signore—how goes it?"

He described how the laborers had cleared the building site and were even now digging the footings for the foundations. He enumerated the crews he'd obtained and the difficulty in getting Bernardo Pugliesi to agree to run two crews.

Dario Rossi stopped him. "Two crews? I don't understand."

"In order to finish this project on schedule, gonfaloniere, I'm doubling the number of men on each crew. Each trade master—all but Pugliesi—has agreed to this."

"Twice the workers . . . ?" Rossi's eyes seemed to lose focus. "But this means . . . twice the labor expense."

"It does, signore."

Even as Rossi's face paled, Enzio Borroni's seemed to brighten. "Ah, but this is wonderful news." He grinned at Rossi. "Twice the men, twice the progress. Whatever you need, master builder, just ask for it. Our generous patron, here, has agreed to provide. The contract specifies as much, does it not?"

"It does, signore."

"Other than the difficulty with your master carpenter, I am well pleased," said Fabiano. "Now let us hear about your trip north."

Amadeo described his visit to Carrara and the necessity of renting the site for the duration. Then he quoted the price to rent the quarry and the price for transport.

"B–but three thousand two hundred florins." Rossi's face became as white as a block of statuary marble. "And another five thousand five hundred per year for cartage. That's . . . eight thousand . . . seven hundred— each and every year! On top of everything else." He looked around the table. "It's impossible!"

"It is what we require."

Rossi's hands flew to the top of his head, and he stared at his capo-maestro. "This will ruin me."

Grinning, Borroni faced the gonfaloniere. "But with the income from your mine at Acque Salutari, you should be awash in florins."

Rossi glared at him.

"My lord," said Bishop Ferata to Rossi, "you did agree to pay whatever was required for the duomo's construction. Are you unable to fund these expenses?"

Rossi closed his eyes, took a deep breath. "No," he whispered. "I will pay them."

"I couldn't hear you," said Borroni.

"I will pay," Rossi said, louder. Then his eyes opened, and his gaze fixed on Amadeo. "Signore, for my sake, you must slow these expenditures."

"If I am to complete this task before the Lord takes us both, I must have the resources and men to do it."

"Agreed." Borroni was still grinning.

"Agreed," said Fabiano, followed by Callisto and the bishop.

But Rossi said nothing.

"Thank you, all." Amadeo rose. "I must prepare for my departure. In a few days, if Bernardo Pugliesi doesn't arrive, I am leaving for Lyon to search for a master carpenter."

CHAPTER 17

~ THE FINAL MASTER ~

SEPTEMBER 1469

Amadeo's small entourage climbed into a cart on the Strada delle Campane. Ahead, four mares swished their tails against the flies. Holding the reins, a driver sat in front, with Amadeo and Skender. Four mercenaries armed with pikes and swords sat their horses ahead of them, prepared to provide protection on the long journey.

Yesterday was the last of August, and all day he'd hoped to hear something, anything, from the expatriate Florentine carpenter. But nothing had come. He could wait no longer.

He was sailing to France to search for another master carpenter.

The reins slapped, and the horses yanked the cart over the cobbles. But from behind came the clopping of hooves.

"Wait!" came a familiar voice. "Stop!"

Amadeo spun to look. The rider was Rinaldi Ferata.

"They've arrived!" shouted the bishop. "Pugliesi and his entire crew have arrived."

Moments later, with his armed escort released from duty, Amadeo strode onto the dirt of the building site. A great number of carpenters and foresters milled about a newly arrived cart filled with axes, saws, chains, adzes, and chisels. Bernardo Pugliesi himself was out in the field, peering into the foundation holes the workers had dug. Amadeo ran to greet him.

"Welcome, Bernardo." As Pugliesi turned to face him, Amadeo extended his hand, and they shook. "I had nearly departed for France to find someone else."

"Well, here I am. I thought it over, and though it breaks all tradition, I could never live with myself if I gave up this opportunity." Pugliesi spread his hands toward the foundation holes extending across the field. "This is impressive, my friend."

"How many men did you bring?"

"Sixteen companions and thirty-two apprentices. I learned of a crew from Lucca without work. I traveled to that city to present them the offer, and they accepted. I just hope the Lucchese will not fight with my Florentines."

"Good. When can you start?"

"As soon as the men have lodging and we store our tools."

"Excellent. But tomorrow, you will please ride with me to investigate the forest, sì?"

"I will ride with you."

THE NEXT DAY, AMADEO DRESSED in clothing reserved only for official occasions. He met the master carpenter, also formally attired, and Tancredo, the bald, portly notary. Eager to start, Amadeo's black gelding whinnied and shook its head. Then they began the five-mile ride to the forest owned by Baron Calvino Calabrese.

"Signore"—sweating profusely, Tancredo sat uncomfortably atop his mount—"I hope we don't have much farther to go."

"We've only begun, my friend."

When they reached the forest, the sparrows' chirping filled the treetops. Amadeo and Vittorio dismounted and led their horses on foot so the master carpenter could examine the tall stands of oak at leisure. Behind them, Tancredo sat his horse and let it wander.

"This is close to the city." Pugliesi's wave was expansive. "And these are good trees. The oaks are straight and thick. This entire forest is nearly untouched. It is perfect." He pointed toward the highest branches. "Soon, we must cut the tallest of these for the duomo's roof."

"But we won't build the roof for decades."

"We'll erect a warehouse here to store the lumber. If we cut now, by the time we need it, the wood will be dry enough to use." Pugliesi faced Amadeo. "We cannot use green wood for the roof, capomaestro."

"Ah, of course. But now we must make an arrangement to buy these trees. Let's hope Baron Calabrese is willing."

Mounting again, the three rode through the bordering pine forest.

"This, too, is good wood," said Pugliesi. "We'll need much pine as well."

When they arrived at the baron's hilltop castle, they dismounted in the courtyard. Dressed for a hunt in hightop boots and leather jacket, the Baron Calabrese greeted them. Then Amadeo explained his request to take wood for the cathedral from Calabrese's forests and to set up nearby workshops and a forge.

The baron crossed his arms. "Dario Rossi, the ruler of your city's Signoria, already hunts with impunity on my lands. Now you wish to carve up my hunting grounds, removing two or three square miles of my forest?" He narrowed his eyes. "This cathedral—how long would it take to build?"

Pugliesi opened his hands in apology. "Our lifetimes, signore."

Calabrese scowled and whirled away, muttering to himself.

Amadeo feared he would refuse. What would they do without that forest?

Calabrese spun back. "How much would you pay?"

"Two thousand florins each year."

Only then did a smile lift the baron's lips. "Then sì. For two thousand a year, you may take what you need."

As they left the hilltop castle, with Tancredo's horse trailing far in the rear, Pugliesi turned in the saddle. "I am well pleased with the forest and its location."

"As am I," said Amadeo. "But come. If we increase the pace, we can get Tancredo off that horse before supper."

As they entered the building site later that afternoon, Amadeo was greeted by the clattering of many horses' hooves and the excited voices of yet another newly arrived group—Damiano De Luca, fifteen companions, and twenty apprentices.

"I've come as promised, capomaestro. The best stone mason and mortar mixer in all of Italy." He pushed out his chest. "But on the way here, I decided to present one more request. One I hope you will approve."

"What's that?"

"I wish to become lodge master."

Amadeo sucked in breath and suppressed a frown. He'd been warned De Luca was difficult to work with. "But is that not for the men to decide?"

"Sì, but . . . it is still my request."

"The feeling is that"—Amadeo glanced at him—"that the men will probably choose Vittorio Rivera."

De Luca pressed his hands together. "I . . . see. But if you insist, perhaps they will choose me?"

"Perhaps." Amadeo had no intention of trying to sway the men. He faced the master mason, hoping this was the end of the matter, and smiled. "I'm glad you decided to join us, signore."

"Sì. It will be good to work again. But do consider my request."

The next day, as expected, the men elected Vittorio Rivera as lodge master. De Luca watched with crossed arms and soured face as the men voted his rival to the position. Later in private, he complained to Amadeo.

"It is tradition." Amadeo shrugged. "And we must abide by the vote."

Frowning, De Luca nodded.

But would the mason secretly hold it against him that the architect hadn't forced a preference on the men?

CHAPTER 18

~ AMADEO'S GRAND WELCOME ~

On the following Saturday, with all the major teams in place and all the masters now on site, Amadeo called a grand meeting of the workers. Abuzz with loud conversation, they assembled on the dirt of the former Piazza dei Sole. The day before, he'd arranged with Fabiano to receive funds for a small feast. Tables were set up beside the piazza, where the city's women called orders to each other as they brought bread, cheese, spiced cabbage, and olives. Other tables were laden with apples, grapes, oranges, and amphorae of wine.

When the men had gathered—nearly seven hundred strong, including common laborers, with many more to be hired—he mounted a wagon brought in as a dais. Also climbing aboard were the masters he'd chosen—Vittorio Rivera, master stone cutter and lodge master; Umberto Sabbatini, speaker; Damiano De Luca, master mason; Bernardo Pugliesi, master carpenter; plus master forgers, blacksmiths, and others. He stood atop the wagon and straightened his back.

"Workers of Colpena"—his voice boomed over the crowd—"stonecutters, masons, carpenters, forgers, blacksmiths, barrel makers, ox drivers, laborers, and masters of many trades—I bid you welcome to the building site of the Cattedrale del Figlio sul Mare. Some of you have been working here all summer, and I give you my thanks. Those of you who are newly arrived, I heartily welcome you."

Smiling faces lifted toward him, some young, eager, and bright, some weatherworn from the elements, others older and bearded but attentive. What an assembly of skill, knowledge, and expertise! Who had ever seen the like? He caught his breath and went on.

"My friends, let us never forget that what we build here is a mighty work for God. That is the sole reason most of us will toil for the next forty or fifty years, spending our lives to raise the walls, columns, arches, and roofs, and to fill the niches and bays with art that will glorify our Lord and Savior, Christ Jesus, and educate the populace. At the end of that time, our sweat and blood will have become part of every block, every ounce of mortar, and every inch of height. This, my friends, is our praise, our honor, and our sacrifice for our Lord."

"Amen," shouted Bishop Ferata, standing below the wagon.

Cheers and applause rose all across the square. It continued until Amadeo raised his hands for quiet.

"You all know the rules of the guilds to which you belong. See your master if anyone does not understand them or has questions." He waved to the men on the stand behind him. "These rules call for integrity, personal responsibility, and devotion to duty. We expect everyone to work hard and live well and honorably.

"But sometimes"—he drew in a deep breath—"personal circumstances arise that are beyond our control, situations that bring us hard times. If that happens to anyone here, I now make a promise to you. If any guild worker or common laborer finds himself in difficulty because of such circumstances, and if their guild is unable to help, please appeal to me personally, and I will see what can be done. I make no promises other than that we serve Christ first and I wish everyone to be treated with honor and mercy. But I will at least look into your situation. And if I can help, I will."

With those words, the entire assembly erupted in loud and continuous applause. As he looked out over the multitude of workers, smiles accompanied the nodding of heads. A few hands from the wagon behind slapped him on the back.

When the commotion quieted, he beamed at the crowd. "I understand the women have prepared a small feast, with bread, cheese, olives, and wine. So welcome to the duomo, my friends, take the day off, celebrate our grand work, and steel yourselves for the glorious task ahead."

The entire square burst again into wild cheering. Smiling and nodding vigorously to each other, the men moved to the tables.

"You have made a great beginning." Vittorio laid a hand on his shoulder. "The workers will not soon forget this day."

Amadeo turned and nodded. "Let the other masters know I expect them to be lenient with the guilds' rules. And to bring individual hardship cases to my attention. We must show mercy and compassion to these men who form the backbone of our work."

"I will do so, capomaestro," Vittorio said. "And I already have a case for you. I was about to give a certain baker—Bonifacio is his name—a contract to supply bread for the workers at noon, but he defaulted on his debts to the Rossi bank. For the last month, he's been in debtor's prison. Ten florins will release him and another forty will allow him to buy back enough equipment to meet our needs."

"Thank you, Vittorio. I'll see to the matter." Amadeo fished in a pocket, pulled out ten florins, and called Skender over to take care of the matter. He'd send the rest when he was paid.

Vittorio smiled. "Capomaestro, it's going to be a pleasure working with you."

BEFORE THE LAST LEAVES OF autumn fled the trees, Colpena bustled with furious activity from Amadeo's crews.

Vittorio built a new Piazza del Duomo in the open space where the former church and charred houses and shops once stood. Every day, the kiln at the Montemerano quarry burned stone to make lime. Daily, carts drove back and forth over the few miles from the quarry workshop, stopping along the way at a dry riverbed to fill their beds with sand. In the place where the old church had been, mixers filtered the sand and worked constantly to mix the mortar, barely keeping up with the masons laying stones as they built the new square.

Pugliesi soon lived up to his reputation. In the newly completed Piazza del Duomo, his expanded crew erected a lodge, a workshop for the stonecutters, another shop for the masons, and a forge where the metalworkers would create tools, nails, pulleys, wheels, and other needed items. In addition to the workshop and kiln at the Montemerano quarry, the carpenters built a forge and workshop in the baron's forest. They also made three carts, one for hauling stone from the docks, two for hauling timbers from the forest.

The carpenters then fashioned small cranes that the masons used to lower pallets of bricks into the foundation trenches. In the square, the mortar mixers added sand, lime, and water in just the right proportions. Apprentices carried the mixture in buckets, and cranes lowered them on pallets. At the bottom of the trench, masons mortared the sides with stones saved from demolished houses. The center they filled with stone rubble mixed with mortar, adding more layers as the mortar cured.

All this they accomplished by late October when the last barge, piled deep with blocks of blue-gray bardiglio marble, arrived. Nicola Lombardo's crew and Vittorio's men had hewn the blocks based on Vittorio's templates. Men loaded small wheelbarrows with the heavy stones and rolled them across the wharf to waiting carts. Two teams of oxen rumbled the wagon with its steel-rimmed wheels up the winding Via del Porto to the hilltop. There, laborers stacked the blocks in the new piazza.

They'd barely completed the chancel foundations when winter's cold rains and winds forced the masons to stop. Covering the top of the foundations and the newly cut blocks with manure and straw, the men retired to their quarters for the winter at half pay. The stonecutters finished dressing as many blocks as had arrived before the barges stopped sailing.

Already, he'd seen a few hardship cases the guilds could not address. One man, a hard-working carpenter, explained to the capomaestro how his wife had broken a leg. With her unable to continue as a laundress for local merchants and with three bambini to attend, the family was reduced to poverty. The man's wages simply were not enough to feed them and pay their meager rent, even in a cheap, sixth-floor apartment in the Temestre Inferiore. The guild's rules did not allow for her maintenance.

Out of his own pocket, Amadeo gave them ten florins. This, along with what the carpenter could afford, was enough to tide them over until she healed. When Amadeo handed the man the money, the carpenter had fallen to his knees, weeping with gratitude.

Embarrassed, Amadeo had asked him to please stand.

With the cold weather, Amadeo retreated to his rooms and his desk, where he drew detailed plans for the interior statuary and frescoes. He also visited the men in the lodges and took long walks. Anything to fill the time until work resumed in the spring.

CHAPTER 19

~ ALDO'S PLAN ~

NOVEMBER 1469

"**S**hall we walk on the beach?" Dario gripped the child's hand as their feet clapped the stones leading down to the western docks. For November, the day was warm, and he'd left his cioppa back in the palazzo.

"Sì, uncle." Letizia threw her long black locks over one shoulder and shot him a smile to melt his heart. "We can gather shells."

"I doubt we'll find any, but we can look." He glanced again at his out-of-wedlock daughter, the child everyone knew as his niece. Something inside him longed to tell her the truth, this child whom he'd grown to love like no other.

Love. What a strange word. One with so many connotations and meanings—the carnal desire he held for the women who visited his palazzo almost nightly; also the lust mixed with affection he reserved for Calandra and Bianca, his regular women at the Allegra Taverna; then the love he'd felt for his mother, now passed on. For his deceased father, he'd held an altogether different kind of affection—one mixed with respect, fear, and obedience. Finally, the deep tenderness, warmth, and intimacy he felt with Letizia, this seven-year-old bundle of life beside him.

How often hadn't he wished to bring her into his palazzo to live with him?

But no. Along with Letizia would come her mother, Savina. And what he felt for Savina could no longer be called love. When the two of them were together, they did nothing but fight. Savina was constantly demanding what he could not give. Yet seeing Letizia meant seeing her mother first. He was gonfaloniere, and with a word to Jacopo, men—and even women—disappeared. But he could do nothing to harm Savina. Destroying her would destroy the child.

They left the stone for the beach and stopped on the sand.

"Tell me again about my father," she said.

"My half-brother." He shifted his feet uncomfortably. He hated talking about the lie he'd forced on Savina. "Roberto, your father, was the only child from my father's first wife, but both he and his mother died before I was born. After Roberto married Savina and she had you, he died of some unknown ailment in Genoa."

"I wish I'd met him."

"I didn't know him."

"Look, uncle." She jumped up and down. "A shark."

A dorsal fin broke the surface.

"No, he's a porpoise."

"How can you tell?"

"The shark swims in circles, close to the surface, looking for something big to kill. The porpoise often swims up and down. This one is playful. He only eats small fish."

"I think people are like sharks, don't you?"

Startled, he jerked his head toward her. "Why do you say that?"

"Because some people are always wanting to be bigger, stronger, and take things from other people. But the other people just want to jump around and have fun without hurting anyone. I want to be a porpoise, not a shark."

She looked up at him with such innocent dark eyes, he didn't know how to respond. "Maybe . . . little flower . . . maybe you're right. And sì, you should be a porpoise. Not a shark." His breath caught in his throat.

The bell in the town hall's campanile began tolling. One, two . . . seven o'clock.

"I'm sorry, but I must get you back."

"So soon?"

He shrugged. "To your mother . . . by seven."

"You're already late." Black curls bouncing, she shook her head in mock disapproval.

"And I was supposed to meet my cousin before six."

"Then you're twice in trouble."

"All the more time to spend with you."

They returned to the dock and entered the warren of the Temestre Inferiore with its five- and six-story apartments stacked one atop another. Too many people lived in the lower quarter. And without enough water. Before the Signoria allowed a sixth story on the houses down here—the lower quarter bred like the rats they lived with—the cisterns already had trouble keeping up. Now they were constantly running dry.

Bramante needed to finish his endless water project. And soon.

They turned the corner and stopped at number twenty-eight, Strada degli Innocenti. A scolding voice called from an open window four stories up, "You're late."

"Sorry."

"You're always sorry. Why don't you marry me? Why don't you end this farce?"

He ducked inside the stairwell out of view, kissed Letizia on the cheek, winked, then ran down the street.

"Do what you should, Dario," shouted the voice from above.

When he was out of earshot, he slowed to a walk. She shouldn't make public spectacles. One of these days, she'd go too far. Then he'd have to do something about her.

Minutes later, he entered the Allegra Taverna. He strode past the loud conversations, the lute player, and Mario, the innkeeper, who barely had time to look up from the customers he was serving. Dario pushed through the door to the back room.

"You're late." Aldo sat with an empty wineglass, an empty decanter, and an empty plate.

Waving away the accusation, Dario slid his chair closer to the table. "I was with my niece."

Aldo rolled his eyes. "Don't play games with me, cousin."

"You don't know her as anything else."

"Of course, I don't." Aldo leaned forward on the table. "You're late, and we have serious business to discuss."

Slight, blonde-haired Maria swept into the room, smiling and bearing a plate of beef and bean stew with bread, another glass, and another flagon of red wine.

When she'd gone and Dario began eating, Aldo opened a leather folio filled with papers.

"I thought we agreed not to discuss business here." Dario ate a mouthful of stew so thick, he had to use the fork from his cadenza.

"This is something we can't discuss at the palazzo—something I don't want anyone else to hear."

Dario stopped eating and cocked his head.

"We are broke, my friend," said Aldo. "And it's all because of your funding of this accursed duomo. Not to mention your gambling, your hunting excursions, your frequent parties, and everything you spend in the bordellos."

"Those last two—insignificant. And do you not also partake?"

"But it all adds up." Aldo slapped a piece of paper in front of him.

The figures showed four columns—the outflow for the last year, the income from the bank and shipping company, the amount they had in reserve, and the debts they owed.

Their expenses exceeded their income. Their debts exceeded their assets.

Dario looked up, his fork suspended halfway to his mouth.

"That's right, my cousin. The monies you've given Fabiano to fund this duomo project have destroyed us."

"But . . . what about the mine income?"

"As I've tried to explain, we have contracts for ships on their way to foreign ports loaded with alum. But they won't reach their destinations for months. And they won't bring back any payments for even more months. We just started shipping alum in June, and even those quantities were small. It will take time to build up that business."

"So right now we're broke?"

"That's about the size of it."

As if to punctuate their dilemma, a ship's bell clanged out on the docks, followed by another and another. Changing of the watch.

Aldo slapped both hands on the table. "I want you to stop funding the duomo. We can't afford it."

"You know I can't do that."

"I know of no such thing. It's foolishness. You never asked me if I agreed to it. You just did it."

"It's what I have to do. And I would remind you, I own eighty percent of the bank, the shipping company, and the mine."

"As you keep saying." Aldo pulled the papers back. "You will not buy your salvation, Dario. You don't even have a soul to bargain for."

"Everybody has a soul."

"Bah! The priests have poisoned your brain."

"I know I have a soul. As do you. I can't tell you why or how, but deep within me, I know this. And without this duomo, I am . . . damned."

Aldo stared at him. He shook his head and closed his eyes. "And because of that notion, so is our business."

"Isn't there something—*anything*—we can do?" Dario opened his hands.

Closing his eyes, Aldo dropped his head into his hands and massaged his brow. "I was hoping it wouldn't come to this. That's why I wanted to discuss this here, away from eager ears at the office."

"Wouldn't come to—what?"

"One of our sea captains—a good sailor, he is—approached me a month ago. He sees the cargo we haul, the gold we bring back, and he's put it all together. He knows our situation, Dario. And he gave me an offer I've been mulling for quite some time. One I hoped we'd never have to use."

"What?"

"Before he turned to captaining merchant vessels, he was a mate aboard a privateer off the French coast in the employ of Spain."

"A pirate's mate?"

"Some would call him that. His name is Vico Vecoli, and he offered to find a ship of Moroccan origin. He'd crew it with foreigners—probably Moroccans—who are familiar with the trade. He wants to go into business with us as a privateer."

"You talk as if this were a legitimate enterprise?"

"Listen. Here's my idea: We buy Vecoli a ship of his own. In return, he gathers a crew of foreign privateers. We split the spoils of whatever cargo he takes, sixty for us, forty for them. But here's the difference— what if he only preyed on ships of Pisan origin? What if only ships leaving Pisa's harbors, run by Pisan shipping companies, were intercepted and looted? Think what that would do to their shipping companies? Who would the Pisan merchants then turn to?"

"Pisa is a client state of Florence. We'd need to be careful."

"With a Moroccan crew, no one would suspect anything."

"But . . . we don't have a shipping branch in Pisa."

"I propose we start one. We send two of our four ships there at once and open an office. And we do this *before* Signore Vecoli begins this venture."

"Do we have the money to buy another ship?"

"No. But we have a line of credit with the Medici Bank."

"It's already overextended, and I'm reluctant to tap Lorenzo for more money. Since his father died last winter, Lorenzo has barely begun to consolidate his power."

"He'll give us more. I'm certain of it. It will plunge us deeper into debt, but"—Aldo waved his hands—"there's no other option."

"What does this Vico Vecoli get out of it?"

"After a number of years . . . ownership of the vessel."

Dario stared at his half-eaten plate of stew. The plan was brilliant. Not only would they garner immediate income from the cargo of Pisan ships, they'd gain business from Pisan merchants looking for safer carriers. He was a bit troubled that Lorenzo's money would fund the looting of Lorenzo's own client city, but his patron would never find out. "Sì. Let us fund this privateer and see if that doesn't bring us a change of fortune."

Then he thought back to what Letizia had said earlier. *Some people are always wanting to be bigger, stronger, and take things from the other people they live with.*

He and Aldo were the sharks, weren't they?

And little Letizia and people like her—they were the porpoises.

PART II

~ La Cattedrale Del Figlio Sul Mare ~

CHAPTER 20

~ THE CEREMONY ~

APRIL 1470

Finally, spring's warm breath kissed the streets and byways, leaves burst full and green from the trees, young birds cracked out of their eggs, and cicadas buzzed long into the evening. Stonecutters resumed work, and masons again descended the foundation holes while apprentices lowered pallets of wall stones and buckets of mortar and rubble after them.

Then came the day Amadeo had planned since the fall—the grand ceremony when the cornerstone would be laid and the bishop would bless and name the duomo.

All the city seemingly now gathered beside the chancel's foundation, spilling onto the field where open holes still yawned, guarded with rope. Crowds backed up even into the new Piazza del Duomo. Vendors worked the crowd, hawking slices of panini drizzled with olive oil and herbs. But most were waiting for the feast to follow.

Amadeo ascended last onto a wooden stage his carpenters built for the occasion. Dressed in his best brown, gold-hemmed tunic with its starred white shoulder piece, he joined hawk-nosed Fabiano in a ruffled green blouse and white hose; dour-faced Enzio Borroni in his customary black; portly, smiling Callisto Mancini in his frumpy merchant's robe; and Dario Rossi, wearing tight red calze, a gold shirt with silver thread, under a jacket with billowing slashed sleeves, his head topped by a black, tri-cornered hat.

In his official green robes and tall bishop's miter, Bishop Ferata shot a furtive glance at Amadeo before fidgeting and turning away. He faced red-robed Cardinal Gonzaga, also topped by a miter. Two minor priests in white cassocks flanked them. Behind stood two halberd-bearing Church guards in ceremonial black calze, shining brass chest armor, and plumed helmets.

Ferata whispered something in the cardinal's ear, to which the man frowned, waved a dismissing hand, and flashed an instant smile to the crowd. Apparently unhappy with the exchange, the bishop crossed his arms, uncrossed them, and glanced again in Amadeo's direction. What was the matter with him?

"What a day for you, signore," said Callisto to Amadeo. "What a day for the city."

"Sì, let's hope it inspires the men."

"This afternoon and tonight, there will be feasting, drinking, and dancing in the streets. And the guilds, not the Rossis, are paying for it."

Amadeo rubbed the back of his neck. "Such a day may also do me some good."

"You work too hard, Amadeo. Sometimes, it's good to relax and savor life."

"I suppose you're right." He smiled. "You are always right, my friend."

The gonfaloniere stepped to the front and motioned to three musicians standing to the side. Two of them raised horns to their lips while the third beat a drum. With this salvo, the crowd quieted and turned their faces to the dais.

"Friends and fellow citizens of Colpena," said Rossi, "what a glorious day for us, for today we lay the cornerstone of our city's great duomo."

The crowd cheered and clapped until the musicians' cacophonous blaring and beating called for silence. Rossi then introduced the men on the platform. When he said Amadeo's name, the cheering began again, causing the musicians again to play.

"We will now place the cornerstone." Rossi nodded to Amadeo.

Amadeo approached the corner of the southeastern chancel, where waited the underlying foundation rock that the masons had perfectly leveled and smoothed. Taking a trowel, he scooped some of the previously prepared mortar onto the surface. He positioned the selected stone, scooped excess off its sides, and tapped it on all corners with the trowel handle. Smiling, he stood.

The crowd cheered. Again, the trumpets and drum quieted them.

As Amadeo returned to the dais, Bishop Ferata seemed to grow increasingly restless. To the creaking and groaning of boards, Cardinal Gonzaga crossed to the platform's front.

The cardinal scanned the crowd and spoke. But he appeared so winded no one could hear him.

"Louder," shouted Ferata from behind.

Gonzaga drew a deep breath and began again. "It's time to officially name and dedicate the duomo."

But even Amadeo, being closer to the cardinal than most, could hardly hear him.

"Lord have mercy. Christ have mercy. Lord have mercy. Let our words here today be recorded in Heaven. In the name of Pope Paul II and the Holy See, I dedicate this duomo to the Blessed Virgin, and I name it the—"

"Stop!" Amadeo stepped forward. "No!"

Gonzaga's words trailed to a stop. As fast as his bulk would allow, he spun to the capomaestro. Gonzaga's face was set, his jaw muscles hard, his eyes fixed. "Outrage," was all his lips could whisper.

"You've broken the contract." Amadeo spoke quietly so only those around him could hear. "And I can no longer work on this project." He whirled and walked across the boards, his heart thumping, his face breaking out in sweat. Jumping onto the cleared ground behind the site, his feet led him toward the Via del Porto. But his eyes beheld the street before him as in a dream, as if wrapped in fog, and he walked woodenly as in a trance.

How could they do this? As the Church's representative, Ferata had signed papers before a notary agreeing to the name and dedication. Was it all a ruse to get him to start the work, hoping he'd go along when they changed the name in public? Well, he wouldn't—*couldn't*—go along.

Tears welled up in his eyes. The greatest project of the age, the biggest duomo in all history, and they marred it with subterfuge.

"Wait, my friend!" Callisto ran up beside him. "Come back."

"Why?" By the time Amadeo's glance met Callisto's, his tears had dried on skin hot with anger.

"Fabiano has called a halt to the proceedings. The crowd is in tumult. He asks for everyone on the building committee to join him at once for a conference."

"To convince me to accept what I cannot?"

"Perhaps not. Let's discuss it."

Amadeo glanced back toward the platform. The committee members were, indeed, heading toward a small shop on Via Santa Croce. From the crowd came murmurs, gestures, excited voices. "All right," he breathed. "Let's see what they have to say."

As they started back together, Callisto shook his head. "This is bad, signore, very bad. Somehow, we must get you out of this."

"Get me out of what? The cardinal broke the contract, not me."

Callisto grabbed his hand and spun him to a stop. "Listen, my friend, and take heed. If you are not careful, Gonzaga will brand you a heretic. He did it to others in Barcelona before he came here. Then, instead of watching you build the duomo, we will watch you burn at the stake."

To keep the curious away, the Church soldiers stood guard a few feet from the small leather shop they'd chosen for the meeting. Amadeo, accompanied by Callisto, swept by them and entered.

Gonzaga's heavy-lidded eyes narrowed at Amadeo. One of the priests scraped a bench free of pouches, belts, and bags and dragged it over for the cardinal to use as a seat. Rossi and Borroni winced as the boards buckled and groaned, but the bench held.

Fabiano cleared his throat. He bowed first to Gonzaga, Ferata, then to the others. "This is unprecedented, my lords. I don't know what to do."

"What we should do"—Gonzaga was still huffing after the walk—"is proceed with honoring the Virgin by naming the duomo for her and blessing it in her honor."

"That is not what the contract states." Amadeo's words passed his teeth slowly, deliberately. "Bishop Ferata agreed in writing to what we would name the church and to whom it would be dedicated. It appears you now wish to break our agreement."

Fabiano closed his eyes, pressed hands to his temples, and faced Amadeo. "I agree this is not what was written, my friend. But can you not—"

"No! I will work only for what I agreed upon. It is to Jesus, not Mary, that I will dedicate my life's work." He folded his hands across his chest.

The cardinal and bishop gasped.

Surprise widened Borroni's eyes.

Callisto leaned toward Amadeo, touched his arm, and whispered, "Be careful, my friend."

And Rossi looked from Amadeo to the priests, his expression bemused as if he was enjoying the proceedings.

Fabiano opened both hands and shot questioning looks from Callisto to Rossi to Borroni. "Somebody, please tell me—what are we to do?"

"A contract was signed, was it not?" Rossi questioned Fabiano. "Should we not live up to it?"

Gonzaga's eyes blazed. "It is the Church, not some heretical builder, that names such a building. And it is the Church that decides to whom it will be blessed. That contract should never have been signed."

"Sì, your lordship." Fabiano glanced at Rossi, his gaze furtive and skittish as if he were trying to decide which way to move in this battle of men more powerful than he. "I admit, it was unusual in its provisions. But it was signed, was it not? Signed by Bishop Ferata's own hand."

"I warn you, Puccini"—the cardinal's hands tightened into fists, clicking his rings together—"proceed with this, and you will regret it."

"Can I suggest a compromise?" Callisto raised a finger. "One that might satisfy both parties."

Fabric rustled as everyone shifted toward him.

"Please, signore, we are open to suggestions." Fabiano waved both hands. "Anything."

Callisto touched Amadeo's arm again. "What if we name the cathedral according to the contract"—he then offered a supplicating palm to the cardinal who was frowning—"but dedicate it today to the Virgin? In that way, nothing already said in public will be refuted or undone. And both parties will get something."

Gonzaga sucked in air. His mouth opened as if about to speak, but then it closed. He stared at the ground.

Amadeo was about to reject the suggestion when Callisto whispered in his ear. "Take the offer, my lord. A hundred years from now, the name will be remembered, not the dedication. We must get you out of this situation. Your very life is at stake."

Amadeo swallowed. "I agree to the suggestion."

Fabiano sighed out relief and braved a glance to the cardinal. "What does the Church say, your grace? This sounds like a reasonable compromise. May I remind everyone the crowd is waiting? We cannot postpone the ceremony to another day. I fear what the people will do. This is unprecedented."

Ferata stooped and whispered in the cardinal's ear. But the churchman winced, bent forward, and seemed to stare off into a corner. The bench groaned dangerously.

Silence filled the lodge, broken only by men hawking street food outside and a rising murmur from the crowd.

"All right." Gonzaga glared at Amadeo. "You have put the Church in an impossible position, master builder. Today, I will agree to dedicating the duomo to the Blessed Virgin, but name it as written in your abomination of a contract."

Fabiano clapped. Borroni nodded. Rossi smiled and winked at Amadeo.

"If we are all in agreement, let us resume the ceremony at once." Rossi started toward the door. "Before the crowd riots."

As fast as Cardinal Gonzaga could waddle, they hurried back to the dais. When they mounted the platform, the crowd cheered.

But Gonzaga sat dour-faced, panting and brooding in the chair made especially for him. He held a conversation with Ferata, whose eyes opened wide, but who nodded.

Then Bishop Ferata, not Gonzaga, stepped to the fore. He swung his silver censer back and forth, sending clouds of incense over the cornerstone.

"In the name of the Father, Son, and Holy Ghost," said Ferata, "under the powers given me by the Holy Catholic Church, I bless this duomo in the name of the blessed Holy Virgin."

The crowd cheered. Drums beat. And horns blared for silence.

Ferata grabbed the handle of his aspergillum, dipped it in a basin of holy water one of the priests carried, and sprinkled it thrice toward the cornerstone. "And in the name of the Father, Son, and Holy Ghost, I christen this duomo the Cattedrale del Figlio sul Mare."

Again, the crowd erupted. But now, even the drums and horns couldn't silence the people.

Ferata tried to finish, but the crowd wouldn't stop. Looking with exasperation to the cardinal, he opened his hands in a symbol of surrender.

As the committee filed off the platform, Gonzaga stilled before Amadeo, his massive shadow swallowing him in darkness. "I will remember this day, capomaestro. And I promise you—someday, you will regret what you did here."

CHAPTER 21

~ SIDE TRIPS ~

AUGUST 1470

The calmer seas of spring had brought with them barges from Carrara loaded with rough-hewn bardiglio marble. Men had unloaded the blocks onto carts that clattered a mile and a half from the Via del Porta up the hill to the Piazza del Duomo and the waiting stonecutters.

By mid-June, one masonry crew had finished laying the foundations for both transepts. The second crew had already raised six feet of the chancel's walls.

Each wall was composed of an outer and inner face of bardiglio marble. The blocks were each a foot thick. The seams between blocks were so tight, the mortar so thin, Amadeo marveled at the precision with which they fitted together. Between the marble facing lay a two-foot-wide layer of mortar and rubble.

Vittorio took Amadeo's drawings and created templates from which to cut the stones. He gave these to Umberto Sabbatini, the speaker, along with instructions for the correct angles, height, depth, and a hundred other details. Sabbatini then communicated this to the stonecutters, masons, and carpenters.

Once a month or so, Speaker Sabbatini even traveled to Carrara with new templates to explain the details to the men stationed there.

But at the end of June, Fabiano complained that the building fund was empty, and he could no longer pay the workers. Amadeo complained to Rossi, who said he'd have the funds in a week or two.

At the end of the following week, a breathless Fabiano arrived at Amadeo's house bearing a large sack. "Late last night, a mysterious ship pulled into the eastern port. They unloaded it in the dark. I don't know where it came from, but I suspect it was Rossi's." He plopped the heavy bag onto the table. Hundreds of gold ducats spilled out. "This morning, the gonfaloniere gave me this. It should cover all arrears."

Amadeo and Fabiano stared at the pile of sparkling gold coins.

Fabiano shrugged. "Just be happy he now has the funds."

Amadeo decided not to ask questions.

Soon, the noise of axes hewing stone, hammers striking chisels, apprentices singing, and trowels slapping mortar onto blocks filled the work site.

Day by day, week by week, the walls rose.

EARLY ON A HOT AUGUST morning, Amadeo stepped as usual from his rooms onto the Strada delle Campane. But waiting outside his door was Simona Mancini holding a wicker basket, standing next to a two-wheeled carriage with Skender holding the reins and Amadeo's own black gelding in harness. The gelding pawed the cobbles, eager to go—but to where?

"Buongiorno," sang Simona's lilting voice. "I'm here to rescue you from yourself. Today, we're going on a special jaunt."

Taken aback, he said, "But I have men to oversee, plans to—"

"When, Signore Amadeo, was the last time you left your work and just relaxed? Hey?"

"I–I—"

"Just as I thought." She grabbed his hand and led him toward the carriage.

"She told me you were going for a ride." Skender opened both hands in apology. "And that I must prepare the carriage."

Amadeo jammed hands on hips and laughed. "I am defeated. Sì, signorina, I'll join you on your adventure, today. But I must be back before noon."

"Tsk, tsk. You must let the day happen. Let's not worry about coming back before we've even started."

"All right, but where are we going?"

"To a special place. All of today will be a surprise."

"Then lead on."

After Amadeo helped her climb into the carriage, he took the reins. And, leaving Skender behind, they rode down the Strada del Nord, through the wall gate, and then, at Simona's direction, turned left onto a trail leading north. No sooner had they left the city than she directed them onto the first of two sand spits connecting the mainland with the nearby island.

"We're going to Monte Argentario?"

"Sì, have you been there?"

"Only once. It has no decent rock for building or forests for timber."

"Ah, but you see it only through a capomaestro's eyes. Today we will see it through mine."

Some five miles from the city, she directed them onto a narrow road leading to Porto Ercole, a small walled town. He'd only seen its tower from across the water.

"This town is as old as Colpena," she said. "But we will continue on."

"You are mysterious, Simona. Has anyone ever told you that?"

She cocked her head to the side, winked, and smiled.

They drove a narrow dirt road hugging the coast, past rocky glens and steep ravines lush with vegetation. Where the path forked, she directed them up a steep incline. It ended some fifty yards from the main path.

"Now we hike to the top."

"Hike?"

"Sì. Good for the heart, good for the soul. The view from the summit is wonderful." She grabbed the basket.

Amadeo tied the horse to a bush where it could eat. To the cicadas' incessant buzz, he followed her up a close, narrow track between the pregnant leaves of flowering holm oak, occasional stands of cactus, and explosions of the low-growing macchia, the thick-leafed evergreens so prevalent here.

By the time they reached the top, a climb of some six hundred feet, Amadeo was sweating, breathing hard, and wondering if Simona would consider resting.

A cool wind brushed past, carrying the scent of the salt sea. Below, seagulls soared in circles and cried to one another.

"Here we are." She waved her hands toward the barren rocky summit.

Amadeo faced south toward Colpena, where the city crowded its promontory. Whirling to the island's northern side, he saw a jagged rocky shoreline winding off into the distance. To the west, whitecaps crested over the Tyrrhenian Sea, and the sun sparkled off blue-green waters.

"Now we'll have a picnic." She led him to the one boulder where they could both comfortably sit. But the only position he could find forced his right leg against her left.

She opened her basket. "We have Sicilian cheese, prosciutto, ham, bread, and grapes. And, of course, wine."

He said a short prayer, thanking God for the food, the day, and Simona, then asking him to bless the building of the duomo.

She uncorked the bottle and filled one of two goblets she'd carefully wrapped in cloth. As they clinked their glasses together, she laughed. "To our feast on the mountaintop, no? Did you ever imagine yourself doing this when you got up this morning?"

He smiled. "I did not. And, Simona, I admit—as in every time we meet—you have brightened my day with joy." As he said this, the heat from her leg ran tingling to his head.

She blushed and nodded.

A few dark clouds rolled overhead, washing cool air around them.

They drank and they ate. Afterward, Simona wrapped the lunch's remains and gently folded a towel around the empty glasses and bottle, returning all to the basket. Then she clasped hands in her lap. "What will you do after you finish your grand duomo, signore?"

"What do you mean?"

"Your life—what will you make of it without your work?"

He shrugged. "I will build something else. But building the duomo may take my entire lifetime."

"No, Amadeo, that's not what I meant. When you are old, who will greet you when you come home? What about your children?"

"Children?"

"Sì. Do you not want sons and daughters?"

"I—I am not certain. They would only interfere with my work."

"Ah, but you are missing the greatest part of life, I fear. You dedicate yourself to God, to building your grand cathedral, but should there not be more?"

"What I have . . . it's enough."

She laid a hand on his leg and lifted her face to him. "If ever you change your mind, Amadeo," she whispered, "I'm here for you."

Her words sent another wave of tingling through his loins, to his chest, and his heart beat faster.

As if sensing his discomfiture, she slid off the rock, whirled, and motioned him to follow. "Now we'll go for a swim."

"Swim?"

"Sì. I have brought what we need. You can swim, can't you?"

At his nod, they descended, retracing their steps to the carriage and their waiting horse. She directed him to drive back to the main road and then west for another mile to a spot where the road again forked. This time, they took a lower path leading to an isolated cove and a beach covered with gritty sand. Just before the beach, someone had built a small shrine to some nameless saint, complete with a roof, seats, and wooden statue. But the weather had badly ravaged and rippled the wood.

With nowhere for his horse to escape to, they left him untied to forage the vegetation along the edge. She threw Amadeo a bundle wrapped in leather cord. "You may wear that. Stand on the other side of the carriage and face away from me, as I will face away from you."

Feeling uneasy that she was only a few yards away and doing the same, he stripped and pulled on what was only a breechcloth with a leather cord to tie it up. When she called out that she was ready, they stepped out from behind the carriage and faced each other.

She wore only another breechcloth with an armless cloth shift over her torso. For the first time, he saw her bare legs and arms, slender and shapely. "These make for good swimming." She waved a hand over her outfit. "Either that, or we wear nothing."

"Better this." He smiled.

"Then let's go." She ran over the hard sand, splashing up to her knees in the cold sea.

He was right behind her.

They plunged into water that took his breath away. She swam out to a small spit of smooth sand, crawled up, and splayed herself in the sun's warmth. Crawling up beside her, he noticed how the thin wet cloth clung to her breasts and hips. He lay beside her, his heart thumping. For what seemed an eternity, they lay together in the sun, side-by-side.

This was all premeditated, wasn't it? To get him out here with her, alone, to see her like this?

And now he wondered about his vow of chastity. Was it really in the service of God? Or was it only an excuse to keep from involving himself with someone like her? She was beautiful, and she wanted him. He tried to envision a life with her at his side, and the very thought filled him with joy.

A drop of cold rain splattered on his chest. A chill wind washed his skin, and he opened his eyes. Dark clouds had swept in from the west.

"Uh-oh." She sat up. "Looks like a storm. We'd better get back."

By the time they'd swum back through the cold sea and were running up the beach, frigid, slanting rain drove against his skin, leaving him shivering.

His horse had already found its own cover, shoving its nose under an elm.

They grabbed their clothes from the carriage and ran for the only shelter—the shrine.

Huddling under the roof, they stood side by side, shivering as the downpour continued.

"I–I'm cold," she whispered.

"Me, too."

"H–hold me." Violent tremors shook her. "Please."

Hesitating only a moment, he wrapped his arms around her shoulders and pulled her against him. The naked flesh of their arms touched. She laid her head in the crook of his shoulder, her warmth taking his chill away. Their legs entwined.

For the longest time, he held her like that, their bodies close, her breath warm on his shoulder, her hair falling across his back. He lifted her head, her clear, brown eyes wide. Eyes that smiled into his.

Her lips parted.

He leaned down, and their mouths pressed together in an explosion of tingling warmth. Cupping her head, he kissed her again, longer, deeper, until he pushed away. His breath came fast, and his heart raced. At that moment, his desire to take her was so strong, he pushed her further away and stepped back.

"We can't," he whispered.

Just then, the rain stopped, and the sun came out.

"I think we should go home now," he breathed.

She nodded, but longing filled her glance.

As the carriage trundled over the path, they hardly said a word. His heart was still leaping, his hands unsteady on the reins.

By the time he drove her to her father's small palazzo, only a block from Rossi's own, dusk had fallen. He left the carriage and helped her down. As they stood facing each other in the twilight darkness, he was about to turn away when she reached up, let her fingers glide over his lips. Again, he bent his head down, and their lips pressed tightly together.

They parted. "You need someone, Amadeo," she whispered. "And I need you."

He closed his eyes, nodded. Feeling lightheaded, he climbed back into the carriage.

On the ride home, he tried to control his racing heart, the feeling of euphoria on which he seemed to float.

WELL AFTER MIDNIGHT, HE WOKE sweating, his heart pounding. All he'd thought about since leaving Simona was the time he'd spent with her and the possibility of taking her for a wife. But now he feared that, in the space of a single day, he'd lost focus. Not once since leaving the mountaintop had he thought about the duomo or what he needed to do tomorrow.

He leaped out of bed, his night shift rustling around him.

The day had been well calculated, hadn't it? She was desirable, willing, and available. But to become involved with her now would suck the energy from him, divert his attention from this great work to which he was pledged.

Walking into the garden in his bare feet, he stopped in the moonlight.

How easy it would be to succumb to what she wanted. And how treacherous for what he was made to do. His knees buckled and hit the flagstones.

"Save me, O God," he whispered, "for a life dedicated only to you. I am an unworthy creature, filled with lust—or is it love?—for a woman. She's a good woman, I know, and she fires in me a deep desire to care for her and keep her close. But I know you also have a plan for me to build this great duomo for your glory. O Lord, in your Son's name, please help me focus on the work and nothing else."

When the cold of the stone began creeping up his thighs, he stood.

In the kitchen behind him, he heard movement and whirled.

Tears running down his cheeks, Skender watched from the shadows.

CHAPTER 22

~ A NIGHT OF MISFORTUNE ~

JUNE 1472

With the late-afternoon sun behind him, Amadeo Puccini stood in the Piazza del Duomo holding his dividers and gazing east. It was the first of June, and the chancel walls were already thirty-five feet high with the transept walls not far behind. Spiral stairs built into each corner allowed the workers access to scaffolding suspended from wooden supports sticking out of holes in the walls.

The sound of the work had its own composition, one he lived and breathed, that brought music to his soul. On the ground, the companion stonecutters' axes and chisels chopped on the bardiglio, precisely hewing each gray-blue block. Laborers grunted as they lifted heavy blocks from the cart and dropped them, thudding, onto pallets. Then a creaking treadwheel crane raised the pallets to the scaffolding's highest level where apprentices carried the blocks, one at a time, over squeaking planks to the masons.

On the floor below, the mortar mixers poured lime, sand, and water into a wooden trough, where their shovels slurped and turned the mix. The mixers' apprentices then hauled buckets of mortar to the pallets. Other apprentices removed buckets at the top. Their feet tromped across the scaffolding until they passed the buckets to the masonry companions. Then came the slap of mortar on stone, the scrape of trowels as the masons removed the excess, followed by the clink of trowel handles tapping the blocks into place.

It all fit together in a kind of workers' symphony.

The music was marred only by frequent complaints from Damiano De Luca that the blocks he was receiving from Vittorio's crew were not big enough. Or not square enough. Or coming too fast. Or not fast enough. But every time Amadeo investigated, he found no truth to De Luca's complaints.

"They come from Carrara," Amadeo had explained for the hundredth time, "and the stonecutters square them. It is the way it will be. And if you need more men to keep up, perhaps we should find you more apprentices?"

"No, signore," said De Luca. "I will manage."

The sounds of the duomo's construction had become part of Colpena's daily life. And since the arrival of the mysterious foreign ships, Rossi's funds had kept the work going. Amadeo dared not ask from whence came the money. He'd heard rumors, but what the gonfaloniere did was his business. Between him and his God.

"The work proceeds, does it not, architect?"

Amadeo whirled. Dario Rossi himself had crossed the square to stand behind him. "It does, and we are making good progress. Better than expected."

Rossi nodded. "You are dedicated to your work, capomaestro. I'll give you that."

"It is all for God's glory, gonfaloniere." Today, Rossi wore only a simple brown tunic and sandals without calze. Was he going to frolic among the commoners?

Tilting his head to one side, Rossi raised an eyebrow. "Have you ever in your life done one thing—*anything*—that didn't drip with virtue?"

"I have, signore. Far too many times. And I've always regretted it."

"Glad to hear it. No one should be perfect, should they? Or what would the world look like? Call me Dario."

"All right, then, Dario. You may call me Amadeo."

"Do you have a woman in your life, Amadeo? One whom you bed?"

Taken aback, Amadeo shook his head. Never would he mention Simona in Rossi's presence. And, of course, he hadn't *bedded* her, as Rossi put it.

"Ah, too bad. You are missing one of life's greatest pleasures—to have a woman beneath your loins."

"Should such a thing not be between a man and his wife?"

"So the priests would say. But then what do they know of life's pleasures, hey?"

"I take my pleasure in my work. That's all I need."

"But what if there is more, Amadeo? Have you not pined for a lusty, naked beauty writhing beneath you?"

His face warming, he turned away. A young apprentice scurried out along the scaffolding, as lithe and agile as a monkey. Why was Rossi baiting him? Did he want to proselytize his sins? How Amadeo lived was his business.

"Ah, well, if I've offended you, I apologize."

"Apology accepted, gonfaloniere."

Behind him, Rossi's footsteps echoed across the piazza.

Leaving the architect and the noise of construction, Dario strode across the square to Via Santa Croce, then descended the steps into the Temestre Inferiore. Surely, the man had a weakness. No one could be so virtuous, so seemingly pious and dedicated to God. Someday, he would find that crack, however small, and pierce his righteous armor.

This afternoon, he was looking forward to seeing Letizia, but now, as they did too often lately, his thoughts shifted to Colpena's alliance with Florence. Only last year, small deposits of alum had been found near Volterra. A few leading Florentine citizens had owned part of the mine. But after the estimate of deposits increased, Volterra voided the contract and took over the mine. In response, Lorenzo hired a condottiere, Montefeltro of Urbino, whose mercenary army laid siege to Volterra. The town surrendered, and that should have ended the matter.

But then Montefeltro's troops ran wild. They pillaged, murdered, and raped. For Volterra, it was a great humiliation. For Lorenzo, it was a total disaster.

Though Florence now had access to this small source of alum, it wasn't enough to satisfy its wool trade. To keep his larger ally happy, Dario had given the Florentine merchants a five percent discount on all purchases of alum bought through Rossi Shipping and Transport.

For many months after Dario's concession, he'd heard nothing from his friend. Had the gesture been too little? Then last week, two dozen crates of oranges, four barrels of wine, and two wheels of Sicilian cheese arrived at Palazzo Rossi from Florence—Lorenzo's belated expression of appreciation.

Still, Dario worried that circumstances could change, and someday Florence could turn against its smaller ally. The privateer he and Aldo had hired was still preying on Pisan shipping.

If Lorenzo ever found out that Colpena was behind it . . .

Colpena needed a condottiere of its own, a seasoned military mind with an army at his disposal that the city could rely upon at a moment's notice. Dario must start looking for such a man. All Colpena had to defend itself was its city guard, a mere one hundred and fifty strong.

At number twenty-eight Strada degli Innocenti, he climbed the staircase to Savina Udinesi's apartment and knocked. Savina opened the door, took one look at him, and stepped back.

He entered.

Fiery dark eyes bored into his. "You want to see her again, don't you? Not me, only her, this niece you have created?"

"Please, Savina, let's not do this."

"You send me money, and I thank you for that. But let us marry, you and me, so I, too, can live in your fine palazzo. You have no sons. Let me give you sons. We can be happy together as man and wife, I think."

"We could never be happy together. You, of all people, should know that. Just let me see her today. Then I'll be gone."

"She's not here. And no. I'll not let you see her. Not until you agree to marry me."

Dario stared at her, the heat rising to his face. "It will never happen, woman. You know it won't. You were a whore. I could never marry a whore."

Her nostrils flaring, she planted hands on hips. "Your daughter knows what I was, Dario. I told her. She thinks that after *Roberto* died"—she spat the word as if to emphasize its untruth—"I went out into the streets until you took pity on me and sent me money."

"Why did you tell her that? You should never have told her that."

"She needed to know. And I'm sick of all these lies."

"Where is she?"

Pushing past him, she entered the hallway. "He bears a child out of wedlock," she shouted. "And he calls her his niece."

"Don't do that! Stop it."

"She's not here, and I'll shout to whoever I want." She cupped her hands around her mouth and shouted. "Out of wedlock. With me—"

He whirled her back into the apartment. Then, as if it moved of its own accord, his palm slapped her across the face. She rocked back, her eyes wide and fearful. A hand gingerly touched her cheek. Her fingers rubbed the raw skin. She gawked at him, then slunk back. "Don't ever . . . ever come here again."

"I'm sorry, Savina. I—"

Both of her hands hit his chest, pushing him into the hallway.

The door slammed in his face. His heart beating fast, he stood unmoving, staring stupidly at the wood. Down the hallway, doors opened. Heads poked out.

He turned aside, hurried to the stairway, and descended the steps two at a time.

Out in the street, he wandered the lanes, not caring where he went. She couldn't keep Letizia from him. That wasn't going to happen. And if she wasn't more discreet, he'd have to do something about her. He hated the thought, but—what else could he do?

He stopped at a taverna, one unfamiliar to him, where the men there didn't know who he was without his noble dress. He ordered wine. Before he realized it, he'd drunk almost the entire bottle. Then he ordered another. Soon, it, too, was gone. He ordered a third.

Men young and old came and went from a room upstairs. When he asked the proprietor what went on, the man leered. "Rosaria and Sandra. You interested?"

"Pretty? Young?"

"Sì."

After he'd taken his turn upstairs with Rosaria and he'd pulled his pants back on, she asked for payment. But when he reached for his purse, he discovered it missing. He faced the prostitute. "Someone's robbed me. Someone downstairs in the taverna."

"You don't have the money?"

"No. But don't you understand? I've been robbed. I'll have a servant bring you what I owe later."

She opened the door and called down the hall. "Donato! Come here."

Dario wouldn't wait for whoever Donato was. He pushed past her into the hallway where a heavyset man was barreling toward him.

"He can't pay," she called from behind.

"How many times do I tell you?" came Donato's gruff voice. "Ask for the money first." The man's bulk nearly blocked the hallway. He focused on Dario, his wayward customer, and grinned.

Dario tried to push past him, but Donato slammed his back against the wall. "If you don't have the coin, my friend, you pay with your flesh."

A fist slammed into Dario's jaw. His head smashed into the wall. Stunned, he tasted blood.

"You don't know who I am, friend," said Dario. "Stop, or you'll regret this."

"A big man, are you? Well, all I need to know is you can't pay." Another fist punched him in the stomach. Dario gasped and slumped to the floor.

"I . . . am . . . the gonfaloniere."

Donato guffawed. "And I'm the pope. Here's my blessing." A shoe kicked him in the chest, and he could no longer breathe.

Then the blows landed so fast and hard he couldn't think. All he knew was pain. Kicks on his legs, his arms. A foot punched air from his chest. Putting his arms over his eyes and bringing his knees to his ribs, he tried to present a smaller target and protect his head.

The next kick slammed his head against the wall so hard that stars popped before his eyes.

Then the world went black.

Shivering violently, he woke—crumpled in a ball, his face and hair matted with dried blood, every inch of his chest, arms, and legs throbbing. The stench of rotten food filled his nostrils, and he gagged.

Something furry touched his hand, and he jerked it away. Leaden lids pried themselves open.

A rat's tiny eyes stared into his. Its nose wriggled.

He pushed up with both hands. The rat scampered into a pile of refuse. Needles of pain shot through stiff, unresponsive forearms. Was he in a quintana?

He tried to stand, but so great was the explosion of pain shooting through his head, he thought for a moment he would pass out.

Two steps. Then three. He began to walk. Stepping out into the lane, he discovered it was morning. Had he spent the entire night in the alley?

Unable to walk straight, he staggered from side to side through the streets. When passersby saw him, they averted their faces in disgust.

"A drunk," they said, spitting the words, or, "a beggar."

Somehow, he climbed the steps to the old wall and found the Via delle Rose. He turned left onto the Via delle Trombe and stumbled onto the Piazza del Duomo—straight into a well-dressed crowd.

Was it Sunday morning already? Was this the morning service?

Dressed in his green robes, a tall bishop's miter topping his head, Ferata faced the crowd of worshipers. He swung his silver censer, throwing clouds of incense toward the people.

Dario staggered forward three paces and stopped.

Most of the Signoria and the Thirty were here—Enzio Borroni; Marcello Esposito; Callisto Mancini and his daughter, Simona; Rocco Marino; Fabiano Trentino; and, of course, in the front row, Amadeo Puccini. Their faces wrinkled with disgust.

No one recognized him. Not one person. Did he look that bad?

He brought a hand to his face, felt the clotted blood, the hair stuck to his cheeks. His face was a broken mass of pain.

Finally noticing something was wrong, the bishop lowered his censer and whirled toward him.

Then came the first words of recognition, not from Ferata, not from any of those on the Signoria or the Thirty, but from Amadeo Puccini. "Rossi?" questioned the capomaestro. "Is that you?"

"Sì."

Puccini rushed from his seat, followed by Grazziano who appeared out of nowhere. Then four men he recognized as sycophants. A small crowd began helping him across the square toward his palazzo.

He shook off their hands. "I can walk."

"Someone, get a physician," said Puccini, and one man ran to do his bidding.

Dario stopped, weaved on his feet, and stared at the capomaestro.

Puccini, the righteous.

Puccini, the upstanding citizen, the one who could do no wrong and never slept with a woman, who only spent his time building monuments to God.

Puccini, the one who worshiped while Dario wallowed drunk in the lower quarter with the whores, was robbed and beaten, and spent his nights in the quintanas with the rats.

And in that moment, Dario knew that someday, somehow, he must put a crack in that armor, split it apart, and bring low the man inside.

Days later, when Dario had somewhat recovered, with only a black-and-blue face remaining, he dressed in his finest official clothing. He conscripted four men from the city guard, and they marched into the lower quarter.

Leading the way, he slammed open the doors to the taverna where Donato had beaten him. The soldiers pushed in after him.

Upon seeing Dario, the innkeeper gripped the top of his head, and his mouth opened. "Please, gonfaloniere"—he spluttered, nearly in tears—"we didn't know it was you. I'm sorry. Very, very sorry."

"Where's Donato?" he said. "And Rosaria?"

"I don't know, signore. Please, they left as soon as they heard it was you. They've disappeared."

"Put him in the city dungeon for a week." Dario paused, considering. "Make that two."

The guards seized him and searched the building. But the two he sought had fled.

Back in his palazzo, he sent Jacopo to search for them.

Two weeks later, the battered and bloated bodies of a man and a woman floated up on the spit of sand leading to Monte Argentario.

CHAPTER 23

~ THE RECEPTION ~

AUGUST 1472

Dario stood on his top-floor balcony, looking down the western slope to the setting August sun. Music and conversation drifted up from below. A cool sea breeze brushed his face. Tonight was his grand reception and party to celebrate a fourth successful year for Rossi Shipping and Transport. In the last four years, the company's fleet had expanded from four to fifteen ships, seven of which were dedicated to shipping only alum. Three more vessels he'd purchased from Spain were due to arrive any day.

Aldo's secret plan to prey on Pisan shipping had worked beyond all expectations. Within months of the privateer's operation, customers realized that every vessel departing Pisa and flying a Pisan flag was at risk. He and Aldo added another privateer and put Piombino on the list of afflicted ports. The insurance rates for companies operating out of those two cities soared. Business for the Pisan and Piombini merchant ships plummeted. But when those same customers contracted with Colpenese or Genoese vessels, their goods sailed safely to their destinations. Aldo's ploy helped Genoa as much as it did Colpena, and no one knew which city, if either, was behind it all.

The music floating up to the balcony from the grand hall's open windows increased in tempo. He needed to go down soon.

All of the Signoria, some of the Council of Thirty, and everyone of importance in Colpena would be here tonight. Some were even now exiting their carriages in the piazza below. Also arriving were dignitaries, important customers, and business prospects from Pisa, Lucca, Sienna, Rome, Genoa, and Florence. He hoped Lorenzo himself would be here tonight. He'd put up as many of the most important guests in his palazzo as it had rooms for.

After his debacle in the lower quarter earlier this summer, rumors about the episode had spread. So tonight, to placate the contadini, besides the formal party for shipping customers and foreign dignitaries, he was throwing a grand celebration for the commoners in the streets, with music, dancing, free food, and wine. Aldo had objected, and it had cost a fortune. But the goodwill it would produce was beyond price. Anything to help the people forgive and forget.

To rule a republic, one had to keep the people on one's side.

He took a last sip of wine and left the balcony.

As Dario stepped into his grand ballroom on the palazzo's first floor, Callisto Mancini approached, dressed in his usual understated brown robe and white calze. "My lord, I do believe you have invited half of Italy here tonight." The musicians had taken a break, and the noise of hundreds of conversations now echoed in the vast hall.

With a smile, Dario nodded. "Perhaps it will improve even more the fortunes of our shipping company."

A short man with a heavy black beard, Teofilo Gallo from Genoa, strode over and raised a glass. "Whatever Pisa's and Piombino's sins have been, it has brought both our cities great fortune." He looked around the room conspiratorially and whispered, "Let's hope it continues."

Dario hoisted his glass and beamed. "May Genoa's trade do as well as ours."

Shawm and curtal woodwind instruments, accompanied by a flute, a lute, and a male singer, began again. Dario had encouraged the vocalist to sing as many bawdy songs as he knew. All in French, of course.

"Where did you get these musicians, my lord?" asked Teofilo. "They play a most pleasing concert."

"They're from Flanders. They were on their way to Rome when I convinced them to stay for this affair."

"My compliments." Teofilo bowed, then left to visit with the Florentine delegation.

"If only he knew what they were singing." Callisto smiled, then strolled to another corner.

Bishop Rinaldi Ferata soon took Callisto's place, bringing his glass to Dario. "I would like a word, signore."

"Sì, whatever is on your mind?"

"Are those women in the far hall who I think they are?"

Dario glanced toward the courtesans he'd hired. Dressed as modestly as their professional wardrobes would allow, they sat quietly—discreetly, he thought—out of the way. "They are there, bishop, for the single men. To make their nights more enjoyable during their stay. They will not attend tonight's dinner."

"Is it not unseemly to bring them into the company of decent men and women?"

"Would you like one to accompany you tonight, bishop?"

Grimacing, Ferata shook his head. "Now I would speak with you on another matter. It has been three months since your, ah . . . accident . . . during the Sunday morning service. Considering all that has taken place"—he shuffled his feet—"to put it bluntly, you have not been to confession, signore."

Dario stiffened. The last thing he needed was for the Church to know more about his private affairs. "I feel it best that I bring my sins only to God. The last pope pardoned me, did he not? For past, present, and future transgressions? So why should I burden you with what has already been forgiven?"

"I see." The bishop narrowed his eyes. "Well, then, I will not trouble you about it again."

As the bishop melted into the crowd, Dario scrunched his face in disgust. How little backbone some men had! But the bishop's pliable nature suited Dario.

Aldo had been glancing in his direction, and after the bishop departed, his cousin approached. "This morning, the Pisan ambassador was at the southeastern dock asking questions."

Dario raised an eyebrow. "He won't learn anything there. Has he gone to the western jetty?"

"Not yet."

"Good. Tell Jacopo to shadow him. If the ambassador does try to talk with anyone where it matters, have Jacopo and one of his men show their presence. Perhaps that will discourage loose tongues?"

"I wish he hadn't come. I don't like this."

"Sì, but if I hadn't invited him, it would look suspicious."

By the time Aldo nodded and moved away, Lorenzo stood filling his glass by the table. Dario crossed the room to Colpena's greatest ally. "Ah, my friend, I'm so glad you could come."

"I just arrived. I wouldn't miss your grand celebration for all the incense in Arabia."

"Perhaps you and I and Aldo can slip away for some fun tomorrow night, hey?"

"Good. I'd like that." Lorenzo glanced around the room and lowered his voice. "This business with Pisan shipping is becoming increasingly troublesome. Have you heard anything about who's behind it?"

Swallowing, Dario shook his head.

"I would give a thousand florins to know who it was. I suspect the Genoese."

"It's possible."

Then Lorenzo spied the Roman ambassador, excused himself, and left.

After Lorenzo departed, Dario breathed easier. Had this piracy business gone too far? Perhaps they should end it?

But now the guests had all arrived. Appetizers of cheese, bruschetta, ham, and prosciutto had been laid out on tables for all to partake. And, of course, plenty of wine. It was time for Dario's grand announcement.

Stepping to the top of the stairs where everyone could see him, he motioned for the musicians to stop playing. He clapped his hands. When he had everyone's attention, he spoke as loudly as he could. "I welcome this august group to my palazzo. I hope you will all have an enjoyable visit to Colpena. But before we eat, I would like to dedicate this evening and the days that follow to the Rossi Shipping and Transport Company and to the Rossi Bank, with which you all have some interest. We are grateful for a successful four years. With God's help—and yours—we pray for many more. Let us now eat. I'm told we are having spaghetti with hare sauce, followed by wild boar."

The men and women clapped quietly, then strolled toward the ballroom.

Dario hung back as his guests passed. Each had an assigned seat, placed according to their status and relationship with those seated beside them—the Pisans and Lucchese were separated, of course.

As he was about to follow, Tonio Rizzo, the Pisan ambassador, blocked his way. This was one conversation Dario had been hoping to avoid.

Rizzo, a fat, bearded man, wearing one red and one green calze, planted a hand on his billowing red blouse. "Before dinner, signore, I would like a word."

"Sì, Signore Rizzo. You are welcome to my time."

"The city of Pisa does not understand what is happening to its shipping."

"And neither do I, ambassador. It is most unfortunate."

Rizzo frowned. "I'm here to tell you, signore, that we suspect a plot to increase the trade of Genoa or Colpena. We can prove nothing at the moment, but somehow I will get to the source of this mystery. I've already warned Signore Gallo, and now I warn you"—he breathed in deeply—"whichever city is behind this, Pisa will not stand idly by. We will send an army and a fleet to punish the perpetrator."

Dario flashed him a look of shock. But the threat of military action gave it all the sincerity he needed. "Let's not make unwarranted threats, ambassador. I assure you, I know nothing of this business. Let there be peace between our cities. We, as well as Genoa, are the innocent beneficiaries of these privateers. For the safety of the high seas, we would like these ruffians caught as much as you. Think, signore. At any moment, these pirates could also turn against us. Meanwhile, we stand ready to assist your merchants to get their goods to market."

"Just the same, I am investigating."

As the ambassador left, Dario wiped a hand across his brow—he was perspiring.

The evening was warm and getting warmer.

CHAPTER 24

~ TROUBLING NEWS ~

JULY 1475

Amadeo climbed the spiral stairs and stepped out onto the high scaffold. Up here, a light breeze carried away the midsummer heat. Had it already been six long years since they'd begun? In that time, the exterior walls of the chancel and both transepts had risen almost eighty feet, a much faster pace than normal. Another two or three years and the first section of the walls would be complete.

Walking out to where the masons worked, he was well pleased with their progress. The crunch of trowels sinking into mortar, the slap of mortar on stone, the tapping of stones—all of it warmed his heart.

Creaking boards announced the approach of an apprentice carrying two buckets of mortar, suspended from a yoke on his shoulders. Flattening himself against the wall, Amadeo let the youth pass.

Below, the foundations for the arcade columns were dug, filled with mortar and stone, and cured. Carrara would soon start sending the larger blocks of bardiglio for the column bases. These would require more skill from the stonecutters to dress. They'd construct the massive four-part piers from precise sections. When those columns began to rise and when a final coat of cement covered the surface, each would appear as if four separate columns had joined, back-to-back, to form one massive pillar.

He looked west, past the ropes and stakes marking the place where the nave walls would soon rise. The eventual entrance seemed an impossible distance from where he stood.

"Master architect," came De Luca's familiar voice from far down the planking. "I would have a word."

"Sì. I will join you." Amadeo walked along the platform, stepping around the masons as they troweled mortar onto blocks or worked on the gap between the inner and outer faces. He stopped before De Luca.

"The blocks are not square, signore. See this gap."

Amadeo knelt. On one corner of two different blocks, he did indeed see a gap, perhaps an eighth of an inch. "But look everywhere else." He swept his hand over the rest of the wall. "Once in a while, the blocks will chip. We do not want to throw them out. They are good, solid blocks. The mortar will fill in the cracks. The gaps are small and acceptable."

De Luca shook his head, put hands on hips, and frowned. "Were I lodge master, I would not accept such shoddy work."

"Please, Damiano. These gaps are so minor as to be trivial."

His face grew red. "This is not . . . trivial."

"Please?" Amadeo opened his hands. "For my sake? For peace?"

De Luca turned away, muttering.

A bell sounded below, and the men who weren't working from a bucket wet with mortar began heading down. Women had brought wine, bread from Bonifacio's bakery, and a hot meal of beef stew in buckets.

After Amadeo descended the spiral stairs to the bottom, Vittorio took him aside.

"The man is impossible." Vittorio waved up at the scaffold and De Luca. "I cannot work with him."

"But you must. As I must. He is skilled. He is all we have."

"Still, he is impossible."

THAT EVENING, AS HE SOMETIMES did, Amadeo took Skender to a ristorante on the Piazzeta dei Fiori where the chef served thick Sienese pici and roasted guinea fowl. They found a table on the street, and after receiving glasses of wine, they ordered. Then they watched the swallows scream and chase each other through the narrow lane.

No longer just a houseboy, Skender was now a handsome young man of nineteen. Amadeo had tried to teach him how to paint, but the lad had no interest. He was content just to serve.

"I thank you, capomaestro, for this meal at a ristorante."

"For all your hard work, Skender, you deserve a special night out once in a while, a night when you don't have to cook."

"You are too kind. None of the other nobles or merchants treat their servants as good as you."

"I'm not a noble. And you are more a friend than a servant."

Skender smiled.

As they waited in the cool of the evening, a group of six young men and women approached from down the street. They sang loudly, shoved each other, laughed, and careened from side to side.

"They're drunk," whispered Skender.

One couple, a bit less rowdy than the others, clung to each other as they walked. Suddenly, they stopped, kissed passionately, and separated.

As their faces parted, Amadeo recognized blonde-haired Simona Mancini, smiling as though she were the happiest woman in Italy.

The young man beside her was black-haired, muscled, and dressed like a fop, with a ballooning shirt, pointed shoes, plumed hat two feet tall, and different colored calze on each leg. When the man's arm slipped around her back, squeezed her rear, and yanked her close, heat flushed Amadeo's face.

As they neared his table and she glimpsed Skender and him, Simona's smile vanished. She whipped her face toward the opposite wall, walked faster, and pulled her surprised companion to greater speed. Then she grabbed the young man's hand, and they broke into a run until they'd turned the corner.

Amadeo stared at where she'd gone, his jaw muscles tightening.

"You're upset?" queried Skender.

"Sì."

"You love her."

Shaken, Amadeo jerked a startled face to his servant.

"It's obvious, signore. You should marry her. Then she'd give up such as him."

"I have no room in my life for a wife."

With a steady, widening gaze, Skender sat up straighter. "I don't understand. You know you love her. But then you say you can't be with her. This will lead only to unhappiness, capomaestro. For both of you. Even I know that."

"What am I to do?" Amadeo shrugged, a helpless feeling pressing down on his shoulders and arms. "I do love her. But the duomo—that is my life. That is the task God has given me. What room is there for anything else?"

"I don't know, signore." Skender shifted to face the empty street. "I simply don't know."

A week later, Callisto Mancini pulled Amadeo away from the noisy building site to a quiet bench at the Piazza del Duomo's shady end.

"I bear troubling news about my daughter. And about Cardinal Emilio Gonzaga."

Amadeo's breath caught in his throat. "What news?"

"I'll start with Gonzaga. He's become something of a zealot, vowing to purge all heresy from the Church. If you remember, he came from Spain, where they carried that kind of thing to an extreme. It was only because Gonzaga's brother married into Roman nobility that the last pope brought him here from Barcelona."

"What zealotry do you speak of?"

"It concerns an incident with a young priest." Rubbing his jaw, Callisto frowned. "The man had been speaking indiscreetly, questioning the selling of indulgences and accusing certain churchmen of simony. Word of it came to Cardinal Gonzaga's ears."

"Who hasn't questioned the selling of bishoprics and even cardinalates for money? And where in the Bible does it say one can pay to be absolved of one's sins?"

Callisto's mouth opened, then closed, and his hand dropped to his side. "You must never speak such sentiments. Never, my lord. This young priest did just that. Gonzaga then held a trial before a triumvirate of like-minded cardinals. They convicted the priest of heresy. Then they threw him in the dungeon and tortured him until he confessed and recanted."

His own mouth now open, Amadeo stared at Callisto.

Amadeo had copied the Bible in his own hand from the Latin Vulgate, and he'd read it. Few men, even priests, had ever done so. After his studies, one thing was clear to him—the men of the Church had created traditions far beyond, and perhaps even in opposition to, what Christ and the Apostles had taught. When he recognized the corruption the Church had brought the faith, he was deeply troubled—

Troubled by the indulgences, the selling of the forgiveness Jesus freely gave by his death on the cross.

Troubled by simony, the selling of church offices to unholy men who sought only personal profit and power.

And even more troubled by the worship of Jesus's earthly mother as if she were the equal of the Son of God himself.

And now, when one clear-eyed, honest dissenter dared speak the truth about those troubling practices, the Church used a hammer to squash him.

"I see you are distressed, my lord." Callisto laid a hand on his shoulder. "So take heed. Beware, you do not express similar sentiments to the cardinal—or even to the bishop."

"I thank you for the warning. But what is this news about Simona?"

Callisto shook his head, his eyes losing focus, his gaze wandering across the yard. "She's become involved with a group of young men and women of whom I do not approve. They carouse. They keep her out half the night. She comes home drunk, smelling raw, with teeth marks on her neck and arms. I know the young man with whom she has become infatuated. He is of low character, living off his parents' money, with few prospects."

"Sì, I saw her once in the streets with him."

With a somber nod, Callisto let out his breath. "So I'm sending her away." But his words seemed to carry regret.

"Away?" Amadeo's heart skipped. "Where to?"

"Her aunt lives in Avignon. I'll send the girl to live in France, far from this boy who mauls her and gets her drunk and does whatever else he does with her in the wee of the night."

"To France?"

"Sì. I thought you should know."

"Thank you, signore. Perhaps it's for the best."

After Callisto left, Amadeo sat and stared across the piazza, feeling not at all that her leaving Italy was for the best.

But why did he feel this way? Had he not given her up? They weren't together, wouldn't be married, and he had no claim on her.

So why was he reeling, feeling lightheaded, as if he'd just learned his father had died? As if someone had just slammed a board across his forehead?

He'd given her up. Yet he couldn't get her out of his head. Or out of his heart.

CHAPTER 25

~ A DIFFERENCE OF OPINION ~

DECEMBER 1475

After Amadeo received the letter from the courier, he hurried back inside to warm himself before a crackling kitchen brazier. A winter storm off the coast had brought cold whistling winds and driving rain. Holding the missive before the fire, he recognized the slant of the writing, the thin curlicues that could only belong to Simona. This was the first letter from her since she'd left. With trembling fingers, he broke the seal, unfolded the parchment, and read.

My dearest Amadeo,

How lonely it is for me here in Avignon. My aunt means well, but she is a woman most severe and far too strict. I am rarely allowed to leave the house without an escort. She must think me a terribly loose woman for the way she keeps me locked up.

I admit that, when I was with Roberto in Colpena, he and his friends were wild and unruly. We did things I had never done before, things I should never have done. And that night last summer when I was with him and we kissed beside your table, I saw how appalled you were to see me that way. You had every right.

But I've changed. From now on, I'm going to be a different woman.

I've vowed never to see Roberto again. Since leaving Italy, I even learned that, at the same time he was seeing me, he was seeing two other women. Can you believe it? What a cad!

Aunt Riccarda sometimes invites young people to supper. I am quickly learning French, and last week, she allowed two young men into the house. One of them, with dashing black hair and eyebrows and deep black eyes, brought his lute, and he sang for us. As we ate a dinner of fowl with onions and truffles in butter, I couldn't keep my eyes off him. For dessert, we had pastries. The French wines are not as good as ours, but I think I drank my share that night. That dinner was my aunt's attempt to lessen my boredom and my loneliness here. But she hovered over us every minute, and though I enjoyed it immensely, she hasn't invited the two young men back.

How I wish I were back in Colpena, and that you and I could start over again. How I wish you would change your mind and make room in your life for more than your duomo.

Please write.

Your dearest friend,
Simona Mancini
26 Rue des Rois, Avignon

The smell of perfume arose from the parchment still in his hands. His heart beat faster. She still wanted to be with him, wanted a future together. Even after all his refusals and his insistence on a life dedicated to his work.

He laid the letter on the table and shook his head. Even her letter distracted his mind from today's task.

Shoving the work of the last few months into a leather tube, he pulled on his heavy cioppa, scarf, and beret and stepped out into the biting wind. Bending against the cold onslaught, he turned left and made his way to the work site and the lodge.

He pushed open the door and entered the main room. Flaming logs crackled in a brazier beside Vittorio and Umberto Sabbatini. Iron tools hung from wall hooks. Nails filled two boxes. Rope lay coiled between them. In the room beyond, where the workers slept, men slapped cards on a table and called out their bets. In winter, wages were dropped by half for those without work. Card games became a main occupation.

"I've brought my plans for the interior," said Amadeo.

Vittorio nodded and began clearing the large worktable.

Amadeo slid his sketches from the tube and unrolled them. "Each section is themed." His heart already beating faster, he smoothed the top parchment. "The north and south nave walls, with six bays each, will tell the tale of the Old Testament. This is for the north nave wall."

Inscribed on the paper were the dimensions of six giant frescoes, each thirty feet wide, that would cover the walls. Beside each were descriptions of the contents—the major players and the action. He'd also sketched preliminary designs for each. Between the paintings would stand statues of each fresco's main characters. Above the frescoes was the clerestory with its row of stained-glass windows.

"This is wonderful." Vittorio traced a finger over the descriptions. "From creation to Cain and Abel, to the Tower of Babel, the Flood, the destruction of Sodom and Gomorrah, and Joseph in Egypt"—he raised his head—"you have it all."

Beaming at Vittorio's praise, Amadeo pushed the top parchment aside to reveal his plan for the south wall.

"The Egyptian plagues and the exodus"—Vittorio again moved his finger—"the Israelites wandering in the desert, the conquest of Israel by Joshua, the time of the judges, King David's reign, and the exile to Babylon." Vittorio caught the speaker's gaze. "Sabbatini, this is a condensed history of the Old Testament."

"What a joy it will be to execute these plans, capomaestro," said Sabbatini.

Amadeo pulled another parchment from the pile. "Look at this one for the north transept, what I'm calling the Chapel of the Savior."

"The adoration of the magi and Jesus's birth," said Vittorio. "The miracle of walking on water, the wrath of Jesus against the Temple moneychangers. But what's this on the north wall? The Last Judgment?"

"It's one giant fresco depicting the day of judgment, with sinners destined to Hell on one side and the elect rising to Heaven on the other. In the center, Christ sits on his throne."

"And on the north transept's eastern side, you've got the road to Calvary, the crucifixion, and the ascension."

"What about the south transept?" asked Sabbatini.

"That will be the Chapel of Martyrs. Smaller scenes depicting the death of St. John the Baptist, Saints Stephen, Peter, Paul, and Thomas among others. Eight saints in all. Beside each fresco will be a statue of the individual. There will also be bays with places to light candles for the saints."

"And the chancel?" asked Vittorio.

"Dedicated entirely to Christ. In the center behind the altar and the dais will be a giant statue of Christ rising to Heaven. It will be the crowning work of art in the entire cathedral. For that, I must find the greatest sculptor in all Italy."

"And he is . . . ?"

"I haven't found him yet."

"And for the walls behind it?"

"The choir and dais stand in front. The fresco filling the east wall will start above those so the congregation can see it." He took a deep breath and traced a finger over the parchment. "There, I, myself, will paint three large frescoes depicting the birth, the life, and the crucifixion of Christ. Above that will be a large stained-glass window, a wheel showing more scenes from Christ's life."

"How wonderful!" Vittorio slapped Amadeo on the back. "The central focus is clearly on Christ. All of it tells his story. This is brilliant, capomaestro!"

Amadeo nodded furiously. Vittorio understood. His heart swelled, and his breath came faster. To have someone else feel what he felt when he created this was, well, exhilarating.

Vittorio moved the parchments around, examining each. Beneath were smaller sketches, where Amadeo had further detailed some scenes. "What about the floor tiles? Will there be a design or more illustrations?"

Amadeo dug deeper to retrieve more parchments from the pile. "In the nave's center, the floor will contain twelve large pictures echoing the nearest theme."

"And this plan was approved by the bishop?" Again, Vittorio looked up.

"He gave me initial directions, telling me what he wanted on each wall. But only in vague terms."

"What about spaces for tombs?"

"Tombs? This is a place of worship, not a mausoleum. But I am allowing for crypts marked by plaques under the floors of both transepts."

Vittorio grimaced. "I don't see much of the Virgin here."

Amadeo frowned. "She's in the Adoration of the Magi and the crucifixion frescoes. Isn't that enough?"

"I doubt that will satisfy the cardinal."

"She's a minor figure in the biblical story. I will not make this cathedral into another monument to the Virgin."

Vittorio's eyes widened. "The bishop and cardinal may have other ideas about that."

"I'm sure they'll understand that the purpose of all the frescoes, statues, floor tiles, and stained-glass stories is to educate and inspire the populace. What other purpose should they serve?"

"Amadeo, your heart is true. You are without guile. I just hope the Church has as much respect for the common man and the biblical stories as you do."

Two days later on a Tuesday, Amadeo showed his plans to Bishop Rinaldi Ferata in his palazzo. The bishop looked them over, nodded, and said he'd like to keep the parchments for a few days to show the cardinal when he arrived. Amadeo left the documents.

On the following Saturday, a young messenger handed Amadeo a summons to appear at the bishop's palazzo for a consultation. Dressed in his official clothing, he walked the short distance to the palace on the Via San Christo beside the building site. On the way, he braced himself for what he might expect. He tried to remember Callisto's warning about not arguing with the cardinal on theological matters.

"Welcome, signore." Bishop Ferata opened the door. Ferata had spared no expense in fixing up the palazzo of a deceased Signoria member. Paintings from another era depicted Christ, the Virgin, and the saints with halos—but all appeared flat and two-dimensional, without any of the perspective the new artists were adding.

Behind him stood Cardinal Gonzaga's great bulk. Shifting from foot to foot, the cardinal reached out a hand and tried on a smile. "Let us begin again, master architect, and forget the unpleasantness of a few years ago."

Having not seen the cardinal since the duomo's awful dedication day, Amadeo took the offered hand and nodded.

Ferata led them to a corner of his reception room where high-backed chairs waited in a semicircle and faced a central table holding Amadeo's documents. On the near wall, logs in the fireplace blazed and crackled.

Gonzaga plopped down with a creak and a groaning of wood. Ferata and Amadeo sat opposite.

"Would you like a glass of wine?" The cardinal was nurturing his own goblet. At Amadeo's headshake, the cardinal waved him to a seat. "Then let's get down to business. We are mostly pleased with the plans for the interior you've laid out. But we do have suggestions for some minor changes."

Amadeo swallowed. "And what might those be?"

Ferata knelt to the first drawing. "We like the plan for the nave, but we want the two western corners reserved for crypts."

"Crypts?" Heat tingled up Amadeo's neck, rising in his face.

"One for the cardinal." Ferata waved to Gonzaga, sweating and huffing in his chair.

"And one for myself."

"Go on."

"And in the Chapel of the Savior and in the Chapel of Martyrs, we must reserve the corners for four more crypts. One for the Rossi family, the Borroni family, the Marinos, and the Mancinis."

Amadeo breathed slowly in and out. "You would have me eliminate six frescoes and replace them with tombs?"

"Sì. And on the three frescoes above the altar and choir, we would have you dedicate the panels to the life of the Virgin—her marriage, Annunciation, and her station by the cross. You already have a statue of Christ rising to Heaven in the chancel."

Amadeo gripped the sides of his chair, pinching his knuckles against polished wood while trying to still a rising anger. "Is that all?"

"No. On the floor, we would like your eight tiled pictures to show the history of Colpena, with all the important families, including the Rossis and their role in its founding."

He closed his eyes, trying to remember the warning about the priest Gonzaga had branded a heretic and tortured. What they were asking was to remove the heart of what he'd put together, replacing biblical history with monuments that glorified men, substituting scenes of Christ for those with Mary as though she were equal with God, and making all the floor tiles exalt Colpena's ruling families.

"My lord?" Ferata spoke too loudly. "Will you accept our changes?"

"The bays in the Chapel of the Savior—must they contain crypts? Could we not shorten the two crypts in the nave and put all of them together there?"

Ferata looked to Gonzaga, who shook his head.

"The frescoes of the Virgin that you want me to put above the choir—could we not move them to the Chapel of Martyrs and reduce the number of saints honored?"

Again, Gonzaga shook his head.

His face hot, his heart beating fast, Amadeo tightened his grip on the sides of his chair. "Then . . . I guess . . . this is what must be."

Gonzaga nodded. "Sì, architect. This is what must be."

Numb, he rose and gathered up his parchments. He put one foot before the other. But his legs had become pillars of wood, refusing to bend. And his feet seemed to move of their own accord. He tottered toward the door.

All his plans, all his work to create a consistent, coherent theme, one that taught as well as decorated, were being corrupted by men who seemed to care more about honoring their earthly masters and themselves than about enlightening the masses flooding through the duomo's doors. Worse, their hearts were not with Christ. Instead, they'd turned Jesus's earthly mother into an idol. He thought of the priest they'd labeled a heretic and shuddered.

Admittedly, the work on the chancel frescoes was years away. But he wondered—when the time came, could he actually paint what they asked?

CHAPTER 26

~ A DISASTROUS AFFAIR ~

APRIL 1476

While the swallows dove in circles and shrieked above, Amadeo stopped before the entryway leading up to Palazzo Rossi. He sat on the steps, facing the piazza. Why had Rossi invited him to this dinner? How upset would the padrone be if he just returned home and never showed up?

For the hundredth time, he pulled out Simona's last letter, written four months ago. Every week, she'd written regularly. But after this last letter, all correspondence from her had ceased.

Dear Amadeo,

My aunt has taken a boat up the Rhône to Lyon and left me here alone. She gave strict instructions I was not to leave the house, but I am going insane with nothing to do. She's not here, and I will not be locked up like some prisoner.

I have pleaded with Father to let me come home, but he will not relent.

Bored nearly to death, I sent a note yesterday to Lamar, the young man who often comes with the lute to play at dinner. He is coming tonight, and we will have a private supper, just him and me. The servants have agreed to serve us. When I threatened to leave if they didn't, what else could they do?

In his reply, Lamar said he knows a park by the Rhône, where people sit and just watch the sunset. And wouldn't I like to go there after we ate? I would so like to stroll through the gardens down by the river at dusk.

Why do I write these things to you, Amadeo? Maybe because you are the only person I can really talk to, even though you are far away.

163

But how I long to be back in Colpena and Italy. Can you talk with Father and bend his ear to let me come home again? Though it seems I've been away for years, I still miss you. I miss what we could have had together. Please write.

Simona Mancini

How many times had he read that letter? How often had he worried about that dinner and the lack of correspondence since? His replies elicited no response. Once, he even thought to take the letter to Callisto and show it to him. But no. Revealing Simona's private thoughts would be a violation of her trust.

Folding it, he stuck it in his pocket and tilted his head toward the diving, screaming swallows.

He stood and climbed the steps.

Grazziano answered his knock. "The gonfaloniere says I am to welcome you, master builder, and lead you to the grand affair he has planned upstairs."

"Grand affair?"

"Sì, tonight you are the object of one of my master's frequent, bizarre whims, and I apologize in advance for his behavior."

As Amadeo crossed under the foyer's seventy-foot cavern and began climbing the steps to the second floor, he shot a glance to this servant who seemed to take such liberties with his position. "Apologize?"

"Who can understand the heart of man, signore? It roams from whimsy to folly to debauchery and then to awe and reverence for God. But there's been precious little of the latter around here lately."

Amadeo stifled a smile. How did Dario Rossi ever put up with this man?

When he entered the ballroom, he stopped at the entrance.

"Welcome, my friend." Rossi rushed forward, a glass of wine in one hand. "Welcome to a night of pleasure, entertainment, and abandoning work for the delights of the flesh."

A bit wary of Rossi's admission, Amadeo nonetheless nodded.

The ballroom, like the entryway, was massive. At the near end clustered two dozen of Dario Rossi's young male friends from Colpena's wealthier families. Dressed in foppish ballooning blouses with slashed sleeves, short checkered and striped jackets, and wearing different colored calze on each leg, the men laughed and flirted with a group of young women. He recognized one as the son of Marcello Esposito on the Signoria. Others came from the families of rich merchants, or their fathers sat on the Council of Thirty.

The women's clothing was bright, scant, short above the knees, and open to reveal the tops of their breasts. They all wore high heels.

One black-haired girl of about nineteen, with fetching black eyes and a gold headband across her forehead, approached. "You must be Amadeo?" She'd painted her eyelids so they flashed blue when she blinked.

He bowed. "I am."

"I am Rosina, your companion for the evening."

His companion? He knew what she was. Despite that, he was attracted to her.

She put her arm in his, shot him a coy smile, and pulled him toward the others. Reluctantly, he let himself be led. A smiling Rossi followed.

As they approached the group, Amadeo realized all the women were prostitutes. What was his host planning?

When Rossi clapped his hands, everyone turned in his direction. "May I introduce to you Signore Amadeo Puccini, the capomaestro of the duomo."

The young men rushed forward and spouted their admiration for the work he was doing. He tried to be gracious but felt uncomfortable with their flattery, however sincere.

"And now," said Rossi after a time, "let us eat."

Their host ushered them across the vast space to long tables at the far end.

Rosina guided him through the crowd to a seat beside Rossi. Next to Rossi sat a black-haired, tan-skinned woman from Istanbul, apparently Rossi's escort for the night. No doubt she'd once been a slave.

He decided to be courteous, stay for the meal, engage in enough conversation to please his host, but then leave. What they were planning later, he wanted no part of.

While a musician strummed a lute, three others blew on a shawm, a curtal, and a flute. A fifth kept time with a drum. Despite his vow to be only marginally involved with this affair, he found the music pleasing and joyful.

"Capomaestro"—soft and pleasing as any musical instrument, Rosina's voice caressed his ear—"how high are the walls now?"

"Over a hundred ten feet for the transepts and the chancel area."

"And," said Rossi from the opposite side, "I see the walls are rising on the nave."

"Sì. The foundations were finished this spring. The nave walls are already seven feet high."

"Good progress, to be sure," said Rossi. "But try some of this wine. It's from Siena."

Amadeo took the goblet a servant had just filled and sipped. "A good vintage."

A dozen servants entered, bearing trays from which they dished ravioli smothered with olive oil, herbs, and cheese. As he ate, Rosina kept sliding her hand along Amadeo's leg. Each time she did so, he pushed it away.

Perhaps it was the quality of the wine or his discomfort from the woman's hand, but when the second course came, he was on his third glass. The servants brought wild boar, with onions fried in sugar and leeks cooked in butter. Admittedly, the food was delicious. By the time he'd finished, he'd downed a fourth glass.

"Now," said Rossi after the meal, "let us dance."

Despite his objections, Rosina pulled him from his chair, and they followed the others to the floor.

As the music's tempo increased, Amadeo found himself stepping with the courtesan to a sprightly tune. They danced down the line, moving in and out, exchanging partners, until he ended up back with her. As he danced with the row of laughing, smiling couples, the blood seemed to rush to his head.

After more wine, dancing, and intervals for conversation, servants began snuffing out the candles in the holders lining the walls. He turned to Rosina. "What are they doing?"

"Getting ready for the best part."

"What's that?"

"Where you and I and all these young men and women find each other in the dark."

"I don't understand."

Some of the couples were beginning to kiss.

"You know"—she eased a little closer—"we get together."

Heat rushed to Amadeo's face. He was beginning to understand. Yet he raised a questioning glance to her.

"We couple, silly."

For one brief moment, he pictured himself and this beautiful inviting woman making love. Sì, he wanted her. What would it feel like? Would he enjoy it?

His heart beat faster.

But no.

He shook his head, took two steps back. Like water boiling down the sides of a kettle, his anger at Rossi's trap exploded.

He whirled and stalked toward the door, some one hundred feet distant. Before he'd made it halfway, Rossi raced to his side.

"Don't leave, capomaestro. Why don't you take her? Be with her tonight?"

Amadeo kept walking. "I'll have no part of this. Why did you invite me here tonight? To bring me down to your level? Or just to embarrass me?"

"Not at all. I brought you here so you could have a bit of fun."

"Fun?" He waved toward the ballroom, becoming darker as more candles were extinguished. Some men and women were undressing and moving to cots the servants were setting up. "I'll have no part of this . . . this abomination." He strode toward the door.

Rossi's hand grabbed his arm and spun him around. "Stay, architect. Drop this façade of being the good and righteous man. Be like everyone else."

"Façade?" Amadeo stared into his host's eyes. "This is who I am, gonfaloniere. You've tempted me tonight, I admit. But I hope never to become like you or your hedonistic friends. What you're doing here tonight—it does not glorify God."

"And you, Puccini, what you do only glorifies yourself." Rossi released Amadeo's arm.

Clenching fists at his side, Amadeo stepped away. "If you remember, one reason I became master builder was to pay for your sins. But even funding twelve duomos would not be enough to absolve you of the transgressions you continue to accumulate. You are unworthy to be the padrone of even one duomo's construction."

Rossi's jaw muscles tensed. "You cannot enjoy life, architect. You are incapable."

The words stung, and Amadeo felt tears welling up in his eyes. He pointed at the men and women kissing and pawing at each other in the dimming light. "This . . . this . . . it's unrestrained debauchery. It's unworthy of anyone calling himself the gonfaloniere of a city or the padrone of a grand duomo. I'll have nothing to do with it." He strode toward the door.

"Someday, architect"—Rossi's voice, now filled with anger, followed—"I'll find the crack in your armor. You're a fraud, and I'll prove it."

Amadeo pushed open the door and entered the hall at a near run, his heart beating fast, tears obscuring his vision. Why had he let Rossi goad him to tears?

"I apologize again for my master," came Grazziano's soft words from a chair in the hall. "He's incorrigible, I fear."

Without turning his head, Amadeo nodded. He raced down the long flight of steps, across the foyer, and into the cool night air.

There he slowed and breathed deeply, glad to be away from the sordid business above. Why had he let that man twist a knife into his soul? And why, for even one moment, had he felt a desire to join them? Never again would he attend something like that in Palazzo Rossi.

His initial instincts had been right. Rossi was like a stain of dark oil on white satin. Everyone around him became so soiled, no amount of washing could cleanse them.

CHAPTER 27

~ FOR THE LEAST OF THESE ~

Later that night, still upset over his moment of weakness and Rossi's attempt to corrupt him, Amadeo couldn't sleep. Long after Skender was breathing softly on his kitchen cot, Amadeo knelt at the foot of his bed and clicked open the lock to the trunk he'd bought years ago. Made of solid oak, it now held his most valuable papers and personal items.

He pulled out the book he himself had copied and smelled the leather binding. Too many months had passed since he'd opened this book.

Carrying it to the garden table, he lit the four candles on their high stands. As the wicks sputtered, his hand reached out to the glass of wine he'd nursed earlier. He sipped and set it back.

Years ago, on a six-month visit to Florence, he'd spent time at the San Francesco monastery in Fiesole, where the Franciscan monks had welcomed him as one of their own. When they discovered he could read and write Latin, they let him make his own copy of their New Testament and Psalms.

Tonight, the heavy vellum pages crackled at the seams as he turned them to the book of Matthew and the words Jesus spoke about the coming judgment.

When all the nations are gathered before the Lord, He will separate the people as a shepherd separates the sheep from the goats. At his right hand, he will gather the sheep. And on his left will be the goats.

Then the King will say to the sheep on his right, «Come, for you are blessed by my Father. Your inheritance in the Kingdom awaits. It was prepared for you from before the creation of the world.

«For when I was hungry, you fed me. When I was thirsty, you slaked my thirst. When I was a stranger, you invited me into your home. When I was naked, you clothed me. When I was sick, you cared for me. And when I was in prison, you visited me».

But the ones declared as righteous replied, «Lord, we never saw you hungry or thirsty and gave you something to eat or drink. When were you ever a stranger, and we showed you hospitality? When were you ever naked, and we gave you clothing? And when were you ever sick or in prison, and we visited you»?

And the King replied, «Verily, I say to you, when you did it to one of the least of these, my brothers and sisters, you were doing it to me»!

From several streets over, the bell in the town hall campanile struck. Once, twice, thrice . . . nine times, ten times.

Amadeo set the book down. When he'd been in that tower prison just below that bell, he would have appreciated someone visiting him. The days were long, the nights longer, and the company confined to the guard.

By building the duomo, he was spending his life in service to God. But didn't these words in Matthew call him to something more? Certainly, he'd helped many workers who came to him in need. But was that enough?

He shut the book, blew out the candles, and returned the tome to its chest. Tomorrow, he would make amends.

It had taken half the morning for him and Skender to gather what he required. Behind him, his servant's arms bore what Amadeo couldn't.

When they arrived at the town hall and the first set of steps, they met Dario Rossi coming down. The most powerful man in Colpena stopped. His annoyed glance scanned them. "Where are you taking those goods, Puccini?"

"To the prisoners in the tower."

Apparently stunned by the response, Rossi only stared at him with opened mouth.

Amadeo continued to the main assembly room where they climbed the long set of spiral stairs. Their feet echoed up inside the narrow winding column. After a long ascent, they reached the cells.

Luigi, the heavyset guard who never seemed to shave, rose from his chair before a locked door. "What are you doing here?" He glanced at the bundles in their arms as if they bore muskets.

"Bringing blankets, food, and wine to the prisoners."

"B–but . . . why?"

"Because our Lord Jesus commanded it, my friend."

Taken aback, the guard frowned. "Only relatives allowed. And I must watch whatever goes on in there."

"Do you know who I am, Luigi?"

The guard scratched the stubble on his chin. Suddenly, recognition widened his eyes. "The capomaestro?"

"Sì, and once you watched over me when I was here. Now, I'm bringing a bit of cheer to whoever you've got locked up today. Please, let us pass."

The guard nodded, rattled his keys, and opened the door. They entered the first level with locked doors leading to three cramped cells. "We only got three in the tower right now."

When the guard opened the first cell, Amadeo set a flagon of wine, a loaf of bread, and a blanket on the floor.

"This here, Roberto," said the guard, "is the capomaestro of the duomo."

The surprised inmate, bearded and unwashed, gushed his thanks and fell on the bread.

As Luigi led them away, he said, "Roberto owes Rocco Marino two hundred florins and hasn't paid him. He's a bachelor. The next one's Arturo Costa, a spice merchant. He owes Marcello Esposito another tidy sum. Also a gambler, I think."

When they entered and the guard announced the identity of the prisoner's benefactor, Amadeo distributed his gifts. Costa took them, looked up, and said, "Thank you, capomaestro. This is unexpected. And welcome. But I fear for my wife. While I'm locked up in here, I cannot work. She may have nothing to eat. Can you do something for her?"

Amadeo took down her address and promised to try.

The last prisoner was accused of slandering Enzio Borroni. His time would be up in a month. But he waved the gifts away. "I thank you, but my family provides me with everything I need. You should take these to the poor wretches in the civil dungeon. They're in far, far worse shape than any of us up here."

As they left his cell, Amadeo thanked the man for his honesty and the information.

"I've never seen the like." The guard shook his head. "Bringing gifts to prisoners. No one ever does anything for me. And if I don't pay twenty florins to a certain signore by next Friday, I may end up here as well."

"Are you, too, a gambler?" asked Amadeo.

"No. A loan to replace the clothing me and my wife wore out. We couldn't afford to buy more."

They entered Arturo Costa's cell once more, and Amadeo gave him the third loaf and blanket. As the guard opened the tower door to let them back down the spiral steps, Amadeo presented the guard with the last flask of wine. He also counted out twenty florins from the purse at his belt.

Tears wetting his eyes, Luigi grinned and bowed. "You don't know what this means to me, signore. Nobody ever does anything like this for me."

Before they descended, Amadeo asked, "How many are in the civil dungeon?"

"Fifty or sixty. No one keeps count. But they're a lower class of criminal. In for robbery, adultery, murder, debts, and the like. You'll need a lot more than a handful of goods to take care of that lot. In fairly bad shape, they are."

Amadeo nodded. He'd have to save money for several months to distribute gifts to that many souls.

They descended the steps, left the town hall, and walked to the building site.

"It was a good thing you did today, my lord." Skender was beaming.

"When I have more funds, we'll go to the civil dungeon where the need is greater. But tomorrow, we must go to Florence."

"Why?"

"It's time to find sculptors."

Nodding, Skender left to buy produce for dinner, and Amadeo to oversee the day's construction.

When Amadeo fell into his bed that night, he felt as if he'd washed himself clean of the depravity—and his desire to give in to it—from the night before.

CHAPTER 28

~ THE SCULTORI ~

JUNE 1476

As the rains pounded his cape and thunder rolled over the Tuscan hills behind them, Amadeo and Skender hurried the last few yards up to Settignano. They'd spent days traveling the roads through Montalcino, Siena, and yesterday, to Florence. Now a stream gushed down the cobbles, washing over his sandals, wetting even the calze clinging to his calves.

He stopped to ask directions. A teenage girl peeking through the crack of an opened door pointed him down the lane. At a stone house with a weathered bench in front, he knocked.

A young man of about twenty-six opened the door. His tanned face bore the scars of marble chips, and black hair fell to his shoulders. "Sì?"

"Are you Clemente Pisano?"

"I am."

Amadeo introduced himself and Skender.

"Please, signori"—a smile crinkled the man's eyes—"come in out of the rain."

They entered, shook water from their capes, and passed them to the young wife, who set them on racks before the fire. She brought each a glass of wine, and Amadeo thanked her.

"To what do I owe a visit from the capomaestro of Colpena's duomo?" asked Clemente.

"I understand you are a sculptor of some renown, and that you have your own bottega here in Florence?"

Clemente's eyebrows rose. "To call us a bottega does our group too much credit. I myself have only finished a few pieces for the baptistery of Santa Maria del Fiore. Likewise my companions."

"I saw your statue of St. Stephen yesterday, and you are too modest. How many others work with you?"

"Four sculptors and three fresco painters. But we don't always work together. We do meet occasionally to exchange ideas and techniques. We all hold similar views about art."

"With whom did your group study?"

"Some with Donatello for a few years before he died. The others with Ghirlandaio."

"And what commissions are you working on now?"

Clemente frowned and shot a glance to his wife. "None, signore. We await a fresco project from Rome."

His blonde-haired wife stepped forward. "But six months has passed since the cardinal promised work to your brother. And that was only for him and his painters. Nothing for you scultori. And no word from him since."

Clemente shrugged. "I cannot deny it."

"I need sculptors now, Clemente. Would the scultori in your bottega consider moving to Colpena to work on my duomo? I can promise many years of work with wages at four to six florins a month for each man, depending on skill, plus bonuses for completed projects. I'll need painters later."

His wife rushed to Clemente's side and whispered in his ear. Clemente rubbed his chin. "My wife says I should accept. But may I ask a question?"

"Of course."

"I and my scultori compatriots are exploring a new attitude toward the marble. Signore, we don't want to go back to the old ways. Some of the old sculpture traditions present man as bound to religion in fixed ways. They fail to show humanity as we really are. We want to be free to express our creativity without the constraints of the past."

Amadeo's pursed his lips. "I don't understand what you're saying."

"Recently, my chisel wants to carve man as he was made by God, showing the human body as God designed it—naked and free, with muscles and tendons and chest and loins open to the sky. I want to show man's full range of emotions, not just in stylized worship with halos surrounding heads, but in striving, grieving, honoring, hating, fighting, and in love. At the same time, I want my carvings to show the honored position God gave man in the world. We are all made in the image of God, signore—but you know that, I'm sure. And in all my work, I want that to shine through. And, of course—though some have called it the devil's work—my painter friends are using the new technique of perspective to create the illusion of depth. Sì, I, and all my friends, believe these new attitudes and techniques—far better than the old ways—more accurately and realistically express the human condition, its emotions, joys, fears, and desires."

"Like Donatello's *David*?"

"Sì. But that work was flagrant and immodest."

"I agree." Amadeo examined the floor. This sculptor was thoughtful, honest, and skilled. But would the bishop and cardinal go along with these new ideas? Clemente's *Stephen* was naked above and below the waist, where clung a narrow strip of marble loincloth. But it allowed the sculptor to show muscles, sinews, and a body expression impossible to portray when covered with clothing. Clemente's *Stephen* raised one hand to Heaven even as the other fended off the stones that would soon kill him.

Amadeo gave a decisive nod. "If you come to work on my duomo, I'll give you all the freedom to carve as you please. As long as the work reflects that man was made in the image of God and it's reverent."

Wide smiles broke Clemente's and his wife's faces. "Then I would be glad to accept your offer. I'm sure my scultori friends would, too."

They shook hands, and Amadeo provided initial funds for traveling. The rest of the morning, they talked about the kinds and numbers of statues Amadeo needed. As with the others, upon arrival, Clemente and his crew would join Colpena's Mason's Guild.

After Clemente's wife served lunch, Amadeo and Skender returned to Florence. Tomorrow, they'd leave for Colpena.

He'd achieved what he came for—a bottega of sculptors willing to dedicate themselves to the duomo. And he couldn't wait for them to start.

A WEEK AFTER AMADEO HAD returned to Colpena, he paced beside the western dock and a newly arrived barge bearing the first stones for the columns. As gulls shrieked above, the sun heated the stones beneath his sandals, releasing mist from last night's rain. He fidgeted as this new treadwheel crane Pugliesi had designed fastened its clamps on one of the largest block yet, weighing three tons. Only two weeks ago, using the old crane, they'd lost an entire block into the harbor when the clamps suddenly released.

Employing a series of interlocking gears, Pugliesi had designed a new type of machine able to pivot its boom so loads from the barges could be hoisted, swiveled, and dropped directly onto the cart or piled on the wharf. This was far superior to the former method using ropes to pull the load sideways from the fixed boom, hoping to cross the distance. As usual, two men walking inside the giant treadwheel powered the raising and lowering of the load.

When the first two bases for the piers settled in the cart without mishap, Amadeo exhaled his relief.

Then oxen trundled the load uphill.

At the duomo, Vittorio waited with his stonecutters. As soon as another crane brought the first granite base to the ground, the master stonecutter rushed over with a pair of dividers and a ruler, and he measured.

"Precisely as ordered." He rose from his squat and motioned to the companions. They would now file the surfaces and polish them smooth using an iron plate, a whetstone, and finally a rottenstone.

In five locations within the chancel and transepts, the foundation holes for the columns had already been dug, filled with mortar and stone and the mortar cured. As each arriving column was polished smooth, the masons would mortar them in place. A row of piers would soon rise to support the galleries bordering the transepts and chancel.

Damiano De Luca approached. "When will you start the dome foundations?"

"Next week."

"We are stretched as it is, working everywhere at once."

"I'm sure you'll be able to keep up."

With masons working high on the scaffolding rising with the walls, De Luca was constantly busy. The dome foundations would be massive, much bigger and wider than the arcade columns. The foundations didn't take as much skill, but a few masons were still needed down in the trenches.

A cart topped the Via delle Trombe and rumbled over the cobbles. Amadeo rushed to greet yet another batch of new arrivals. "Clemente! Welcome to the Cattedrale del Figlio sul Mare and enough work to keep you occupied for decades."

"That's music for my ears, capomaestro." Clemente introduced him to the others—Brizio, Ercole, Filipo, and Gaetano. All appeared as young and bright and strong as Clemente and eager to begin.

Amadeo led them toward a house with rooms for rent. "You will be pleased to hear that, two weeks ago, we received a barge full of white statuary marble from Carrara."

Clemente slapped the shoulder of a companion beside him. "White Carrara marble, Filipo. As good as being with a woman, no?" He faced Amadeo. "Filipo once compared cutting on the white marble to being with a woman. We've never let him forget it. But before we carve, master builder, we'll have to study the figures we're to make and ponder our approaches. I like to model in clay before I carve. Others will make drawings from different angles."

"I'm eager for you to start." Amadeo stopped before the house wherein the men would stay. "Though we're years away from needing statuary, by starting now and storing what you create, the moment the niches in the walls, chapels, and lunettes are ready, we'll be able to fill them."

"We are all eager to begin. Good it will be to once again have stone beneath my chisel." Leaning closer, Clemente lowered his voice and whispered. "Don't tell the others, but Filipo is right. Cutting on perfect, white Carrara marble is almost like being with a woman."

Amadeo grinned.

CHAPTER 29

~ MURDER IN FLORENCE ~

APRIL 1478

Dario followed his host through the doors of the Palazzo Medici, then turned right onto Florence's Via Larga. From the campanile in the Piazza Duomo came the deep tolling of bells. Today, the streets were unusually crowded with those who'd stayed after Easter for the coming Feast of the Ascension.

This was Dario's third day in Florence, and he hadn't yet been able to pry Lorenzo free from business to break away for one of their usual nights out. Yesterday, he'd attended a boring luncheon Lorenzo had thrown at his Fiesole villa in honor of the seventeen-year-old Cardinal Raffaele.

Today was Sunday, and he and Lorenzo, dressed in their finest robes, strolled with a small entourage toward the cathedral of Santa Maria Del Fiore for mass. Behind them, Lorenzo's brother, Giuliano, dawdled with Francesco de' Pazzi of the rival Pazzi Bank. Recovering from eye problems, Giuliano had left the house late and lagged far behind.

"I'm glad you came, Dario. It's time we had a long talk."

Dario nodded, wondering what his host had to say.

"I applaud your success with the alum mine and your shipping company, but I believe Colpena needs to return the friendship Florence has lavished on its smaller cousin."

"In what way?"

"Wool is our biggest industry, and all our wool needs to be dyed. But I've heard complaints about the price of alum from your mine." Lorenzo shot him a severe glance. "Should not friends receive better treatment than that given to foreigners like those in Venice? Or London? Or Flanders?"

Dario swallowed. "I suppose you're right."

"Then why not give our wool customers a much bigger discount than a mere five percent?"

"An excellent idea." It wasn't, but he had to pacify Colpena's greatest ally. "As soon as I return, I'll see it's done."

A wide smile crossed Lorenzo's lips, and he extended a hand.

Dario took it, and they shook.

The smile vanished, replaced by a frown. "Have you heard anything about this piracy business, Dario?"

He shook his head.

"It's become a thorn in my side. I'm advising Pisa to build a navy to protect themselves."

"Probably a good idea."

"Sì. I've even advanced them funds to defray the cost. You need always look to the welfare of your city, Dario—and to that of your closest allies—as I look to mine."

"You've been a good friend to Colpena, Lorenzo."

"Thank you. But, Dario, another matter's come to my attention." Lorenzo laid a hand on Dario's shoulder. "Reports from Colpena trouble me." He removed his hand, his frown deepening the crinkles around his eyes. "One must sometimes put aside the pursuit of one's personal pleasure for the welfare of others and one's city. Having a rare bit of fun is one thing—wallowing in such sensual excess that it brings us down to the level of the worst commoner is quite another."

Dario swallowed again. "You are referring to that unfortunate incident of two years ago. It will never happen again."

"I'm glad for that. But now we are at the church."

They'd reached the duomo doors, but Giuliano still lagged far behind.

"Follow me," said Lorenzo.

Inside, they walked the nave's length past numerous seated congregants and took seats reserved in front for Lorenzo's party. Dario gawked again at this great structure. He looked up at the dome directly above him. To his right on the giant frescoed ceiling, the devil held one of Hell's unfortunates, his eyes appearing to leer down, directly at him.

Shuddering, he faced the altar. Beside him sat Lorenzo and a dozen friends and followers of the man everyone called Il Magnifico. As the service began, Dario glanced back once more to find Giuliano had taken a seat about ninety feet behind them.

The bishop spoke the introductory rites. Then the choir sang. In the cavernous space, their voices rang and echoed like the music of Heaven. The bishop intoned the liturgy of the Word, followed by the liturgy of the Eucharist.

The sacristy bell tinkled.

"Accepti panem in sanctas ac venerabiles," droned the priest.

The front two rows stood and approached the rail to receive the bread and the wine.

But as Dario entered the aisle and started toward the front, two priests came up fast behind them. One glanced nervously at Lorenzo, then looked away. What was the matter with him?

Dario, Lorenzo, and the others approached the railing to receive the Eucharist from the bishop and his assistant.

But some kind of commotion in back stayed the bishop's hand.

Out of the corner of his eye, Dario caught motion—a hand lurching up from behind them.

It grabbed Lorenzo's shoulder, and Lorenzo whirled.

Dario also spun.

Behind them, the two priests brandished knives. One man slashed out, a sparkling blade lunging for Lorenzo's throat.

Even as Lorenzo jerked back, the knife edge bit into his neck. Wrapping his cloak about his arm, he drew his sword.

Dario, too, yanked his blade from its sheath.

The two priests—now facing a crowd of Lorenzo's supporters with weapons drawn—bolted for the door.

Lorenzo leaped over the altar rail and ran for the sacristy. Dario and his friends followed. Behind them, Dario heard the striking of metal on metal, blades clashing in battle.

The group rushed into the small room where the priests prepared for the service. Coming in last, the poet Poliziano helped another of Lorenzo's friends, apparently wounded. Blood poured from a gash in the man's stomach.

With a resounding crash, Poliziano dropped the bar over the door.

Dario's heart pounded, and he was breathing fast.

Then Lorenzo saw his wounded friend—Francesco Nori—and his face twisted in shock. "Wh–what happened to him?"

"Bernardo Bandini was behind you, coming after you . . . with a sword." Poliziano tried to catch his breath. "Nori stepped in, tried to stop him. Then Bandini stabbed him. He saved your life."

"Nori"—pain scrunched Lorenzo's face—"how can I ever thank you?" But Nori was too weak to answer.

Dario stared at the wounded man. At the rate he was losing blood, he'd be dead within minutes.

Lorenzo wrenched his gaze from his mortally wounded friend. "Bandini did this? He's a Pazzi sympathizer."

"But you, signore," said Dario, still breathing hard. Blood ran down Lorenzo's jacket. "Are you all right?"

Lorenzo touched a hand to his neck, brought it back red. "It looks bad, but it's just a surface wound."

"Who attacked you?" questioned a young man beside Dario.

"One of the priests. And I know him. A tutor for the Pazzis." Lorenzo's glance swept the room. "Where's Giuliano?"

"He was sitting a few rows back," said Dario. Had the assassins also gone for Lorenzo's brother?

From the chancel beyond, the noise of shouting and feet stomping toward the exits had diminished. All was now silent. At length, one of Lorenzo's friends knocked on the door, saying it was safe to come out.

Dario followed the others into the empty duomo with only a few men now guarding the entrance.

Lorenzo's frantic glance swept across the empty aisles. "Where's Giuliano?"

The friend who'd opened the door winced and nodded toward the pews. "Dead, signore. Murdered. Come away, you must not look."

"Who"—Lorenzo's voice choked—"did it?"

"Bernardo Bandini. But the conspirators have fled. Now we must get you to safety."

Lorenzo staggered behind the small crowd. Twice, as though drunk, he leaned on Dario's shoulder for support. They led him into the square, through the street, and back to Palazzo Medici. Once inside, Lorenzo dragged his feet up the steps to his room.

Dario went with the others to a second-floor balcony where they looked down upon an increasing commotion in the streets. People were running toward the Piazza del Signoria with sickles, knives, pitchforks.

"Is the city under attack?" asked Poliziano.

But to that question, no one had an answer.

After the assassination attempt, the city and countryside roiled in turmoil with rumors that various armies were marching toward Florence to complete the attempted coup. Lorenzo sent a messenger on a fast horse to the Duchess of Milan with a plea to send troops. But any response would take days.

Within hours, dozens of supporters flocked to the Medici palace and armed themselves from Lorenzo's extensive armory. The palazzo became a garrison. Dario wanted desperately to leave for home, but necessity demanded he stand with the others in support of his patron. Everyone feared that the faction behind the attempted coup would, at any moment, invade the city.

Dario stayed until the end of the following week when a semblance of order was restored and events became clear.

While the two priests were attempting to kill Lorenzo inside the cathedral, Francesco de' Pazzi and Bernardo Bandini had made a furious knife attack on Lorenzo's brother, leaving Giuliano dead and bloody several rows back.

After those two had fled, only blocks away another assassination attempt was in progress. The target was Florence's gonfaloniere, Cesare Petrucci, eating lunch with the Signoria.

Archbishop Salviati himself led the second conspirator group. He'd hired mercenaries from Perugia, thinly disguised as priests, for the job. But as the archbishop stood before his intended target, the Perugians were inadvertently locked in a downstairs chamber. Without their support, the archbishop became so nervous he could barely speak. Suspicious of Salviati's erratic behavior, Petrucci called for the guards, and the archbishop fled.

As the Perugians escaped, Petrucci barricaded himself and the Signoria in the tower where he rang the bells calling for the citizens to arm themselves and assemble in the Piazza della Signoria below.

The original conspirators, led by Jacopo de' Pazzi, failed to rouse the crowd gathering in the piazza against Medici rule and fled. When enough Medici supporters arrived, the mob broke into the Palazzo della Signoria, killed the Perugians, and dragged their severed heads through the streets.

Behind the assassination attempt was the Pazzi family, owners of the only other major bank in Florence. The failed coup attempted to address past grievances and gain control of the city. News also filtered into Lorenzo's palazzo that loyal peasants in the countryside—armed with sickles, axes, pitchforks, and knives—had beaten back several armed parties marching to occupy the city.

When it was over, Jacopo de' Pazzi's naked corpse hung from a top window of the Palazzo della Signoria. Beside him, the body of Archbishop Salviati, still wearing his purple robes of office, also dangled from a rope. The two priests who attempted to slay Lorenzo were caught, stripped of their robes, castrated, and also hanged.

Dario trembled at the mob's increasing violence. It seemed to feed upon itself as they turned against the guilty and innocent alike. As if to display trophies of their rage, the crowd scattered its victims' body parts across the Piazza della Signoria.

A week later, a still-shaken Lorenzo stood with Dario on his balcony watching torrential rains pound the streets. "The rain has washed away the grain harvest." Lorenzo's jaw was set, his expression grim. "The people now say God himself is angry at what's happened."

"I can't believe the violence that's been unleashed." Dario shuddered. "I've never seen anything like it."

"They tried to kill me." Lorenzo gripped the iron railing with white knuckles. "And seize the city. But this conspiracy went far beyond the Pazzis. Archbishop Salviati was involved. Pope Sixtus and I have never been on good terms. I fear the pope himself was behind it." Lorenzo's face twisted with pain. "What am I to do, Dario?" He shook his head and closed his eyes. "The most powerful man in Christendom is now my mortal enemy. And I don't want to fight."

"I don't know, Lorenzo." But as he shifted to watch the river pouring through the street, a sinking feeling warned Dario that the worst was yet to come.

When it seemed safe to leave the city, Dario left a grief-stricken Lorenzo and rode for home. Fearing the violence that was spreading like a plague through the countryside, he hired a squad of ten armed men to accompany him.

As his horse clopped along a dusty road, Dario pondered the previous events with a growing sense of unease. When he thought about the depth of the conspiracy and the crowd's uncontrolled rage, he shivered.

Lorenzo had rarely spoken of his enemies. His conspirators were men pretending a deep friendship with him. Men who attended Lorenzo's grand luncheon and sat beside their host. Men who projected warmth, wore smiles, joked, and shook hands with him.

The depth of their treachery was staggering.

Then there was the rage of the populace. Dario always thought the people of Florence had loved the Medicis. Indeed, he often wished Colpena's masses admired him as much as Florence's admired the Medicis. Lorenzo often admonished Dario to keep the people's welfare first. But this attempt on Lorenzo's life had released such passion among the commoners—not only against Lorenzo's rule but against all the upper classes—it stripped away Dario's assumptions about his own security.

With this in mind, he returned to Colpena by way of Arezzo. In the city square, as vendors hawked panini drizzled with olive oil, he sought out a certain tall thin man with a goatee—Baldassare Fanucci, a condottiere renowned for his military adventures.

"Signore," said Dario, "with the turmoil recently unleashed in the countryside, I may soon need an army to defend Colpena."

The condottiere chewed a hunk of cheese and nodded.

"How many men can you raise on short notice to come to Colpena's defense?"

"Two thousand," said Baldassare between bites. "Perhaps three."

"And how much will it cost?"

"Thirty thousand florins to start, my lord. More if the campaign is lengthy."

Dario swallowed but nodded. "I'll send a messenger if I have need."

"I will await your call."

SHORTLY AFTER ARRIVING IN COLPENA, Dario met with Aldo. They agreed to increase the Florentine discount to twenty percent on all alum purchased from the mine.

"Their wool merchants are our biggest customers." Aldo grimaced and shook his head. "This will cut heavily into profits."

"We can afford it. What we can't afford is to lose Lorenzo's goodwill."

"Agreed."

A few weeks later, the bishop made an urgent request to appear before the Signoria, and Dario called the council to meet in chambers.

A pale-faced Bishop Rinaldi Ferata, waving a document in one hand, stalked back and forth before them. Dario had never seen the bishop so upset.

"Signori," said Ferata, "the events in Florence have shaken all Tuscany. And now we learn, without a doubt, that Pope Sixtus IV himself gave his blessing for the attack on Lorenzo and his brother."

Gasps issued from everyone at the table.

The bishop shook the paper in his hand. "When Sixtus learned how the Florentine mob killed and hung his archbishop, still in his robes, from a Palazzo della Signoria window, he flew into an uncontrollable rage. And he issued this abomination of a decree."

Ferata then read the papal bull demanding that Lorenzo de' Medici be turned over to Rome for a long list of crimes, including blasphemy, murder of the archbishop, and sacrilege. The bull excommunicated not only Lorenzo, but also Florence's gonfaloniere, the Florentine Signoria, and every citizen in Tuscany, including all its priests and bishops.

"Signori, this is so outrageous . . ." Barely able to speak, Ferata lifted his glance. "But the next part will be of special interest to you Rossis."

"Why?" demanded Dario, his heart beating faster.

"The Holy See has seized the assets of both the Medici Bank and the Rossi Bank in Rome."

Lightheaded, Dario breathed in slowly. He turned to an open-mouthed Aldo.

"I've been in communication with Cardinal Gonzaga." Ferata stared at the papal document as if he'd pulled it from a chamber pot. "And we will not stand for this."

"What can anyone do?" Callisto leaned forward in his chair, hands spread as though to repeat his question.

"All the priests, bishops, and churchmen in Tuscany, including Florence, have decided to excommunicate the pope and his followers."

A stunned silence followed.

"Does this mean war?" breathed Fabiano.

"Quite possibly," whispered Callisto.

"It must not," said Enzio Borroni. "We have no army to defend us."

"If necessary"—Dario slapped a hand onto the table—"we'll purchase one. I've already made arrangements. But we must get the people behind us." The memory of the Florentine mob running wild through the streets after the attempted coup still chilled his blood.

"I agree." Callisto faced the bishop. "Once you've fashioned your response detailing what the pope has done and how you will excommunicate him and all his cronies, give it to me. With our new, marvelous printing press—this miracle machine from Gutenberg—we can print two hundred posters and nail them up in every square. When the people see this pope's outrageous actions and the town crier repeats it every night, they'll be on our side."

"Sì," said Dario. "Let it be done."

Dario's worst fears were soon realized. Weeks later, the pope declared war on Florence and, by implication, on Colpena. Word also arrived that King Ferrante of Naples was sending an army north to join Rome's smaller force.

That same day, Dario sent a messenger on a fast horse to Baldassare Fanucci in Arezzo with an urgent plea to bring troops for Colpena's defense.

CHAPTER 30

~ PROGRESS ~

AUGUST 1478

Amadeo walked from the hot afternoon sun into the shade of the open-sided structure Pugliesi had built for the sculptors. Around him came the striking of hammers on chisels. Marble chips plinked like shaved ice onto a growing pile on the floor.

Only last week, the mercenary soldiers who'd finally arrived in the city had billeted the inns to overflowing. All the workers now complained. Even while strolling here from his quarters, he'd passed dozens of armed men from Arezzo. As a group, they were rude, boisterous, and spent most of their time in the bordellos and tavernas.

Skender also reported rumors that the streets were no longer safe for women alone.

Surely, Rossi was overreacting by bringing in this force. Was the pope really going to send an army against Colpena when he had Florence in his sights?

Amadeo approached Clemente, standing atop a wooden platform surrounding a six-foot white block of statuary marble. Stripped to his waist and sweating despite the shade, he held a hammer and a punch, the first tool for removing sections of marble before precision shaping began. Charcoal lines marked where the punch would strike. Beside him on a table sat the smaller clay model of the Apostle John he'd fashioned these last three months—St. John raising one hand, a stylus in the other, his glance toward Heaven, a tablet on his lap.

When Clemente heard Amadeo's footsteps, he glanced aside.

"It's a fine block," said Amadeo. "Pure and milky white."

Clemente smiled. "I've been studying it for weeks." His gaze returned to the marble. "But now I must begin." He laid the punch against a corner and struck slowly, seven times. Chips flew away. Pausing to examine the result, he struck again. More chips plunked onto the floor.

Amadeo walked down the line past the other four sculptors. Like Clemente, most had barely begun shaping their marble. For months, they'd been drawing, molding clay, and thinking through their projects. Brizio, Ercole, and Filipo were working on blocks the size of Clemente's, to become saints for the chapel bays. Gaetano, the least skilled of them, worked on a smaller piece for a niche.

Nodding to each man, Amadeo continued through the Piazza del Duomo. He stopped to watch masons add the last layers of rubble and mortar for the nave foundations. He smiled. Everywhere along the cathedral's entire outline, the work proceeded. With double the crews, progress exceeded his wildest expectations. He stepped through the gap where one of the façade doors would go.

Walking beside the rising nave walls, he slowed under the center of the future dome. On every side but the nave, massive piers for the arcades were already sixty feet high and climbing fast. And they'd only begun them last year. The stonecutters at Carrara couldn't ship the column sections fast enough. Roof vaults would eventually rest atop the columns and join the walls. Already above him, the chancel and transept walls were complete at one hundred and twenty feet, and—

Footsteps approached from behind.

"Your presence is requested in the tracing house," said a young out-of-breath apprentice.

Amadeo followed the youth to the piazza and entered the tracing house Pugliesi had built beside the lodge. There, Vittorio Rivera and Umberto Sabbatini greeted him. Wooden patterns for pieces of the stone vaults lay cut, stacked, and ready to ship to Carrara for the stonecutters there.

"What can I help you with?" Amadeo put hands on hips.

"We want you to remove Damiano De Luca from the position of Master Mason."

Amadeo sucked in breath. Not again. "Why?"

"He's constantly undermining our authority," said Speaker Sabbatini. "I tell the men what Vittorio wants, and Damiano gives them different instructions. I give him new instructions, and he ignores them. But if I bypass him and tell the men directly, he becomes angry."

"And he won't stop complaining about the blocks from Carrara," said Pugliesi. "There's nothing wrong with them."

Amadeo closed his eyes and grimaced. "I know. He's shown me hundreds. All are acceptable."

"Well?" said Vittorio. "What are you going to do about it?"

"I'll speak with him. Again."

"It will not be enough."

"It must be. His entire crew is working for us." Amadeo sighed. "I will talk with him."

At day's end, Amadeo took De Luca aside. "We simply must come to an agreement about who is in charge, Damiano."

"I am in charge of the masons."

"Sì, but Vittorio is lodge master, and Sabbatini is speaker. I give my instructions to Vittorio, and he gives them to the speaker. They are then explained to you, and—"

"Do not treat me like a child, capomaestro."

"Then listen to my speaker. Carry out his instructions. And do not countermand what he says. He's following my orders. Is that clear?"

De Luca pursed his lips. "It's bad enough we have to live with these scum soldiers from Arezzo, filling the inns with their foul mouths and their arrogance. Now I have to grovel before a man who does not know his—"

"Is that clear, Damiano?"

"I should have been made lodge master, signore."

"But you weren't. And now you must follow Vittorio's orders when Sabbatini relays them to you. If you don't . . ."

"Then what?" The man crossed his arms and narrowed his eyes.

"I'll have to find someone to replace you."

He huffed and shook his head. "You could never—"

"Do not try my patience." Then Amadeo softened his voice. "You are highly skilled, Damiano, and I need you. Let us come to an understanding. Please?" He stretched out his hand.

De Luca frowned but took it.

As the master mason walked off, Amadeo hoped that would be the end of it. For who could he get to replace this man?

CHAPTER 31

~ ACCOUNT TROUBLES ~

NOVEMBER 1478

As Dario gripped Letizia's hand, their footsteps echoed through the empty ballroom. As it had all through the tour, her glance bounced from wall to ceiling to floor, feasting on the frescoes, the high cross-beams, the tile designs. After years of refusal, Savina had finally relented and allowed his daughter to see him. She was sixteen now, and today was the first time she'd ever been inside Palazzo Rossi.

"What kind of dwarves, uncle?" She gave him one of the smiles that melted his heart.

"Talented dwarves. Ones that know how to juggle, perform feats of magic, and put on plays."

She clapped her hands. "It sounds wonderful. When will they arrive?"

"My man Fiorenzo is on his way back with them now. Maybe in a few weeks."

"Where will they live? Here in the palazzo?"

"Next door." Dario smiled. After hearing that a troupe of performing dwarves had passed through Padua, he knew he had to have them. "I bought the small house beside me. Workers have ripped out the walls and rebuilt the place for small people. They'll be my court fools, my permanent acting troupe. And every Saturday night, they'll perform for the crowds in Palazzo dei Rossi."

Letizia clapped again. "I must see them."

"If your mother allows it."

"She will. What great fun." Her smile split her face, and she clapped once more.

The bell in the town hall's tower rang. Dario counted seven strikes and looked to his daughter. "It's time." He led her toward the hallway and the stairs.

"I'm so glad you brought me to see your palazzo. Mother says you should marry her and bring us both here to live. Why don't you, uncle?"

He felt the heat rising to his face. "I wish I could, but it just wouldn't work out." They were on the steps now, father and daughter descending together.

"Then I could see the dwarves every day."

"Th–they . . ." Thinking of all the years he'd lost with her, all the years she could have lived here instead of with her mother sent a pang of regret closing his throat. "They won't want to perform every day. You'd probably get tired of them."

"I'd never get tired of performing dwarves."

At the bottom, he helped her on with her coat, then motioned to one of his younger servants standing by the door. "Aurelio will take you home now."

"Not you?"

"It's best if I don't see your mother again. From now on, one of my servants will pick you up and drop you off."

She frowned. "I wish you two would get along."

Dario shook his head. "It's not to be, little flower."

"You haven't called me that in a very long time." Then she walked up and hugged him.

He returned the hug, then pried her arms from his back. At sixteen years, she was almost a young woman. "I'll see you soon."

"When? Not as long as last time?"

"No. That was your mother's doing, not mine. You can come again next week."

Aurelio led her away, and he left for his meeting with Aldo.

Dario waited by the old wall with the harbor far below. A chill November sea breeze whistled through cracks in the stone. Even wrapped in his wool cioppa, he shivered. Aldo had summoned him to talk about the latest round of bad news. Lately, Aldo brought nothing but bad news.

After sending his urgent missive to Arezzo, Dario had waited four anxious months for Baldassare's army. Finally, in the first week of August, two thousand soldiers had marched into town from the north. But he soon discovered that, besides paying the condottiere his thirty thousand florins, the city was also expected to feed and lodge the soldiers.

To pay the army, they'd raised taxes on the citizens. Almost every day since, he'd heard complaints. Even Signoria members had to pay their share, and although he was gonfaloniere, everyone knew the Rossis were the wealthiest in Colpena. His portion was thirty percent of the unusual expense, with the Borroni and Mancini families, as next richest, paying one-tenth each.

Of course, the Rossi Bank had two sets of books, with a second set presenting a much leaner financial picture to the city tax collector. And since most city business came first through the bank, he maintained a third set of public books for the city. This, of course, required a fourth set of private city books. In the good times, funds flowed easily and quietly from the city to the Rossis' personal account. But now, with the city in trouble, the reverse was happening. Only he, Aldo, and Fortunato, his trusted accountant, ever saw those private ledgers. And Fortunato, having seen what happened to those possessing indiscreet lips, would remain forever silent.

At the same time, the shipping business was tapering off. With the threat of war, looting, and rampage looming over Tuscany, merchants in Lucca, Pisa, Piombino, Florence, and Genoa were reluctant to risk sending their precious goods anywhere. Even the wool trade and orders for alum declined.

As a result, he'd had to pare his frequent hunting excursions in the countryside down to once a week.

In August, Naples followed Rome by seizing the Rossi Bank branch in that city. Afterward, all business with Naples ceased.

In September, the Neapolitan army marched north up the coast, passing so close to Colpena that Dario could see the troops tromping in the distance. Weeks later, they laid siege to the town of Colle. Only two weeks ago, they captured it, and Colpena's trade with the rest of Tuscany ceased. Last week, news arrived that Naples' army had taken Siena and would winter there.

Then panic broke out. Merchants closed their doors. Customers stopped buying anything but food and wine. Even those became scarce. Fishermen still went out each day but found fewer buyers for their catch. Some wealthier citizens left the city, hiring mercenaries to accompany them, seeking safety in their well-stocked country estates.

"We're in trouble," said Aldo from behind.

Dario whirled to his cousin. "It's about time. It's freezing out here."

"Next time, let's meet back at the inn. If we keep the doors closed, no one will hear us."

"How bad is it?" Dario stepped closer.

"Our branches and all our business in Rome and Naples—gone. In all Tuscany, no one's buying alum, hiring ships, or sending goods anywhere. But we're spending a fortune keeping this army fed and this duomo construction funded. In short, we're going broke."

"What about our reserves?"

"Five thousand florins and dwindling fast. In a few weeks"—Aldo raised both hands—"it will all be gone."

Dario frowned, and his gaze wandered toward the harbor. It was winter, sì, but ten ships sitting at anchor was more than he could ever remember. Ten ships without customers, with crews wanting to be paid. Five more would soon return from their last voyages to join them. Then the entire fleet would sit idle. And Baldassare's army was costing him, personally, seven hundred florins a month. "What can we do?"

"I suggest you ask Lorenzo for another loan."

"I'll try. But Florence may be in the same shape as we are."

"There are also big expenses we can stop."

"Such as . . ."

"Your weekly hunting trip. You've pared it down from two, and that's good. But it's still too much. You're paying for grooms, horses, stable boys, dog masters and kennels, and trackers. Then there are these outlandish, expensive meals you set up in the forest for everyone who joins you." He shook his head. "Dario, you're serving rare wines in silver goblets, some of which don't come back. You're paying a troupe of cooks, servants, and laborers to haul boar, pheasants, pastries, and an entire kitchen out into the woods, just to impress your rich friends."

"We must keep them happy and on our side."

"But right now, we can't afford it. This must stop."

"All right. For now, I'll stop the hunting excursions."

"What about the maintenance of all the horses in your stable and the dogs in your kennels? Can you sell some of those animals?"

Dario winced. "No. And who has the money to buy them now, anyway?"

"Then there's the gambling."

"I enjoy it. And I usually win."

"Rarely. Last week, you lost five hundred florins to Marcello Esposito. The week before, it was two hundred. The week before that—"

"All right, all right. I'll forgo the gambling."

"That leaves us with the biggest expense of all." Aldo faced him, his expression severe.

"What?"

"The duomo. Stop funding it. Stop paying the workers."

Dario's shoulders slumped. "Are you sure? Only a few weeks until—"

"Until all our reserves are gone."

He closed his eyes. "All right."

That evening, Dario sat at his desk with a quill and parchment.

My dearest Lorenzo,

Truly, I am sorry for your loss. The murder of your brother, Giuliano, was tragic and despicable. May you someday exact the revenge you require on the perpetrators.

But I write now in my capacity as gonfaloniere of Colpena, responsible for my city's welfare. The income from our shipping and alum businesses has all but ceased. Our bank and most of Colpena's businesses suffer. Nothing is imported or exported.

Only the food and wine merchants survive. I fear what will happen when their supplies run out.

In short, within a few months, the city and the Rossi Bank will exhaust all reserves.

It is with great reluctance, but with dire need, that I now ask your assistance. You have been a great friend and ally to Colpena and to me, personally. Now is when we need your help the most.

Thus do I request that the Medici Bank transfer to the Rossi Bank a sum of thirty thousand florins at your earliest convenience. Such a loan would keep us solvent, allowing us to feed and lodge our condottiere and his army through much of next year. We will pay it back when the situation returns to normal.

Your friend and ally,
Dario Rossi, Gonfaloniere of the Signoria in Colpena

For some time, he stared at what he'd written. Then he folded the parchment, sealed it with wax, and called for a messenger.

He decided to hold off telling Puccini about any of this. Let them all work on his grand indulgence until Fabiano's fund was empty.

CHAPTER 32

~ THE DWARVES ~

DECEMBER 1478

Late in the afternoon, two days before Christmas and more than three weeks after he wrote Lorenzo, Grazziano knocked on Dario's bedroom door. When Dario gave his servant leave to enter, he was lying in bed next to Signora Delfina Costa. Even though he'd banked the fire high, the room was still cold.

"My lord"—Grazziano averted his eyes from the bed—"your assembly of small persons has arrived."

"My dwarves?"

"Sì."

A smile spread slowly across Dario's mouth. "I'll come right down."

After Grazziano departed, Dario stood and began pulling on his loincloth, calze, and shirt.

Behind him, Delfina slipped out of bed and dressed.

When Puccini had requested that he help the woman because her husband was in the tower prison, Dario had investigated. She was indeed without funds, barely surviving, and possessing little to eat. He'd used the occasion to go to her apartment.

"If you will resume gracing my bed for the next two years," he'd said, "I will pay your rent and ensure your larder is always full. At the end of that time, I will also pay your husband's debts to release him from prison. A fair exchange, no?"

She'd closed her eyes and staggered back against the wall. But, of course, she'd agreed.

Now she was dressed and standing by the door, ready to leave.

"Tomorrow afternoon, my dear?"

"But tomorrow is Christmas Eve."

"So?"

She lowered her head toward the floor. "I'll be here."

He followed her downstairs. While he got into his coat, she pushed hurriedly through the door.

A moment later, he stepped out into the Piazza Rossi. There stood long-lost Fiorenzo, his red hair unkempt, his clothes dirty and unwashed. Around him were gathered one dozen dwarves, none taller than Fiorenzo's waist.

Dario's smile stretched wider the corners of his mouth.

Dwarves. What a novelty!

A small crowd had stopped in the square to gawk at the dwarves' stripes, their polka dots, frumpy hats, and baggy pants. They wore full backpacks, appearing as if at any moment the loads would tip them over backward.

"I sent you out over a year ago," said Dario to Fiorenzo. "Since then, I've been sending you money constantly. Where have you been?"

"I chased them across most of Europe. They never stayed in one place long enough. Then I became ill. Then I had to convince them to come with me."

Dario squinted. "Or did you have yourself a merry time with my florins, visiting every bordello and taverna in every city along the way?"

"No, signore. And once we entered Tuscany, we had to avoid the bands of ruffians popping up everywhere. You don't know what it's like out there now."

"Ruffians?"

"Sì." Fiorenzo shook his head. "Civil order has broken down everywhere."

Dario frowned. If that was true, things were worse than he'd imagined. At least here, they had Baldassare's soldiers to keep order. He faced the dwarves. "I am Dario Rossi, your patron and gonfaloniere of this city. Welcome."

A dwarf with a pointed white beard stepped forward, his miniature hands on hips. "I'm Vasilica, and I speak for the group. Your man said you wanted performers. He offered free food and beds. But he wouldn't say how much we'd be paid. Lodging and meals are not enough. We only perform for cash. How much?"

Taken aback by such demanding words coming from one so small, Dario scratched the back of his head. "What do you require?"

"Seventy florins a performance. On top of meals and lodging."

Dario gasped. The dwarf was lying, and Dario bargained him down to thirty. Still too much, but he could afford it, he thought, even if the Rossis were going broke. And any day now, he'd receive the loan from Lorenzo.

After they'd shaken hands, he ushered the group to the house he'd prepared for them. Only last week, he'd paid workers a final five hundred florins to remake the place. It now held smaller rooms, lower ceilings, and tinier doors. Dario had to duck to enter. Inside, the workers had also fashioned smaller beds and chairs. He glanced at Vasilica, hoping for some compliment.

"It will do." Vasilica gave a dismissing wave. "When is our first performance?"

Dario winced. At least the dwarf could have said something about all the efforts he'd made to accommodate them. "Tomorrow night after the service in the square."

"On Christmas Eve?"

"Sì."

"So be it."

ALL THE NEXT DAY, THE town crier walked the city, advertising the free performance of dwarves in the Piazza Rossi right after the bishop's Christmas Eve service.

After his tryst with Delfina Costa, and as dusk fell, Dario wrapped himself in a heavy jacket and brought Letizia up from the Temestre Inferiore to the Piazza della Signoria for the service.

Bishop Ferata, dressed in his official green robes and topped with a high miter, performed the usual rites. Without a church, the bishop was still holding services in the open. But many had fled the city, and the crowd tonight was smaller than usual.

The choir sang. The bishop read the Christmas story, followed by more singing from the choir. Then the square emptied, and the crowd walked the single block to Piazza Rossi, where workers had spent the day erecting a small stage.

For the last year, Dario had been looking forward to the dwarves' appearance. But he didn't know what to expect. The dwarves walked onto the stage wearing the exaggerated, somewhat irreverent, costumes of a king and his court. But everything they wore was askew. They bowed with a flourish. Then they began acting out some kind of comedy. But it was bawdy, laden with foul language and obscene gestures.

He glanced at Letizia. A silly grin pasted her face.

As Dario continued to watch his dwarves, his face grew warm. They made fun of nearly everyone in any kind of authority—the nobility, the rich, the city leaders, and especially the clergy. He glanced to the side, where Bishop Ferata stood, his arms crossed, his expression increasingly dour.

Behind Dario, some in the audience, mostly the contadini and poorer folk, were laughing heartily. But many richer merchants and members of the Thirty were whispering to each other, shaking their heads, and leaving. Only half the original audience remained.

The night was turning into a disaster.

He faced the performance and forced himself to bear it. One dwarf, playing the part of a peasant, swatted a board across the rump of another dwarf playing the part of a king. Then he made crude jokes about the size of the king's various body parts. The crowd's laughter came less and less often.

After the performance ended, Dario closed his eyes and took a deep breath. As the crowd dispersed, he heard their mumbling.

When he opened his eyes, Bishop Ferata stood before him, his face red, his eyes wide. "That was the most disgusting, ill-conceived, inappropriate display of vulgar, foul, and despicable behavior ever performed in this city in public. And on Christmas Eve! I hope you send them back into whatever foul hole you found them!"

As Ferata whirled and stalked across the emptying square, Dario tried to remember a time when he'd seen the bishop angrier. He couldn't. He looked down at Letizia.

"I didn't understand it, uncle," she said. "They turned mean. I didn't like them."

"Sì, they were mean. I'll have to send them back. Let's take you home." All he could think about was how much money he'd spent to renovate the "dwarf house" and keep Fiorenzo searching for them. All of it—wasted.

As they crossed Via delle Rose heading toward the old wall, a man's footsteps pounded up from behind. Dario turned. A leather bag was strapped across the man's shoulder.

"Signore." Sweat poured down his forehead, and he bent forward, breathing heavily. "I bear . . . a message from Florence."

Dario smiled. At last—some good news. "Let's have it."

The man opened his bag, pulled out a wax-sealed parchment, and passed it to him.

With shaking hands, Dario broke the seal.

My dearest Dario Rossi, Gonfaloniere of Colpena,

It is with great regret that I respond to your request for funds. Florence, too, is facing a dire situation with the Neapolitan army encamped just to the south. Our condottiere reports weekly skirmishes with the enemy. Thus, at the current time, I am unable to send what you request. Let us pray for an early end to hostilities so we can both resume normal business affairs.

With great regards,
Lorenzo de' Medici

His heart pounding, Dario lowered the letter. Without some kind of miracle, both the Rossi Bank and the city of Colpena would soon be bankrupt.

CHAPTER 33

~ A SEASON OF DISCONTENT ~

MARCH 1479

With spring came cicadas droning, swallows shrieking, and flowers bursting from the ground. It was time to resume work on the duomo.

All winter Amadeo had been looking forward to this day. In a few minutes, he'd meet with Vittorio to discuss that very subject. He'd just pulled on his beretta and put his hand on the latch when Skender rushed through the door.

"They're leaving." Eyes wide, Skender carried a loaf of bread.

"Who's leaving?"

"The army. Even now, they're marching down the Strada del Nord."

Amadeo was afraid of this. Rumors had reached him that the city could no longer pay the condottiere what he asked. Only a month ago, the city guard had left their posts, insisting that, without having their lodging and meals paid, they would no longer work.

"Army or no, work on the duomo must continue." He stepped out into the Strada delle Campane.

Two men ran down the street toward him, and he backed against the building to let them pass. In their hands, they carried loaves of bread. Thieves? To his right, the baker, his son, and the baker's assistant chased after them, wielding knives.

The army hadn't even passed through the north gate. Was the city already in chaos?

He walked the distance to the Piazza del Duomo and entered the main lodge. There, Vittorio Rivera waited with Speaker Sabbatini, Damiano De Luca, and Bernardo Pugliesi. When he entered, they stood, but he waved them back to their seats. Why were they all here? He'd only requested to meet with Vittorio and Sabbatini.

Some of the companion stonecutters who couldn't afford rooms in the nearby inns lived in the lodge. Vittorio now asked these men to leave the main room so they could talk.

After Amadeo sat, he examined the faces of his masters. All were somber, troubled. He'd come to discuss starting work again. What was wrong?

"I'll come right to the point, capomaestro." Vittorio's gaze was downcast, his rough hands clasped on the tabletop. "For the last two weeks, Fabiano has not paid us. And now the men say that, if they do not receive what's owed them, they'll go home."

"Home?" Amadeo felt his heart skip a beat.

"Most have homes elsewhere."

"Of course. But if only they continue working, I promise they'll receive their back pay when the situation settles."

"You don't understand." Sabbatini shook his head. "Without funds, they cannot pay for lodging and food. In their home cities and villages, they at least have a roof over their heads. And their families would feed them."

Amadeo closed his eyes, took a deep breath, and opened them. "Can they wait till tomorrow? I'll talk with Rossi this afternoon."

"I'll ask them," said Vittorio. "But I doubt talking with Rossi will do any good. Rumor has it that both he and the city are broke."

Amadeo faced Vittorio, his jaw tightening as grim determination fought with a sinking feeling that the situation was spiraling out of control. "We cannot stop. The work must go on."

Vittorio opened his hands. "See what you can do."

Nodding, Amadeo left at once for Rossi's palace.

Grazziano admitted Amadeo to a sitting room. "I'll tell him you're here. Perhaps he can tear himself away from his latest whore long enough to talk with you. That's about the only profession these days that's unafraid to practice its trade. But now the women want bread, cheese, and wine, not florins."

Amadeo raised an eyebrow. The city was in chaos, and Rossi was still sleeping with his whores?

Out in the hall, he caught a glimpse of a scantily clad young woman heading toward the entrance carrying a loaf of bread and a bottle of wine.

Long moments later, Rossi entered, his hair disheveled, his face flushed. "What can I do for you, capomaestro?"

"You can pay my crews and my masters so we can resume work."

Rossi slumped into a seat opposite him. "I wish I could." He traced the scrollwork on the chair arm, and his voice softened. "But with the turmoil throughout Tuscany, business has come to a standstill. The city has exhausted its funds. I cannot pay the army. And this morning, the mercenaries left." Worry creased his brows. "I fear what will come of it. The Neapolitan force is nearby. If they get news of this . . ."

"But . . . the duomo? If the men are not paid, they cannot eat. They will leave."

"I don't have the funds." Rossi stood and walked to the window. "I'm sorry, Amadeo."

He thought of the harlot who'd just left, of the full larder Rossi surely had, of his stable of horses, kennels of hunting dogs, and many servants still in his employ. Somehow, he had money for those. Feeling as if he'd been kicked in the gut, Amadeo turned his back and walked out.

When he told the news to Vittorio, the lodge master's face scrunched in pain. "I can afford to stay in the city. But most will now leave. I . . . I'm sorry, Amadeo."

"I . . . I understand."

"Someday, this war will end. Things can only get better from here, capomaestro."

"I suppose you're right."

But Vittorio was wrong. Things got worse. Much, much worse.

After the lodge master delivered the news to the workers, most departed the city with their tools. Some larger, bulkier items they left behind the locked doors of the tracing house or the forge. Only a few stonecutters and sculptors, those with money to purchase food, remained in the lodge. Of Amadeo's masters, all but Vittorio left the city.

Within days of the army's departure, order broke down. Gangs of men bearing swords and knives roamed the streets at dusk, robbing anyone foolish enough to venture outside. By midafternoon, most houses and shops barred their doors, and the people hid inside.

The cost of wheat increased tenfold, as did the price of most other foodstuffs. The baker closed his oven to the neighborhood, and Skender had to fry unleavened flatbread over a fire on the kitchen floor. The vintner shuttered his doors, opening it only after peering through a crack to verify if the customer was somebody he recognized. It was the same with the other vendors. Gathering together in a group with hooks and spears, the fishmongers alone fought back long enough to sell their wares to those brave enough to venture out when the fishermen returned at dusk with the day's catch.

Suspicion and fear hung over the city like a thunderhead pregnant with storm.

Several times in the following weeks, Amadeo took his sword and left the house to wander through the empty work site, if only to assure himself nothing had been vandalized. In every street, he passed faces troubled with worry. Was he imagining it, or were some now gaunt with starvation?

Without work, without his lifelong project to occupy him, he paced his tiny garden. He couldn't concentrate long enough even to paint. What was his life without the ringing of hammers, the slap of mortar on stone, the padding of feet on scaffolding? What purpose was there to hiding in his house, waiting for an end to a chaos beyond anyone's control?

Skender, too, was restless, wanting always to go out despite the danger. Every afternoon when Skender left to buy food, Amadeo worried for his safety. But his servant was now a strong young man of twenty-four, and when he strode out the door, he carried Amadeo's sword, a foot-long knife, and a courage born of youth.

About a month after the gangs ran unopposed through the city, someone knocked loudly on the door at midday. Amadeo grabbed the sword and peered through a crack to see who it was.

Callisto Mancini stood in the street.

"Capomaestro"—the tall, gray-haired man nodded to Amadeo as he entered—"it's no longer safe in Colpena, and there's no telling how long this will go on. Tomorrow, I'm leaving for my country estate. We have food there, and I've hired ten of our former city guards to bolster the villa's defenses, so we'll be safe. I'd like you and your servant to join us."

"Sì, Callisto, I'll go with you. Anything to get away from this . . . this place of inaction and worry." He faced his servant. "Skender?"

The young man nodded.

On the journey, they received news from other travelers that roving bandits and thieves, emboldened by the breakdown of civil authority, roamed with impunity. But the travelers arrived at Callisto's Fair Fields estate without incident.

For the first few weeks, Amadeo released some of the tension that had plagued him these last months. The villa was well provisioned, with its own wheat fields, vegetable gardens, and a small herd of cattle. A full-time staff kept the place mostly self-sufficient. The ten guards they'd brought added to the five regulars, ensuring they were well protected.

Each night, Callisto feted him with sumptuous meals of pasta, onions, beans, fowl, hare, beef, and wine. Skender attached himself to Callisto's cook and learned many new preparations.

During the day, while Callisto worked in his garden or read from his extensive collection of Roman and Greek texts, Amadeo tried to occupy his mind.

But as the weeks passed, he found himself unable to work, adrift and without purpose. He'd brought parchment, styluses, ink, canvas, brushes, and enough herbs and plants to make most of the colors he needed to paint, but he couldn't concentrate.

Now thirty-seven years old, he'd spent ten years of his life working on the duomo. Completing it had become his single purpose in life. But the work, his reason for being, had come to a standstill. And with no prospects for resumption, he was lost.

One afternoon, Skender approached him. Amadeo had sat unmoving on a bench for hours, simply staring across the garden. "You must paint, signore. Or draw. Or design. Or do anything but this—" The young man had waved his hands in frustration.

"I know, Skender," Amadeo had said. "If only I could . . ."

Skender's face then carried such a look of pain, Amadeo even went to get his sketchbook. But it was no use. He just stared at the page, his pen unmoving, his mind bereft of a single idea about what to draw.

Walking slowly and without a goal, he began wandering the roads leading away from the farm. He cut across fields and climbed hills only to sit for hours staring aimlessly across the vineyards, wheat fields, and orchards. He tried to pray, but even that wasn't working for him.

"O Lord, please end this war," he said. "Help me to endure this idleness, this uncertainty, and this...accursed impatience. Above all, please end this conflict."

But every bit of news they received only confirmed that the situation everywhere was worsening.

The summer dragged on, and Tuscany lay paralyzed by fear of the Neapolitan army and the roving bands of ruffians. At Fair Fields, they were safe. But without work, Amadeo was like a staved-in wine barrel— empty, hollow, and without purpose.

On a warm day in early October, a messenger arrived from Colpena, rested briefly, then left for another villa to the north. That night, Amadeo and Callisto sat as usual for supper. "I'm worried about you, Amadeo," said his host. "All you do is mope about and wander aimlessly, doing nothing productive."

"If I can't make progress on the duomo, I am . . . lost."

"This chaos—it will end, capomaestro. It always does."

"I hope so."

"But now I must tell you a bit of news. I've been recalled to the city. The Signoria is meeting to discuss whether there's something, anything, we can do to restore order. I don't know what that might be. The city has no funds to pay the guard."

"When are you leaving?"

"Tomorrow. I'll take five soldiers with me. The rest will stay here. I'm sorry to leave you here alone, Amadeo, but it can't be helped." Then Callisto winked. "But perhaps, something will come along to cheer you up, hey?"

Amadeo nodded, wondering what Callisto could possibly mean.

The next day when Callisto rode off with the soldiers, Amadeo fell into a dark well of despair from which even Skender couldn't rouse him.

He tried to pray. He stalked the fields and hills. He wandered the roads. But nothing helped. Without the duomo, a deep melancholy gripped his every waking hour. The walls and columns weren't rising. Statuary wasn't being sculpted. Marble wasn't arriving at the dock. Suddenly, life had no meaning.

And he knew what he was feeling was terribly wrong.

It was a late-November afternoon, seven months after he'd arrived at Fair Fields, when Skender came running into the garden where Amadeo sat staring at the fountain. "Riders are approaching, signore. Six men with spears and a hooded figure—foreigners, by the look of them. This could be trouble."

Amadeo leaped from the bench and ran into the house. He and Skender grabbed swords and joined all ten remaining guards at the entrance. Perhaps a show of force would dissuade whoever was approaching from attacking.

But the riders kept coming. As they neared the villa, the hood fell away from the caped figure. It was a woman.

When they slowed, dismounted, and led their mounts at a walk, he lowered his sword. A hostile force wouldn't have done that.

Then the caped woman's features became clear, and his heart leaped. Simona!

By now, she must be nearly thirty. But the six years they'd spent apart had only heightened her beauty.

"Amadeo?" Surprise lifted her voice. Her smile brightened even her eyes.

"Simona, what are you doing here?"

"My aunt refuses to let me live with her any longer. She sent me home."

He grasped both her hands and examined her brown eyes, the smoothness of her cheeks, the brightness of her smile. "I—I've missed you."

"And I, you."

He pulled her close, and despite a warning sounding deep within him, his lips found hers.

CHAPTER 34

~ SIMONA ~

NOVEMBER 1479

When they parted, Amadeo's heart beat faster, and he felt light-headed. Even after all this time apart, Simona still held his heart captive.

"Why are you here at Fair Fields with Skender?" Simona nodded at the servant who smiled back. "And where's Father?"

He explained how Callisto had brought them out of the city for their safety but was then recalled. "I haven't heard from him for nearly a month."

"We knew about the troubles here in Tuscany. That's why my aunt hired so many mercenaries to escort me. So you're here all alone?"

"Sì."

A wide smile lifted the corners of her mouth. But it turned to a frown. "Oh, Amadeo, I'm so sorry about that night you and Skender were eating at your table and I let that rogue of a boy lead me to do what we did."

"It's all right. No need to apologize."

"But I must. For some time, I've realized that all these others"—she waved her hands—"meant nothing to me. All this time—it was you I wanted."

He nodded, feeling a rush of heat to his face. How quickly she intoxicated him. Had the aimlessness, the worthlessness, of these last months made him more vulnerable to her? But he didn't care. Within the space of a few minutes, she'd brightened his world and relieved his melancholy.

"Come." He gripped her hands. "Let's feast on the best dinner Fair Fields can offer. Then let's talk."

Normally, he ate with Skender, but tonight his servant worked in the kitchen with Callisto's country chef and served them.

"You've filled out, Simona," said Skender as he carried two plates into the dining room. "French cooking must agree with you."

She blushed and shook her head. "I prefer Tuscan food. But, Skender"—she wagged a finger at him—"it's not polite to mention a lady's figure."

"Sorry." He disappeared into the kitchen.

"Why did your aunt tell you to leave?" Amadeo's fork stabbed a cheese ravioli.

"I could no longer obey her." She lowered her eyes. Then she spoke so softly he could barely hear her. "I was going insane, the way she kept me locked up. When she caught me going out through a window one night, she flew into a rage. Then she said I couldn't live in her house any longer."

Amadeo smiled at the picture of Simona slipping out the window to escape her aunt. "You're a naughty girl, I think."

She tried to smile in return, but the smile vanished. "I–I'm afraid I am."

After supper, bundled in jackets, they strolled through the garden, hand in hand, and listened to the hoot of a distant owl.

"You don't realize, Simona, how much your coming here has lifted my spirits. I've been terribly down this last year."

"Without your work?"

"Sì. It's so much a part of me that without it . . . I–I don't know who I am."

She grabbed his hands and whirled him to face her. "So I make you happy?"

"Very much so."

She beamed, and they walked again. She began swinging his hand. "Father sent me a note saying I should meet him here. But now that he's still in the city, I'm glad."

"So he knew about your coming?"

She stopped, frowned, and nodded.

"Well then, let's make the best of it before he returns." But the moment the words escaped his lips, he realized how they could be interpreted. He shot her a glance. She was looking at him intently, questioning. "I–I only meant—"

"I know what you meant. We'll become the best of friends, Amadeo. The very best."

He breathed out. "We will."

THE WEEKS PASSED, AND AMADEO and Simona spent every day together. This was far different from his previous visit to Fair Fields. Back then, he'd been preoccupied with his drawings, sketches, and designs. Now, he lived and breathed Simona.

As if by magic, she banished his melancholy. She intoxicated him.

In the last week of December, Amadeo received a message from Callisto. The city was slowly regaining control from the ruffians. With the promise of a future abatement of taxes, a group of wealthier citizens, including the Rossis, had personally paid half of the former city guard to resume their duties. As a result, Callisto decided to stay and look after his business. Though the gonfaloniere didn't yet have funds for the duomo, elsewhere in the city, trade was creeping back to normal.

But most of Tuscany was still in turmoil, and Callisto encouraged Amadeo and Simona to stay at the villa until he arrived, possibly in a month.

Yet time passed, and he did not come.

When the messenger sat his horse in the yard, ready to return to Colpena, Skender stood beside him holding the reins of his own mount. "You don't need me here any longer, capomaestro." Skender's glance shifted to Simona. "And it's safe enough now to return."

Amadeo nodded, realizing that since Simona had arrived, he'd all but ignored his servant and youthful friend.

After Skender's departure, Simona filled his every waking moment. Gone were all thoughts of the duomo, the plans lying unfinished in his house, the workers scattered to their homes across the country, the blocks of bardiglio lying abandoned and unmortised under straw and dung. If he couldn't work on his duomo, he would fill himself instead with her.

During the warmer afternoons, the two walked hand in hand through the fields. Or they sat in the garden. On the colder days, they played chess at the dining room table. Or they played the card game frussi, and at the end of each round, Simona seemed always to have the greatest number of the raisins they used for betting.

Sometimes, they retreated to the library and read to each other from Callisto's vast collection. They read from the latest Italian poets, or, with Amadeo's knowledge of Latin, he read from Roman history or philosophy.

In the library's far corner, Callisto had built a pillow- and felt-lined reading nook. A window let in light, and when they filled the brazier with hot coals, it was much warmer than the rest of the house. There Amadeo and Simona would often go to get warm and hide from the servants.

One afternoon in the reading nook, as she lay her head on his lap, he read from Poliziano's translation of Homer's *Iliad*. As he read, he wondered, and not for the first time, why she had gained so much weight.

Halfway through the day's chapter, she reached up and pushed his book aside. "Kiss me," she said.

He looked down into her eyes, bright and inviting, and he bent over.

When his lips touched hers, an explosion of energy swept over his shoulders and down into his loins. They parted, and he was breathing faster.

"Take me, Amadeo." She sat up and peered at him with longing. "Please."

How easy it would be to take her right now, here in this secluded nook. So often in these months together, he'd wanted to feel that warm enticing body pressing up against his own. And now here she was, throwing herself at him.

But no. He'd taken a vow. He couldn't have her out of wedlock. And something deep inside him warned that, while the duomo remained unbuilt, he could never marry, never be with a woman, no matter how great his desire.

"No." He slid away from her on the cushioned bench. "I think we should stop."

For one frozen moment, she stared at him. Then her nostrils flared. "Sometimes, signore, you're as cold as a fish." Her voice rose. "Here I am, needing you, wanting you, and all you do is push me away. You're incapable of loving anyone or anything. Anything except your cold, unfeeling duomo, and now you don't even have that."

Her words cut deeply. Tears forming in his eyes, he just shook his head.

Seemingly oblivious to how she'd wounded him, she pushed open the door and left him alone in the cushioned hideaway.

That evening, she didn't come down for supper, but the next day, she apologized and smiled sweetly. Then their argument the previous afternoon seemed to have happened in another lifetime.

And they began all over again.

Once more, the episode repeated itself. It, too, ended the same way.

Except for those times, he spent the next two months at Fair Fields floating in a cloud of near-perfect bliss.

Then, in late March, as twilight sent shadows across the garden and sparrows chirped an evening symphony, Amadeo sat playing chess with Simona by candlelight. At the sound of footsteps, he looked up.

Callisto had returned. And he was smiling. "I have wonderful news for you both."

"You're back." Simona ran to him, and they hugged.

"What news?" asked Amadeo, standing.

"The war is over. By a brave and stupendous act of selfless diplomacy, Lorenzo de' Medici sailed alone to Naples and arranged peace with King Ferrante. He basically bought the goodwill of the people of Naples, spreading florins around like flower petals. He even freed the hundred galley slaves who'd rowed his boat to the city. In the end, Lorenzo's charm, and perhaps fear of the latest Turkish incursion to the south, changed Ferrante's mind. The king agreed to peace, and Naples recalled its forces. And without Naples' army, the pope can no longer war against us."

The news slapped him across the face, forcing him awake. Suddenly, as if it were a dream, the world he'd made here with Simona receded. And the world he'd left behind pushed forward out of the mist, razor-sharp and focused. "What of Rossi? Can he fund the duomo again?"

"Soon, capomaestro, soon. Some of his merchant ships have already set sail loaded with alum. And merchants are again exchanging money at his bank. So I advise you to return to the city at once. You should recall your men. In another month or so, by the time they've returned, you should be able to resume work."

His heart leaped. After a year of idleness, the crews could start again. He swept a hand through his hair. "Truly wonderful news, signore." Then he gazed at Simona and saw her downcast look. "What's wrong?"

"Now you'll leave. Then you and I . . ." She whirled away from him.

Callisto glanced from his daughter to Amadeo and back to Simona. "Did you tell him, Simona?"

Still facing away, she shook her head.

"No?" Callisto's voice rose. "You didn't tell him?"

"No, I didn't."

"Tell me—what?" Amadeo arched a puzzled look to his host.

Callisto winced and rubbed between his eyes, then let out a long breath. "The reason her aunt sent her away was because my daughter is pregnant. If she does not marry, I'm sending her to live in the convent of Saint Elizabeth just east of Colpena."

His breath caught in his throat. He stared at Simona who still didn't dare look him in the eye. Of course. How blind could he be? That was why she'd gained so much weight.

"I–I'm sorry, Amadeo." Callisto's voice softened. "She should have told you. I let you two be together, thinking"—he waved his hands—"I don't know what I was thinking. Maybe that if you saw her and knew her situation, maybe you'd renounce your vow and the two of you . . ." He turned away. "You need a wife, capomaestro, and I thought my daughter would be the perfect mate for you. That was presumptuous. I'm sorry."

Now he understood why she'd thrown herself at him so many times. If they'd slept together, he'd have broken his vow. Then she probably thought he'd marry her. And he might have.

She jerked a tear-filled glance to him. "I'm sorry, Amadeo. But I do love you. I've always loved you. Can you not see that?"

Emotions swirled in his head like someone mixing colors of paint. He did love her. He knew that, had always known that. But now the duomo was calling him back. His life's work could resume, work far more important than any one man's personal happiness. In such a life, how was there room for a woman? Or a child?

His eyes wet, his voice came as a strangled whisper. "I–I can't, Simona. My . . . my work."

Her shoulders slumping, she spun away from him. She shuffled across the garden into the night.

The next day, he wanted to say goodbye to her, but she wouldn't come to see him off. With a somber Callisto looking on, Amadeo mounted a horse. And, with three mercenaries at his side, he rode for Colpena.

CHAPTER 35

~ THE OX-HOIST ~

NOVEMBER 1480

Half the city was out in the streets celebrating the feast of the four crowned men. Behind Amadeo in the column of marchers, drums beat, fifes played, and trumpets sounded. Nearly a year had passed since the war ended, and today, he felt like singing.

For the men building the duomo, November 8 was the most important feast day of the year. All the holidays provided the workers a welcome and needed diversion. Amadeo once calculated that, after all the religious feasts, the men worked two hundred and seventy days each year. Accounting for weather, maybe only two hundred.

Earlier that morning, he'd attended the bishop's mass in the Piazza del Duomo. Dressed in his official best, the capomaestro then marched behind the bishop who led the grand procession by holding aloft a brass crucifix studded with gems. Behind him, Vittorio bore a tall felt banner, woven with gold and silver thread and the images of the four crowned men. As the procession marched back up Via del Porto toward the duomo, Amadeo smiled and waved at the crowd. They'd been marching for at least two hours and had made one full circle of the hilltop.

Several times along the route, a man or a woman he'd once helped would rush out from the crowd, approach him, and gush their thanks. He remembered all of them.

In the third century, went the tale, four stonecutters—Claudius, Castorius, Symphonarius, and Nicostratus—had just converted to Christianity. But when Emperor Diocletian asked them to carve a statue of the god Aesculapius for him to worship, they refused. The Roman emperor then locked them inside lead coffins and threw them into the River Tiber. Now on every November 8, guilds all across Europe celebrated the martyrdom of those four brave men, now regarded as saints.

A smiling Bishop Ferata brought the marchers to a halt on the Piazza del Duomo, where he climbed atop a chair. "Let the celebrations begin!" he shouted.

The crowd cheered and headed for tables, where the city's women had provided bread, cheese, olives, spiced cabbage, and wine for all. Other tables were piled high with apples, grapes, and oranges. The Signoria, the Council of Thirty, and the Church had paid for the event, but with so many attending, they couldn't afford meat.

After they'd eaten, Amadeo and Vittorio followed Pugliesi to his workshop. Amadeo had given the master carpenter his studies of Brunelleschi's wondrous lifting machine—the ox-hoist. Now, Pugliesi was ready to construct a duplicate.

"It's a truly marvelous device." Pugliesi smoothed a parchment with his sketch of the machine. "The blacksmith is already making bearings for the pulleys. I've ordered an elm tree five feet in diameter from Portugal that should arrive any day now. The Pisan shipbuilders are making a rope over six hundred feet long. And we're going to need special reinforced tubs from our barrel maker for the machine to haul the mortar and masonry to the top of the dome."

"How does it work?" Vittorio frowned at the complicated diagram.

"On the ground, a fifteen-foot-high frame will hold horizontal and vertical spindles. Each vertical spindle rotates the horizontal spindles through cogged wheels. Two oxen walking in a circle will turn the vertical shaft. Because of the cogs' differential nature, this movement will slowly lift even the heaviest load. Brunelleschi's ingenuity was that the vertical cog can mesh with another, larger wheel on a horizontal axis. But it can only connect with one cog at a time. One cog raises the load. The other cog lowers the load. A screw lifts or drops the rotor to change the gears so they mesh with the right cog." He looked up with a smile. "The result is that, with the mere flip of a handle, we can reverse the lift's direction—either up or down. We don't have to unyoke the oxen and turn them around to reverse direction."

"What prevents the rope from catching fire as it goes through the pulley?" questioned Vittorio.

"We'll drench it with sea water."

"Truly an amazing device." Vittorio stood back with hands on hips. "To not have to unhook and turn the oxen—think of the time this will save!"

"It's key to building the dome," said Amadeo. "When can you finish it?"

"It's complicated. Assuming I get the elm, I'll work on it all through the next few winters."

"Good. We've dug the dome's foundations, and we're only a few years away from needing this."

From outside, the drums, trumpets, and fifes started up again.

"Perhaps we should rejoin the celebration?" asked Amadeo. "The men would appreciate our presence."

The others smiled and headed toward the music.

CHAPTER 36

~ THE CIVIL DUNGEON ~

A few days after the celebration, Amadeo, Skender, and three hired servants arrived at the town hall early in the morning. All bore backpacks and arms full of bread, cheese, and wine. Descending the stairs, they arrived at the civil dungeon. By now, the guards were familiar with Amadeo's thrice-yearly visits. He needed at least four months to save up enough to buy the quantities of food needed to make a difference in these squalid underground quarters.

He handed the guard the two florins for their admittance. That was the price he and the head guard had agreed upon. The first time Amadeo had tried to enter the lower prison, he'd been turned away. The man had insisted that, unless Amadeo bore a pass from someone on the Signoria, he couldn't enter. But even after Callisto signed such a pass, the head guard balked. That's when Amadeo and the man settled on the price of two florins. Later, he learned such a bribe was customary.

The iron doors creaked open. Out washed a stench so bad it stole the breath from his lungs. Carrying a torch to illuminate the darkness, Amadeo entered.

Men and women—dirty, sick, and starving—were chained by the ankles and wrists along every yard of wall, tied even on posts sticking up from the room's center. There must be a hundred prisoners down here, with little water and few buckets for waste. Their clothing hung in rotting strips from bodies emaciated by starvation, neglect, and loss of hope. Twice a day, the guards brought them a thin gruel for sustenance, barely enough to keep them alive.

As fast as they could, Skender and his hired servants distributed food to the prisoners who fell upon the bread and cheese like animals. From a single large amphora, Amadeo poured a cup of wine for anyone who had a clay cup. For those who didn't, he handed them a cup from the ones he'd brought.

"Thank you, capomaestro," came a broken voice from the wall. "You are God's angel sent to Hell."

Suppressing tears, Amadeo nodded and continued pouring wine.

When they'd given away everything they'd brought, he led his group back to the door and poured a last cup of wine for the guard.

"Guard"—he handed over an extra florin—"there are two corpses on the far wall. I'd appreciate it if you could remove them at once. Also, if you could please empty the waste buckets . . . ?"

The head guard pocketed the coin and agreed to do so immediately.

As they headed back up the steps toward fresh air and light, Skender said, "No one should be treated like those people down there."

"Sì, my friend," said Amadeo. "And let's hope none of us ever ends up there." But as the words left his mouth, a cold shiver began in his shoulders and crept down his back.

Why had he said that?

CHAPTER 37

~ A BAD VINTAGE ~

JANUARY 1482

Dario shuffled up the steps to the second-floor dining room without enthusiasm. Tonight, he would eat in the palace with Aldo; Aldo's wife, Elnora; their thirteen-year-old daughter, Desideria; and six-year-old Rosalva. With Elnora constantly complaining about Dario's and Aldo's frequent nights out, once in a while, Dario ate at home.

Six male servants and Grazziano waited on the room's perimeter. Above, on the twenty-one-foot ceiling, fauns flirted and danced with nymphs in a forest. On the walls, gilt-edged mirrors and crystal candelabras vied with portraits of long-dead ancestors, now black with age and candle soot.

Taking his seat at the table's head, he nodded to Adriano, the headwaiter, a tall, severe, but competent servant. Adriano clapped his hands, and the others scurried through a far door toward the kitchen. Grazziano remained standing in the corner.

On Dario's right sat Aldo, nursing a glass of wine. Opposite him on Dario's left sat his cousin's wife and daughter.

"We met Marcello Esposito's granddaughter today," said black-haired, plump Elnora. "And she's a lovely child. Perhaps she could come sometime and play with Desideria?"

Dario glanced at Aldo's daughter, a smaller version of her mother, with long, black hair and small, flashing eyes. "Would you like that, child?"

"Very much, signore," said Desideria. "So few children come here to play."

"Sì," added her six-year-old sister.

Dario faced Desideria. "What if, instead of dwarves, we hired a few minstrels and performers to entertain us while we ate?"

Aldo frowned. "How would we pay for them?"

"They'd cost but little. We have the funds. The mine is producing well. And the shipping company is bringing in more income than we ever dreamed." He spread his hands as if to encompass all of Colpena. "Why not spend some of our good fortune to bring in a bit of diversion?"

"Jugglers?" Desideria's eyes widened. "And musicians?" She looked to Rosalva whose eyes were gleaming.

"Sì, children. To brighten our meals and bring some life into this dismal room."

"Let's discuss it later." Aldo's scowl deepened.

Adriano entered with the other five servants bearing trays and pitchers. He opened the trays' lids, set them on the nearby sideboard, and brought Dario the first platter bursting with penne pasta, covered with wild boar sauce and sprinkled with herbs. He scooped a generous portion onto Dario's plate.

Another servant, a new man hired only yesterday, poured wine into Dario's goblet. When he'd filled Dario's, he moved to Desideria's.

She grabbed her glass and drank deeply. "I'm so glad you allow me to drink wine now." She smacked her lips.

Aldo smiled. "Just don't drink too much, my dear. Look, you've already downed half of it."

The servant filled Elnora's glass, then rounded the table to Aldo.

"A bit later." Aldo waved the man away.

Setting the decanter on the table, the servant left the room with too much haste.

Dario must have a word with Adriano about servants practicing a bit more decorum in the dining room.

"Musicians, Dario?" Elnora raised her glass, then set it down again without drinking. "I suppose that's a bit less bizarre than your ill-fated dwarves."

"What other man of renown in Colpena, Siena, or even Florence could boast his own stable of musicians?"

She rolled her eyes. "What if your shipping business falls off? I heard in the market today that, for the last six months, there haven't been any pirate raids on Piombino or Pisa. They said that's because Pisa has built warships. What if Pisa starts taking commerce away from you like before?"

"Rossi Shipping and Transport is well established now. I think we'll keep most of our new business." No one but he, Aldo, and Jacopo knew about their funding the privateers and the end of that arrangement. The two captains had recently approached them, saying that to continue the Pisan raids had become too dangerous. Too many times, they'd been chased by brigantines equipped with cannon. One shot had even swept a deck before they escaped. After that, both captains vowed to stop sailing against Pisa or Piombino. They would henceforth plague the French and Spanish coasts.

"We won't keep anything if we don't pay our dues to the Wool Guild," said Aldo. "I saw our names on the list of miscreants yesterday."

"An oversight." Dario's fingers flicked away Aldo's objection. "I'll pay it this week."

"I've heard of men being imprisoned for less. Let this not become an issue for our enemies."

"I'll pay it." The importing, carding, and dyeing of wool, as in Florence, was one of Colpena's main industries. As bankers, the Rossis belonged to the Guild of Money Changers, but their membership in the Wool Guild was even more important. Only members of the Wool Guild could sit on the Signoria.

As Dario reached for his wine, he noticed a contorted expression on Desideria's face. "What's wrong, child? The meal not to your liking?"

Her eyes widened, and she appeared to be gasping for air. Then her hands went to her throat. "The wine"—she stood, knocking her chair backward—"something's . . . wrong."

Aldo threw his chair aside and raced around to her side of the table.

Dario eyed the red liquid in his goblet, set the glass down, then glanced around the room. The new boy—where was he? He said to Adriano, "Find the man who served this. Don't let him leave the house."

"At once, signore." Adriano ran toward the servant's door.

Then Dario whirled to Grazziano. "Get the physician."

With a nod, Grazziano bolted across the room to the exit.

Rising, Dario hurried to the child. She was clutching her throat, gasping for air. Elnora stood by helplessly, her hands pressed to her mouth, her face twisted with fear.

Rosalva began wailing, and one servant led her away.

Her face pale and sweating, Desideria's feet buckled beneath her. She collapsed into Aldo's arms.

Aldo turned a contorted face to Dario. "What's happening to her?"

"Poison," whispered Dario.

They took her down the hall to her bedroom and tried to get her to drink water. But soon, she lost consciousness. An hour later, by the time the physician arrived, Desideria's heart had stopped.

Aldo's daughter was dead.

The tears of mourning soaked every corner of the palazzo's second floor. The moans and wails from Elnora tore at him. Nothing he could do would comfort Aldo, whose tear-streaked twisted face looked from Dario to Elnora to Dario as if he couldn't believe what had just happened.

Dario stared at his niece's face, white and unmoving in death, and wept. He couldn't remember the last time he'd wept.

Someone had just tried to poison him and his entire family. Someone with a grudge. Instead, they'd taken the life of his niece. Was it an assassination attempt? Or something more?

Time passed, maybe an hour, and he realized he must act. Wiping his face, he left Aldo and Elnora. He found Adriano and quizzed him about the servant who'd poured their wine.

"Gone, my lord." Fear marked Adriano's normally expressionless face. "The others said that, right after he served you, he ran out the servants' door. No one's seen him since."

"Where did he come from?"

"From the lower quarter, signore. He claimed he once worked in the Sagese palazzo."

"And did he?"

"I–I don't know. We didn't check."

Dario frowned. "From now on, every new servant is to be given a thorough background check. I'll deal with you later."

His face ashen, his hands shaking, Adriano bowed and backed away.

Dario pulled on his coat and hat and left the palazzo. He stepped into the cold harbor wind.

What if this was the beginning of a coup like the one in Florence? What if, even now, an armed force was heading toward the city to complete the transfer of power?

His heart beating faster, he ran the two blocks to the town hall and raced up the steps. "The captain of the guard," he shouted. "Where is he?"

Two soldiers rose from seats where they'd been sleeping. "Signore?" questioned a youth not much older than Letizia.

"Bring the captain here at once."

The soldier nodded and ran out the door. Long moments later, the captain, a middle-aged soldier with a paunch, clattered in.

"Call out the guard," said Dario. "Close the city gates and put every man you've got on the walls. There's been an attempt on my life and the lives of my family. My niece is dead. Someone may be attempting a coup."

"At once, signore." Wide-eyed, the man bowed and ordered the two on duty to begin rounding up every soldier.

As they bolted into the night, Dario remembered the chaos and fear that swept through Florence after the attempted assassination on Lorenzo. Would the same happen here?

Satisfied that the guards were following orders, he wound his way down to the Temestre Inferiore. He threaded narrow lanes in the dark, stopping at a house on the Corsia Pescivendolo. Climbing to the fourth story, he knocked on the door to apartment number fifty-six.

He waited. When no answer came, he pounded his fist on the wood, louder, longer. Finally, the door creaked open.

"Signore?" The candle in Jacopo's hands lit the alarm on his face. "What brings you to my home so late?"

"My niece has been poisoned. Sh–she's . . . dead." He sucked in breath. "I want you to discover who did this. And I want them killed."

THREE WEEKS AFTER THEY'D BURIED his niece, Dario stood on a corner of the old wall in the rain, looking over the Temestre Inferiore. A brisk sea wind whipped sleet around his coat and legs.

He gazed at the harbor below. Four ships were docked, waiting until spring before sailing again. Waiting, always waiting. That's what he was doing now. Waiting for the missing piece that would brighten his life. Waiting for the name of the man—or men—who killed his niece and tried to kill him.

Glancing both ways along the wall, he snugged his cape closer and shivered. Where was Jacopo? They'd agreed to meet here half an hour ago. Tonight he also waited for Jacopo.

Lately, an unease, a restlessness, seemed to fill Dario's every waking moment. First was the attempted assassination and coup. On the night when Desideria was murdered, the city guard had manned the walls. A force of some five hundred armed soldiers had, indeed, marched toward the city. But when they saw the closed gates and soldiers with crossbows manning the walls, they turned and fled. If the poison had killed him and Aldo, no alarm would have been sounded, and that force would surely have seized the city.

But where did those men come from? Tonight, he hoped Jacopo would tell him who they were.

The coup was thwarted. But the affair left him restive, on edge.

But something more was wrong. Something profound was missing from his life, and he couldn't identify it. The only time he felt content was when he was with Letizia. But she was now twenty, and lately, when he'd taken her to a trattoria to eat, she appeared distant, bored, even uninterested.

Then there was Puccini. He was surely part of Dario's discontent. The man's self-righteousness, his single-minded devotion to his God and his duomo—it ate at Dario. Puccini must have some weakness, some fault that would show him to be like everyone else. No one should set himself as far apart from the rest of humanity as Puccini. Someday, Dario would bring him down.

Footsteps approached, and Dario whirled.

"Sorry for being late, signore." Jacopo's breath spouted white mist. "I misread your reply and went to the wrong overlook."

"We'll meet in places like this from now on. Not at the inn. Last time, though I couldn't prove it, I think Calandra was listening at the door. What do you have for me?"

"I regret to say that, after a month of searching, I have no leads. The servant, this Agapetto Moretti, has simply disappeared. He never worked for the Sagese family. That was a lie. He might have caught a ship north. One did sail the next morning for Genoa. But it hasn't returned. If it does, I'll interrogate the captain and ask whether Moretti booked passage."

"What about the soldiers sent to invade the city? Who bought them? Where'd they come from?"

Jacopo shrugged. "I've asked—all up and down the hills, I've asked—and nobody in the villages will say. It was dark, and the force wasn't flying a banner."

Dario slammed a fist into a palm. "Could Enzio Borroni or Rocco Marino have been behind this?"

"Possibly." Jacopo wiped rain from his face. "But we can't prove anything."

"Could you ask their servants if this Agapetto had ever been seen in their households?"

"I will do so. Discreetly, of course."

"No matter how long this takes, Jacopo, even if it takes years, we will find whoever was behind this and give them the justice they deserve."

"Sì, my lord. One's family is sacrosanct."

"They wanted more than my family, Jacopo. They wanted the city itself."

CHAPTER 38

~ FERATA'S RELICS ~

JUNE 1482

In the dark, breathing the stale hallway air outside number twenty-eight, Strada degli Innocenti, Dario waited. Just inside the apartment behind an open door, Letizia and her mother were arguing.

"I don't want you going out with him," said Savina to her daughter.

"You don't have anything to say about it," Letizia fired back. "I'm twenty now. And whether you like it or not, I'm going to spend the afternoon with my uncle."

"Uncle?" Savina faced Dario. "When are you going to tell her, Dario?"

He shrugged. "Tell her what? I don't know what you're talking about."

As Letizia turned a questioning look to her mother, Dario shot Savina a warning glance. "Don't."

"This farce has gone on long enough." She waved him inside. He hesitated but entered the musty, one-room apartment. Bare, cracked walls, a bed, two chairs, and a table. He hated entering her place. Then she shut the door.

"Don't do it, Savina."

"Why not? You're never going to marry me. Someone needs to tell this girl that you . . . are not . . . her uncle." She took a deep breath, grabbed her daughter's shoulders, and spun her around. "This man is your father."

Letizia's mouth opened, and she stared at him. "Is that true?"

Dario squeezed his eyes shut. Damn that woman for her indiscretion. He opened his eyes, caught Letizia's stare, and nodded.

"B–but what about my father? My father, Roberto?"

"He made it all up." Savina sneered at Dario. "The man never existed."

"All these years . . . you let me believe I was your niece." She whirled to her mother. "But then . . . so that's why you've been pestering him to marry you? Because when you were on the streets . . . he was . . ." She put hands on top of her head. "No! He was one of your customers? But how do you know *he*"—she pointed at Dario—"was my father?"

"For two years"—Dario barely heard Savina's whisper—"he was my only client. That's when you were born. Then he stopped keeping me."

"So . . . you lied. You *both* lied to me." Tears filling her eyes, Letizia twisted away from them. "I hate you. I hate you both."

"I didn't tell you"—Dario's heart was pounding—"because I didn't want you to think the worst of me. And I could never marry this woman. We don't get along."

"Get away from me, both of you." Then she ran out the door and down the hall.

Dario stood before Savina, his fists clenched, his jaw muscles tightening. "You shouldn't have done that. But maybe it's for the best. Now that she knows, when she calms down, I'll bring her into the palazzo to live with me."

"You will not." Her eyes wide, Savina planted her hands on her hips and cocked her chin. "You wouldn't."

He headed for the door. "She's old enough to leave you. And if she's living with me . . . you don't need my support anymore."

His words rocked her back. As if her legs failed her, she grabbed the doorframe. "You're cutting me off?"

"Consider it done." He tromped down the stairs, hoping to catch up to Letizia.

But out in the street, there was no sign of her.

For hours, Dario wandered the lower quarter but never found his daughter. He ducked into a taverna, drank a few mugs of beer, and decided he'd return to Savina's tomorrow and pick up his daughter. He headed for home.

As he crossed the Piazza del Duomo, he paused to look at the duomo's progress. After the yearlong hiatus, Puccini had worked his crews furiously to catch up. Dario wanted the cathedral finished, sì, but the man's dedication and single-minded focus irritated him. And for some reason, his visits to the dungeon bearing gifts grated most of all. The capomaestro had to have a flaw, some sin that marred his public appearance of righteousness.

Still, Dario was pleased that the arcade columns for the transepts and chancel were complete. So were the massive foundations for the dome. Now the workers were building wooden structures—centerings, Puccini had called them—to hold the rib vaults for the roof. The nave walls were also rising. All of it was building an impregnable defense against the fires of Hell.

Leaving the work site, he turned left onto the Via san Cristo. At that moment, Bishop Rinaldi Ferata left his palazzo steps.

"Signore," Ferata called across the square. "Glad I am to have caught you. I would have a word."

Dario stopped and waited.

"Some while ago, I invited you to view my collection of relics. Since you are here, would this be a good time?"

Dario nodded. Anything to divert his mind from what Savina just did. "Please, bishop. Lead on."

Beaming, Ferata ushered him up the steps. Far smaller than Dario's own palazzo, the bishop's house boasted a few frescoes on the walls, a handful of sculptures, and some faded paintings of the former occupant's long-forgotten ancestors. He followed Ferata up a central flight, down a hall, and into a room that might once have been a library.

Eight tables filled the space. On each stood a reliquary atop black velvet fringed with gold thread. Each reliquary, made of gold and silver, some with embedded rubies and emeralds, held a holy object. The first was merely a holder for a rugged wooden cross about two feet long.

Dario raised his eyebrows at his host. The cross looked like something that had washed up on the beach.

"That crucifix was made by St. Thomas and rescued from India. It's worth over three thousand florins."

"Three thousand florins?"

"Sì. While others of my profession spend money on jewelry, expensive furniture, and the pleasures of the flesh—rare wines, sumptuous banquets, and—"

"Whores," added Dario.

Ferata shot him a disapproving look. "While they waste their florins on such, I spend my income on rare objects of great spiritual value—holy artifacts. Take, for instance, this gold coin." He opened the doors of a reliquary to reveal a coin. Removing it, he handed it to Dario.

Dario recognized Latin and a faded picture of some Roman emperor. "What is it?"

"There's a high likelihood this could be the very coin Jesus held up when he said: 'Give to Caesar what is Caesar's, and give to God what is God's.' That's Tiberius Caesar on the front."

Dario stared at it. "How do you know it's the same coin?"

"I have a certificate of authenticity saying this came from the same fund the Apostles used to buy their food. If nothing else, Jesus and the Apostles held this in their very hands. It's worth one thousand florins."

Dario moved to another table without a reliquary, where lay a ragged, thread-worn robe, faded to a dull gray. "And this?"

"St. John wore that robe on the day of his death on the island of Patmos."

"What's it worth?"

"It's one of my most valuable possessions. Four thousand florins."

Dario's eyes widened. "But what good is all this?" He spread his hands toward the tables. "Why have you spent a fortune collecting these items and hiding them away like this?"

Ferata narrowed his eyes and frowned. "They are of great historical and spiritual value, signore. Some claim that relics such as these still hold the power of the Holy Ghost from their original owners. And indeed, sometimes when I am alone with them at night and I lay my hands on them, I can feel their power coursing through me."

Dario tried to stifle a smile. Did he really believe this? "So that's why you do it?"

"There's also this: the common people will pay great sums to view them. Why, I've heard that the bishop of Mainz once took his relics on a tour. The commoners gave him coin after coin to view his collection. He thereby garnered enough donations to help finance the construction of his cathedral."

Dario's breath caught in his throat. Going from table to table, he looked with new eyes at what Ferata had gathered. "Have you ever taken these on such a tour?"

"No. I would need one item of such great value that it, alone, would draw the people in. None of these rises to such a height."

"And if you had such a relic, would you consider giving such a tour?—if the money went to the Church, of course."

"I might. It would be a shame not to let others feast their eyes on the wonders I've gathered."

"Very interesting, Ferata. Thank you for showing me this."

Smiling, the bishop led him back to the street.

As he returned to his palazzo, Dario wondered how much a tour of relics could bring in. He also questioned whether half of the items in Ferata's possession were really what the bishop thought they were.

But if they could garner as much money as claimed—what did it matter?

CHAPTER 39

~ THE VOYAGE ~

OCTOBER 1482

Just before noon on a warm October day, Amadeo stood on the new terra-cotta tiles below the chancel. He craned his neck to look one hundred eighty feet to the top, where foundation pillars would soon support the dome. From the scaffolding above came the cooing of pigeons nesting in the boards. If they became more of a nuisance, he'd have to bring in falconers. Already, they were making a mess for the masons on the unfinished walls.

The transept's clerestory walls, recessed forty feet from the outer walls, were already thirty feet high, halfway to their goal. Today, carpenters were raising the first roof frames for the north transept using the chestnut Pugliesi had taken from Baron Calabrese's forest during the duomo's first year. For the last twelve years, the boards had been drying in the forest warehouses. Compared with other tasks, the roof would rise quickly. Already, they'd completed the chancel and east transept roofs.

After weeks of laying roof pieces on the ground, the carpenters had assembled and then disassembled the trusses. A treadwheel crane then lifted the parts, one by one, to the top where carpenters reassembled them. Where the truss pieces joined, each contained a mortise, or square hole, into which was fitted a precisely cut tenon from its opposite piece. They joined the whole together with pegs of oak, pounded into strategic holes.

Last year, he'd gone to Bologna to recruit plumbers and roofers. For months, the plumbers had been fashioning slate tiles. As the carpenters worked on one side of the transept, the roofers were hauling the slate to the chancel roof and fastening them to the frame's crosspieces.

Seeing the progress, Bishop Ferata had beamed. "This is wonderful. We can now start holding services in the chancel."

"When the entire structure is under one roof," Amadeo had replied, "we'll replace the terra-cotta tiles with marble."

That was weeks ago. Now he glanced west. Scaffolding covered the entire top of the nave walls, already seventy feet high and rising. He smiled. The cathedral was taking shape.

"Amadeo," came a cry from the west.

A small figure waved from the distance.

As he walked to meet Fabiano in the nave, someone struck a bell. By the time the two met, women had arrived with bread, cheese, and wine.

The stonecutters left their stones. The carpenters made their way across the scaffolding to the spiral steps. And those masons not working on a bucket of wet mortar descended the western scaffolding. Lunchtime at the duomo.

Fabiano passed him a bag clinking with coins. "This is an allowance for the widows of the three men who died in last month's scaffolding collapse."

"Thank you, Fabiano. I didn't have the funds myself, and unfortunately, the guilds do not have a widow's allowance. All the crews will appreciate it, knowing that, if something happens to them, their families will be taken care of. How did you get the gonfaloniere's approval?"

"I have made certain entries in the books that are—how should I put it?—ambiguous."

"You're a sly one, Fabiano." Amadeo thanked him again.

"And here are your funds for travel." Fabiano passed him a larger bag. "Is anyone going with you on the voyage?"

"Skender, six stonecutters, and two guards."

"Well, take care, capomaestro. The season of storms is nearly upon us."

"We'll be back in less than a week."

THE VOYAGE TO CARRARA ON a four-masted galley took a day and a half. He'd brought new templates for the stonecutters working there, and six new men to bolster the crews in the Apuan Alps. The men stationed in Carrara were always glad to see visitors from Colpena, and Nicola Lombardo greeted him like an old friend.

"Tiziana, she married now." Nicola beamed. The sun, weather, and flying marble chips had so darkened and beat his face that his visage appeared chiseled and sandblasted. And each time Amadeo saw him, the years seemed to bend his back a bit farther. "She married a stonecutter. I have four grandbabies, Amadeo! Four nipoti!"

Amadeo congratulated him and introduced the new men, four of whom would work only on statuary.

"I rent new quarry for the pure white marble. We go there now."

After Amadeo had distributed the new templates and instructions to the men at the Battaglino Quarry, he followed the master quarry-man down the mountain then up a narrow road to the southeast. As they climbed, the skies clouded, and occasional thunder rolled over the mountains.

The quarrymaster led him and the new men five miles to a second quarry. He spread his hands toward the giant terraces, where previous miners had cut steps from the white marble. "My new quarry—for statuary only." Four men stood on the highest row, striking mallets on wooden stakes. At the base, two others sawed on one of the blocks while an apprentice poured sand and water into the crack, where the blade ground against rock.

Nicola stopped the sawing and laid a heavy hand on a stocky dark-haired youth. "This is my son-in-law."

Amadeo shook his hand and stepped back. He wiped his brow. It was hot, and he was feeling a bit queasy. Was it the altitude?

Nicola glanced at the sky. "Big storm coming. Today, we quit early."

After Amadeo paid Nicola for the next installment, they followed the new men and statuary cutters down the mountain to Carrara.

But on the descent, it rained so hard, they could hardly see to plant one foot ahead of another. By the time he reached his Carrara inn, Amadeo was shivering violently.

That night, his forehead was burning, and he ate only a few mouthfuls of the inn's stew before turning in early.

The next morning, when Skender saw him, he frowned. "Signore, are you ill?"

He waved off the suggestion, and after a breakfast of bread and cheese that he barely touched, they met the galley captain who would take them home.

But the sailor only frowned at the darkening clouds and roiling seas and shook his head. "We'll wait another day. I don't like the look of these skies."

One more night they stayed, and Amadeo's fever worsened. The next morning, he vomited what little breakfast he ate. Then he and a concerned Skender trudged down to the dock, where the captain decided that, despite the still-threatening clouds, they would sail. They started out in choppy seas under a light drizzle.

At noon when they were far down the coast, the storm that had hovered offshore for days finally hit. The winds bore upon them from the southwest. The captain lowered sail, and they made slow progress keeping the ship headed south. Heaving from side to side, the galley hit the swells with a great pounding. In the cramped, smelly cabin he shared with Skender, Amadeo lay feverish in his bunk.

The return voyage took four days, during which he ate not a morsel of food he could keep down. Once, he remembered opening bleary eyes to see a stranger standing over him with a worried look. Then his eyes closed.

"It's not the plague, is it?" questioned a voice he recognized as the captain's.

Someone put a hand to Amadeo's forehead, pressed it, and pulled it away. "No. Some kind of fever. He's been delirious, you say?"

"Sì, signore," came Skender's worried voice. "Thinks he's back in Colpena."

"Keep a cloth on his forehead, lad. Try to get some nourishment in him."

"Will he be all right?" asked Skender.

"I don't know," came the voice. "But it doesn't look good."

By the time they docked at Colpena's western port, Amadeo was drifting in and out of consciousness. When he was awake, Skender hovered at his bedside with a wet cloth on his forehead. His servant tried to get broth through his cracked lips, but he just couldn't eat.

"Where are we?" Amadeo asked when men came to lift him off his bed. The ship was rocking more gently now.

"The western harbor, signore," said Skender. "And now we must get you to your own bed."

As sailors carried him up the hill, rain wet his face. Somewhere across the western sea, thunder boomed. When he opened his eyes, the sky overhead threatened with dark, menacing clouds.

Before they reached his house on Strada delle Campane, his world turned as black as the thunderheads above, and he knew no more.

CHAPTER 40

~ RECOVERY ~

NOVEMBER 1482

Time passed in a confused, feverish fog. Amadeo barely remembered sipping spoons of broth, swallowing bread soaked in stew, and feeling gentle hands wiping his forehead with a cold cloth. Consciousness would briefly return, and he would again drift into restless dreams, filled with images of men climbing scaffolds, masons troweling mortar, and carpenters drilling holes. In his dreams, he cried out, urging the men on.

He relived entering a ballroom, where young men and women were undressing, kissing, and pawing at each other as the lights dimmed. Beside him stood Dario Rossi, grinning and waving him to join in. In the nightmare, he tried to run, but his feet were weighed down with bardiglio. Rossi and the others only pointed and laughed at him.

After a deep, dreamless sleep, he woke, and the fever was gone. He opened his eyes to a smiling woman standing over him. Light streamed through the bedroom window, sparkling in her eyes. Was it morning?

"You're awake?" she said.

"I am." He tried to focus on this wavering image—this woman in the habit of a sister novitiate. Was it an angel? "Who are you?"

"I'm Simona, silly."

"Why . . . are you here?"

"They let me leave the convent to minister to you. A mission of mercy." She called over her shoulder. "Skender, he's awake."

"How . . . long?"

"Three weeks, signore." Skender entered the room.

Amadeo turned his head.

Smiling, his young servant knelt beside him. "We've been very worried about you."

"The duomo . . . how is it—?"

"Never you mind about your cathedral." Simona brought a wet wash-cloth to his face and began washing his cheeks. "Vittorio Rivera is taking care of everything."

He nodded. But sleep called, and his eyes closed.

THE NEXT DAY, HE KNEW how a caterpillar must feel after living in a cocoon and breaking free, reborn into new life. The fever was gone, and his appetite had returned. Now, he could sit up in bed long enough to eat a bowlful of Simona's delicious chicken and dumpling stew.

But even with two braziers burning, the bedroom remained cold. "What's happening outside?"

"The weather has turned," she said. "The puddles froze last night."

"And the duomo?"

"Vittorio will tell you everything. But tomorrow, not today. You need more rest."

"Thank you, Simona." He reached a hand across to hers and squeezed. "Yesterday, I thought you were an angel. Today, I know you are."

She smiled and pressed her lips to his forehead.

After eating, he stood on wobbly legs, circled the bed once, then fell under the covers to sleep again.

WHEN VITTORIO CAME TO SEE him later, Amadeo nearly burst with questions.

"We stopped work for the masons," said the lodge master. "Too cold for the mortar. The uncured blocks are under straw and dung. The carpenters are still working on the north transept, and the plumbers are half-finished laying slate over the north transept roof."

"And your stonecutters?"

"Working inside the lodge. The companions are still finishing blocks from the last shipment. But after the storm, Carrara sent only one more barge. The sea captains have stopped their regular routes until spring."

"So we should put the nonworkers on half pay until spring."

"Already done."

"You see, Amadeo"—a familiar voice entered the room—"you are not indispensable."

"Gonfaloniere!" Amadeo sat up higher in bed.

"Sì." Rossi moved to his bedside. "I came to say I'm glad you've recovered. And I brought this." He laid a wheel of cheese wrapped in paper at the foot of the bed.

Amadeo stared at the cheese and at the padrone. So startled was he that no words came to him. "Th–thank you . . . Dario."

"You are welcome. I wish you a speedy recovery. Without its capomaestro, how will my indulgence ever be finished?"

"Indulgence, signore?" Amadeo scratched the stubble on his face. "I would call it, first, a cathedral. A duomo rising for the glory of God. Do you not think so?"

"Sì, of course." Rossi took a step back from the bed. "A cathedral first. An indulgence second."

Then Simona burst in and waved them all away. "Enough for today," she said. "Thank you for the cheese, gonfaloniere, but the capomaestro is still very weak and needs his rest."

Within the week, Amadeo was able to sit at the table with Skender and Simona. By now, she had abandoned her novice nun's garb for more familiar clothing.

One afternoon, when Skender went out to buy food for the night's dinner, Amadeo and Simona sat opposite each other, drinking hot water with lemon, cloves, and a dash of wine.

"I never told you"—Amadeo's gaze found the bottom of his cup—"how sorry I was to hear that you lost your baby."

"How could you? I've been in the convent since you left me at Fair Fields. That was—what? Three years ago?"

"Sì." He swirled the lemon in the tea, then caught her gaze. "How has it been for you in the convent? I mean—do you like it there?"

"I . . ." She lowered her glance and seemed to search for words. "Maybe I'll get used to it. The sisters are nice to me. They want me to take the vows to become a real sister like them."

He caught his breath. "Will you?"

"I don't know. No one will marry me now that I'm no longer a . . . a virgin. And I'm getting older. The sisterhood may be the only thing left for me."

Amadeo nodded. Implied and not spoken was that if he would have agreed to marry her three years ago, he could have saved her reputation. Then her life would have taken a different course. Not only hers, but his. "I'm sorry I couldn't . . ."

She pushed back from the table and walked to the window. "I still love you, Amadeo," she whispered. "No matter what happens, I don't think that will ever change."

He stood, walked up behind her, and held her. "I know. And soon, if you become a nun, we'll both be under vows of chastity."

She whirled to face him and laughed. "How strange life is, capo-maestro. Who would ever have expected things to turn out this way?"

"Who, indeed?"

CHAPTER 41

~ CHARGES ~

APRIL 1486

Standing precariously one hundred and eighty feet atop the dome foundations, Amadeo tried to take his mind off the document in his pocket. Was this some kind of test from God? Things had been going well, maybe too well. But the baseless accusations in his pocket cast doubt on everything he'd done.

With a few moments left before the meeting, he'd climbed up here to take comfort in the finished octagonal ring that would soon support the dome's weight.

Pugliesi's marvelous ox-hoist had easily lifted the heavy stones. Still, it had taken three months for crews to place the eight blocks, each weighing over two tons, atop the four giant pillars. The dome's supporting pillars were forty-five feet long by ten feet wide and carried most of the weight. But where the blocks met in open space, masons had built arches extending from the floor and meeting at keystones. The arches and keystones supported the open-space junction. A third arch would soon reach from the tops of arcade columns in the transepts, chancel, and nave and meet at the keystones.

Around him, feet now tromped on scaffolding, and masons called for more mortar while the echoes of chisels chipping at stone rose from below. Above, the exterior roofs over the chancel and both transepts were complete. Plumbers had already installed drainpipes leading to sculpted gargoyles that would spout rainwater away from the building. His sculptors had fashioned the traditional heads of dragons, demons, and monsters to carry off the effluent.

Complicated rib vaults now reached from every column, wall, and on top of the dome-support pillars—all meeting at central keystones above him. The interior ceilings built upon these great arches were nearly complete, needing only plaster.

He spun to the west. The nave walls were complete at one hundred and twenty feet. The arcade columns were complete at eighty feet, and arches already extended from these to meet the columns hugging the nave walls.

They had surely accomplished a massive amount of work in a short time.

Despite this, Bramante had written his letter leveling a withering criticism.

Amadeo felt again the parchment inside his pocket. Time to answer its charges.

He crossed the scaffolding to the spiral steps and descended. He traversed the nave and turned right toward the town hall, toward his accuser and the Signoria.

In the hallway outside the meeting room, he sat opposite Bramante in a tense silence.

Then the doors swung inward, and the sergeant-at-arms's welcoming voice echoed from beyond. "I introduce the Signore Basilio Bramante, architect in charge of the city waterworks. And the Signore Amadeo Puccini, capomaestro of the duomo."

Amadeo followed Bramante through the open door and took a seat before the Signoria's long table. All were present: Bishop Rinaldi Ferata, Enzio Borroni, Callisto Mancini, Dario and Aldo Rossi, Marcello Esposito, and Fabiano Trentino.

"We welcome our two architects to this special meeting of the city council." Rossi held a bored expression as his glance sought Bramante. "We understand you have a list of charges to level against your colleague? Please read them."

Bramante stood, cleared his throat, and lifted his document. "I, Basilio Bramante, architect in charge of—"

"Sì, sì. Let's skip your lengthy introduction and get straight to your accusations."

Bramante scanned down the page. "I hereby charge Amadeo Puccini, capomaestro of the Cattedrale del Figlio sul Mare, with gross professional incompetence, moral failure, and bribery of public officials."

Frowning, Callisto faced the architect from Urbino. "That's quite a litany of crimes. What proof have you for any of this?"

"I'll start with professional incompetence. The Signoria was given the plans for the dome, was it not?"

Nods from around the table.

"Well, my calculations tell me that, after this bungling fool of an architect places all the stone required to complete his monstrous dome atop his inadequate four foundation pillars, the dome's weight will collapse the outer walls."

"Signore, your calculations are in error," said Amadeo.

"And I say the walls will buckle outward under the lateral stresses."

"And how"—Callisto waved a hand—"would you fix this problem you say exists?"

"I would attach flying buttresses to all the outside walls."

"Unsightly and unnecessary." Amadeo shook his head.

Fabiano looked from Bramante to Amadeo. "If he is in error, capomaestro, please explain why."

Rossi, Ferata, and Borroni nodded in agreement.

Amadeo smiled at his accuser. "I don't need buttresses, signore, because columns are taking their place. Even now, more sections are being cut in Carrara, and when they arrive, we will ring even the outside walls with columns. If you had taken the time to look closely at the roof, Basilio, you will see thick overhangs, especially at the point where the arches meet the interior walls. That, my friend, replaces the buttresses. The lateral stresses are accounted for."

Bramante huffed. "But the weight of the stone required to finish the dome—"

"I'll be using lighter material. Following Brunelleschi's path, after the first sixty feet in height, the entire dome will be made of bricks. Much lighter than stone."

Callisto smiled toward the others at the table. "I think that fairly answers the objection, don't you?"

All but Borroni nodded. He merely frowned.

"You have also charged the capomaestro with moral failure," said Callisto. "If you have any proof of this, I'd like to hear it."

Bramante cleared his throat and looked away from him. "This is a rather delicate matter, Signore Mancini, yet it must be addressed. I apologize in advance for this . . . but it concerns Puccini and your daughter."

His eyes narrowing, Callisto slapped both hands on the table. "Whatever you say, architect, you'd better have proof. If you malign my daughter . . ."

Bramante turned to the others on the Signoria. "I have it on good authority that, during the war with Naples, Puccini and Signore Mancini's daughter spent many months together at Mancini's Fair Fields estate. For much of that time, they were alone. During that period, she became pregnant. But the cad didn't marry her, and the poor girl went into a convent where she subsequently lost the child."

Amadeo stared at him, his face red. How could he?

Rossi focused on Callisto. "Is this true, signore?"

Callisto's jaw muscles tensed. "It is not." His gaze swept to the others at the table. "Some of you also have unruly children, so I know you will understand when I tell you Simona became pregnant in Avignon while staying with her aunt. Her aunt then insisted she return to Italy, and I agreed. This was during the war, and I had encouraged Amadeo to stay at my villa until the city was safe again. If I remember correctly, most of you also abandoned the city for your country estates." He wagged a finger at Amadeo's accuser. "This is a scurrilous charge, Bramante, and I do not appreciate your using my family's personal troubles as ammunition against your rival. You have overstepped your bounds."

"That explanation certainly satisfies me," said Dario Rossi.

Indeed, that man would be the last one to object to a charge of moral failure.

The other members of the Signoria also nodded.

"What about this last charge—that of bribery?" Ferata frowned at Bramante. "Please explain this."

"About ten years ago, the capomaestro ascended the stairs to the prison tower. The guard there had standing orders to refuse admittance to anyone who was not a friend or relative of the inmates. We can only speculate at the capomaestro's motives, but his relationship with the inmates was neither. So he gave the guard twenty florins and bribed his way in. Since then, he's regularly been going to the dungeon to visit the miscreants there while spreading similar bribes."

"This is outrageous." Amadeo rose to his feet. "Skender and I took bread, cheese, wine, and sometimes blankets to give to the prisoners. The first time when the guard let us in, he mentioned no one ever did anything for him and that he was in debt with no way to pay it. So I gave him twenty florins out of Christian charity."

"What about the guard in the dungeon?" asked Bramante, one thick brow rising.

"I do give him money each time I go. Otherwise, I couldn't go down. And I do give the head guard an occasional bottle of wine or a loaf of bread. But I benefit in no way from these visits. They are simple acts of charity. And, I might add, apparently customary."

The bishop frowned at Bramante. "Surely, you wouldn't begrudge the capomaestro the act of bringing gifts to the prisoners? Jesus, our Lord and Savior, admonishes us to do that very thing. And if, in the process, he's helped out a fellow Christian, even a guard, with an occasional gift of money or wine, I don't see how we could construe that as a bribe. Your charges are miserly and mean-spirited, signore. And, I might add—unchristian."

"Bramante, now that you've brought up the subject of professional incompetence." Callisto's face was still red. "When will you finish your endless water project? Long ago, you promised to complete it. Yet the years pass. And still, we wait."

Taken aback at the sudden turn of questioning, Bramante sputtered. "I–I've had difficulties keeping workers. N–no one wants to spend all day in the dark hacking through solid rock."

Callisto faced the Signoria's other members. "I move we dismiss these charges and end this meeting at once."

"I second that motion," said Ferata.

The others agreed.

Bramante only stared at Amadeo, spun on his heels, and stalked from the room.

CHAPTER 42

~ IN THE PALAZZO OF IL MAGNIFICO ~

JUNE 1489

The bedroom door creaked open, and Grazziano stepped inside. "Signore, you have a visitor."

Dario glanced up from the saddlebags he was packing for his trip. He was looking forward to several nights of wild revelry in Florence with Lorenzo. "Who?"

"Your former 'niece' whom you've transformed into a daughter. She's in the foyer."

Whirling away from the bed, he rushed down the hall and descended the stairs two at a time. He hadn't seen Letizia for seven years, ever since she'd run out of her mother's apartment on the Strada degli Innocenti and never returned. When his feet hit the bottom landing, he slowed.

Before him stood a slim woman in her late twenties with long, black hair and flashing eyes. How she'd grown! But her clothes were ragged at the edges, her face gaunt, and her hands red and raw.

"Letizia!" His voice echoed in the cavernous space. "How wonderful to see you!"

"I wish I could say the same—*Father.*"

The way she spat out the word *father* made him jump. "You shouldn't have disappeared, Letizia. I was willing to bring you into the palazzo to live with me. But are you eating? You look thin. How are you surviving?"

"I do fine for myself. I wash clothes for a rich merchant."

"Who?"

"You don't need to know."

Dario would find out. He would have her followed and, with a quiet conversation to her employer, ensure she was well taken care of. "Won't you come in and eat something? Please, stay awhile."

"No. I'm here to give you some news, and then I'm leaving. My mother, your lover"—tears welled up in her eyes, and her voice broke— "she's dead."

Dario grabbed the bedpost for support. "Savina, dead? How?"

"After you stopped sending her money, she returned to the streets and began selling herself again. She had no way to live . . . my mother." She faced away, tears wetting her cheeks. Then her gaze snapped back. "Two nights ago, one of her customers argued with her over payment for her . . . services. He became violent. Then he strangled her. The constable is looking for him now."

He released the bedpost and glanced at the floor. The last time he'd tried to contact Savina, she'd moved, and no one could tell him where she'd gone. He looked up. "It was her choice to return to that life, was it not? In the end, she was really nothing but a cheap whore."

Her face reddening, her tears drying up, Letizia narrowed her eyes at him. Fists clenched at her sides.

"I . . . I'm sorry, Letizia, I shouldn't have said that."

"I don't want your apologies. They're meaningless. I'll never again believe anything you say. All my life you lied to me. Everyone I cared about has lied to me. And now"—a sneer, too much like Savina's, flicked across her mouth—"sì, I think we should never see each other again. Don't try to find out where I work, because I'm looking for something different."

"What kind of work?"

"That's none of your concern."

"But I want to see you again . . . little flower. Please?"

"Don't ever call me that again. You've caused enough suffering and misery in my life. And for everyone whose life you've ever touched. I'm never going to see you again."

She spun on her heels and bolted through the door, slamming it.

He ran after her, followed her down the steps.

But she broke into a run and disappeared around the corner.

Entering the palazzo again, his feet seemed made of stone. For seven years, he hadn't seen her. And now she turned up only to say she'd never see him again.

Beside him, Grazziano shook his head. "What bitter crops we reap from seeds so thoughtlessly sown."

He whirled toward his servant, intending to rebuke him.

But Grazziano had turned his back and was striding away.

ON THE FIRST DAY OF his trek to Florence, Dario led his traveling group. Horses' tails swished at the flies, hooves clopped and raised dust on the road, and four city guards behind continued a never-ending cavalcade of bawdy jests. For the first ten miles, the capomaestro and Skender rode in the rear with Dario's two servants.

Dario let the guards take the lead and dropped back beside Puccini. He must find some diversion to take his mind off what Letizia had said. "Tell me, capomaestro, what draws you to Florence?"

"I'm looking for a great sculptor to do a major work for the center-piece behind the altar. I plan to visit a certain bottega, where I've heard Lorenzo de' Medici encourages talented sculptors."

"Capomaestro, I know the very place."

Beside them, strips of cane held grapevines to their wooden posts. The green rows of vine wound, layer after layer, around the hillside. Smoke rose from a farmhouse chimney in the valley below.

Dario smiled and went on, "I've walked through Lorenzo's sculpture garden in the Piazza San Marco, and I've met the bottega master. A promising young sculptor there by the name of Michelangelo Buonarroti is someone you should meet. His work is like none other."

"Thank you, gonfaloniere. While I'm there, I will seek him out."

"Please, call me Dario."

"All right . . . Dario. And what is your purpose for this trip?"

"To visit my friend Lorenzo. To do a bit of business. And perhaps to enjoy some of Florence's more exotic entertainments." Dario spun in the saddle to face him. "Where are you staying?"

"I will find a suitable inn."

"Oh, but you mustn't. I'm sure Lorenzo will put you up. His palazzo on the Via Larga has many guest rooms. And it's not far from San Marco."

Puccini sat, stiff and looking straight ahead, in the saddle. "I would not presume to—"

"Nonsense. When Lorenzo discovers the reason for your visit, he'll personally want to escort you to his sculpture garden. And Michelangelo also stays at his palazzo. But you'll have a hard time finding him there. He's almost always at the bottega."

"I'm in your debt . . . Dario."

"Think nothing of it. But now, ride with me up front. Another three days of travel lie ahead of us, and it wouldn't do for the illustrious capomaestro of Colpena's duomo to ride with the servants."

Puccini nodded—reluctantly, it seemed to Dario—and followed him to the front of the column, where they picked up the pace. Dario actually felt better at having just now done some good for someone. He smiled. Letizia was wrong in saying he caused misery and suffering in the lives of everyone he touched.

A bit later, he wondered if he could convince Puccini to join him and Lorenzo when they went out at night. But no. The capomaestro was too righteous. He would never let himself be led into any kind of sin.

Or would he?

THEIR HORSES' HOOVES CLOPPED TO a halt on the cobbles before the Palazzo Medici. Hot and dusty, Dario dismounted and handed a servant the reins. After the recent troubles, Lorenzo now posted two guards at both street entrances, and one ran inside to get their host. As Dario expected, Lorenzo warmly welcomed them both and insisted Puccini stay in the palazzo.

But when Lorenzo put the capomaestro in a room next to Dario's, a bit of confusion—or was it hesitation?—appeared to cross Puccini's face. Yet Puccini accepted.

Their second-floor rooms were spacious, each with a large window, an enormous fireplace, a four-poster bed, and a dresser. But without a hallway, to get to Dario's room required one to enter and leave doors on opposite sides of his room. Every room on the eastern wing was laid out thus. Privacy in the Medici palazzo was nonexistent.

That evening, after they'd washed and rested, the three of them ate in Lorenzo's upstairs dining room with Lorenzo's son, Piero, attending. While Dario and Lorenzo talked, Puccini sat unusually quiet. This was only the second time Dario had met Piero, and the youth was his usual morose self.

"What do you know about this preacher, Savonarola?" Dario queried his host. "I hear he's shaking things up."

"He'll come to a bad end, if you ask me," said Piero, speaking for the first time.

"Why is that?"

"Because he doesn't know his place. He will incite the *populo minuto* to violence and set them against us. And he values too much the Church's importance."

"But if he speaks for the Church, should we not listen to him?" Puccini also broke his silence for the first time. "Is not our first allegiance to Christ and his Church?"

Piero's glare was unsettling. Was he always that objectionable? "Our first allegiance is not to the Italian Church, but to family and business. I'd put them above all these corrupt priests, cardinals, and popes."

"How old are you, Piero?" The boy was getting on Dario's nerves.

"Seventeen."

"You should be careful when speaking with such certainty about matters as delicate as this. The Church needs our support, my youthful friend, because through them we are granted absolution from our sins. They may be corrupt. But then so are the rest of us."

"I doubt they can deliver on the promise to absolve anyone of their sins." Piero, his face hard and set, now focused his glare on Dario.

"Ah, but the pope says they can. And I believe this with all my heart."

"Anyone who believes such nonsense is a fool."

Dario took a deep breath. "Are you calling me a fool?"

"That's enough, Piero." Lorenzo raised a hand. "Please be civil."

"This man is an idiot." Piero pushed away from the table and faced his father. "His reputation precedes him, and if he is the bulwark of support for the Church, well—he proves my argument." He rose and stalked from the room.

When they were alone, Lorenzo apologized profusely. "I don't know what to do with him. He's often abrasive and lacks common social skills. What will happen when he takes over after me?"

Dario had no answer to that question. It had been on his mind recently as well. With Piero in charge, would Florence still be Colpena's staunchest ally?

After an uncomfortable silence, while Dario cooled his anger, Lorenzo spread his hands to placate his two guests. "Speaking of Savonarola, I think it's time I hear this new preacher. I understand he's quite entertaining. The day after tomorrow, he's preaching at San Marco. Would you two like to join me?"

Both agreed to accompany their host.

"Good. And tomorrow, Amadeo, I'll take you to my sculpture garden."

"I look forward to it."

After Puccini retired to his room for the evening, Dario turned to Lorenzo. "Do you want to go out tonight? I've been looking forward to this for some time."

Lorenzo tilted his head toward the floor, pursed his lips as if considering, but then smiled. "Why not? I haven't had a night out with that kind of fun for some time. You're a bad influence, Dario."

Dario smiled, and the two descended the stairs to the Via Larga, where Lorenzo turned right and led them to one of his favorite bordellos. But he limped most of the way. When Dario asked about it, Lorenzo admitted his gout was getting worse each year.

At the bordello, the young woman Dario was paired with left him sweaty but satiated. Afterward, he and Lorenzo visited a series of tavernas, where they consumed bottle after bottle of wine, more than Dario had drunk in weeks.

It was late when he finally staggered up the stairs and dropped, fully clothed and barely conscious, onto the bed.

CHAPTER 43

~ OF MARBLE AND GLASS ~

The next morning, Lorenzo led Amadeo to San Marco. Rossi, who had stumbled through his room late last night, had still not risen, and Amadeo thought Lorenzo appeared puffy-eyed and hungover. At the monastery, they walked the length of a long hall under a loggia into an oblong garden. Lorenzo guided him on a path toward a pool and fountain, where the statue of a boy pulling a thorn from his heel spouted water from his mouth.

"I bought this garden for my wife, Clarice. But she passed away, and now I've asked Bertoldo di Giovanni to use it as a school for sculptors. Follow me."

They stopped at the porch of a large building in the garden's center, where a number of young men worked at tables. Beside them, an open loggia enclosed the garden's walls, under which sculptors chipped at marble blocks.

A white-haired older man, so thin Amadeo thought he might blow away in a strong breeze, approached and held out a hand. "Welcome, Il Magnifico, to your bottega."

"It's your school, Bertoldo, not mine."

When they'd shaken hands, Lorenzo said, "This is Amadeo Puccini, the capomaestro building Colpena's duomo."

The old man's eyes widened. "And what brings you to a bottega dedicated to sculpture?"

"I'm looking for the best marble artist in the land. Colpena's duomo will be possibly the greatest ever built, and to carve the centerpiece behind the altar, I need someone of exceptional talent."

"You know who he should see?" Lorenzo winked.

Nodding, Bertoldo motioned for them to follow. Under the loggia's roof, he led them to where a young man held in his hands a mallet and chisel. Before him on a low table, a figure had nearly emerged from a block of white Carrara marble about four feet high. The sculptor slowly circled his work-in-progress, examining it from all angles.

Even though the statue was not yet complete, the figure of a woodland faun emanated power, grace, and beauty. Its hooves dug into a stump, and its naked body twisted back behind it, extending delicate fingers for a ripe cluster of grapes just out of reach. In the faun's face and eyes, Amadeo saw beauty, longing, and—impish joy? The work wasn't even finished, but the figure had already come alive. How could anyone make something so real out of nothing but a block of stone?

"Michelangelo," said Lorenzo, "I've brought someone who might be interested in commissioning a work from you."

"And if all your work is as impressive as this"—Amadeo waved at the faun—"then I've found whom I'm looking for."

When the young man turned, the plainness of his face—with its large nose, it could not be described as handsome—surprised Amadeo. But under a mop of curly dark hair, the eyes burned with intelligence.

After Amadeo explained the project, Michelangelo said, "How big will this centerpiece be?"

"At least seven feet tall, big enough so people in the back pews can see it. I'm envisioning the figure of Christ on the day of his ascension."

The sculptor's eyes brightened. "Sì, signore. I might be interested. But I cannot commit to anything until I've finished my work in progress here."

"Of course." Amadeo beamed. "Would you be willing to sign a contract today?"

Michelangelo looked to Bertoldo, who nodded. "Sì, signore. I will sign."

Sometime later, as Amadeo left the garden with his host, Amadeo clutched the contract to his breast. "I've never seen sculpture like that. He will breathe new life into everyone working on the project. Thank you, Lorenzo."

"Don't mention it. Buonarroti is one of my protégés. When he's not working, he has a room in my palazzo. But I rarely see him, because"—Lorenzo smiled—"he's always working."

When they entered the Palazzo Medici, Lorenzo went to look for Dario, and Amadeo excused himself. He had one more item of business to attend to in Florence.

Leaving Skender behind to shadow the palace's chef, he wended his way through narrow streets to a house on Via Benedetta. He knocked. A servant admitted him into a dark interior, leading him to a sitting room, where waited a thin, blond-haired man with a pointed goatee and pockmarked cheeks. Above him, a window with multicolored glass split the light, spewing a hundred colors across the floor.

After introductions, Amadeo pointed to the window. "Is that your work, Gervasio Fontana?"

"Sì, and to what do I owe the honor of a visit from the capomaestro of Colpena's grand duomo? I hear it will be a duomo to outshine all others."

"We approach the stage where I need a glass master. The clerestories in both transepts and the chancel are ready. And the praises of your work as master glassworker have reached my ears." Then he unrolled the parchments with the clerestories' diagrams.

When Fontana studied them, a smile as bright as the multicolored window above lit his face. "I've just returned from six years in Genoa, but I'm willing to pack my bags, gather my team, and begin at once. Marta"—he called to the other room—"bring cheese and wine. I have another commission."

As they ate, Amadeo explained that Fontana needed to hire more than one team. At first, he frowned, but then his face lit up. "My compatriot, Elmo Siciliano, is also looking for a commission. I believe I could convince him to join you."

"Good. Let us seal our agreement in writing."

Moments later, Amadeo and Fontana found a notary down the street and signed the contract.

On his way out, Amadeo passed his new master a small bag of florins. "Tell Siciliano I'll give him the same terms as you and I signed here today. Give him half of this as a down payment."

"I cannot wait to begin this work, signore."

They shook hands, and Amadeo left, happy to have concluded his business in Florence.

But as he turned a corner, one of the most beautiful women Amadeo had ever seen stepped out from an alley. Young, with a lithe, slim body and flowing black hair, she glided to a stop before him. Unlike those of the other prostitutes, her giornea was understated blue silk. When she blinked, her painted eyelids mesmerized, enchanted, and drew him in.

Against everything he believed in and stood for, he wanted her.

"Only two florins, signore?" she said. "And I'm yours for the afternoon."

He should have run. Instead, he stood there, unmoving, his heart beating faster. What would it be like to lie with a woman? With this woman? Who would know whether he spent the afternoon with her? For two florins, he could, for once in his life, be like other men. His desire for her rose up like a stream of water shooting from a fountain. But then he thought of Simona.

He took a step back.

"You want me. I can see that." She smiled, and he wanted her even more.

But he shook his head. He stepped aside and broke into a run. When he reached the corner, he looked back. She was still standing there, watching him.

He turned and walked fast toward the Via Larga.

THAT EVENING, A GRINNING ROSSI approached him in the upstairs stairway. "Would you care to join Lorenzo and me? We're going out to partake of this city's extraordinary nighttime pleasures."

For one frozen moment, Amadeo wanted to say yes. Tonight, he wanted to experience everything that Rossi did.

Rossi raised an eyebrow. "I can see you're considering it. Please come with us, Amadeo."

His fingers bit into his palms until they hurt. "No, gonfaloniere, I will not."

"Are you sure?" Rossi placed a hand on Amadeo's shoulder. "Would you not like a woman between your legs tonight?"

Again, he hesitated, wondering once more what it would feel like. But again, he shook his head no.

"Just this once? I won't tell anyone."

Amadeo whirled and pulled away from Rossi's hand. He raced to his room, entered, and dropped to his kness before the bed, his heart pounding.

Then he whispered, "Dear Lord, help me resist these carnal desires and this man who tempts me so. Forgive me, for tonight I do so much want to join him."

CHAPTER 44

~ SAVONAROLA ~

The next morning, Amadeo followed Rossi and his host inside the San Marco monastery. Above, the campanile's bells tolled, announcing the beginning of the service.

Rossi's eyes were red and puffy, and even Lorenzo appeared a bit dazed. Had either of them slept at all last night?

Colpena's ruler now wore an expensive red giornea, with ruffles, green and red calze on his legs, and a yellow jacket trimmed with gold thread. Fancy clothing for a visit to hear a preacher.

They joined the back of a large crowd swelling into every open space of the monastery's vast garden. Standing motionless beside a pulpit up on the dais, a black-caped man with a receding chin and a jutting nose peered down at folded hands, as if in prayer. Around Amadeo crowded nobles, merchants, laborers, monks, priests, and contadini. Too many people for the space.

Lorenzo, pushed ahead by the pressing bodies, turned back to Amadeo and Rossi. "My grandfather Cosimo rebuilt this monastery for the Dominicans. Before that, it was in terrible shape."

A voice from somewhere nearby answered. "That's what you can do when you've stolen all the power in the world and everyone else's money."

Lorenzo's glance searched the crowd for his accuser, but even Amadeo couldn't see who'd spoken with such disrespect for Il Magnifico, as many called him. In the crowd, people were constantly shifting for a better position, sending eager glances toward the dais. Its mood was watchful, tense, restless.

When the murmuring died down, Amadeo looked toward the caped figure at the far end.

"My friends," began the monk, "there are tyrants in this world who rule us, not by God's power, but by their own." Savonarola's voice boomed out with authority. "For far too long have they ruled the cities and lands of this earth, creating laws, not for the glory and expansion of God's kingdom, but for their own personal benefit. But if you wish to create good laws, first you must obey the laws of God, for all laws depend on eternal law."

Near Amadeo, the crowd stood mesmerized, hanging on every syllable. Amadeo himself felt a certain kinship with the man on the podium.

"The power held by the ruling classes has corrupted them. For every man is a weak vessel, and if the spirit of the living God does not inhabit his being, he will surely fall prey to and serve the Evil One. And such, I fear, is what has happened to those who rule us in this age."

Ahead of him, Amadeo could see Lorenzo shifting uncomfortably from foot to foot.

"This corruption has manifested itself in wanton and flagrant sins of the flesh. So debased have some of these men become, that they now take it as their right to lie with prostitutes; to lie with and sodomize each other; to attend glutinous feasts, getting drunk, while the common folk starve and go thirsty; to drape themselves in expensive jewelry, furs, silks, and linens. And all the while, they ignore the Word of God."

Rossi moved up beside Lorenzo, put a hand on his host's shoulder, and whispered something in his ear. Lorenzo shook his head and continued facing the podium. Rossi spun around as if to find an exit. But the bodies pressing in close trapped them. Even if they wanted to, there was no escaping this sermon.

"This corruption is like a plague spreading among us. It has infected the ruling classes and now even the Church—this Church that promises false absolution if only we will give them some of the florins we have earned by the sweat of our brows and the calluses of our hands."

From some of those around Amadeo came gasps, startled expressions. But others—the contadini and laborers—were murmuring approval and nodding their heads. Savonarola quickly left that subject and found a new target.

"This plague has even infected us, the common people. Who among us has not seen the new works of art, these paintings and sculptures that glorify human flesh and human sin? Who among us has not felt titillated with desire at their nakedness and their sinful themes? But where in all this art is God? Where is Christ? And who hasn't heard of the new books that fill the mind with fanciful tales and rhymes? Instead of glorifying our Maker, they only entice us further into our fallen human condition. Who among us has not coveted the fine silks, calze, plumed hats, and furs paraded so brazenly by the wealthy?

"Rubbish, I say! All of it is the Devil's rubbish, and we put up with it and want it only because our leaders have led us to believe in it, these leaders who feed an unholy obsession with the pleasures of the flesh and the possessions of this world. But this is not God's way . . ."

On and on like this, the message went. Amadeo never wanted it to end. By the time the preacher had finished, he was carried away, drinking in every word.

Savonarola was right. The ruling classes, people like Dario Rossi and Lorenzo de' Medici, had surely led them astray. They wallowed in their sins and thought nothing of it. And yesterday, Amadeo had felt temptation like never before. Was some of that Rossi's doing and Rossi's previous attempts to corrupt him? Or was it Amadeo's own carnal desire, finally rising up? A sinful desire that Savonarola blamed on corrupt authority?

Only with Savonarola's attack on the new art did Amadeo disagree.

Finally, the sermon ended.

Then from the crowd around him came excited voices from the peasants, heated arguments from the wealthy. He sensed a charged atmosphere, and the enthusiasm he'd felt only a moment ago morphed into a restless unease.

Had Savonarola just drenched the crowd with oil and lit a match to it?

Beside him, Rossi appeared shaken. His hands found the top of his head, and—was he trembling?

"I need to leave here," Rossi said to Lorenzo. "Now."

"I thought we could eat lunch at a small trattoria nearby."

A pale-faced Rossi shook his head. "I need to get out of here. I'll meet you later at the palazzo." Then he began worming through the masses toward the doors.

"The preacher seems to have affected him," said Amadeo.

"Sì. That man was not what I thought he'd be. Piero may be right. If he continues speaking in this manner, he's going to cause trouble. It wouldn't take much, and he could whip this crowd into violence. Some of what he said borders on . . . sedition." Lorenzo pointed Amadeo toward a far exit. "Follow me. Perhaps some wine and good food will get the taste of that rebel out of our mouths."

CHAPTER 45

~ THE BEGGAR ~

After Savonarola's sermon, Dario arrived back at the Palazzo Medici. But all he wanted to do was escape. The Dominican's message had left him with a pounding heart, a sweaty brow, and a creeping sense of doom. It was as if the man had crafted a sermon especially for him.

In his room, he grabbed a purse of gold florins and returned immediately to the Via Larga. Then he wandered aimlessly, always walking, not caring where he went.

Within the space of a week, Letizia had appeared, bringing news of Savina's death and blaming him for it. Then she said she hated him and would never see him again. Grazziano's words also rang in his ears, something about bitter crops and recklessly sown seeds. He'd certainly sown a lot of seeds. And most of the crop he was now reaping would be better left in the ground. Then today, of all days, Savonarola had pointed an accusing, damning finger straight at him. What's worse, the Dominican monk had said the Church could not absolve anyone of their sins.

Surely, the man was wrong. He had to be wrong.

These monks—Dominicans and Franciscans, alike—brought nothing but bad news.

Well past noon, he stopped at a trattoria, sat at a table, and ordered some bread, cheese, and a bottle of Chianti. He only nibbled at the bread but finished the bottle, then began walking again.

A beggar approached on the street. A festering sore marred one of his cheeks, and the stench of his unwashed body befouled the air for yards. Rotting, threadbare rags hung from his emaciated frame. Something black and putrid stained the man's entire front, and when he stuck out a grimy hand, pleading for alms, Dario recoiled. "Get away from me, beggar!"

As Dario scowled, the man shrank back, hung his head, and scuffled away. This city had too many beggars, and Colpena had the same problem. They should round them up and drop them somewhere far out in the country. When he returned home, he'd bring the matter up with the Signoria.

On the next street, brightly clothed women wearing high heels smiled, winked, and called to him. He chose the youngest and prettiest and went upstairs with her. But when she undressed and he saw the rash covering her belly, he suspected disease. He decided not to go through with it and left.

Back in the street, he wandered until late afternoon, ending in an unfamiliar part of the city by the farthest eastern wall. At a second taverna, he drank another bottle of wine, then continued roaming. Inside an open doorway, men with black beards and turbaned heads—North Africans?—sat on cushions, smoking from tall pipes. He entered a room filled with pungent, sweet-smelling smoke.

At first, the proprietor didn't want to admit him, but when Dario brandished more gold florins than the man probably made in a month, he was ushered to a seat. While the turbaned customers stared, the owner gave him a lump of something gooey and black and told him to place it in the pipe bowl. Dario followed instructions and lit the substance with a taper.

Moments later, he found himself in a kind of waking dream. The room swirled, its colors brightened, the sounds became softer, fuzzier, and when he thought of Letizia and Savina, he started to laugh. Suddenly, their plight didn't seem nearly as important as it had only moments ago.

He smoked all of the tiny brick and called for another. The proprietor frowned and shook his head, but Dario insisted. After finishing it, he weaved through the seated patrons and somehow floated back onto the street. Nothing seemed to matter anymore, not his daughter, not Savonarola, not even doom itself. When another beggar approached and asked for alms, he laughed and spat in the open hand.

Evening had long ago fallen, and Dario wandered slowly, aimlessly, through torch-lit streets until his feet took him to another taverna. Plopping himself at a table, he quickly drank another bottle of wine. But when he got up to leave, he could barely walk, and the buildings' shadows swirled, darkened, and became grotesque. The torches reaching out from their wall sconces threw starbursts before his eyes.

Staggering into a narrow quintana between houses, he collapsed, senseless, onto the cobbles.

He woke, shaking, huddled in a ball in a dark alley. From the main street beyond, light streamed in, hurting his squinting eyes, illuminating a square near the entrance. Beneath him, cold stone pressed against a bare left shoulder and arm, against bare buttocks and a leg. His hands slid down shivering thighs. He was naked! Some kind of rough fabric lay over him. He grabbed a handful of cloth stiff with grime and swiftly released it.

Rags! Someone had stolen his clothes and left him naked under filthy beggar's rags. His hands groped around the stones for his purse, but of course, it, too, was gone. Something bit him on the arm. Fleas!

He tried to stand, but fog swelled his head, tried to get out. Staggering, he placed a hand on the wall for support. Suddenly, he felt ill. He dropped to the ground and retched.

Kneeling on all fours, naked and trembling in the shadows, with a violent tremor slithering up and down his body, he retched again.

Apparently, all he had to wear now were these filthy, flea-infested rags lying on the quintana floor. He couldn't walk naked into the streets.

A family of rats scurried to his right, and he shrank back.

What choice was there? He reached down and pulled the beggar's garment over his head. Its stench was unbearable, but it was all he had. Stiff with dirt and grime, something black and putrid had stained the whole of its front.

Oh no!

These were the very rags belonging to the disgusting beggar he'd passed only yesterday.

He imagined how, back at the palazzo, he'd have the servants fill a tub with hot water and scrub his skin until it was raw. Only then did he feel the itching from the fleabites. While he slept, they must have feasted on his face, arms, and legs.

He touched a painful spot on one cheek where they must have sucked all night. But then he realized the wound was too deep. Something bigger had bitten him there. A rat?

Hunger wrenched his stomach. Yesterday, he'd eaten only a light breakfast and just nibbled at the food he'd bought. The rest of his nourishment had been liquid. After retching, his stomach was now empty. He was hungrier than he could ever remember.

Where were the beggar's sandals? He searched everywhere but—nothing. He was as far from the Palazzo Medici as he could get. He'd have to walk barefoot most of the city's length.

Shuffling from the alley, he emerged into a street full of people. Instantly, those around him recoiled and backed away. Upon seeing him, the expressions of the young couples dressed in their new calze, expensive cioppas, and gamurras changed to sneers, revulsion, disgust. One man, a green-robed priest, threw a coin at his feet before holding his nose and hurrying off.

Dario picked up the silver fiorino and held it in his palm. What could he buy with a nearly worthless fiorino?

Moving on, he found the going slow and painful. He'd barely gained two blocks when the rough cobbles had cut the tender soles of his feet. Jutting cobblestones twice stubbed his toes. With injured feet, his progress became slower yet. At this rate, how would he ever cross the city before nightfall?

An old woman hunching along in better rags saw him, stilled, and threw another silver fiorino at his feet. Silver fiorinos. Nearly worthless coins.

He considered telling someone who he really was. But no one would believe him. His only hope was to reach the palazzo before dark.

But his feet hurt so badly, he couldn't walk. Plus, he must have slept through most of the day, because the sky was already darkening. And with half the city still to cross, he'd never make Lorenzo's palazzo tonight.

Hunger and thirst so gripped him, he became lightheaded. He pulled out the few coins he had. Was it enough to buy a hunk of bread?

A woman with a jade necklace, wearing a fur gamurra, saw his open palm, wrinkled her nose, and stopped. "Beggar, when was the last time you ate?" The instant she spoke, he recognized her. This was the wife of the master of Florence's Wool Guild. Last year, he'd met her at a party Lorenzo had thrown. She'd drunk too much wine and had even flirted with him while her husband scowled from the corner. He mustn't let her recognize him.

"Two days ago." He hunched down and tried to disguise his voice.

"Here." Careful not to touch his palm, she dropped another silver fiorino into his hand and hurried off.

This was now enough for some bread and cheese and some cheap wine. He took his money to the nearest trattoria and plopped into a seat at an outdoor table.

The proprietor rushed over, waving and crying out. "Get out. Go away. You cannot eat here."

"But I have money." He held up his open palm.

"I don't serve your kind here." The man hit Dario's hand, flinging the coins into the street.

Falling to his hands and knees, Dario scrambled after them. He needed that money. If he didn't eat soon, he didn't know how he could go on.

When he'd retrieved the coins, he limped farther until he found a street vendor willing to sell him half a loaf of stale bread, a small wedge of cheese, and half a bottle of cheap white wine. But three silver fiorinos was too high a price for what he got.

Clutching his purchases, Dario shambled off into an alley and slumped down. He scraped as much mold from the cheese as he could. As his teeth bit into the bread, tearing off huge chunks, he sighed. He followed this with guzzles of wine and bites of cheese. When he'd finished the bottle, he curled up and slept.

The next morning, he hobbled through bustling markets and streets busy with vendors and buyers. Everywhere he went, people shrank from him, threw him sneers, and wrinkled their noses. Once, a crowd of children followed, pelting him with garbage and stones. He grabbed a vendor's broom. And, with the man following and yelling, "Thief!", he hobbled after the urchins until they scattered.

It was nearly noon when he stumbled down Via Larga and reached the gates of Palazzo Medici. He breathed out his relief. Finally.

He stepped up to the guard at the door.

"Where do you think you're going, beggar?" queried the burly man with a stubbled face. Brass armor covered his chest, and one hand held a six-foot pike topped with a jagged point.

"Don't you know me? I'm Dario Rossi, gonfaloniere of Colpena. I'm Lorenzo's guest."

Both guards burst out laughing. The burly man was barely able to hold his spear for his mirth. "And I'm the Count of Bologna in costume. Get along now. We don't allow beggars on this street."

"You will let me inside the palazzo"—he tried to stand up straight—"or you'll regret it."

The guard shoved the point of the pike toward Dario's gut. "At first, it was good for a laugh, beggar. Now you need to leave."

"I'm not leaving until you call my host, Lorenzo de' Medici, to the door."

The first man said to his companion, "Should we get the constable?"

The second guard, a young blond-bearded man in his twenties, added his spear to his companion's. "If I was you, beggar, I'd be getting off this street before we puts you in the Stinche."

"B–but I'm the—"

The second man's spear pressed into his chest. Then the first guard clamped a viselike hand around a fistful of his rotten tunic and, after at first ripping a bit of the stiff fabric, dragged him down the street. A hundred feet later, the guard shoved him so hard Dario fell face-first toward the gutter. He scraped his hands on the stones to keep from hitting his head.

"If you come back, you're going to the Stinche." Then the guard left.

Shaking all over, Dario drew himself to a sitting position. This was intolerable. In his present condition, how was he ever going to convince anyone who he was? Those guards would pay for this. As would that beggar now walking around in Dario's expensive clothes.

Too exhausted to move, not knowing what to do or where to go, he sat motionless and cross-legged on the street corner. Passersby crossed the street on the opposite side to avoid him. He had no money. He was starving. Giving up, he actively started begging. Two people dropped silver fiorinos. But as evening approached, he received no more, not even enough to fill his stomach.

Facing yet another night on the streets in filthy rags with an empty stomach, he rubbed the bottoms of his aching feet. When he brought his fingers back, they were red.

"God," he said to the sky, "I curse you. I damn you for bringing me to this."

A minute later, footsteps pounded down the street and slowed in front of him. Fearing someone had called the constable but too tired to run, he raised weary eyes.

"Dario?" came Lorenzo's bewildered voice. "Is that you?"

"W–what's happened to you?" Puccini stood beside Lorenzo, his face twisted in disbelief and disgust.

"I–I passed out in an alley. Then I was robbed."

"Help me get him up," said Lorenzo.

By the time they traversed the Via Larga back to the palazzo and passed the fearful, effusive apologies of the two guards, Dario's feet were bleeding again.

Upstairs, servants prepared a tub with hot water and soap. As he scrubbed himself and downed bites of fresh bread, Sicilian cheese, and aged prosciutto, Dario heard how Lorenzo had sent men to search every bordello and taverna in the city for his missing guest.

"You're over forty years old, Dario, and you're the gonfaloniere of your city." Lorenzo frowned. Beside him, Puccini sat inside the guest room, shaking his head. "And look what you've done to yourself. Having a bit of fun is one thing, but this"—he waved a hand toward the flaming pile of rags the servants had thrown into a nearby brazier—"this is beyond the pale."

Dario stopped scrubbing long enough to take the glass of wine from the bench beside him. Before he drank, his gaze found Puccini's.

The capomaestro was staring at him. Suddenly, Dario hated the man with a passion so great, the goblet nearly slipped from his hands.

Puccini, the righteous.

Puccini, the celibate.

Puccini, the man who'd never be caught lying with a woman, who'd never stagger drunk through the streets.

Puccini, the man who'd dedicated his life to serving the Church through his work—his excellent, perfect work.

Puccini, who selflessly brought food and blankets to prisoners.

Someday, Dario would find his weakness. And then Dario would bring him down.

CHAPTER 46

~ A SUMMER EVENING ~

AUGUST 1491

Late on a hot August afternoon, Amadeo entered one of the new workshops Pugliesi had built on Colpena's Piazza del Duomo for Gervasio Fontana, the master glassworker. The second glass master, Elmo Siciliano, and his team occupied another workshop next door. Inside Fontana's shop, even the open shutters couldn't dissipate the kiln's heat. On a huge, whitewashed table, Gervasio had drawn the details of a single stained-glass window on what he called a cartoon. This cartoon showed John, Mary, and Peter kneeling at the foot of the cross. The picture was broken into small sections, with a code indicating the color for each.

After nodding in greeting, Gervasio reached thick gloves into the kiln and pulled from it a red-hot iron knife. A sheet of glass with its sections already outlined in white lay on another table. With the hot iron point, Gervasio began cutting along the lines until he'd separated a piece.

At another table, assistants used grozing irons to further shape previously cut pieces to the exact forms required. Farther down, more assistants painted the pieces in colors of azure, violet, ink black, jade green, and sunflower yellow.

"Gervasio," said Amadeo, "what's in your paint that makes it so brilliant?"

"Ground glass, wine, and pigments that are a trade secret. But as you can see, those jewels"—he pointed to a pile of brilliant blue gems—"are sapphires. We'll grind them and mix them into a few sections. Then they'll sparkle like no color you've ever seen. When we fire the pieces in the kiln, the paint melts and merges with the glass. Sometimes we also paint the back to give it shading and depth."

At a final table, young apprentices added lead strips to fit together hundreds of painted and kiln-fired glass shapes to form a single stained-glass window for the clerestory. Each windowpane was six feet by twelve. Once complete—like the other five panes Gervasio had finished and the four done by Elmo—all would be disassembled and reassembled on the duomo floor. Then workers would carefully raise the final panes into position.

"I'm impressed, Gervasio. Is there anything more you need?"

"A cool breeze would be nice."

Amadeo smiled. "I'll ask for one tonight."

He left the workshop and strolled across the piazza, stopping in the space where the duomo's future doors would go. Inside, the clerestory walls for the nave were finished. Even now, carpenters were erecting the nave roof.

The front was ready to receive the façade. The eight columns for the arcades in the nave, four on each side, rose eighty feet, with their arches extending to meet the walls. The place was finally looking like a real cathedral.

Strolling three hundred and sixty feet across the dirt, he reached the dome's center. Soon, workers would lay a temporary terra-cotta floor over the dirt.

From now on, the dome and the façade must be Amadeo's main focus. With the first sixty feet of stone complete, the dome was ready for the masons to start laying bricks.

In the forest, two new kilns were already firing bricks for the dome. Amadeo had made frequent trips there to ensure the brickmakers followed his orders precisely. He needed so many different kinds and shapes of bricks—triangular, rectangular, flanged bricks, dovetailed bricks, bricks with odd angles—that he'd had a barrel maker construct dozens of wooden molds.

To make the bricks, laborers would tread barefoot on vats of river clay until it had the right consistency. The resulting paste was molded with forms, seasoned, and sent to the kilns.

The kilns were heated so hot, it took two weeks for the ovens to cool down. Only then could they remove a load. Each firing created 20,000 bricks, with three weeks between firings.

It was late, and after a long day's work on the dome, workers were already emerging from the bottom of the spiral steps and heading for their quarters.

Amadeo exited through the back and made his way to the Strada delle Campane and his first-floor apartment. Pushing through the doors, he was greeted with the sound of silence. Skender should be making dinner. Something was wrong.

"Skender?" he called.

"Skender's not here." He knew the woman's voice from the garden.

"Simona?" Walking through the hall, he stopped when she came into view. Tonight, she'd abandoned her habit and wore only a simple frock. Her hair was cut short in the manner of all nuns.

"Sì, signore." She smiled and bowed demurely.

"B–but why are you—"

"I was sent on a mercy mission up the coast and came back early. No one knows I'm here. Tonight, we're going to have dinner out. Together."

"B–but . . . where's Skender?"

"Didn't you know? For some time, he's had his eye on a girl living upstairs. I gave him the night off and encouraged him to take her on an evening stroll."

"He told you about Maria?"

"Sì."

He smiled. In only one afternoon, Simona had discovered what it had taken Amadeo months to eke from his servant. "Aren't you breaking convent rules?"

She cast him an impish grin and raised one eyebrow. Even at forty, she held a girlish charm, a playful spirit. The convent didn't seem to have changed that.

"It will be a lovely evening for a walk and a meal outside, don't you think? Freshen up if you need to. Tonight, I'm going to dally with you as long as I want. And I don't know anything about convent rules. Do you?"

Amadeo smiled and went to his room to wash.

THEY ATE IN A SMALL trattoria catering to visiting merchants down by the southeastern dock. Accompanied by a local red wine and frequent glances into each other's eyes, the meal—cooked Spanish-style, with garlic, red pepper, parsley, chicken, shrimp, and octopus over rice—was delicious. The late-August sea breeze cooled his skin. Overhead, seagulls circled and cried to each other in the dying light.

When they'd finished eating, Simona slid a hand across to his and squeezed.

"Aren't you afraid someone will see you?" he said.

"Who, me?" She laughed. "Without my habit, no one will recognize me. None of the nuns come up to Colpena. They're all locked in their chapel or saying prayers in their rooms."

"What has it been like for you there?"

"You've asked me that before. I don't want to talk about it." She frowned and pulled her hand back. "Let's say . . . I'm enduring it."

He peered at his empty plate. What would his life—and hers—have been like if he'd married her long ago? Now here she was, after so many years, pretending as if nothing had changed, as if they could still be together. He reached across and again cradled her hand in his. He liked the feeling of her warmth melding with his.

Smiling, she caught his gaze.

But who cared what had happened before this moment? Tonight, he was with her, and all the years seemed to fall away. He'd spent so much energy looking to his eternal future, now that he was with her, every moment seemed precious, beyond price.

Sometimes he envied Dario Rossi. Right now, why not live for the moment, grab every pleasure, every bit of life while he still could? "I'm glad you stopped by to spend tonight with me. It's been a . . . a long time. I've really enjoyed it."

She nodded but said nothing. Her eyes appeared moist. Were those tears forming?

"Come," he said, rising. "Let's go for a walk."

"I'd like nothing better."

He paid, and they walked onto the wharf, where seven of Rossi's merchant ships sat at anchor, more than he'd ever seen for this time of year. Rumor had it that the shipping business was again in trouble, with some of their orders returning to Pisa, Livorno, Piombino, and Genoa. But tonight, who cared?

"What's to become of us?" asked Simona as they neared the jetty's end.

"What do you mean?"

"I'm forty years old. There's only one person in the world I ever really wished to marry, and he's—"

"Chaste." He focused on the harbor waves washing against the pilings. Was it worth it? All those years of dedication to God's work. All those years of denying himself what other men took for granted and sought so earnestly—the love and companionship of a woman. Was it even the right thing to do?

"And now." She laughed again. "Now I, too, have taken a vow of chastity. Isn't that something? Isn't that—"

Suddenly, she whirled toward him and looked deeply into his eyes. The moment hung, suspended in midair. Her hands grabbed his head, and her lips moved toward his. Then they kissed.

The heat from her lips, the force behind her desire, energized him and filled him with longing. He didn't pull away, didn't ever want to pull away. Instead, he embraced her and kissed her back.

When they parted, he was breathing heavily, and his heart was beating faster. He peered into her pupils, searching. He kissed her again.

They separated, staring into each other's eyes, his hands wrapped around her back.

"It's time to return." He mustn't let this go any further, or he didn't know where it would end—ah, but he did know, didn't he? And he couldn't let that happen. "Where will you stay tonight?"

"I should return to the convent."

He agreed, and they began the trek back up the Via del Porto, holding hands all the way, his heart thumping in his chest.

When they reached his house on Strada delle Campane, only flickering torchlight lit the street. From somewhere nearby, a man plucked strings on a lute. She entered, then emerged from a back room, once again wearing her habit. "Keep these for me, will you?" She passed him the simple frock she'd used to shed her identity as a nun.

He accompanied her to the door. Outside, the cicadas competed with the lute player.

"This is goodbye."

"Sì." He held both her hands. "If you can, please come again."

Her gaze snapped up. "I will, Amadeo. I will."

He wanted to kiss her again, but the nun's garb was inhibiting. "Goodbye, Simona." He squeezed her hands.

She let go of his grip, stepped through the door, and spun back. "Goodbye, Amadeo."

CHAPTER 47

~ THE END OF AN ALLY ~

MAY 1492

Hunching against the wind and rain, Dario crossed the shifting dock and boarded *The Saint Anne*, one of the new, sleek, four-masted galleys. As a crewman ushered him to an open hatch, the hull creaked and moaned, and the ropes ground back and forth in their moorings. A late-spring storm had blown in, rocking the ships anchored at the dock.

A sudden burst of rain pattered across the deck behind him as he descended the ladder and stepped into the cabin. Before him waited Aldo and Bettino Scutari, the emissary and part-time spy he'd sent to Florence weeks ago.

"What news, Bettino?" asked Dario, wiping rain from his forehead. "It's been a month since I expected your return."

The thin, middle-aged man wearing a floor-length gray giornea shook his head. "Bad tidings, signori. Bad indeed. Lorenzo de' Medici is dead."

Dario reached his hand to the bulwark for support. Lorenzo, dead? His friend, mentor, and Colpena's strongest ally—dead? He found a seat and, aided by the deck's sudden shifting, plopped into a chair. "What happened?"

"He took sick with the gout over a month ago and retreated to his estate at Careggi. I was stuck in Florence, unable to learn what happened until recently."

"What about the loan?" Aldo questioned. "Did you get him to sign anything before—?"

"No. The gout was so bad, when he was still in Palazzo Medici, no one would let me see him. But you need to hear about the omens preceding his death. Very bad, these omens."

"What are you talking about?" Dario frowned.

"Two weeks before he left for Careggi, the city's lions in their cage under the town hall's loggia mauled each other to death. That same day,

279

a new lantern had been installed atop the dome of Santa Maria del Fiore. But that night, lightning struck the lantern, knocking one of the marble balls from its perch. The ball crashed to the street and shattered on the northwest side, the side pointing to Lorenzo's house."

"Bad omens, indeed," whispered Aldo.

"Sì," said Bettino. "But the news only worsens. After Lorenzo died, his son, Piero, immediately claimed his father's position. He's calling in all the family's debts. Instead of granting us a new loan, he insists we pay back the one his father gave us—at once."

Dario shifted to Aldo. "Can we pay it?"

"No." Aldo waved at the emissary. "Thank you, Bettino. You may go."

When the two were alone in the cabin, Dario lowered his head into his hands. "This is terrible. What's the state of our business?"

"I've told you before, cousin, but you don't listen. I wish you'd take more interest in this. Our shipping business has been declining for years, and the duomo's expenses just keep mounting. They're eating us alive."

"We need to keep funding it. That expense is not negotiable."

Aldo shook his head. "The only thing I can think of is to return to piracy."

Dario looked around the cabin. "Is that why we're meeting here?"

"Sì. Do you agree that must be our next step?"

Dario closed his eyes and sighed. What else could they do? He nodded.

Leaving through the door, Aldo returned a moment later leading a short, blond-bearded man with a weather-beaten face. "This is Captain Cleto Violante, and he's expressed an interest in working for us. I've already explained what we need from him."

Dario shook his hands. "And what wages would you be asking, Captain Violante?"

"Why, thank the stars you asked, signore." When Violante smiled, one of his front teeth was missing. "When we've settled accounts, I'd be wanting ownership of this here vessel, *The Saint Anne*. Mighty fine name for a privateer, don't you think? Ownership and one-half of all booty captured."

"One-third, only." Dario arched a glance to his cousin. "Who owns this ship?"

"We do," said Aldo. "Captain Violante has been sailing it for us for years."

Dario turned back to the seaman. "One-third, only. And you must rename it and make it over to look like a different vessel. Your crew must not know you work for us. You must find different men. Foreign men."

"Sì, I will take it to Barcelona and recrew there. That will be my base."

"You agree to a third of the booty?"

Violante scowled, scratched his beard, but nodded.

"And you must not return to Colpena after your voyages," said Aldo. "Sell the booty and deposit the funds with the Rossi Bank branch in Barcelona. That way, no one can trace it back to us."

"That I can do."

"Then we have an agreement," said Dario. "But one more thing. We need the money fast. I authorize you to prey on anything that moves on the water—except if it's one of our ships. Or if it's Genoese or Venetian. We don't want a fight with Genoa's or Venice's navy. Can you do that?"

Violante grinned. "That I can do, signori."

They shook hands, and the captain left. Outside, the rain spattered against the creaking hull.

"How can we trust this man to give us two-thirds of the booty?" Dario rubbed his forehead.

"We can't. Let's just hope that what we receive makes up for our lost income."

"And that our shipping business picks up." He stood and went to the door. Before he left, he spun back. "What about Piero's demand for repayment? Can we hold him off?"

"For a while. He's certainly not making any friends by calling in his father's loans. I doubt he's going to get it all back."

"Aldo"—Dario shook his head—"I fear we've lost a great ally in Lorenzo."

His cousin nodded. "Without Florence's backing, who will keep Siena's army from our doorstep?"

"I don't know."

They left the cabin for the rain-washed deck.

Two months later, Dario was pleased to receive a shipment of ten thousand gold ducats, the settlement of a deposit Captain Violante made in Barcelona. Apparently, three French merchant ships had been waylaid off the coast of Corsica by an unknown privateer. With more prizes expected in the months to come, he told Aldo he was going to put half in the strongbox under his office floor.

"I think Captain Violante is honoring his part of the bargain," he told Aldo. "Perhaps he's the best investment we ever made."

CHAPTER 48

~ THE ATTACK ~

NOVEMBER 1494

Just as Dario was about to leave Palazzo Rossi for a night at his favorite bordello, a breathless Bettino Scutari rushed into the foyer.

"Did you just arrive from Florence?" asked Dario.

"I did, signore. Once again, I bear bad news."

Dario closed his eyes. He feared what his spy would say next. "About the French?"

"Sì, they've defeated the Neapolitan army at Rapallo. It was a total rout. King Alfonso is fleeing back to Naples."

For two months, all Italy had been abuzz with news that the French king, Charles VIII, had led an army of hardened warriors, accompanied by the vaunted Swiss Guard, across the Alps into Tuscany.

Hearing the seasoned fighters of northern Europe—they even had cannons—had decimated the Neapolitan force came as no surprise. The Italian version of warfare was to hire mercenaries who postured, positioned, and outmaneuvered. But when it came to real battles . . .

Aldo ran in from the street. "Did you hear the news? The talk is all over town." Only then did Aldo notice Bettino.

Dario waved to the emissary to continue.

"After the French victory"—Bettino shook his head—"their army overran the garrison at Fivizzano and put everyone there to the sword. Piero, the fool, rode into the enemy camp and tried to negotiate with the French, but the mission was a disaster."

"In what way?"

"He capitulated, handing over the cities of Pisa and Livorno, getting nothing in return. When he returned to Florence, the Signoria was so angered, they refused to let him into the town hall. Instead, they rang the bells of the campanile. Crowds gathered and turned ugly. The end

283

result—Piero was forced into exile. The Medici family rules Florence no longer."

"Piero, gone?" Aldo was smiling. "Then we can forget about our debt to him."

"The same thing others said after his departure." Bettino nodded. "But when I saw that even the servants were abandoning Palazzo Medici, I took a room at a nearby inn. Days later, crowds ransacked the palace. Fearing they'd torch the building, the Signoria took it over. Then the Signoria itself looted the place of all its treasures."

Dario thought of all the paintings, sculptures, and the extensive library of ancient literature Lorenzo and his father had collected over the decades. What a staggering loss! But perhaps the Signoria would safeguard what they stole. "I'm guessing that isn't the end of your tale?"

"Eight days after Piero's flight, Charles occupied the city with twenty thousand soldiers. He rode in wearing golden armor and a crown atop his head. The Signoria caved to his every demand, including a fine of one hundred and fifty thousand florins to finance the occupation. Throughout, I hid in my room, fearing the soldiers who roamed everywhere. About two weeks later, the army left, headed for Naples."

"But that means . . ." Aldo's eyes widened.

"They'll march down the coast road. Right past us." Dario could feel the blood draining from his face.

"But they're traveling slowly," said Bettino. "And they may forage a bit through the country, stripping the farms of livestock and the orchards, vines, and fields. I'm guessing they won't show up here for at least two weeks."

"Will they lay siege?" asked Aldo. "Or demand a ransom?"

Bettino only shrugged.

"With Piero gone, who's running Florence?" Dario rubbed his temple.

"The Signoria says it's in charge, but everyone now looks to Savonarola. His latest sermon attracted fourteen thousand people. He continues attacking the ruling classes, blaming their decadence and mismanagement for the city's current troubles. He says the French invasion is God's revenge. I'm guessing he'll soon be ruling the city."

"Never," said Dario. "He'll bring it to ruin."

"More so than now?" Bettino gave him a wry grin.

"You arrived by ship?" Aldo questioned.

"Sì, and as we left the dock at Pisa, French soldiers were pouring into the city from the north, and French ships were filling the horizon."

"The French navy?" Dario's breath quickened. "How many vessels?"

"Too many to count. Rumor has it that their fleet captured a number of Italian merchant ships and conscripted them. They also recently sank a pirate ship with all hands aboard. As a result, the captain of our merchantman was in such a hurry to sail, he left a quarter of his cargo on the dock."

"From where did that pirate ship hail?" asked Dario.

"Spain, I believe."

Dario exchanged glances with Aldo. It could belong to none other than Captain Violante. Had they just lost another source of income?

Bettino opened his hands in apology. "I wish I could have brought better news."

"Thank you, emissary," said Dario. "We appreciate what you've learned. Of late, the news from up north has been sparse."

Bettino nodded and left.

Dario faced his cousin. "We should have hired mercenaries to protect the city."

"It's too late for that now, isn't it?"

"Sì." Dario closed his eyes and rubbed his temples. "We must fortify the northern wall as much as possible. And station the city guard on the ramparts."

"What if we arm the citizens?"

"Laborers and merchants? Armed with swords, spears, and knives against a real army?" Dario shook his head. "The French army is professional. They have cannons. And if they lay siege, we'll quickly run out of water." He slammed a fist into a palm and swore. "Bramante and his endless water project. Now is when we'll need that water the most."

"What if we put Puccini on improving the fortifications? No one would be better at it."

"Sì, our task now must be to defend the city against the French."

It was late afternoon when the Signoria met in an emergency session and made their request to Amadeo. "But I'm not a defense engineer." He gripped the top of his head and shook it. "I'm a builder of cathedrals and a painter."

"If the French take the city," said Callisto, "they'll loot it, rape our women, and set it ablaze. Then your cathedral will have no workers, no one to worship inside it, and no city to support it. You are the only choice to be master of our defense works. Take the job, Amadeo."

Reluctantly, he agreed. Having walked the wall's length many times, he already knew what was needed.

"The northern perimeter"—he faced the Signoria—"where the city wall borders the land bridge with the mainland—that's the weakest point. That's where they'll attack."

"Can you bolster it?" Callisto wore his usual, understated merchant's robe.

"With a lot of help. But I can do nothing about protecting the spring. It's too far outside the walls." Bramante's project would have created an underground link to the spring, hidden from any besieging enemy. Long ago, the walls should have been extended to encompass their only source of water. Now, it was too late.

"We'll put everyone in the city at your disposal, capomaestro," said Callisto. "If the French breach the walls . . ." He shook his head.

"I understand. I'll do my best."

Amadeo spent the next weeks in furious activity, none of it on the duomo.

While Bramante was ordered to hasten his water project, the entire city became laborers under Amadeo's command. He put the duomo workforce—now at one thousand strong, plus the city's shopkeepers, prostitutes, merchants, and laborers—to the task of making cheap bricks from pounded earth mixed with cattle dung and marsh reeds. With these hastily constructed, unfired bricks, his masons constructed an additional five-foot layer on the northern perimeter's outer wall.

The masons also added another ten feet to the wall's height. For a hundred yards to the west and east of the land bridge, the walls already rose directly from the sea. So by bolstering a single three-quarter-mile section of wall, he was able to present a formidable defense against any land attack. That attack would most certainly be preceded by a cannon barrage.

Their greatest weakness lay in an assault from the sea, from small boats loaded with troops rowing across the bay. But without a great number of small craft to ferry those troops, that approach seemed unlikely.

Three weeks after dedicating themselves to fortifying the walls, the enemy still had not yet arrived. They'd obviously taken their time in pillaging the countryside.

Now he walked atop the northern ramparts, inspecting the finished work with Callisto beside him.

"As usual, you've done an impossible task in a short amount of time, capomaestro." Callisto looked over the edge at the new layer of thick, earthen bricks.

"But is it enough to stop a cannon barrage?"

"We'll soon find out. Our scouts report that the enemy will arrive tomorrow."

As the bells in the town hall's campanile tolled without ceasing, Dario looked out from the city's northern wall at the troops massing on the flat and gasped. Never had he seen so many soldiers in one place. Just when he thought the flow would stop, another banner led in yet more men. The noise of clinking armor, neighing horses, and rumbling wagons silenced even the cicadas.

Beside him on the wall walk stood most of the Signoria and Puccini, their new master of defense. Dario was grateful for Puccini's expertise, but it galled him that the capomaestro was receiving so many accolades for his work. Wasn't it Dario's money that supported the city in this dreadful hour? Shouldn't Colpena's citizens offer just as much appreciation to their gonfaloniere and padrone?

Stretched thin all along the northern wall on both sides of him stood the city guard. Since the chaos a few years ago, they'd increased the numbers to three hundred. But what was that compared with the thousands upon thousands of seasoned soldiers massing on the plain below?

Three men bearing a white flag approached the main gate. One called up for a parlay. Dario, Borroni, and Callisto—the war council assigned by the Signoria—left the wall, descended the steps, and entered the tunnel under the barbican between the inner and outer portcullises.

A guard creaked open the wall of heavy iron bands forming the outer gate. Just outside the safety of the tunnel, Colpena's war council met the enemy delegation by torchlight.

"What do you want?" Dario crossed his arms.

The leader—his legs and arms wrapped in sparkling chain mail, his chest covered with shining brass—put hands on hips. A sneer lifted one corner of his mustache. "I bring a demand from King Charles VIII, king of France. We have sunk the privateer in your employ and captured your Captain Violante. The king wishes you to know that, but for the crime that Violante admitted under torture, we would have bypassed your city. We now know it was your city that's been preying on our supply ships."

Borroni whirled to face Dario, his jaw muscles tensing.

Callisto shook his head and scowled.

"We deny the charge," said Dario. "I ask you again, what do you want?"

"We demand that you open the city gates and let us in. You must also pay a fine of twenty-five thousand ducats for the loss of our supply ships. In return, we'll spare the lives of your Signoria and your Council of Thirty. That's all we can promise."

Dario's face became hot. His hands formed into fists. "Open the gates so your men can rape, kill, and plunder our fair city? Never. Tell your King Charles—never!"

"Then so be it." The knight stalked back to the grassy flat, where waited the French host.

When they were safely inside the barbican, Borroni grabbed Dario's arm and pressed him up against the wall. "What have you done, Rossi? Piracy? So the rumors were true."

Dario shrugged off the arm and kept walking.

"If not for you, gonfaloniere"—a tone of unusual anger had entered Callisto's voice—"the French might have bypassed Colpena. The enemy doesn't know it, but our cisterns hold only a single week of water. Your actions have put Colpena's very existence in jeopardy."

"There will be consequences for this." Borroni spat to the side. "I'll make sure the whole city knows what you've done."

THE FIRST BARRAGE BEGAN IN late afternoon. Amidst the roar of cannons, Amadeo rushed to the top of the ramparts to determine how his defenses were holding up.

"Get down, capomaestro." A guard, huddling beneath the balustrade with a sword in his hand, waved. "You must protect yourself."

Shrugging off the suggestion, Amadeo ran to the parapet's edge and looked down. A cannonball thudded heavily into the wall to his right, sending clods of dirt flying. The thick, pliable earthen bricks were absorbing the blows even better than he'd hoped. The ball had embedded itself in the still-wet bricks. It never penetrated the stone wall behind it.

He smiled and headed for the stairs. They could bombard all they wanted. At this rate, it would take weeks for them to knock down the walls.

But then he frowned. Long before that, Colpena would drink the last of its water.

FOUR DAYS LATER, DARIO STOOD atop the balcony of Palazzo Rossi with Aldo beside him. To the west lay the bay formed by Colpena's promontory and Monte Argentario. Stretching in a line across the western harbor were twenty French galleys that had appeared overnight. Three of Dario's own merchant ships had docked only yesterday and sat now at anchor. The rest, having unloaded and fearing the appearance of the French fleet, had fled down the coast.

"Can those ships ferry the army to our shores?" asked Aldo.

"I doubt it. Where would they get all the small boats they'd need? But those vessels could dock at the port. Then we'd have to fight whatever force disembarked."

Behind them, Grazziano coughed, and Dario faced him.

"Your presence is requested at the northern wall, signore," said Grazziano. "Apparently, the French want to talk."

Dario left at once. Joined outside by Borroni and Callisto, he followed the Strada del Nord down to the main barbican, where again they met the armored knight under the portcullis.

"Having trouble with your cannon, Frenchman?" Dario grinned.

The knight stretched to his full height and spat to the side. "The king tires of wasting his cannonballs on your worthless city. Thus, he has agreed to a new demand. If you will pay a fine of twenty-five thousand ducats—florins will also be acceptable—he will take his army on to Naples. If you do not agree, our ships will lay waste your harbor, and we will continue the siege with just enough men so that, before spring, you will be eating your own children and drinking the water you pass from your own bodies."

Callisto whispered urgently in Dario's ear, "We need to talk."

"Give us a moment to consider this," said Dario. The three retreated to the tunnel under the gatehouse.

"If paying twenty-five thousand florins will end the siege and save the port," said Callisto, "we must pay them."

Borroni spread his hands, the gold trim of his black tunic dancing. "How can we trust the French to do what they say?"

"If we pay the ransom, they'll depart," said Callisto. "Or they'll never get another ransom from another city again. But if they lay siege, we'll run out of water—possibly tomorrow. Bramante and his cursed water project!"

Dario frowned. "We don't have twenty-five thousand florins. The Rossi bank can only come up with six on short notice. The city treasury has barely enough to survive the winter."

"I have about three thousand," said Callisto.

"And I, two." Borroni grimaced. "I'm guessing we could raise another four from the rest of the Signoria and five more from the Council of Thirty. Maybe that will be enough?"

The others nodded, and Dario led them back to the knight, his mail gleaming in the bright sunlight beyond the wall. Dario presented their offer.

The soldier narrowed his eyes. "I'm authorized to take a lesser amount in exchange for lifting the siege. Twenty thousand . . . will perhaps be enough for that. But the port"—he grinned—"ah, that's another matter. You should never have preyed on French ships, my friends."

Dario swallowed, looking to the others. They both agreed. What choice did they have?

Later that afternoon, city guards delivered heavy bags clinking with twenty thousand gold florins to the smiling French knight. An hour later, the enemy army began breaking camp and filing away to the south. Shortly thereafter, the twenty French ships in the bay opened fire on the port. Their cannons boomed in a continuous cavalcade, their thunder echoing off Monte Argentario and back to where Dario and Aldo stood on the balcony of Palazzo Rossi.

First, the enemy's cannons sank the three merchant ships docked at the western wharf. Then their cannonballs ripped into the jetty itself, chewing up planks and pilings, some balls even smashing into the defense towers of the city gate beyond.

When they'd finished destroying the eastern dock, the ships raised sail and took up positions to the southeast, where they opened fire and destroyed the smaller dock there.

By the time the bombardment was over, a mass of broken, jumbled timber floated out on the bay. Planks and pilings, some of it on fire, drifted in disarray. Some of the waterfront area itself lay in shambles, with a few inns, warehouses, trattorias, and houses reduced to rubble.

The entire bombardment lasted only three hours. When it was over, Colpena's main trading link with the outside world was gone.

As the French sails disappeared over the southern horizon, Grazziano appeared beside them. "Ah, what a bitter harvest we do reap."

Dario whirled on him. "You've said that before. Be careful, servant."

"As you say, signore." The man bowed and left them alone.

"He's right," said Aldo. "It will take months to rebuild the harbor, months with no income coming in. Maybe we should never have engaged Violante?"

"We did what we had to do." Dario's jaw tensed, and he stalked from the balcony. Now that the danger had passed, he wondered whether any of the bordellos would be open this evening.

CHAPTER 49

~ CENSURED ~

JUNE 1495

Throughout the long winter, news had filtered back from Florence that Savonarola had indeed taken control of the city. Along with these tidings came occasional copies of the monk's sermons that Amadeo read again and again.

"King Charles VIII is God's instrument of judgment against the tyrant rulers of the city," the monk had said, and, "People of Florence, repent of your sins. For too long have you gloried in the pleasures of the flesh, turning your back on God. You follow the hedonism and materialism of the tyrants to your own destruction."

Amadeo had agreed with many of the truths Savonarola's sermons taught. But as he reread the monk's words and pondered what was happening in that city, he became increasingly uneasy.

Too often, Savonarola placed blame on the upper classes, on people like the Medicis, the Rossis, and lately, even on artists, sculptors, and painters like those Amadeo himself had hired. Reports had arrived that bands of Savonarola's followers were going door-to-door, collecting paintings, sculptures, and books that did not, in the monk's mind, glorify God.

Today in Florence, even a poem or a painting about a woman or a sculpture of a nude boy as a fountain's centerpiece had become works of the flesh, works to be destroyed. It was a disturbing trend. One Amadeo hoped would never reach Colpena.

When the French had attacked, work on the duomo had already stopped for the winter. For this, Amadeo gave thanks to God nearly every day. Almost as soon as the enemy fleet had left, the Signoria began restoring the western port. Amadeo had sent his carpenters and masons to help.

But when the warm rains of March washed the streets and the wharf lay yet unfinished, trade with the outside world was still at a standstill. Without a functioning port, most of the city's businesses were still closed.

Rossi's dwindling funds were still able to pay the duomo's workers, but he complained constantly about it to Fabiano.

When April's flowers sprouted from his garden, Amadeo paced the streets, took long walks in the country, and sometimes even went down to the dock to help.

Only Skender's marriage to the girl upstairs provided some relief from his angst at being without work. He'd attended the wedding, glad for his servant to have found happiness. In the ceremony, Skender surprised him to tears when he took on the last name of Puccini. He only hoped Skender would not take his bride and move away. Amadeo's first-floor apartment had only one bedroom.

In early May, the city received a welcome, but belated surprise. Bramante finished his long-awaited water project.

Amadeo joined a select delegation, carrying a torch and crouching his way along a five-foot-high rock tunnel leading from the springs outside the northern walls. They passed a sluice gate under the city walls, then followed the tunnel for nearly a mile to a huge, underground reservoir cut into solid rock beneath the city's center. There, a six-foot diameter shaft led straight up. Amadeo and a few hearty adventurers climbed a narrow access ladder beside a chain pump Bramante had constructed. The vertical shaft opened onto a huge cistern on the Via dei Fiore, capable of holding five million gallons.

After the tour, Bramante's crew had dug a temporary shaft to remove the rock between the spring and the sluice gate. Water gushed through, they opened the gate, and the reservoir filled. Then the chain pump, powered by oxen on the surface, began filling the cistern. At long last, Colpena's water problem was solved.

Later, they'd held a ceremony to celebrate the opening of the waterworks, where Amadeo had congratulated Bramante on an impressive feat of engineering.

Bramante now even talked of routing water to a few piazzas, where he would build fountains, an extravagance in a city that, until now, had always been desperate for water.

Shortly afterward, workers restored the southeastern dock and began work on the western wharf.

In mid-June, the city rejoiced when word arrived that the French army was marching home on a route through the center of Italy, bypassing the coast road.

Merchants reopened their doors. Ships again sailed. And a load of bardiglio arrived at the newly rebuilt southeastern dock.

Finally, work on the duomo resumed.

On a Tuesday in late June, Amadeo received a summons to report to the Signoria. He had no idea what it was about. A bit anxious to leave work on the dome, he nevertheless entered the town hall, ascended the stairs to the Signoria meeting room, and waited.

He hoped this wouldn't take long. Today, they were installing the first of the sandstone rings that would encircle the dome at thirty-five-foot intervals, and he needed to be present. Iron clasps would connect each octagonal sandstone block to the next section. The rings would keep in check the outward thrust from the dome's weight and allow them to build the dome without scaffolding.

The sergeant-at-arms opened the door and ushered him inside.

Sitting at their long table, the seven Signoria members faced their visitor.

"To what do I owe the honor of this meeting?" he asked.

Callisto Mancini smiled and looked to both sides. "Amadeo, we have discussed your performance as master of Colpena's defense works, and . . . the city is well pleased."

He bowed. "I only did what seemed logical, necessary, and right."

"Nevertheless, I now speak for the committee, and indeed, the entire city. For your expertise in defense, for saving Colpena from a bombardment that almost certainly would have resulted in its capture and possible destruction, we have decided to award you, Amadeo Puccini, with the city's first-ever Citation of Honor. Please step forward."

Stunned, Amadeo moved closer to the table.

Callisto placed around his neck a silver-threaded ribbon holding a silver disc on which was etched, "For the Expert Defense of the City."

"Along with this, we are also awarding you one thousand florins."

"I–I don't know what to say." He rubbed his thumb across the smoothly etched disc. He recognized the work, molded and pounded out by one of the city's goldsmiths. "Thank you."

"You're more than welcome."

Clutching his award, he left. Then he wondered: If he used the money to build a room for Skender and his bride, Maria, how much would he have left to feed the prisoners?

As Dario watched the capomaestro leave the room, his face grew hot. He was the only Signoria member not in favor of this award. But the others were adamant, so he went along. Dario had spent all his reserves keeping the duomo funded and rebuilding the port—money in the strongbox that he'd held back from the ransom demand. And for that sacrifice, what did they give him? Not even a thank you. "If there is no other business," he said, "I move that this meeting—"

"Ah, gonfaloniere," said a grinning Enzio Borroni to his left, "but there is other business."

"Oh? What?"

"Let me do this," said Callisto, facing Dario. "I'm sorry to report that the five of us were forced to meet earlier today before you and Aldo arrived."

"What?" Sitting beside Dario, Aldo jerked upright. "Without us?"

"Sì," continued Callisto. "What you two did by entering into piracy on the high seas was"—he shook his head—"dishonest and dishonorable. It endangered the very existence of Colpena. It was enough, even, to strip you, Dario, of your leadership and your title of gonfaloniere."

Dario caught his breath. Surely, they wouldn't.

"But the title has been in your family for generations, ever since your great-grandfather founded this city after the Sienese destroyed the first settlement. Out of respect for your predecessors, we have refrained from that. Instead, we voted to give both of you an official reprimand, documents of censure for your actions."

Dario's heart was beating faster. Sweat dripped off his forehead. He glanced from one to the other at the table beside him. This was treasonous.

Aldo's face had gone white, and he stared straight ahead.

Callisto passed a document to each of them. Dario didn't even glance at his.

"We are also imposing a fine of five hundred florins on each of you," said a grinning Borroni.

"You may pay Fabiano at your leisure," said Callisto.

"Are we finished?" asked Dario.

"Not quite. Word has spread of what you did—that the city would have been otherwise spared had you not engaged in piracy. Because of that, many people have approached me—commoners, merchants, and nobles, alike—to ask that you Rossis be removed from the Signoria." Callisto closed his eyes, again shook his head, and opened them again.

"We're lucky mobs aren't rioting in the streets right now, calling for your heads. Dario, the Signoria rules at the pleasure of the people, and this body must give them a semblance of justice. To mollify them, we have instructed the town crier that, for every day of the next month, he will announce your censures and fines on every street corner and piazza. He will also announce the award we've given to Amadeo for his brilliant work in saving the city from destruction."

Dario peered at Callisto, not believing what he heard. Private censure was one thing. But public humiliation? And every day for an entire month?

Borroni's grin was more than Dario could stomach. His glance fixed on the room's far walls, his hands gripping the sides of the table.

"Now the meeting is adjourned," said Callisto.

As the others stood and left, Dario sat motionless, his hands forming into fists.

Aldo was last to depart. He bent down and whispered, "I'm sick of this. You've brought me nothing but poor profits, sleepless nights, and now—dishonor."

"If you remember, piracy was your idea," Dario fired back. Aldo said nothing, only whirled and left.

Still sitting, Dario crumpled the document of censure so hard, his knuckles ached.

On the same day they gave Puccini an award, they dared to censure him. And the five hundred florins he and Aldo were fined would funnel directly into Puccini's pocket. On top of that was the public humiliation.

At that moment, the hatred he felt for the capomaestro was so great, if the man were to walk into the room, he feared it might turn to murder.

Dario needed the duomo finished to complete his indulgence. He would wait for that. But someday, somehow, he would bring about Puccini's downfall. Of that, he was now more certain than ever.

UNDER LEADEN-GRAY SKIES THAT MIRRORED his mood, Dario walked the short distance to his palazzo, his head down, his steps slow. His life was falling apart. What did Grazziano keep telling him? Something like, "The seeds you sow, you must also reap."

He trudged up the steps one at a time, barely able to lift his feet. Things could only get better from here. How could they possibly get any worse? He pushed open the door.

"Grazziano?" he called.

No answer. Odd. Grazziano was always waiting for him. He was nothing if not reliable.

He crossed the entryway and turned the corner.

There on the floor—a body, prone and unmoving. Grazziano's gray hair sprawled over the tiles.

Hurrying over, Dario knelt. "Grazziano? Are you all right?"

Had he had some kind of stroke? By now, he must be in his late seventies, and lately, he'd been complaining of headaches.

No response.

Dario laid two fingers on his neck—cold.

His hand jerked back.

Grazziano, his longtime servant and part-time conscience, was dead.

Dario slumped to the floor beside his faithful servant. He stared at the corpse.

After what seemed an eternity, he rose and went in search of a bottle of wine.

CHAPTER 50

~ MICHELANGELO BUONARROTI ~

APRIL–DECEMBER 1497

Amadeo pushed through the door into Vittorio's stonecutter's lodge, where he'd heard the new man had gone. Instead of seeking out his capomaestro, Michelangelo had headed straight for the nine-foot block of marble Vittorio had picked out for him. Everyone in the workshop had already stopped what they were doing to watch the new sculptor they'd heard so much about.

As Amadeo approached, Michelangelo circled the block, eyeing it as if he were buying an expensive horse.

Nearby, a smiling Vittorio watched.

His hammer tapped the block in several places. "Rings like a bell. Good. But what does it look like in the early-morning sun?"

"Translucent, signore," said Vittorio. "I've heard of your test and made certain that all our statuary marble meets it."

"Good." Still, he circled. Finally, he turned to face the men watching his inspection.

Amadeo stepped forward with an open hand. "Welcome, Michelangelo Buonarroti, to the work site of the Cattedrale del Figlio sul Mare. Long have I anticipated your arrival." The face of the man before him was rough, lined, perhaps even ugly. The nose had once been broken, but the eyes—they gleamed with intelligence and fire.

The sculptor shook Amadeo's hand. But then, as if drawn by a magnet, his gaze returned to the marble. "I'll have to build a rotating platform around it. And can we move it outside? During the summer, I like to work outside."

"Certainly," said Vittorio.

"No offense, master stonecutter, but if we can get it outside by morning, I'll verify your findings at sunrise."

Vittorio nodded.

Michelangelo's gaze was fixed on the marble. "I've already made drawings. Hundreds of them from all angles—Jesus turning, one hand rising to his Father in Heaven, his eyes alight with the glory he's about to see. I'm excited to begin."

The man's eagerness and love of his work was contagious. Amadeo could see it already brightening the other sculptors' eyes.

"For this project, I'll make a clay model first. I'd like to begin tomorrow." At last, Michelangelo faced Amadeo and Vittorio. "Thank you for this. The climate for artists in Florence now is not good."

"In what way?" asked Amadeo.

"Savonarola." Michelangelo shook his head. "Just before I left at the beginning of lent, his bands of 'blessed innocents', accompanied by guards with swords, were going house-to-house throughout the city. They collected books of the ancient Greek and Roman philosophers, books of poems by Boccaccio and Petrarch, and the writings of Cicero, Pulci, Poliziano, and others. Poliziano was my friend." Again, he shook his head. "His poetry . . . does not deserve this. They also confiscated paintings of naked women by Botticelli—beautiful, priceless works of art. They confiscated flutes, violas, and lutes, and any work of art depicting a Greek or Roman god. They even grabbed sculptures of nudes, some of which I myself had sculpted—I was in Palazzo Medici when this began, and I hid many works in the cellar before I left. Everything Savonarola deemed profane they threw onto a great pile in the Piazza della Signoria. To this, they added wigs, false beards, perfumes, rouge, and even jewelry. Then they doused it with oil and lit it on fire. The monk called it a 'bonfire of the vanities', and I fear it is the death of culture in Florence. No, my friends, right now is not a good time for artists in that city."

"Are the people in favor of this . . . this atrocity?" asked the sculptor Clemente Pisano, his arms crossed, his jaw tensing.

"Savonarola has driven a deep wedge through the populace. Some embrace his fanaticism. They aid him willingly. But many others hide their true feelings, fearing to be branded a heretic. Someday, he'll go too far, and it will end badly."

Michelangelo drew a hand through his hair. "But now I'm in Colpena and have left all that behind." Smiling, he again faced his block of white

Carrara marble. "Now I have a good stone for my chisels to work, and that makes me happy, indeed."

AMADEO WAS IMPRESSED BY THE speed and urgency with which this master scultori worked. Within three weeks' time, he'd made a three-foot-high clay model of Christ's ascension built on a wire frame. With Pugliesi's help, he then built a rotating wooden platform surrounding the block in the piazza.

The day came when he put chisel to marble, and then the chips flew. This sculptor worked like no other. He carved from sunup until long after everyone else had gone home. After supper, Amadeo would often stroll into the Piazza del Duomo only to find Michelangelo's block surrounded by torches and the sculptor's mallet striking his chisel in a regular series of blows, followed by a pause, a quick examination of the result, and then more blows.

More than once Amadeo pleaded with him. "Do take a rest, signore, and have some supper," he'd say. "No one can work at such speed all day without nourishment and rest."

At such times, Michelangelo only grunted, eyed the marble, and continued working.

The effect this new sculptor had on the others was infectious and energizing. All the artists on the duomo—the glassworkers, painters, and sculptors—often came to watch him in his glorious act of creation. It was as if God himself guided the man's chisel, revealing layer after slow layer of the masterpiece beneath.

Thus, did the summer pass.

For his own part, Amadeo oversaw the placement of the second sandstone ring up on the dome's rising bricks. The workers now went up in the morning bearing their lunch buckets of bread, cheese, and wine and weren't allowed to descend until nightfall. After one man fell to his death, they also put in place a rule requiring that their wine be diluted by a third—the same as for pregnant women. The very act of navigating the stairs to the scaffolding on the dome's highest level was exhausting. And the workers had begun to spend too much time on their noonday break descending and ascending the spiral stairs.

Amadeo himself climbed the dome once each day, inspecting the placement of the bricks. Every few feet, they now laid the bricks in a herringbone pattern. This was one of Brunelleschi's secrets to building an octagonal dome without scaffolding. The interlocking irregular pattern held the bricks in place while they dried.

After he'd done what he could on the dome, he descended and continued overseeing construction of the façade.

Skender and his wife now occupied two rooms attached to Amadeo's apartment. He'd bought the space, had a wall removed, and fixed it up for the newlyweds. Maria, a quiet girl with black hair and dark eyes, devoted to Skender, often helped in the kitchen. Amadeo had increased Skender's wages and was glad for Maria's placid company.

For Michelangelo, his prize sculptor, the months passed in a frenzy of work. Day by day, Christ revealed himself in the marble.

Then, one day in late June, news arrived that Pope Alexander VI had excommunicated Savonarola. Michelangelo's—and Piero's—prediction about the man had proven prescient.

Once, Michelangelo had spoken of the French mercenaries who'd visited the New World and who'd left the departing army to stay behind in Florence. The ships of exploration had apparently brought back new animals, foods, and plants. They also brought with them what people were calling the French Disease. Marked by sores, rashes, fever, and headaches, it spread quickly through the bordellos. Savonarola had called it God's judgment on wanton sexual excess.

When the first chill winds of October blew in, the sculptor moved the block inside, where he continued working at a furious pace, surrounded by braziers, lanterns on poles, and heaps of white marble chips lying across the floor.

Finally, in late November, he put away his chisels and began polishing. By the time December's rains chilled the bone and even six braziers could not keep the lodge warm, the work was finished.

Carefully, with Michelangelo supervising every step of the way, workers removed one of the workshop walls and carried the statue to a cart, where they bundled it in rugs and tied it securely. Oxen then trundled the piece to a temporary position at the back of the chancel.

The next day was Sunday, and half the city gathered inside the duomo to dedicate Michelangelo's statue. By now, all the roofs were in place and the arches finished. Above them, the dome had risen to such a height that the circle of open sky had considerably diminished. Stained-glass windows covered most of the holes in the clerestory for the transepts, chancel, and even parts of the nave. As the sun shone through, multicolored beams bathed the gathering below.

With worshipers crowding the duomo, a smiling Bishop Ferata dedicated the statue, then preached a message on Christ's ascension.

Throughout, a smiling Amadeo stood next to Michelangelo. They took the bread and wine together. When the assembly began breaking up, he turned to the sculptor. "Your work will stand for generations as the duomo's centerpiece—a work of art like none other in all Colpena."

"You exaggerate, capomaestro," said Michelangelo. "But it was a pleasure working here." Michelangelo looked up at the dome, the arches, and down the nave's long aisles. "This is a worthy home for any work of art, a masterpiece in itself. I commend you on its design. Architecture, it seems, requires its own brand of demanding artistry, and you, signore, have excelled at it."

Amadeo thanked him for the compliment and bowed.

The next day, the entire crew of artists bid Michelangelo a grand farewell in the Piazza del Duomo. But as his horse clopped over the stones of the Strada del Nord, Amadeo was sad to see a man of such artistic vision leave their presence.

CHAPTER 51

~ THE DOME CEREMONY ~

OCTOBER 1506

The day's ceremony marked the dome's completion, and as Amadeo walked the center aisle beside rows crowded with parishioners, the crowd's murmurs and the shuffling of thousands of feet echoed through the open space.

"A great accomplishment," said someone as he passed.

But he only nodded. He'd spent thirty-seven years working on this cathedral, twenty on the dome itself. He was now sixty-three years old, no longer a young man. In another seven or eight years, his work here would be complete.

"Congratulations, capomaestro," said another, a wool merchant on the Council of Thirty.

Terra-cotta tiles now covered the duomo's entire floor. Stained glass gleamed in every window, and the painters he'd recruited from the rest of Clemente's bottega were completing the frescoes he'd planned so long ago. Statuary that his sculptors had been working on for decades was even now being taken from warehouses and placed in niches and bays. The façade itself would soon be complete.

In the front row, he found a seat before the altar that workers had constructed for Bishop Ferata. Behind the altar, Michelangelo's *Christ Rising* had been moved to its final position.

Beside him sat Aldo Rossi, Vittorio Rivera, Callisto Mancini, Dario Rossi, and farther down, Enzio Borroni. Nearby sat the entire Signoria and the city's most prosperous merchants. As much of the town as could fit had crowded behind them in the nave, the aisles, and the transepts, filling every available space.

Donned in his green robes and wearing his high miter, Ferata walked the center aisle to the front, waving his smoking censer all the way. Beside him, Cardinal Gonzaga, red-robed, ponderous, and bearing an official scowl, tried to keep up. Both took high-backed seats under the chancel, facing the crowd.

When Ferata opened the service and began the Rites of Introduction, the entire congregation responded. Ferata's words boomed through the great cavern of the duomo like the voice of God himself. Hidden in their stalls at the back of the chancel, the choir sang. Their voices echoed off the walls as if from a throng of heavenly angels. The newly installed pipe organ boomed out notes, adding an impressive accompaniment.

But as Ferata launched into the Liturgy of the Word, including the profession of faith, Amadeo's gaze landed not on the bishop, but on the arches, columns, half-completed frescoes, and partially filled niches. Here, indeed, was an offering to God. Here was his life's work, the sweat and toil of his every waking moment for thirty-seven years, now marching toward completion.

Ferata spoke from one of the Psalms on the subject of giving glory to God, but Amadeo's thoughts wandered instead to the blank wall at the back of the chancel—where he himself would paint the final frescoes.

There, Gonzaga wanted him to glorify Mary, to deify her as if she, too, were a god. But Amadeo was intent on his original plan—frescoes honoring Christ.

After the choir again sang, Gonzaga stood from his chair and waddled to the front. When he spoke, the cardinal's thin voice lurched Amadeo back from his musings.

"Above all, you must hold fast to pure doctrine," warned Gonzaga, "in thought, in word, and in deed. Bishop Ferata is right that we must always give God the glory. But we can never do so if we wander from the teachings of the Church. That is about the only thing that preacher in Florence, that Savonarola, has said that I agree with. And that is the reason I have started my Inquisition—to bring to justice those wayward souls who have dared to trample on the truths proclaimed by the Church."

Inquisition? Had he said the word *inquisition*? Had not Ferata mentioned something a few months back about the subject? What Amadeo had heard of the Inquisition going on in Spain right now was frightening. With Gonzaga in charge, this could not be good.

By the time the fat cardinal resumed his seat, a queasy feeling writhed in Amadeo's stomach.

Ferata concluded the service with the Eucharist. When he announced it was time for the feast, the room emptied, everyone eager for the bread, cheese, olives, and wine laid out on the tables outside in the square. Today, there was even smoked ham.

With Signoria members and some of the Thirty at his side, Amadeo left the duomo for the street. Everyone wanted to be seen with the man who'd completed the great dome that rivaled Florence's. Only Bramante, glaring at him from an aisle, avoided him.

"A great accomplishment, Amadeo." Callisto clapped a hand on his back as they entered the piazza.

Bands of musicians, with fifes, horns, and drums, started playing and marching behind the different banners of the Wool Guild, the Stonemason's Guild, the Stonecutter's Guild, and the minor guilds.

"There's quite a bit of work yet to do." Amadeo waved a hand toward the sky. "The lantern atop the dome. The campanile. The façade."

"Ah, but this is a day for celebration. You have completed the dome, and that is a feat worthy of great praise."

Amadeo nodded and followed the others toward a table laden with food reserved for the richer merchants, nobles, and city leaders. Besides ham, it included capons. "What is all this business about an Inquisition?"

"Haven't you heard? From now on, you need to be careful, my friend. Gonzaga is the last man to be put in charge of such a thing. He's too much of a zealot."

"I'm not worried. What can he do?"

Callisto grabbed Amadeo's arm and stopped him. "Did you not hear about the spice importer in Siena and what happened to him?"

"No."

"He was only a merchant. But at the end of a service much like this, he told those beside him that the Eucharist bread and wine were not really Christ's body and blood after we eat and drink it. As proof, he spit the half-chewed bread out of his mouth and showed it to everyone. When Gonzaga heard the story, he had the man arrested, thrown in prison, and tortured until he confessed to a long list of sins. Before a tribunal, the broken merchant then admitted that the transmutation of the Eucharist host was indeed real. Then Gonzaga had the man beheaded."

Amadeo stared, open-mouthed. "B–but that's outrageous. Why is he doing this?"

"My opinion is that Gonzaga is responding to Savonarola's charges that the Church has become corrupt. So instead of cleaning up the obvious sins of the flesh among his own priests and himself—the whoring, the gluttony, the simony, the fondness of the priests for shiny, expensive things—he's focusing on Church doctrine. It's what they're doing in Spain where he came from."

Amadeo shuddered. "This is not . . . God's will. It can't be."

"Don't ever let anyone hear you say such a thing." Callisto lowered his voice nearly to a whisper. "We live in strange times when men like Gonzaga can sit in judgment on men far more righteous than he. Take care, Amadeo. Take great care."

Stunned by the news, Amadeo followed the others to the feast.

At that moment, he decided to delay painting the fresco on the chancel's back wall. He must save that for last.

CHAPTER 52

~ THE FORTUNES OF LUCK ~

OCTOBER 1508

Dario studied his cards, glanced briefly at the three men across the table, then back at the hand he'd just been dealt—the six and seven of hearts. The braziers surrounding them crackled with the new logs that Tommaso, his host and one of Colpena's richest merchants, had thrown in. He welcomed their heat.

He'd lost much tonight. But what did it matter? With each hand, the stakes had been rising, and soon, any deal now, his luck would turn. The stake had risen to two hundred florins per deal, with a limit of six hundred per round. Two nights ago, he'd won a thousand florins at primero. Last night and tonight? He'd lost twice that much.

It was his turn to vie. "Supremus, fifty-five." He was betting he'd get an ace.

Guffaws came from the other three at the table.

"Going for broke, Rossi?" Marcello Esposito was the only other Signoria member at the game.

"Just playing my cards."

"Or playing for luck." Tommaso, the current dealer, dealt two more cards to each player.

Dario picked up the four of diamonds and the ace of hearts. His heart raced. Finally, his luck had turned. He added another two hundred florins to the pot in front of him. "Supremus, fifty-five," he repeated.

The others narrowed concerned eyes at him, and the dealer, as required by the rules, gave him one new card. He turned in his four of diamonds. Slowly, he picked it up. A Jack . . . of . . . hearts. In disbelief, he stared at it. The card had put him over. Couldn't he for once get a winning hand?

Tommaso continued to deal around the table. The next two players passed. But Marcello checked his hand and vied another two hundred. "Chorus, eighty-four."

When Dario passed, they all showed their cards.

"Tough luck, Dario." Marcello, the winner, pulled in Dario's pot. "It just hasn't been your week, has it?"

He fingered the two hundred florins he had left. When the night began, he had two thousand in his pocket. He pushed back from the table. "I'm broke. Guess I'm out. At least for tonight."

The others waved goodbye, and he left the palazzo for a chill October evening. Down by the southeastern dock, a ship's bell rang. Twelve bells. He yawned. When was the last time he'd slept?

He hadn't gone fifty yards when Aldo appeared on the cobbles ahead. "I've been looking all over for you." Irritation edged his voice. "I have terrible news."

Dario scowled. "Do you ever bring good news, Aldo? Could you just once track me down in the middle of the night to tell me how *great* things are going?"

Aldo drew him to a stone wall that bordered the winding lane and overlooked the wharf. "One of Borroni's ships docked in port today. Its captain reported that last week, when we had such bad weather here, the storm to the south was worse. Much, much worse. His vessel barely avoided being capsized by giant waves south of Sicily. Many ships were apparently lost."

Dario closed his eyes. "What are you saying?"

"Six of our galleys are long overdue. Last week, all of them would have been passing through that area near Sicily on their way back to port."

"How much overdue?" He raised weary eyes to his cousin. Six ships was one-third of their fleet. If they lost six ships loaded with cargo . . .

"Over two weeks."

"Is there any chance they'll come in?"

"Little or none. But that's not all."

"What else?"

"You remember how I said that production from the alum mine has been diminishing?"

"Sì, and you said they discovered a new vein."

"Well, that vein has petered out. Each month, the mine is producing less and less alum. We can no longer meet the orders we're receiving. Soon, it will give out altogether. Dario, we're facing financial disaster."

He gripped the stone wall. Besides the shipping business and the bank's money-changing profits, the alum mine was their major income source. "So our reserves are dwindling again?"

"Sì."

"How long before they run out?"

"Six months, maybe less."

"What can we do?"

"I don't know. I'm out of ideas."

Dario gazed over the moonlit whitecaps, where the waves broke far out at sea. Here on the southeastern shore, Colpena's promontory offered little shelter from the waves. "I can't think about this tonight. Let's talk tomorrow."

"All right. But we need to do something soon."

THE NEXT MORNING, DARIO AVOIDED meeting with Aldo. He hadn't been at his desk for three days, and right now, he couldn't face columns of figures, questions from his accountants, or anything business-related. Didn't he pay four men to take care of that for him? Instead, he slept late, walked for half the afternoon, and then dressed for a party that evening at Callisto Mancini's palazzo.

Callisto's affairs were mild compared to most events he attended. But tonight, this was the only diversion available, and he needed to get away. He couldn't face yet another business problem.

When Dario arrived, he went straight for the wine.

"So glad you could come." Callisto wore a full-length white toga, an affectation at his own parties. "I'd like to introduce you to someone." He led Dario to a tall thin man with bronzed skin and a white goatee. "This is Rifat Basara, a spice trader from the east."

As Callisto moved on, Dario shook hands with the man who looked like some sort of Arab—not a Turk. "What kind of spices, Signore Basara?"

"Ginger, garlic, cumin, paprika, saffron, and cinnamon. Your host is unaware of it, but my main trading interest lies not in spices, but in ancient relics."

"Relics? As in religious relics?"

"Yes, my lord." A sly smile crossed his lips. "And in these European Christian lands, relics can be greatly profitable for the man with the sense to own them."

Dario tilted his head. "Have you brought such relics with you?"

"At the inn where I'm staying, yes. I obtained one particular relic at great cost, hoping to find a suitable buyer rich enough to afford it. It is of such great importance to the Christian faith, I predict it will bring its owner vast profits."

Dario remembered Ferata's collection of relics, how proud the man was of them, and the tale of how the bishop of Mainz used them to finance his duomo's construction. "May I see it?"

The other frowned and glanced around the room. "Let us stay a bit," he whispered, "so we do not offend our host. When the time is right, we'll both leave. I will show it to you tonight. But let's keep it a secret between us, hey?"

Dario nodded, they separated, and he waited until dinner was served. Afterward, he mingled with the other guests, several from the Signoria. The rest were merchants, wool and spice traders, and a visiting cardinal from Rome.

Finally, the mysterious Arab whispered it was time. Dario allowed him to depart first, waited a few minutes, then announced his own departure.

Outside, a smiling Rifat Basara waited. "Now, I will take you to my inn."

As Dario followed him down the hill, he wondered if the man was be a charlatan, a thief trying to lure him into some dark alley, where compatriots waited to rob him. "Are you an honest man, Rifat?"

The Arab shot him a frown. "I am that, my lord. If I were going to rob you, would I take you to the best inn in town?"

Indeed, they'd already stopped before one nicer hostel near the docks.

Dario apologized for his suspicions as they mounted the steps to Rifat's room. Inside, a dark-skinned woman wearing gold arm and ankle bracelets and a silk nightshirt fell to her knees and bowed.

"This is Farah, my slave."

Upon seeing the girl, Dario relaxed. If Rifat had employed a muscular manservant bearing a sword, he would have turned on his heels and left. "So what is this relic you say is so important?"

Rifat smiled and went to a strongbox in the corner. From a cord around his neck, he produced a key and unlocked it. The hinges creaked, and the chest opened.

After reaching inside, he brought out a wooden box about eight inches long and five wide. He placed it gently on a table.

"What I have here, my lord, are two of the original spikes the Roman soldiers used to nail your Jesus to his cross. I have documents of authenticity proving they are what they claim to be, passed down from the centurion who oversaw the execution, to the sons of the man who sold them to some Syrian Christians in Antioch, who then sold them to Daedulus Eliades, a rich merchant from Crete. That man's sons, grandsons, and great-grandsons inherited the relics. For generations, the Eliades family held them, eventually selling them to me."

Only after this introduction did he open the box. Inside, lying on a bed of black silk, were two, six-inch, badly corroded spikes.

Dario looked at them with wonder. If what the man said was true, would the masses spend their hard-earned fiorinos to see them? But of course, they would. He narrowed his eyes and examined this relic-bearing Arab. "Let me see this document of authenticity."

Rifat took a wooden tube from the box, pulled out a yellowed scroll, unrolled it, and laid a coin on each edge to keep it flat. "It's in Latin, Aramaic, and Greek. I've made a translation into Italian here." He produced a more recent document describing what it said.

Dario examined the original. The writing was incomprehensible, but it was definitely old and in three different languages. Was the man telling the truth? He didn't know. And suddenly, he didn't care. What mattered was what he could do with this—authentic or not. "How much are you asking for it?"

Rifat cleared his throat, stood up straight, and said, "Twenty thousand florins, my lord."

Dario burst out laughing. "Ten thousand and it's a deal."

A scowl further darkening his countenance, Rifat shook his head. "This is priceless, my lord. I cannot part with it for that. Eighteen."

"Twelve."

In the end, they shook hands on fifteen thousand florins.

THE NEXT AFTERNOON, AFTER HAVING convinced Aldo of the merits of a venture into religious relics, Dario paid Rifat and took the box with the Nails of Christ to Bishop Ferata's residence. After hearing that Dario had purchased a religious artifact of great importance, Ferata nearly drooled as he led the gonfaloniere into his private sanctum.

When Dario finally explained what he had and after he opened the box to reveal the Nails of Christ and after he unrolled the document of authenticity, Ferata's eyes widened, and his breath came faster.

"So my offer to you, bishop, is this: I propose that you add these Nails of Christ to your collection and then take the entire thing on a tour of Italy. The proceeds you will send to me, and I will use them to pay the duomo's expenses. When the tour is complete and you have been to every city willing to host you, I will gift these relics to you as part of your collection. What do you say?"

Ferata could not hide the eagerness in his eyes. Yet he said, "But the agreement with Cardinal Gonzaga for your indulgence was that you must fully fund the duomo."

"I bought these relics, did I not? And you yourself said you could not show your collection without the addition of some great and important piece. Well, here I am providing the key that unlocks your collection for the world to see. So it really is my money funding this."

Ferata hesitated only a moment. "I think it meets the condition. This contribution that you, alone, have paid for—sì, it meets Gonzaga's condition." Ferata smiled. "These Nails of Christ are a collector's dream. Sì, I believe I will go on such a tour."

They shook hands, and Dario walked home with the hope that soon their financial troubles would end.

But as he crossed Piazza Rossi, a small crowd had gathered around the steps leading to his palazzo. "What's going on?"

"This monk, here, was asking for you earlier today." The man who spoke was the owner of a nearby leather shop. "He said he came all the way from Salvia, but he was sweating, breathing heavily, and now he's dead."

Rossi threaded his way through the people. When he gazed down at a body lying face up on the cobbles, his heart leaped. The face held the same angelic visage with the scar, but older. The body possessed the same clubfoot. Beside him lay a cane.

How many years had it been since he'd seen this man, this apparition bearing messages of doom? "Are you sure he's dead?"

"Sì, signore," said the shopkeeper.

"What a shame." But Rossi was not feeling at all sad that this monk would never again accost him with words of eternal warning. "Someone, call the constable to take the body." He stepped around the corpse and climbed the steps to his palazzo.

But as he climbed, his heart began pumping wildly. Why had this man come to his doorstep? Sweat formed on his brows. Dario had the indulgence, did he not?

A chill began in his neck and slithered down his back.

Had the monk come to deliver yet another warning before he died?

CHAPTER 53

~ FRIENDS AND LOVERS ~

APRIL 1509

Amadeo arrived home late to find Skender and Maria had set a table for him in the garden with spaghetti, olive oil, cheese, and sausage. But after he washed and joined them, they were both quiet and appeared to avoid his glance. Skender, in particular, fidgeted with the wine bottle before he finally poured it.

"What's wrong, Skender?"

"We have something to tell you, signore," said the slight woman with jet-black hair and eyes. But when he glanced at her, she looked down.

"What is it?"

"Signore"—Skender examined his folded hands—"long ago, you gave me my freedom, did you not?"

"I did, and you have worked for me willingly ever since. I truly appreciate it."

"But that means I can go wherever I wish and do whatever I want, does it not?"

"It does." His stomach churning, Amadeo feared what Skender would say next.

"Maria's uncle in Pisa recently died."

"Oh, I'm sorry to hear that. Do you want to go to the funeral? Is that it?"

"No." Skender shook his head. "Her uncle owned an outfitter's shop that serves the ships there. It's done quite well. But his wife died several years ago. And they never had any children."

Amadeo nodded. He now knew what Skender was going to say, and he steeled himself.

"In his will, he bequeathed the shop to Maria's father. But he can't run it because he's got his own shop here in Colpena."

"So my father wants Skender to run it." One of Maria's hands clasped her husband's. "He's giving it to Skender as a belated dowry."

"Which means you'll be moving to Pisa." Amadeo smiled. "You have my blessings. Both of you. I will sorely miss you, but you can't give up such an opportunity." He slapped Skender on the shoulder. "You're going to be a rich merchant, Skender. I know it."

With tears in his eyes, Skender stood, walked over, and hugged him. "Thank you, signore."

"But what will you do without us, capomaestro?" Worry crinkled Maria's forehead.

"I'll find someone else to cook and clean for me. But no one will ever be able to replace you two."

Then she, too, hugged him.

Two weeks later, Amadeo stood on the cobbles on the Strada delle Campane as Skender and Maria held the reins to the horse he'd given them.

Skender was now fifty-three years old, and he'd lived most of his life in service to Amadeo. He and Maria had tried to have children, but they must have been too old when they married, as no sons or daughters resulted from their union. Their plan now was to take in one of the younger orphans who roamed the Pisan streets, make him an apprentice, and start a family.

"I don't know what to say, signore." Skender's eyes were moist, and his glance couldn't focus on Amadeo's. "We may not see each other again for years."

"I know your heart, Skender, and you don't have to say anything." Amadeo's chest constricted. This parting was like losing a son. "A simple goodbye will do."

"Then goodbye, signore." Skender held out his hand.

Amadeo shook it, but then Skender hugged him. When they parted, Maria hugged him as well.

While Skender held the reins, Maria mounted. Behind the saddle was tied a bulging knapsack.

At the corner, they stopped and waved goodbye before disappearing onto the next street.

After they'd gone, Amadeo returned to an empty kitchen and listened to the silence.

Family.

Until those two had come to live with him, family was something Amadeo had never experienced. His mother died when he was barely five. And after his father had sent him, at the age of thirteen, to be apprenticed to Leon Battista Alberti in Florence, he'd been apart from his father and brother.

With them gone, the house seemed empty, lonely.

He'd lied about hiring someone else. No one could replace Skender and his bride. From now on, he'd probably eat at trattorias or skip supper altogether.

Two months after Skender's departure, Amadeo returned home late one night to find candlelight flickering from the kitchen.

"Ciao?" he called, placing a hand on the dagger he always wore. "Is someone here?"

The candlelight grew, threw shadows around the corner. It entered the hall.

His hand slid off his dagger hilt.

Before him stood Simona, her hair now gray instead of blonde, but still falling to her shoulders. Her flashing brown eyes still held the energy of youth, belying the woman of sixty smiling before him. Tonight, she'd abandoned the nun's attire for the simple gray frock she'd left earlier.

"Simona, what are you doing here?"

"I renounced my vows and left the convent."

For a moment, he simply stared at her, bereft of words. "B–but . . . why?"

"Because I never belonged there. And life's too short to stay where you don't belong. And because I heard that Skender and his wife left you."

"That Skender . . . left me?" His heart began beating faster. She'd done that for . . . him?

"Don't act so surprised, capomaestro. I keep in touch with my father, and he told me." She waved toward the garden and his office. "And after looking around, I see you desperately need someone to clean up after you. What did you eat tonight?"

"I haven't eaten yet."

"And it must be ten o'clock. I've got some food ready in the kitchen. It's cold, but I can heat it up." She started to turn, but he gripped her hand and stopped her.

"Simona . . . ?"

"Sì?" She faced him, her eyes searching his.

"What do you plan to do? Now that you've left the convent. I mean . . . where will you stay?"

"Are you asking me to live here?"

"N–no. That wouldn't be . . . seemly."

"No, it wouldn't, would it? I'll sleep at my father's palazzo. But I plan to be here every night to cook your dinner for you and to keep you company until you tell me to get out. Unless, you . . ."

"Unless I—what?"

"Never mind. We've been through that before. You're wedded to your vow of chastity and your duomo. You always will be. You've no room in your life for a wife."

"Simona, I . . ."

"What are you trying to say . . . capomaestro?" When she looked into his eyes, his determination to keep his lifelong vow simply melted.

"That my work on the duomo will one day come to an end. Perhaps in another three or four years. And then . . ."

"And then—what, Amadeo? What are you trying to say?"

"I'm asking you . . . that when I finish the duomo . . . if you will then . . . will you marry me?"

She stared into his eyes, her expression one of disbelief. Or was it shock? "Marry . . . you?"

"Sì. Will you marry me?"

"In three or four years?"

"Sì."

"That's the strangest marriage proposal I've ever heard." Her eyes were moist now, smiling and filling with tears. "You know the answer to that question. It's sì! Of course, I'll marry you. I'll wait another ten years if that's what it takes."

They embraced, and Amadeo's lips found hers. When they parted from the kiss, tears blurred even Amadeo's vision. "It won't be long, Simona. We've mostly interior work to do now. The façade is complete. The frescoes—"

Her finger pressed against his lips, stopping him. "Quiet now. No more talk about the duomo. It's time you eat."

As he followed her into the kitchen, the one word that kept coming to him was—*family*. That's what he'd just invited her to become a part of. Amadeo and Simona. After forty some years, plus a few more to complete the cathedral, they'd finally be together as a family.

That night, he sat down to warmed-over ravioli with hare sauce, cheese, white bread, and wine. And when Simona left near midnight, he felt as if the heavens had opened and showered him with God's mercy.

PART III

~ The Death of The Master Builder ~

CHAPTER 54

~ A BELATED REVENGE ~

OCTOBER 1512

On a chill October morning, dressed in their finest colored calze, wearing expensive fur and silk, and with hats plumed with long feathers, Dario's invited guests gathered in a forest clearing. Holding their horses' reins, each sipped wine from a silver goblet his servants had poured.

They had assembled two miles inland from Colpena on land owned by Baron Calabrese. Every so often, Dario sent Calabrese a barrel of wine or a wheel of cheese or a hundred pounds of wheat to mollify him. Calabrese had never actually agreed to let him hunt here, but the man was too weak to object. And besides, the chase usually took them far from the baron's lands.

Dario was looking forward to this day. Income from Ferata's relics tour had completely replaced his funding of the duomo. The relics had become so lucrative, he'd even been able to route some of the money into the Rossi Bank's reserves. For once, Aldo was happy. And with the creative accounting he was so good at, Dario could keep Ferata forever in the dark.

Ferata was scheduled to end his tour this month, but the bank now had a comfortable cushion.

Nearby, the dog master held the leashes of ten hounds, each three feet tall at the shoulders and straining to begin. But the trackers hadn't yet sounded their horns with news of game.

When the servants began collecting the goblets, Dario mounted his black stallion.

Standing high in his stirrups, he glanced over the crowd of nobles and rich merchants. He knew everyone, and these excursions, besides being highly entertaining, helped cement his leadership and spread goodwill. Many of the Signoria and the Council of Thirty were here. Despite his frequent complaints about the expense, so was Aldo. Even Rocco Marino and Enzio Borroni had joined them. For who could miss out on a grand hunt such as this?

Dario leaned across to Fabiano Trentino, sitting astride a spotted gelding. "Who is that bearded attendant with Marino? His face seems vaguely familiar."

"Why that's Agapetto Moretti. He once served Marino many years back but has been away. I hear he's spent some time in Genoa."

Dario's heart leaped against his ribs. "Agapetto . . . Moretti?" The man was many years older, with a beard and a lined, grizzled face. But he was indeed the servant who'd poured the poison wine in his palazzo— was that thirty years ago?

"Signore, is something wrong?"

"No. Nothing's wrong." Dario gripped the reins tighter.

"A beautiful day for a hunt, don't you think?"

"Sì." But Dario's gaze was fixed on Agapetto. "Better still when the hunter spies the prey he's been looking for."

Fabiano turned a questioning glance to him. "But the game hasn't been spotted yet, signore."

"Ah, my friend, but it has. And it's staring us in the face."

A distant horn sounded. The tracker had found the hart's trail.

Fabiano stared at Dario as if he were bewitched.

The dogs began barking, Dario spurred his mount, and the hunt began.

The chase lasted most of the morning until the hounds cornered a sixteen-point buck. As custom decreed, the others stood aside while Dario shot the animal with his bow.

After attendants gutted the carcass and tied it over a stiff branch, the entire group met back at the starting point, where servants had prepared a lavish lunch on tables with more wine.

But during lunch, Dario's glance returned again and again to Marino and his new groom. He barely touched his food.

It was dark, and as Dario's feet creaked over boards on the deserted wharf, waves slapped against the pilings below. Here at the western dock, two lanterns surrounded by clouds of insects illuminated the hooded figures of Aldo and Jacopo, already waiting.

"Why did you call us here?" demanded Aldo, throwing off his hood. "Why couldn't we meet after the hunt?"

"Because I discovered today the identity of the person who killed your daughter and who tried to kill me."

Aldo's jaw tensed, and his hands formed into fists. "Who?"

"Rocco Marino. The groom with him today was Agapetto Moretti. He's aged and grown a beard. After all this time, Marino probably thought no one would recognize him. So Agapetto did, indeed, work for Marino. When he tried to kill us all, he failed, killing your daughter instead."

Aldo smashed a fist into a palm.

"Sì." Dario faced Jacopo. "You know what to do. Before the week is out, I want them both dead."

"A member of the Signoria?" Jacopo frowned and swatted something biting his neck. "Marino will be a difficult target. Guards man the entrance to his palazzo, and he rarely leaves. He even runs his wine and cheese business from the ground floor."

"Marino, especially, I want dead. Even if you have to get inside his palazzo to do it."

Jacopo shook his head. "This is more dangerous than anything you've ever asked of me. I'm not as young as I used to be. I may have to take someone else, younger and stronger."

"Whatever you need to do, do it!"

After Aldo headed for home, Dario stopped off at a taverna and had a few glasses of wine to celebrate his coming victory. As he sipped, he smiled. Would the attempt on his life, after thirty long years, finally be avenged? Events were in motion now. And nothing anyone could say or do could stop the revenge he'd waited so long for.

Well after midnight, he crossed Palazzo Rossi and approached the steps to his front door.

A figure draped in black stepped from the shadows.

"Flames, Dario Rossi," said the voice, young and vibrant. "I've seen you . . . in the flames."

"N–no, no!" he backed away, his heart leaping like a caged animal.

"You still have time. You can still turn from this course you've set." The monk was in his midtwenties, with jet-black hair and bright eager eyes.

"W–who are you? Why are you here?"

"I know you, Dario Rossi. God sent me a vision, and I walked all the way from Orvieto to bring you the news."

"N–no." He backed away a few steps. "Not again."

"You must stop what you're doing. Turn from your evil ways."

"But I have an indulgence. I paid for the duomo. My sins are forgiven."

"Your sins have risen like a smoking black pall, rising even to the angels and befouling the very doorstep of Heaven."

"Leave me alone. Go away."

"But your passage to the eternal fires—I'm warning you now, Dario Rossi—it will open via the plague. Sì, the black death is coming for you."

After running up the steps, he smashed his key against the lock and missed. Trying again, it slipped into the hole, and he turned it. He didn't want to hear any more.

"You can still save yourself. There's still time."

"Go away! I have the indulgence." The lock clicked. He pushed on the door. It crashed open, sending mad echoes through the cavernous entryway.

Sweat poured off his forehead, burning his eyes.

Slamming the door shut, he rammed his back against it with all his might. The last muffled words he heard from outside were: "You . . . have . . . nothing."

His heart was a hammer pounding so hard against his ribs, he feared the bones would break. But he didn't even have the breath to scream.

JACOPO LOOKED BOTH WAYS DOWN the dark street. Marino lived on the city's eastern slope among the richer merchants' houses. Jacopo nodded to his companion for tonight's work—a dockworker in his midthirties named Aroldo, muscles bulging under his shirt. Heavily in debt, Aroldo had killed men before. He was eager for the job.

From high on the rooftops, an owl hooted, the only sound in an otherwise too-quiet night.

Moonlight illuminated an ugly scar across Aroldo's left cheek—no doubt from one of his frequent tavern fights.

Warily, Aroldo eyed the open window. Then he threw the grappling hook. But the iron claw only clattered against the second-story railing before landing—loud, too loud—on the cobbled street.

Jacopo sucked in breath and shot a glance at the palazzo's only other open window. But no one stuck their head out to investigate. And no cry of alarm went up.

He waved his accomplice to continue.

The dockworker reeled in the rope, swung the hook several times, took aim, and threw again. This time, the hook caught on the rail with a harsh clink. Aroldo tied the bottom to a nearby railing, tautened the rope, and began climbing. Faster than Jacopo could ever have done, he reached the top. After peering inside the room, he signaled for Jacopo to follow.

Jacopo grabbed the rope, put his feet on the first knot, and pushed himself up to the second knot.

He was no climber. And age made this kind of exertion more difficult, but Aroldo had insisted the knots would help.

As he climbed, he thought about the groom they'd killed only moments ago in the stables. He felt no remorse. Even as the man sank to his knees and pleaded for his life, Jacopo ran his knife through the man's stomach, then slit his throat. Agapetto Moretti, the poisoner of children and attempted assassin of the Rossis, now lay dead on the stable floor.

Fortunately, tonight, no other grooms slept there.

Long moments later, breathing and sweating heavily, he gained the balcony.

Aroldo glanced through the open door. "Which room is Marino's?"

Jacopo bent over his knees, trying to catch his breath. He was getting too old for this kind of work. He held up his hand to wait. When he'd recovered, he said, "I'm not sure. I wasn't able to learn much about the layout only that his bedroom is on this floor."

Aroldo grunted, and they crossed the library floor. A few tables held a handful of books and busts of ancient Romans. A few chairs beside the tables.

Pushing open the door, they entered a dark hallway. The torches had all gone out. Good.

Jacopo looked right, then left. No guards. But they'd probably be stationed on the ground floor, not up here. He slid his one-foot knife out of its leather sheath and turned right. Aroldo's blade was already out.

They crept down the hall, but the next door was closed.

He pushed. Creaking on rusted hinges, it slowly opened.

There in bed sat a middle-aged woman reading a book with a candle illuminating the room. She was alone. For one frozen moment, their glances met.

Her eyes widened. Then she screamed.

Aroldo rushed at her and, with two quick blows, knocked her senseless onto the quilt.

A set of footsteps raced down the hall. Jacopo jerked the woman's bedroom door open again and came face-to-face with Rocco Marino.

Marino's mouth opened, and he backed against the opposite wall. "Guards!" he shouted.

Jacopo's blade plunged, catching him full in the chest just below the rib cage. He jerked up, twisted the blade, then yanked it out, his hand now wet and sticky.

Then he slit the man's throat.

More footsteps—too many—pounded up the stairs from below.

"Quick!" he shouted to Aroldo. But his accomplice was already running. They turned left and entered the library. Quietly, he pulled the door shut behind them, hoping the guards wouldn't notice.

If only they could make it down the rope before—

The door burst open, and four men with swords rushed in.

Jacopo backed up. Too late to go down the rope. They must stand and fight.

But Aroldo—the fool!—ran onto the balcony. Two soldiers followed close behind. Even as he leaned over to grab the rope, their blades dropped him to the floor.

Now was the time to attack. Eyeing the nearest guard, Jacopo feinted to the right, then lunged to the left with his knife.

Out of nowhere, something slammed into his side.

The other soldier! But how . . . ?

Even as he looked down, a second sword sliced into his abdomen. He waited for the pain, but, strangely, he felt only a dull ache, growing sharper by the moment.

He slumped to his knees, life leaking out of him.

A third blade was sweeping in from the side. He saw it clearly, aimed for his neck. With the way it came on, from all his years of experience, he knew its trajectory, where it would land. It would cut his head clean from his body. Everything was happening in slow motion now, and he could do nothing to stop it.

The floor rolled, tumbled, then came to a stop. Helpless in the moment before his world went dark, he saw his headless body lying six feet away.

CHAPTER 55

~ CONSEQUENCES ~

NOVEMBER 1512

In the streets outside the Signoria council chamber, the crowds chanted, "Down with the tyrant! Out with the Rossis!" Too much did they remind Dario of the Florentine crowds and how they ran wild run through the city after the attempt on Lorenzo de' Medici's life.

Inside the room, the six remaining Signoria members met in an emergency session, each man shifting uneasily in his chair. The sergeant-at-arms had barred the town hall doors leading to the piazza. They'd called for the city guard to arrive in full force, but none had arrived yet. With the noise from the crowds so loud, Callisto ordered a page to close the windows.

"This is intolerable," said Enzio Borroni. "Look!" His finger pointed, and everyone's gaze fell on the empty chair that was Rocco Marino's. "We must decide what to do about the murder of one of our own."

"I agree, but before we vote, we must appoint someone to replace him." Strain tightened Callisto's voice. "We cannot proceed with only six members."

"Agreed," said Fabiano Trentino.

"I nominate Arturo Costa, the spice merchant," said Borroni. "The Council of Thirty has already put him forward as our next candidate."

Dario's heart raced. "But he was in prison for debts owed to Marcello. How can we allow someone who's defaulted on his debts to sit on the council?" Was this why Costa was waiting in the hall? Had the Signoria already consulted the Thirty without his knowledge?

"Someone paid those debts." Borroni grinned in his direction. "And after he left his gambling days behind, Arturo's business is booming. He's now one of the city's richest men."

"I agree, and I second the nomination," said Callisto. "Gonfaloniere, the rules require that you pass the bowl."

Dario swallowed. He had no choice. "The question is whether to allow Costa on the council. I see the beads are already before you. White for yes. Black for no." He dropped a black bead into the bowl, stood, and walked the bowl down the line to receive the votes.

Bringing the results back to his seat, he counted. "Four white. Two black." He stared at the beads. "Arturo Costa is the new member of the Signoria."

When Dario said no more, Callisto spoke. "Sergeant, let in the new member."

After Arturo Costa took his seat, he glared at Rossi. The man surely had a store of grievances against him. And this was the man, above all others, that the Thirty had put forward?

When Callisto Mancini shook his head at the newcomer, Costa lowered his glance. "Gonfaloniere"—Callisto pointed toward the window—"listen to the uproar in the piazza. The people are in revolt. They know what's happened here, and they're calling for your head. We must give them justice. What are we to do?"

Dario thought quickly. "Let us throw a week of feasting and celebration in the streets—a grand party with free food, drinks, and jousts. A feast the likes of which our city has never before been. Such a display of largesse will surely mollify the people. Then they'll forget all about this incident, and life will return to normal."

Borroni slammed a fist on the table. "No!"

"The city treasury doesn't have the funds for that kind of expense." Fabiano shook his head.

"I agree," said Marcello Esposito. "And we cannot hide what has happened here with bribery. Justice must be served."

"Justice?" Now, Dario slammed his own fist on the table. "Where was the justice in the poisoning of Aldo's daughter? In the attempted assassination of me, Aldo, Aldo's wife, and his children?"

"That was long ago." Callisto opened his hands. "And the people are focused on today's events. They see only this blatant attack by your man Jacopo on a member of our body, and they demand justice. As does the Council of Thirty. And, Dario, the evidence cannot be denied. What happened years ago is not on trial here."

"It should be."

"What is the procedure to elect a new gonfaloniere?" asked Borroni. "I suggest the time for that is now."

Noise from the piazza below replaced the sudden quiet in the room as everyone faced Borroni.

"The procedure," came Callisto's low voice, "is that the existing gonfaloniere must leave the room and the remaining members vote. Is that really what we want to do?"

Dario stiffened in horror as every head but Aldo's nodded.

"Dario"—Callisto was almost whispering—"please leave the room."

While the discussion and vote proceeded without him, Dario sat in the hall. Time seemed to stretch on without end. Jacopo's incompetence had brought not only his own death but also disaster to the Rossis. Dario should have replaced him years ago.

Now, for the first time in his career as the unofficial lord of Colpena, events were spinning out of his control.

After an eternity of waiting, the doors opened, and Aldo walked out.

"Aldo, what happened? What's going on?"

But his cousin merely glared at him and continued walking down the hall without speaking.

"Aldo!"

He disappeared around the corner. Slow footsteps echoed up from the stairs at the end of the hall.

Why had he left without speaking? What was going on in there?

An eternity of moments later, the sergeant-at-arms called him back in.

As he walked the room's length and headed for his seat, his legs were boards of wood. Only Callisto dared look at him. A bad sign.

When Dario reached the middle of the chamber, Callisto held up a hand. "Stop there, Dario."

"Can I not resume my seat?"

"No." Borroni was grinning.

"What's going on? As gonfaloniere, I am entitled to my seat on the—"

Borroni huffed. "You are not—"

"Please!"—Callisto waved to Borroni—"let me."

Dario's heart beat faster now, and his face felt flushed. What had they decided? Aldo's leaving in the middle of a session was another bad sign. Bad, indeed.

"After discussing the evidence," said Callisto, "we believe it's clear what went on at Rocco Marino's palazzo. Considering tradition and your ancestors' role in founding this city, we might have overlooked your past misdeeds. But now the city's very welfare is at stake, and a semblance of justice must be served. Even the Council of Thirty has demanded action. Thus, the Signoria has elected me as the new gonfaloniere."

Dario sucked in air and held it. How could they do this?

"In addition, we have removed both you and Aldo—you who were involved in the murder plot—from the council. Hopefully, that will mollify the Thirty and the mob outside. Above all, we must restore order to the city." Callisto swept a hand through his hair. "I'm sorry, Dario. I wish this had turned out differently. But under the circumstances . . ."

He stared at the five men sitting before him. No longer gonfaloniere? No longer in control of the city's finances? He felt faint.

Turning slowly, he staggered toward the door.

"Just be glad we didn't arrest you for murder." Borroni was sneering. "You're getting off easy."

"Sergeant, help him out the back way," said Callisto. "See him safely home and place a contingent in front of his palazzo until things quiet down."

In a daze, Dario walked through the back streets, accompanied by guards. Once inside his palazzo, he drank until he fell unconscious on his bedroom floor.

CHAPTER 56

~ DOWNFALL ~

MARCH 1513

Amadeo climbed the steps to Palazzo Rossi with dread. Few people had talked with or even seen Rossi since he'd been stripped of his title of gonfaloniere. And last week, when the Wool Guild, the Stonecutter's Guild, and the Mason's Guild had invited half the city to present Amadeo with an award for honor, duty, and excellence in building, Rossi hadn't shown up. Perhaps that was to be expected. The award had been acutely embarrassing, but he'd accepted it graciously.

He could only guess what Rossi was like now. Nothing good could come of this meeting. Yet he'd been summoned, Rossi was still paying for the duomo, and he felt he needed to show up.

He knocked, and the new man, Paolo, opened the door. Tall, thin, and brusque, he eyed Amadeo with suspicion, even though this was Amadeo's third visit since Grazziano passed away.

"I was summoned." Perhaps that would awaken some remembrance in the servant.

"The signore awaits you, does he?" Paolo ran a hand through a mane of ink-black hair and stepped aside. Amadeo missed Grazziano's snide remarks and efficient manner. This servant never seemed to know what was going on inside the Rossi household.

Paolo led him to the library, where Amadeo saw Rossi for the first time in a year. He sucked in breath and tried not to show his surprise.

Sprawled over a high-backed chair, the man had grown a paunch, and stubble darkened his usually clean-shaven chin. Below bloodshot eyes hung dark circles. His thinning hair, long, uncut, and mangy, tangled in greasy clumps, and when he lifted his gaze to his visitor, his rheumy eyes seemed unable to focus.

The heavy, cloying scent of some woman's perfume permeated the library.

"Welcome to the man who receives the highest awards from his compatriots, the man loved and fawned over by everyone." Rossi raised a glass of wine, waved it, spilled some, and then drank. "What higher honor could a man not achieve? Why, even the angels in Heaven couldn't bestow more praise. How the people grovel before you. Why, I wouldn't be surprised if God himself on his throne decided to give you an award."

"It was unexpected, possibly undeserved." Was Rossi so jealous that he needed to badger him?

"Do I detect a bit of false modesty? The great capomaestro gladly accepts his great award but in the next breath says it's undeserved? What is false modesty if not pride? Are you prideful, Puccini?"

"Why have you summoned me here?"

Rossi motioned him to a nearby seat. "To see what you're made of. I've been sitting here thinking. Sì, thinking and . . . pondering."

"Are you drunk?"

"Possibly, capomaestro, and here"—he poured another glass of wine, carried it the few feet to where Amadeo sat, and placed it on a low table before him, where it slopped over the edge—"take some yourself."

"No thank you."

"Of course not. You're a man self-contained, self-possessed, and self-righteous. Wine at ten o'clock in the morning doesn't interest you. And you don't need the admiration of men, yet you receive it anyway. You don't need the company of women, yet Callisto's daughter, Simona— what a beautiful wench, no?—she's been throwing herself at you all your life. And you, being the self-righteous prude that you are, simply ignore her advances. Ah, what self-control. Who wouldn't admire such a man?"

"I should leave." He began to rise, but Rossi, still standing before him, pushed him back down.

"Sit. I'm not done with you."

Amadeo glanced toward the door, wondering if he should try to make a run for it. Rossi was more than drunk. His behavior was strange— frightening, even. For the first time, he noticed someone else in the room. In the library's far corner—a woman. Was it her perfume he'd smelled?

"Come forth, my beauty." Rossi nodded in her direction. "He's seen you."

A woman of perhaps twenty-five, dressed in the manner of all prostitutes with high heels, wearing a shift of such sheer satin he nearly saw through it, stepped out of the shadows. Her hips sashayed as she sauntered to a position beside Amadeo. A tongue circled her lips, and she smiled. The rouge on her cheeks marred what was otherwise one of the most beautiful women he'd ever seen. As he watched, she slipped the flimsy garment off her shoulders. It floated to the floor, and her naked body stepped over it. She began to dance, weaving her arms in the air like serpents.

"She's quite something, is she not?" asked Rossi. "And I will make a bargain with you."

"What?" His heart thumping harder now, Amadeo jerked his gaze away from her toward the door.

Rossi pulled a heavy sack from under his chair and plopped it on the table with a muffled clink. Reaching inside, he began dropping gold florins on the table, one after another. "These are for you, Puccini." The coins clinked, rolled, and began piling up.

Amadeo glanced at the growing glittering pile, then at his host. "What are you doing?"

Rossi kept dropping the coins. "I give them to you, Amadeo. Five thousand florins. That's what's in this bag. And it's all yours."

A frown pinched his brows. "In exchange for—what?"

Rossi smiled and waved at the whore. "All you have to do is go upstairs with her. Lie with her, and these five thousand florins are yours. The easiest money anyone ever made."

Amadeo jerked his glance from the coins, the woman, and stood. "I'm leaving."

Rossi rushed forward, a hand reaching out to push him back into his seat.

The whore stopped dancing and retreated to the corner.

As Amadeo backed away, Rossi stumbled, nearly fell, but regained his footing.

"This is unbecoming of you, gonfaloniere." Amadeo glanced again toward the door.

"They took that title from me." Frowning now, Rossi staggered backward. "Don't call me that."

"What's become of you, Dario? Look at yourself. You're wallowing in self-pity, drinking too much, and heading toward self-destruction."

Rossi just stood and glared at him. "Take her. I order you to take her. I want you to be like all the rest of us, Puccini."

Amadeo spun on his heels and stalked to the door. He gave a last glance back in time to see Rossi slump into the chair with glazed, unfocused eyes.

On the way home, he prayed silently for the soul of the man he'd just left.

CHAPTER 57

~ THE COURTESAN ~

APRIL 1513

At the end of a long day in the tracing house, Amadeo had finally finished the cartoons for the last three frescoes. Then his assistants had smeared a thick coat of intonaco to the panel on the main chancel wall. Tomorrow, they'd help him raise the cartoon paper to the wet plaster.

After he'd painted the completed images, even Cardinal Gonzaga must see why these frescoes glorifying Christ, and not Mary's life, were the right design for behind the altar.

He left the tracing house and crossed the distance to the duomo's front. The façade was complete, and most of the statuary now nestled in niches on the outside facing wall. The high arches, the statues of the Apostles and popes, the starburst, stained-glass window—all of it lifted his spirits. He stepped through the massive bronze doors, under the multiple receding arches, and into the nave.

The sun's dying light shot through the façade's stained-glass window, bathing the interior in all the colors of the rainbow. Over one hundred and fifty feet above him, fluted arches crisscrossed the ceiling. On both sides, the great columns formed aisles for the bays, now filled with the frescoes he and his painters had been working on these last five years. Interrupted only by a few monuments to Colpena's prominent citizens, they told the story of the Bible.

Most of the terra-cotta floor tiles had been replaced with marble designs displaying the coats of arms and history of Colpena's wealthy families—his acquiescence to the Church's desires. Light from the setting sun shone through the clerestory windows, hitting the upper part of the chancel. Michelangelo's great statue of Christ's ascension commanded the space behind the altar.

All of it—or at least most of it—bespoke of God's grandeur and the story of Christ.

His heart soared, and he breathed deeply. Before year's end, the duomo, his life's work, would be complete. The vision he'd once had of the finished duomo was coming true. Outside, all that remained was the lantern atop the dome and the bells in the campanile. Inside, only a few statues, frescoes, and a bit of tile work awaited completion. And, of course, the three main frescoes behind the chancel.

It was a grand work for God's glory. And in a few months, it would be complete.

He sighed. It was late, time to go home.

Tonight, Simona was unable to cook his meal. Rossi had apparently emerged from his melancholy and, in an attempt to reenter polite society, was throwing a grand party. Callisto was going with her.

The new gonfaloniere had just returned from Rome, where, in his official capacity, he had congratulated Giovanni de' Medici, one of Lorenzo's sons, on his elevation to the papacy. Taking the name Leo X, Giovanni replaced the contentious, warring Julius II.

Amadeo had declined Rossi's invitation to the party. Never again would he step foot inside Palazzo Rossi.

Instead, he ate his supper down at the waterfront at a favorite trattoria, then returned home early. But when he shoved his key in the lock, the door swung inward. Odd, he was sure he'd locked the door. Shaking his head, he pushed through to the table and lit a candle. Before leaving for supper, he'd placed there a decanter of wine and a list from Vittorio. But he always set the wine bottle on the table's right side, not the left. He was a man who liked everything in its place. Staring at the bottle's new position, he shook his head. He'd been working hard, maybe too hard.

He sat, moved the decanter to where it belonged, poured a glass of wine, and drank. Then he studied Vittorio's list detailing the workers who'd left the duomo now that they'd finished much of the stone and masonry work and the stained-glass work. He smiled. The number of men who'd finished their tasks was proof that the duomo was nearing completion. But by the time he'd sipped another half a glass and counted up how many workers were left and how much they'd cost, the figures were drifting in and out of focus. Surely, tonight he was more tired than ever he could remember. He stood and took a step toward the bedroom.

His legs almost failed him. The room spun, and he grabbed the table's edge for support. Spots exploded across the room.

Something was wrong.

The wine?

He jerked his head toward a glass vessel that seemed to bulge and shrink even as he watched.

Had he been poisoned?

Reeling, he bounced off one wall and staggered into the bedroom.

But as he collapsed onto the bed, a deepening fog swelled inside his head. Then he heard—or he thought he heard—a woman's voice.

"He's out," she said as if from a great distance.

"Good," said a man, the unknown voice echoing as from the top of a deep well. "Now get him undressed, and . . ."

Sleep called, and he heard no more.

He woke in his own bed to a pounding headache. He jerked himself upright, and immediately regretted the movement. His head throbbed. And he was naked.

The faint smell of perfume, a cloying, heavy scent, vaguely familiar, drifted to him. Coming from the sheets? He lowered his face to the bed. Sì, it was stronger there.

Then he remembered that smell—the same scent as that worn by the prostitute Rossi had tried to make him lie with.

What went on here last night?

But he'd been unconscious. He couldn't have done anything with any woman.

An uneasy feeling churned his stomach.

Hurriedly, he pulled on his breechcloth, calze, tunic, and shoes. He washed his face from the basin atop the dresser. The events of last evening had been so unreal—surreal. Were it not for the perfume, the unlocked door, and the moved decanter, he could've imagined it all.

But whatever had happened here, Rossi had been behind it. The perfume was proof of that.

He checked every room, inside his locked trunk, and all his documents. Nothing was missing or out of place. Shaking his head, he grabbed a piece of bread and was heading toward the door when he noticed on the floor—a crumpled paper.

Kneeling, he picked it up, smoothed it, and read:

My dearest Callisto Mancini and Simona,

I regret to inform you that, for some time, Signore Puccini has been leading two lives. Thus do I urge you both to leave Signore Rossi's palazzo at once, without delay, and proceed to Signore Puccini's residence. There tonight, you will find evidence that the capomaestro is not who you think he is.

Unfortunately, because of my position, and because public revelation of my authorship of this missive might seriously harm my reputation, I must send this note anonymously.

—A friend from afar

His heart beating fast, he stared at the note. His hands found the top of his head. Did the bishop write this?

No, this affair reeked of Rossi. And last night, Callisto and Simona had surely received the note, left the party, and discovered him here in bed with one of Rossi's whores. He pressed a hand to his throat, feeling like he might vomit. Was it the aftereffects of the drug or the thought of Simona seeing him in such a compromising position?

He must go to them and explain—*this morning*. But it was also critical that he go to the duomo. If he delayed too long, he'd have to strip much intonaco from the walls and start over tomorrow, leaving a seam.

But first, he had to find out what Callisto and Simona had seen and explain.

Outside, the sun was already high. Whatever drug they'd given him made him sleep half the morning.

He arrived at Callisto's palazzo out of breath and fearing the worst. After he knocked and the peephole briefly opened and shut, the wait seemed like an eternity.

When a servant finally opened the door, a frowning Callisto stood in the hallway beyond.

"What do you want, Amadeo?"

"I want to explain, and to—"

"No explanation can absolve you of what we saw last night."

"B–but you don't understand. I—"

"I do understand, and that's the problem. I am so disappointed in you, words fail me. I suppose it's the times we live in that bring down even the best of us. You were so drunk last night you didn't even wake. And lying with that whore." His face scrunching with disgust, he shook his head. "Simona was in tears half the night. And if you came to the house today, she said to tell you she will never see you again. Neither do I want you associating with my daughter. Ever again. We've nothing more to say to each other."

"Please, I—"

The door slammed in his face.

He stared at the door in disbelief. They wouldn't even listen to his explanation. This evening, he must come back. Sì, no one was thinking clearly now, least of all himself. Tonight, he'd return and again try to explain.

CHAPTER 58

~ THE FINAL FRESCOES ~

On the walk to the duomo, Amadeo tried to still his racing heart. Surely, after Callisto and Simona calmed down, they'd listen to him tonight. Rossi could not get away with this.

Meanwhile, he needed to be at the duomo. Today was the day he planned to begin the final frescoes. Painting the first scene would also help soothe his troubled mind.

By the time he arrived at the work site, his assistants had been waiting for hours.

"I'm sorry for being so late," he said.

The two young men nodded and exchanged worried glances.

With the plaster still wet from yesterday, his apprentices spread out the first paper cartoon on the floor. This morning, he'd start the first scene. *The Birth of Christ* displayed Mary and Joseph kneeling before the baby Jesus, angels singing above, shepherds coming in from the fields, and the three magi approaching. The cartoon was a charcoal sketch. With the paper still on the floor, he poked through with an ivory point, marking points on the drawing for today's work.

Once he'd outlined the profile of the magi, he prepared his paints. He and his assistants mounted the scaffold with the cartoon, and as they held it up, he dabbed the holes with charcoal. After the cartoon was removed, charcoal dots outlined the figures he'd paint today. With brush in hand, he began.

Painting a fresco was urgent, precise work. The paint merged with the wet plaster, and he had to finish all of the wet section today before it dried. If he didn't, they'd have to scrape off the unfinished plaster tomorrow and start over, leaving a seam. It was demanding work, and drying plaster waited for no one. "No coward ever attempted a fresco," went the saying.

After painting until well after noon, he finished a quick meal, ascended the scaffold, and took up his brush again. As expected, the act of painting had quieted the churning emotions of the morning. He was looking forward to straightening out Rossi's mess with Callisto and Simona tonight.

When the sound of footsteps echoed down the nave from behind, he didn't even turn. People often came to gawk at artists working on the duomo.

"What are you doing, capomaestro?" The command from the familiar voice behind was like the cold wind of storm on a hot summer day.

He lowered his brush and twisted on the scaffold. Below stood Cardinal Gonzaga, Bishop Ferata, a tall man in a black cape, and two church soldiers. "I'm painting the last of the frescoes, signore."

"Come down from there at once. We must talk."

Amadeo glanced at his unfinished magi. "If I don't finish this today, cardinal, I will have to scrape off the—"

"I said come down."

He wrapped his brush in cloth, covered his paints, and climbed down the ladder to stand before this unexpected Church delegation. Why had Gonzaga brought armed men with him? And who was the black-caped man? "What can I do for you?"

"Ferata warned me what you've been up to. Last night, capomaestro, the bishop saw your cartoons in the tracing house." Gonzaga sucked in air, the effort shaking his considerable bulk. "Why is this not a scene depicting the life of Mary, as requested?"

"Because, signore, Mary is but a minor figure in the Bible. Christ is the one whom we should be celebrating. And if you would only allow me to paint what I have in mind, you will see—"

"Is not Mary the mother of God?"

Amadeo frowned. "She is Jesus's earthly mother, sì."

"But is she the Mother of God?"

"God has no mother."

Gonzaga narrowed his brows. "Should we not honor her as the one whom the angel Gabriel blessed, who brought Christ into the world, and who takes our prayers to our Lord and Savior?"

Heat rising in his cheeks, Amadeo stood straighter and fixed a steady gaze on Gonzaga. "Mary is not a god, signore. So why should we pray to her? We should only honor her as Jesus's earthly mother."

Gonzaga's eyes widened. "You are saying we shouldn't pray to her?"

He swallowed. "Sì."

"But that is . . . sacrilege. How dare you speak thus about our Blessed Virgin!"

"I have read the Bible, signore, and nowhere do I find a book of Mary. Nowhere." As he gazed into Gonzaga's cold, tiny orbs surrounded by flesh, a chill breeze seemed to crawl over Amadeo's hot forehead. Something deep inside him warned not to go further. Instead, he stood up straighter. "Signore, you have made her into an idol. I challenge you to find one place in the Bible—just one—where it says we should pray to her. No, you will not find it. Mary cannot intercede for us any more than you or I can. Only Christ, the Son of God, can do that. I have thought deeply about this, cardinal, and no, I cannot paint a fresco to glorify Mary in the place of honor when it is Christ himself who should be there—Christ, the only one who can save us."

"How dare you!" said Gonzaga. "You are no priest. You cannot interpret Holy Scripture."

"Blasphemy!" cried the black-robed priest beside Gonzaga. "I've heard enough. This man is a heretic."

"I agree," said Gonzaga. "His own words condemn him." He motioned to the guards. "Take him to the city dungeon. Tell the guards to hold him for trial."

"And tell them this," added the black-robed priest. "Tell them that Ulisse Rua, the Grand Inquisitor, orders that, until we hold his trial, no one is to be admitted to see him."

As the guards grabbed his arms and jostled him down the nave's center, his heart thumped wildly, and his legs nearly failed him. What crime had he committed deserving of this?

IN THE DAYS THAT FOLLOWED, Amadeo thought back, again and again, to that moment when he last saw the sun, breathed fresh air, and ate decent food.

When the guards dragged him down the cold steps to the dungeon, they ripped his world out from under him. The change was so stark, so abrupt, that for a time he lingered in shock—as if he'd entered not just a dark prison, but a deep well of melancholy, hopelessness, and despair.

One moment, he was finishing the duomo, his life's work.

The next, his entire life—everything that made him who he was—was stolen from him.

The days dragged their feet across the wet stone and became weeks. And the weeks crawled on hands and knees, stared into the blackness, and became months.

How many months? He didn't know.

Not once in all the time since his imprisonment did he learn his fate. Not one word came to him. It was as if the world above had completely forgotten him.

He was thinner now than the day they'd dragged him down here. The clothes he'd worn that day—a simple tunic with some dabs of paint—had shredded and begun to rot in the constant damp.

The head guard's name was Raul, and on Amadeo's many trips here over the years, he'd given the man many florins, brought him many bottles of wine. But after the guard locked shackles around Amadeo's ankles and the iron door clanged shut on this stinking hole, Raul's formerly pleasant attitude hardened.

The only kindness Raul now showed him was that Amadeo received a bucket for his waste. Most of the others had no such privilege.

Only the worst and poorest prisoners were sent to the civil dungeon. The tower was reserved for rich merchants, political prisoners, and nobility. As capomaestro, he should have been sent there. Down here, they locked up murderers, thieves, debtors, and heretics. Down here, only a faded beam of light trickled through the single iron-barred window high up the wall. And down here, few lived more than a handful of years before illness or starvation took their lives.

Twice a day, Raul gave him the same bowl of thin gruel he gave the others. For water, he shared a common bucket with the three men chained in his immediate vicinity. When he'd arrived, the other prisoners recognized him, treated him with deference, and bemoaned that his fate had joined theirs.

A single large room held everyone. Prisoners were chained either to the wall or to a series of wooden posts marching down the room's center, leaving barely a two-foot walkway on either side for the guards.

As he leaned back against the stone wall, always damp, always cold, he listened to the weeping, the moans, the raspy breathing, and the coughs around him.

He had plenty of time to ponder the events leading to his imprisonment.

What he regretted most was being unable to explain to Simona and Callisto about Rossi's whore. He tried not to be bitter about that. Someday, maybe they'd figure it out.

Yet what if he never saw her again?

His future was grim. If Gonzaga now employed a Grand Inquisitor, there was no hope of a reprieve. From what he'd heard of these inquisitions, they never changed their minds. Without exception, everyone tried was found guilty. Nowhere else in Italy had he heard of there being an inquisition like this. But what else could one expect from a Spanish cardinal assigned to Tuscany?

To lift his spirits, he tried to remember the last night he walked alone through the nearly finished duomo. Whatever they did, they could never take that away from him. The duomo, his grand work of forty-three years, was his work of love, his monument to God and to Christ. Whatever false doctrine they tried to make him confess, he'd held true to Christ, true to his heart.

Yesterday morning, after hearing for the thousandth time the moaning, the crying, the coughing from his downcast fellow prisoners, he decided to lift their spirits. Every morning since his arrival, he'd begun the day with a silent prayer.

But yesterday, for the first time, he said it out loud so everyone could hear. "Our father who dwells in Heaven, hallowed be your name . . ." he'd begun.

Soon, every voice still able to speak had joined in. And when they'd finished, he heard their whispered thanks. Last night, he repeated the prayer. And again this morning.

For a short while, at least, he'd brought what light he could into the darkness.

CHAPTER 59

~ ALDO'S DECISION ~

JULY 1513

Behind Dario, thunder echoed off Monte Argentario, and rain pounded the cobbles. Entering his former haunt in the Allegra Taverna in the Temestre Inferiore, he shook the rain from his cape. He breathed in the familiar smells of spilt wine, bubbling stew, pungent cheese, and the smoke of tobacco, the curious smoking weed from the New World.

In the corner by the fire, a young man plucked a lute and sang a boisterous drinking song. Just like in the old days.

Mario, the taverna's former proprietor, had long since passed away, as had Calandra and Bianca. He hadn't stopped here in years, and he'd heard that upstairs worked a new woman, a bit older than usual, but reportedly very good in bed. After sixty-seven years of life, he now found all the women he slept with looked younger to him.

Tonight, just as in the old days, Aldo had called him here on business. His cousin had said that the new owner, a young man named Remigio, would gladly rent them their old room.

Dario was glad for this meeting, hoping to smooth things over with his cousin. Lately, Aldo had been brusque and irritable. Tonight, Aldo wanted to discuss business. But perhaps this evening, they could instead drink, eat, and romp upstairs with the new woman. Tomorrow was the time to discuss business.

He could start life anew. He could even be more serious about making money. But not tonight.

Strolling through the seated patrons, he accepted their smiles and nods. But were some of those smiles actually smirks? And weren't a few of them whispering and casting furtive glances his way? Since losing his seat on the Signoria, some of the contadini hadn't shown him the proper respect he was due.

He pushed through to the back room, where Aldo sat with a bottle of wine.

"Well, cousin"—Dario beamed—"this is just like old times, isn't it?"

"No, Dario, it isn't. Not at all."

"What do you mean?"

"We'll get to that in a minute. Coming through the main room, I heard a rumor there's plague in one African port."

Something cold slithered down Dario's spine. "Plague?"

"Our ships trade in Tunis. Very concerning."

"It appears every ten years or so and then goes away. It won't come here." But did he even believe that? The monk's words rose up before him like a wraith.

A young woman stuck her head through the door. When she asked what they wanted, Dario ordered a bowl of stew and another bottle of wine. After she'd gone, he faced Aldo. "You didn't ask me here to pass along rumors."

"No." Aldo swirled his glass. "The reason I called you here is that . . ."

"Sì?"

Aldo drank the dregs in his glass. "I'm leaving Colpena."

"On a trip?"

"No, permanently."

Dario sucked in breath. "But why?"

"Do I really need to tell you? For decades, you've spent all our profits on your duomo. The alum mine is exhausted. The relics income was good while it lasted, but now that, too, has stopped. The shipping business barely keeps us in the black. Even the bank's income has been dropping. Ever since we were taken off the Signoria—people have been sending their money-changing business to Borroni."

"We can make it profitable again. Why would you want to leave when things are good right now?"

"They'll turn bad again. They always do. And then there's your obsession with Puccini."

"What about him?"

"What has he ever done to you that you hate him so much?"

Dario looked away. Puccini was everything Dario was not. The man was saving Dario's soul by building the duomo, sì. But Puccini's very existence was an affront. How could he ever explain that to Aldo?

"While there's still something left, I want my share. I'm going to start over."

"B—but who will run the business?"

"You will. Or you can hire someone. It's about time you took a more active interest in its affairs."

"But you and I have been together . . . all our lives."

"And it's brought me nothing but dishonor, a dead daughter, and this constant teetering on the edge of bankruptcy. I'm done with you, Dario. I'm taking what's mine, traveling to Avignon, and opening a spice-importing business. With my connections among the shippers, I should be able to make a good profit the first year."

Dario closed his eyes and lowered his head into his hands. Aldo . . . leaving? This was the last thing he expected. He glanced up. "Can I say anything to change your mind?"

"I calculate my share to be twelve thousand florins. Not much after so many decades, is it? Tomorrow morning, I'm taking that and my family and boarding a ship bound for Marseilles. Goodbye, Dario." He stood and offered his hand.

Dario glared at it. Finally, he stood, shook Aldo's hand, and then watched his cousin leave.

As the minutes passed, he sat in the empty room, listening to the thunder rumble outside and the voices murmur in the main room. If Aldo wanted to leave, let him. Lately, the man had been irritable anyway. Dario would hire a business manager to replace him. Together, they'd figure out how to generate profits.

He took a long draught of wine. Tonight, he came here for diversion, not to sit, morose and despondent over yet another setback. To Hell with Aldo.

Rising, he asked the proprietor if he could go upstairs with the new woman. Perhaps a romp in bed would lift his spirits. The man winked, nodded, and Dario climbed the steps after him.

Remigio went in first, talked with her, then stepped back in the hall to say Dario could go in.

As Dario entered the room, he was already slipping off his cioppa. The woman's naked back was turned to him. She was older, with long black locks hanging down her back. But older women were sometimes the best. "I hope you don't mind, my dear, if I check you for the French disease. After all the reports I've heard, I really must—"

Whirling, she ripped a blanket from the bed, clutched it to her front, and gasped.

He stared at the woman, recognition coming slowly. "Letizia?" he breathed.

"Father?"

"W–what are you doing here? Why are you engaged in"—he waved a hand across the room—"this?"

"I could ask you the same. Why are *you* here? But of course, it's what you've always done, isn't it?" Her voice rose. "That's how *I* was born, wasn't it? And now that I'm following my mother's profession, you have the nerve to ask me why *I'm* here? It was *you*, Father, who made me like this. Now get out!" She pulled the sheet closer around her. "Leave. You were never a father to me. You pretended to be *my uncle*."

"Letizia, I didn't mean anything by what I said. I'm just concerned for you. I care for you. And I don't want to see you doing—"

"You care only for yourself." Tears welled up in her eyes, and she turned her back to him. "Get out!"

"Please, little flower . . . give me a—"

"*Little flower?*" She nearly shouted. "Don't ever call me that. This"— her hand slid down her body—"is who your *little flower* has become. Now, get out!"

Pulling his cioppa back on, he staggered down the steps, through the boisterous tavern crowd, and out into the storm. The one person he'd loved more than any other, his little daughter, his little flower—how had she come to this? She blamed him for where she was now. Was she right?

Emotions swirled in him like the wind whirling his cape, sending icicles of cold up his back. He welcomed the bite of the rain stinging his eyes. Anything to dull the pain tearing at his insides.

Nothing was the same anymore. His world was collapsing around him. Tonight, he didn't even want to go back to his palazzo. Grazziano was gone, Aldo wanted nothing more to do with him, and Paolo—no Grazziano was he—would already be in bed.

Bending his head against the driving rain, he staggered. He tottered through the downpour, letting the rain hit his face and soak the leather wrapping his feet. He walked until he was so tired, he could walk no more. Then he entered the nearest taverna, slumped down by the fire, and with the cowl of his cape yanked low over his forehead, drank himself senseless.

CHAPTER 60

~ PRETRIAL MANEUVERS ~

SEPTEMBER 1513

Halfway up the steps to Bishop Ferata's palazzo, Dario stopped. He had no idea why the cardinal wanted him here today. One thing he did know—he must start life anew. He was dragging through each day like a man chained to a block of marble. He wasn't sleeping. And only poking at his food. Yesterday, when he'd caught a glimpse of himself in the mirror, a sick and shattered man had stared back. Sì, gone would be the drinking, the whoring, even his vendetta against Amadeo Puccini.

In a moment of clarity, he suspected what troubled him.

Alongside his desire for Amadeo's downfall had grown a spreading black shadow, a dark, soul-eating creature with a life of its own, living within him, driving him on.

It was time to end the vendetta. It was tearing him up inside.

And besides, he'd won. Puccini was beaten, having lost his position and facing a trial he'd surely lose.

Sì, he would turn the page on his old life and begin anew.

Straightening his back, trying on a smile that quickly slipped away, he continued up the steps where the servants ushered him into a sitting room. Before him sat Cardinal Gonzaga and black-caped Ulisse Rua, Gonzaga's Grand Inquisitor.

"Welcome, Dario Rossi." Gonzaga's fat lips spread into a thin smile. "It's been some time since we've talked."

As Dario sat, he looked warily at the Inquisitor. "It has, cardinal. May I ask the reason for this visit?"

"We are preparing charges against the former capomaestro of the duomo, Amadeo Puccini. And we need your help."

He breathed out his relief. "What kind of charges?"

353

"Accusations of heresy, signore." Ulisse Rua's voice was deep, resonant. "And charges of mortal sin. We understand you have some information in that regard."

Was it possible? Were they giving him a sword to cut away the final shreds of Puccini's reputation? But he'd just vowed to do the opposite. "And you want me to help?"

Gonzaga smiled at the black-caped man. "Precisely."

"In what way?"

Rua sat back in his seat. "Let's not play a game, signore. You know exactly what we want."

Dario's stomach tightened, and he gritted his teeth. For most of his life, he'd wanted Puccini's downfall. But the man had already paid his debt. Having spent five months in the dungeon, having been stripped of his position, Puccini would come out a broken man. Dario had seen enough men brought low by even less time in that foul hole. Gonzaga and the Inquisitor were asking him to stab the heart of what would already be a crushed and broken spirit.

And what would be the price for such treachery? Puccini was nothing if not righteous. Whatever Dario said to convict the man of moral failure would be a lie. Was not testifying falsely itself a mortal sin?

"Is something wrong, Signore Rossi?"

"No." He frowned. "I just have to . . . to think about it a bit."

"What is there to think about?" Gonzaga shifted in his seat, and the chair groaned. "There's a rumor going around about what Callisto and Simona Mancini discovered in Puccini's house when they left your party some time ago. But you know all about that, don't you?"

Pulsing throbs of pain began inside his head. His fingers rubbed his temples, but it didn't help.

"I see you have qualms. So consider this: if you help us, I am willing to make a public statement on your behalf, one that would go a long way toward your public rehabilitation."

Lifting his gaze to the cardinal, he took a deep breath. A public rehabilitation? Was it possible? Could he again join the Signoria?

And why would he not trust in his indulgence? In a few days, there'd be a dedication ceremony for the duomo. Then Dario's grand indulgence was assured.

If the indulgence covered the sin of murder, would it not also cover the crime of false witness? And if Gonzaga would help in his public rehabilitation . . .

"Well, signore," said Rua. "What is your answer?"

"I . . ." He took a deep breath. "I'll do it."

A cold shiver rippled across his shoulders. Deep within him, something dark and cold seemed to swell. He gasped. Was this how Judas felt after his kiss condemned the Son of God?

But Judas didn't have the indulgence that Dario did.

When the guards came to unlock his chains and lift him to his feet, Amadeo could barely walk. Where were they taking him? Raul remained grim and silent as he dragged his prisoner across the dank, fetid floor. Out the door, they took him and up the steps. His feet touched only every other step. Then he was in the town hall's main hallway and out into the Piazza della Signoria. Out into the sun.

He squinted in the blazing light. Not once in the long months he'd been locked in the dungeon had he seen the sun.

They carried him down the steps and across the piazza toward one of Bramante's new fountains, built while he was imprisoned. Still squinting, he made out the statue of a fish spouting water into the pool. Beside the pool stood Ulisse Rua. The Grand Inquisitor had erected a fulcrum at the end of which sat a dunking chair. A great crowd of people thronged around the fountain.

"Welcome, capomaestro." Rua's voice resonated, merging with the soft gurgle of water. "Today, in front of witnesses, you will confess your sins."

Two Church soldiers waded into the fountain up to their waists, dragging his legs through the water, thrusting him into the chair. They tied leather straps to his arms, legs, and torso. Another band held his head against the chair's high back.

"Confess that you have blasphemed God, Christ, and the Virgin, and the Inquisitor's court may show you mercy. Confess that you have cursed God."

Amadeo squinted at his accuser. Then he tried to turn his head to see the others in the crowd.

Callisto—his eyes pained, his head shaking.

Simona—crying.

Bramante—smiling.

Dario Rossi—his face white and expressionless.

Bishop Ferata—bearing a somber, pained expression.

"Do it," said Rua, and the chair tilted backward.

Before his head went under, Amadeo held his breath. The seconds passed, and water went up his nose. His lungs burned, and he struggled against his bonds.

Finally, the chair rose. He coughed water, gasped for air.

"Confess," said the Inquisitor.

"I have never . . . ever . . . cursed God." Amadeo coughed. "Or blasphemed against God the Father. Or Christ his Son. Never."

"And against the Holy Virgin?"

Amadeo was silent.

"Give him the fruit." Rua waved, and one soldier reached out and rammed half an apple between his teeth. As soon as the soldier left, Amadeo tried to spit it out, but there wasn't time. The chair fell back into the water.

With him unable to close his mouth for the apple, water poured down his throat. He struggled, writhed, and tried not to breathe. He gagged, but that only caused him to suck in more water.

The chair rose, and he spat the apple out. He retched, coughed and gagged, and retched some more.

"Confess that you have blasphemed against the Holy Virgin and cursed God, and we will show you mercy."

From the crowd, Amadeo now heard angry murmurs. He opened his eyes and, through blurred vision, saw angry faces turned toward Rua.

"End this farce." Callisto faced the Inquisitor. "Everyone knows this man's heart toward God. If you continue, you risk much."

Ulisse Rua shot Callisto a dark look. "Take care, gonfaloniere, that you, yourself, do not come under the Inquisition's attention."

Callisto glared back but said nothing.

Rua nodded, and the chair went under again.

Amadeo lost count of the number of times they dunked him. Whenever they stuffed the apple back in his mouth, he swallowed more water. Twice, he thought he would surely drown before returning to the surface. But in the end, all that the Grand Inquisitor extracted from him was an apology for being rude to members of the Church and another admission that no one should worship the Virgin or pray to her.

Finally, when he emerged, gasping, gagging, and throwing up water, the crowd around the fountain had had enough. They shouted threats. Anonymous missiles of rotten fruit began hitting the Church guards, the bishop, even the Grand Inquisitor himself. The guards tried to force the crowd back with their spears. But as soon as they returned to their positions, the people surged in again.

"You must stop this," said Bishop Ferata to Rua. He wiped pear juice from his face. "He has nothing further to confess."

Ulisse Rua glared at the crowd, at Ferata, and at Amadeo.

"End this," added Callisto. "Or I cannot account for what the crowd might do."

Rua's stony gaze swept the angry faces around him. Then he motioned to the guards who began unstrapping Amadeo from the chair.

"By your own rules"—Callisto waved to Amadeo—"you cannot torture him again. See that you don't."

Rua stared at the gonfaloniere and narrowed his eyes.

Ferata whirled away from the Inquisitor and headed alone across the square.

As soldiers dragged Amadeo back across the piazza toward the town hall, a small crowd followed.

"We're with you, capomaestro," came a voice he recognized as Vittorio's.

"Take heart," came Pugliesi's voice from the other side.

Even though his brush with death had taken the last of his strength, their encouraging words buoyed him. Pugliesi must have returned from his home.

He searched the crowd's faces, and there, moving up beside him, was Simona. Tears streamed down her face.

"I trust you, Amadeo," she whispered. Then she blew him a kiss.

As the guards dragged him up the town hall steps and back down to the prison hole and the darkness, he clung to his last image of her.

CHAPTER 61

~ THE INQUISITION ~

Two days passed, and Amadeo recovered from the dunking. After they'd chained him in his rotting wet rags back against the stone wall, he shivered for hours. The one good thing he gave thanks for was the first bath he'd received in five months. Yet his clothing bore too many holes, and he'd lost a long strip from one sleeve in the dunking.

On the third morning, Raul came for him again, dragging him out of the fetid room and up the steps. This time, they brought him upstairs to the town hall's main assembly room. The guard pulled him down the center aisle of a vast hall filled with people—the Council of Thirty, the Signoria, Dario Rossi, Simona, Vittorio, Damiano De Luca, Umberto Sabbatini— everyone of importance in Colpena. But hadn't most of the masters gone to their home villages months ago? They must have returned for his trial.

The guards made him stand to the left of a table, where sat Cardinal Gonzaga, Bishop Ferata, and Ulisse Rua, the Grand Inquisitor. But when they released his arms, Amadeo tottered and nearly fell.

Gonzaga rose from his chair, caught his breath, and began. "I hereby open the trial in the matter of the Holy Mother Church against Amadeo Puccini, former capomaestro of the Cattedrale della Beata San Maria, for a catalogue of mortal sins, including the worst charge of all—heresy."

"Its name is the Cattedrale del Figlio sul Mare," said Amadeo.

"The prisoner will be silent." Rua glowered. "The day after tomorrow, we are renaming the duomo."

"Who is defending him?" Callisto spoke from the front row behind Amadeo.

Cardinal Gonzaga sat, and the Grand Inquisitor now spoke. "At the end of this trial, the witness will have a chance to answer all charges against him. But his job here, today, is to confess his blasphemy and his mortal sin. He must throw his transgressions on the mercy of the court who will decide his punishment. And I warn the audience—throughout these proceedings, you must remain silent."

Amadeo's jaws tensed. Had the trial's conclusion and sentence already been decided?

Rua looked aside to a Church guard. "Bring in the first witness."

A smiling Basilio Bramante walked beside the guard to a position opposite Amadeo's.

"State what you know to be the truth," said Rua.

Bramante leered at Amadeo. "It is well known that during the war with Naples, Puccini and Signore Mancini's daughter spent half a year together, alone at Mancini's country estate. At the end of that time, she became pregnant. But he didn't marry her, and she entered a convent, where she subsequently lost the child."

"Untrue!" Callisto rose from his seat.

"If the audience will not remain silent, I will clear the court." Rua faced Bramante again. "So you swear he has committed the mortal sin of adultery?"

"Sì."

"And has he ever, to your knowledge, denied the holiness of the Virgin?"

"Frequently, your honor."

Rua smiled, dismissed him, and called the next witness—Luigi, the heavyset tower guard.

"State what you know to be the truth."

The man shuffled his feet, looked away from Amadeo, and frowned.

"Luigi is your name, is it not?" The Inquisitor glanced at some document on the table before him. "And I understand you have information vital to this court's proceedings. Tell us what it is."

Luigi shot an apologetic glance at Amadeo. "On many occasions, the prisoner gave me a bribe of money and wine so he could visit prisoners in the tower cells."

"Why did he do that?"

Luigi's gaze sought the floor. "I don't know."

"So we can add the sin of bribery. What else, guard? Did he ever say anything about the Holy Virgin?"

"Once, he said we should not pray to her or worship her."

"And you swear this to be the truth?"

Luigi glanced once at Amadeo, then nodded.

"Thank you. For accepting bribes, you are sentenced to one year of penance. You will attend mass each Sunday wearing a black headband. Next witness."

Guards led in Dario Rossi.

Amadeo gazed at the man for whom he'd toiled his entire life. The duomo, Amadeo's masterwork, was to have been Rossi's grand indulgence. Was the man now going to testify against him? Rossi's face, gaunt and dark under his eyes, had taken on a jaundiced appearance.

"Tell us what you know to be the truth, Dario Rossi."

Rossi closed his eyes, opened them, and faced the Inquisitor. "On several occasions, I personally heard Puccini claim that the Virgin Mary was not the mother of God, that we should not worship her, and that she did not deserve a place of honor in the duomo." But his voice was flat, droning on in a monotone.

After a few gasps from the crowd, Rua smiled. "That is quite damning. But I believe there is more?"

"Puccini also summoned Callisto's daughter to his house so she could see him naked and lying in bed with a prostitute"—Rossi breathed deeply—"all for the sake of getting even with her after a quarrel."

"Ah, so besides heresy, we can add the sins of lechery, spite, pride, and revenge. Is that all?"

"No." Rossi's glance found the floor, and his voice lowered almost to a whisper. "When he was recovering from an illness . . . after his trip back from Carrara, I heard him curse . . . curse God."

From the dais behind Amadeo came a gasp.

"What were his exact words? And please, speak up so we can all hear."

"Puccini looked up at the ceiling from his bed." But Rossi stopped there and brought trembling hands to his temples.

"Well," said Rua into the silence, "what did he say?"

"He said, 'God, I curse you. I damn you for bringing me to this.' "

Rustling came from the audience.

Amadeo stared, his face contorting in disbelief and pain. How could Rossi lie like that?

"And you swear what you've said is the truth?"

Rossi shifted his weight to another foot, and he whispered, "I—I do."

"Thank you." Rua shot a satisfied smile to Amadeo while Rossi, his eyes downcast, shuffled back to his seat.

"The court now wishes to add its own witness." Ulisse Rua addressed Amadeo. "I have personally heard the prisoner declare that we should not worship, honor, or pray to the Virgin." He shot Gonzaga a questioning glance.

"I, too, heard him say the same."

The Inquisitor turned to Bishop Ferata, who admitted that he, too, had heard the same.

Rua straightened in his seat. "It is clear to the court where guilt and innocence lie. But before we pronounce the sentence, I now ask the prisoner"—he nodded toward Amadeo—"what do you have to say to these charges?"

Amadeo tried to stand straighter. But long months locked in irons on the floor had taken their toll, and he fought to remain upright. "Never once did I sleep with Callisto Mancini's daughter as has been alleged. If you would only ask her or her father, you would know this to be the truth. As for the incident with the naked prostitute in my house"—he shot a glance to Rossi—"someone sent her to hide in my quarters while at the same time calling Callisto and his daughter to go there. I assume they did this out of personal spite, to destroy my reputation.

"And as for the charge of bribery—I did give the guards money and wine, but this is customary and was the only way I could have access to the tower and the dungeon. I did so because I was bringing food to the prisoners there, in obedience to our Lord Jesus's command to visit prisoners and the sick. Most of the prisoners in that hole are ill. Bishop Ferata was present when these same charges were dismissed many years ago." He glanced at Ferata, who closed his eyes and dropped his head.

"But what of the heresy charge?" questioned Rua. "Do you deny saying that we should not worship or honor the Virgin? That we should not pray to her? Do you deny cursing God?"

His heart leaping inside his chest, Amadeo gazed at Rua. They'd manufactured evidence to prove what they wanted to prove. Nothing he said was going to make the slightest difference in Rua's judgment. But he couldn't stomach their lies. The heat rose to his forehead. "Never in my life"—the muscles in his neck tensed—"have I cursed God. That's a lie. And I never said we shouldn't honor the Virgin Mary. She is the earthly mother of our Lord Jesus and deserves our respect and honor. What I did say is that we should neither pray to her nor worship her. She is not a god, and the Holy Scriptures never teach this. She is simply the earthly mother of Jesus."

Rua smiled. "So you have been trained to read the Holy Scriptures, and you count yourself an equal to priests who have studied them for years?"

"I never said that."

"But you think you have the right to read Scripture and interpret it?"

"I do."

Rua addressed the others. "Do we need to hear more?"

"No," said Gonzaga.

Ferata closed his eyes and shook his head.

"While we determine our verdict," said the Inquisitor, "the audience and the prisoner will remain where they are."

The three turned their backs on the court and joined in heated discussion. Ferata appeared to disagree with the other two, and their deliberations dragged on. Finally, they turned again to face the chambers.

Ferata was white-faced. Not a good sign.

"We have reached a verdict." Rua stood and faced Amadeo. "It is the judgment of this court of Inquisition that the prisoner, Amadeo Puccini, has denied and flouted the Church's authority. We, therefore, sentence him to a fine of all his earthly possessions, payable to the Church."

Ulisse Rua narrowed his eyes at Amadeo. "It is also this court's judgment that by cursing God and denying the holiness and worthiness of the Blessed Virgin to receive our prayers and worship, he shall be labeled a heretic. Thus, he is sentenced to a heretic's death by fire. Sentence to be carried out four days hence in the Piazza della Signoria. This court is adjourned."

Amadeo had expected nothing less, yet after Rua had pronounced the judgment, he was stunned. Execution by fire?

Behind him, a deathly silence filled the hall. It appeared the verdict also stunned the audience. He shifted to look behind him.

Simona's hands covered her mouth and nose. A tear ran down one cheek. He caught her glance, and she shook her head, mouthing the word no.

Callisto stared, grim-faced, at the departing Inquisitor, cardinal, and bishop.

Standing nearby was Bonifacio, the baker whom Amadeo had helped so many years ago. The man's face was twisted in pain. His head, too, was shaking back and forth.

Dario Rossi's forehead was creased as if the verdict also surprised him. When Rossi caught Amadeo's glance, he quickly averted his.

"No!" said the baker's voice, breaking the silence.

"No!" shouted Simona.

There followed a chorus of noes, one following another, until it seemed the entire assembly had joined in.

Only halfway to the door, Gonzaga looked back with utter surprise, but the Inquisitor kept walking as if he hadn't heard.

As the crowd's objections died to a murmur, two guards grabbed Amadeo's arms and dragged him out a back door and down the dungeon stairs.

CHAPTER 62

~ THE DEDICATION CEREMONY ~

Dario stood at the front row of the half-filled duomo. Why weren't more people here today? It was two days after the trial, and barely half of the Signoria and the Council of Thirty were in attendance. Even Callisto Mancini was absent. When he'd entered the cathedral, Mancini's daughter, Simona, said Callisto had gone to Rome on urgent business. The man probably couldn't stomach watching Puccini's execution. But today was the grand ceremony to rename the duomo and dedicate it to the Virgin. The gonfaloniere should be here, not shoring up his personal accounts in Rome.

Up on the dais, Cardinal Gonzaga looked feverish. His face ashen, he kept wiping his brow. Beside him, Bishop Ferata threw him worried glances.

Dario, too, stared at Gonzaga. Two days ago, even as Puccini's trial was concluding, one of Dario's ships had arrived from Marrakesh loaded with copper and leather goods. Only after it had tied at the wharf did it raise the plague flag. Armed with crossbows, the city guard was immediately dispatched with orders to shoot anyone trying to disembark. After quarantining the dock, they shot and killed three sailors who'd jumped into the water in an attempt to swim for shore. No one could say if others had escaped into the city before the soldiers arrived. But it wasn't likely.

After hearing that news, Ulisse Rua decided to miss the execution he'd ordered and hastily mounted a horse for Siena.

Last night, Dario had slept poorly.

First, the young monk's warning returned to echo through his head, "The plague is coming for you." After the ceremony, he must enter his palazzo, shut the doors, and not let anyone in until he was sure the city was safe. But he couldn't miss Puccini's execution. Nothing could keep him away from that.

All night, even though the trial was two days past, he was still going over his testimony against Puccini. Seeing him the way he was—emaciated, starved, stripped of everything—Dario actually pitied the man. Dario's revenge had surely been total. The man's righteousness, reputation, even his wealth was gone. The Spaniard's sentence was only what was expected.

But now that Puccini faced the stake and the fire, the reality of the judgment troubled Dario. How could anyone—even Puccini—endure the flesh being burned from his body?

Flames, Dario Rossi. I've seen you . . . in the flames.

He shuddered. No one could wish such a fate on anyone.

Maybe he should have refused to testify. The pope's written document surely granted him immunity from the Inquisitor's authority. But instead of refusing, he'd added logs to the fire being built under Puccini, logs cut from the tree of false witness, jealousy, and revenge.

He shook his head. Why was he still going over this? Puccini deserved what he got.

Gonzaga stood and waddled to the front of the dais. He began to speak, but once again, his words were so strained, so soft, no one could hear him.

"Is there plague in the city?" someone shouted from the crowd.

Gonzaga's eyes widened, and he seemed about to collapse.

Ferata rushed forward, helped the cardinal back to his seat, and took Gonzaga's place. "A ship in the harbor has been quarantined," said the bishop. "That's all."

"But has the plague entered the city?" shouted someone else.

"No!" Ferata shouted, before glancing again at Gonzaga. "The ship has been isolated. We should be safe." Then the bishop began the ceremony.

He waved the censer, sending clouds of smoke across the altar. He intoned a brief prayer. He talked about all the men who'd worked for years on the project and how, for centuries to come, the greatest duomo in Europe would benefit the city. But never once did Ferata mention the architect, the master builder, the capomaestro who'd made it all happen.

The bishop concluded by saying, "I dedicate this duomo to the Holy Virgin. And I rename it the Cattedrale della Beata San Maria."

The bishop's words should have been the final block in Dario's tower of revenge. With today's ceremony, the public gratitude Puccini was owed for a lifetime of focused effort had been denied him.

But it only brought a profound sense of loneliness and emptiness. He'd won, certainly. Puccini couldn't be more defeated. Yet where was the elation belonging to the victor?

The ceremony was barely over when he stood and walked down the center aisle.

Out in the street, not twenty paces from the duomo, he stopped and stared at an unusual sight lying in the gutter at his feet—

Half a dozen dead rats.

"Up with you now," said the guard. "You're getting new quarters."

Amadeo looked with surprise at the man. New quarters? There must be some mistake.

The guard unlocked his shackles, jerked him to his feet, and dragged him up the steps to the first floor and from there to the spiral stairs leading to the tower.

Glancing up, Amadeo wondered if he had the energy for the climb.

"Sì, signore, someone has bestowed mercy on your last two nights on earth."

The ascent sapped his remaining strength. When he reached the tower cells and Luigi, the heavyset tower guard, Amadeo collapsed. The two men had to carry him to his new cell and lay him on a mattress stuffed with straw. It wasn't the large room where he'd stayed previously, but it was a welcome change from the stinking hole below.

The clean bed, the fresh air blowing through the tower window, the sudden quiet after months of living with the coughing, moaning, and weeping of a hundred unfortunates—for some reason, it all brought tears to his eyes.

"Why am I here?" he managed to croak.

"By orders of the gonfaloniere himself." Luigi smiled. "And I'm sorry, signore, for my testimony at the trial. They threatened me with charges if I didn't say what I did."

"I forgive you."

The guard nodded and left.

Only then did Amadeo notice the basin of water on the floor opposite. Next to it was a loaf of bread, a round of cheese, and a flagon of wine. He hurried toward the food like the starving man he was.

At least he'd go to his death washed and with a full belly.

CHAPTER 63

~ LAST VISITORS ~

It must be noon, too early for his next meal, yet the lock clicked noisily in Amadeo's tower cell. He sat up on his straw mattress. Why was the guard here now? Last night, after washing for the first time in months and eating a nourishing meal, he'd slept better than he had in months.

The door creaked on iron hinges, and Luigi pushed it open.

Standing in the entry behind the guard was Dario Rossi.

Surprised, Amadeo at first said nothing.

"May I come in?" asked his visitor.

Amadeo nodded, Rossi entered, and the guard shut the door behind them.

"Why are you here?"

Rossi looked around the cell. There were no chairs, only the mattress. "Maybe to see what's become of you, Puccini. To see the righteous brought low. A while back, I would have taken great comfort in that."

Like a cauldron boiling over, anger bubbled up, heating Amadeo's face. The man before him had destroyed his life and soon would cause his death. "It was you who sent the whore to my house. And you who wrote the note that brought Callisto and Simona to see her with me." Even as his hands formed fists at his side, he tried to quench his ire. "Why did you do it, Rossi?"

Rossi shrugged. But was that pain Amadeo detected in those eyes?

"And I never cursed God. Why did you lie about that?"

"To see you knocked off your perch, I guess. No, that's not it." Rossi waved his hands, his gaze wandering to the ceiling and back. "I don't really know."

"You don't know? You destroyed my life and you don't know why?"

Rossi's head tilted, and he looked away. "Maybe because I . . . I hated you. But I don't anymore."

"You *hated* me?" Amadeo sat heavily against the wall. He unclenched his fists. Amadeo had spent his entire life working for God, living as righteously as human frailty allowed. Yet Rossi had never ceased plotting Amadeo's downfall. Looking at Rossi now, Amadeo saw nothing but a broken, tortured man. What kind of demons had so ravaged the man's soul that he came to hate the very instrument of what he believed to be his own salvation?

Amadeo's anger cooled, replaced by pity. On its face, the situation was bizarre, and a laugh escaped him. "I don't hate you, Dario. In fact, I forgive you for what you've done. Yours is a tormented, restless spirit. I wish only peace, contentment, and happiness for you."

Rossi's mouth opened, but no words came out.

"Y–YOU FORGIVE ME?" ASKED DARIO. How could the man forgive him after all he'd done? No one could be that good.

"Sì, Dario, I forgive you."

"I have the pope's forgiveness, his indulgence in writing, forgiving all my sins—past, present, and future. I don't need yours."

"You don't need it because, by paying for the duomo's construction, you believe you've purchased your way into Heaven?"

"Of course."

Puccini's face contorted into what Dario could only describe as disbelief. "B–but we cannot get right with God by what we do or by how much money we spend."

Lurching, Dario felt his stomach twist. Who else had said that? "But you've spent your whole life doing just that, capomaestro. You've labored nearly a lifetime to build the duomo. If not for your own salvation, then why did you do it?"

"I did it because I was *already* right with Jesus, my Lord and Savior. I did it because building the duomo was my way of showing my love for him. It was my response for what he did for me. There's a big difference."

Dario staggered back. "But the indulgence . . ."

His eyes pained, Puccini shook his head. "With that, I can't help you, gonfaloniere."

No one had called Dario by that title of respect for months. In this context, it stung. Slowly, he turned and pounded on the cell door. The guard let him out, and he began the long descent to the bottom.

He'd gone to the tower on a whim, and now he wondered why. Was it to squeeze some satisfaction out of Puccini's downfall, hoping that seeing once more the destruction of the righteous man who so galled him would alleviate his guilt? Maybe.

What had happened instead was that Puccini had forgiven him and told him he couldn't buy his way out of the flames.

And then he remembered who'd also said that. The monk. And Savonarola.

When Dario reached the street, he headed straight for the nearest taverna.

Late that afternoon, the lock clicked again, and Amadeo sat up expecting his last meal.

Instead, Luigi opened the door to Simona. In one hand, she carried a steaming bucket wafting the scent of beef stew. The other carried a sack with a loaf of bread and a flagon of wine.

His heart leaping with joy, he stood.

She set the food and wine on the floor.

"It's your last night, capomaestro." Luigi rubbed his chin.

They both looked at him.

"Before he left on his trip, the gonfaloniere gave me orders to let his daughter in to see you. She can stay until midnight. Then I'll have to take the signorina out. It wouldn't do to have her still here in the morning when we come for you. That's all I can do for you." He bowed and shut the door behind him.

Simona ran into his arms, and they embraced.

"I've been praying so hard for you, Amadeo," she whispered. "Praying something will happen to end this nightmare. I don't know why Father left. He was the only one who could have stopped this. But he said it was urgent—something about his spice business. I'm sorry he couldn't help."

"I'm afraid nothing can stop this now. But I'm glad you're here. You've made a condemned man very happy."

Moisture welled up in her eyes.

"Please don't cry." He glanced toward the stew on the floor. "That food is driving me to distraction."

She wiped her cheeks, bent down, and brought him his supper. Pulling glasses from the sack, she poured wine for each of them. She'd brought plenty, and they sat cross-legged on the floor and ate. When they'd finished, they sat holding hands, their backs against the wall.

The food tasted better than anything he could ever remember eating. Every bite brought energy flowing back into his limbs.

After a time, she said, "I understand now how Rossi tried to make me hate you by putting that whore in your rooms. I'm sorry I ever doubted you. He's a despicable man."

"Thank you, Simona. All those months in the dungeon, I hoped you'd figure it out."

"Have you heard about Cardinal Gonzaga?"

"No."

"Yesterday, at the duomo dedication, he looked so pale, people thought he had the plague. There's a quarantined ship in port. But it must have been something he ate. He's recovering."

Above them, the tower bell rang, drowning out all speech. The sound vibrated and thrummed through the cell—one, two, three . . . six, seven.

When silence again reigned, she nestled up beside him. "Only five hours left together."

"We'll have to make it last a lifetime."

"We could have had a good life together, Amadeo."

He swallowed. "This evening is all we've been given. Let's rejoice in that."

"After all that's happened to you, aren't you bitter?" She looked into his eyes. "I would be."

Amadeo squeezed her hand and gazed at the darkening shadows. "No. In fact, I'm strangely at peace." He faced her. "Despite the sinfulness of men—their plots, intrigues, and hatreds—I'm content with how I've lived. I spent my life building a grand duomo for God's glory. And no matter what the Church or Gonzaga or Rossi says, the building stands as my love and my testimony for God and his Son. Killing me can never take that away. There's only one thing I regret. I . . ."

"What?"

"You, Simona." He smiled. "I regret not marrying you. Long ago, I should have abandoned my vow. That is my one, my greatest, regret."

Again, the tears welled up in her eyes. Raising a hand, he wiped them away.

He leaned over and they kissed.

Outside, rain pattered against the tower's stone walls.

It was his last night on earth, and he was still weak. They sat and they talked. Once, he even laughed. But every time the tower bell added an hour to the evening, it subtracted an hour from their time together.

When the bell struck twelve, Luigi opened the door with apologies.

He embraced her. They kissed for the last time. A tearful Simona hurried out the door.

Then Amadeo was left alone with his thoughts.

What would it be like, he wondered, to leave this life and enter the next?

What he feared was the getting from here to there—the skin burning off his bones, his insides boiling. He shuddered. He must focus only on what lay beyond. For no matter how much suffering the fire's flames inflicted, that was only temporary.

Beyond lay an eternity of bliss.

CHAPTER 64

~ THE EVENTS IN THE PIAZZA ~

The next morning, Dario woke from the worst nightmare, the worst hangover, he could remember. Staggering out of bed, he found the washbasin on the table and threw water on his face. In his dream, a vast lake of fire had boiled around him. It rose in great wavering plumes, red and black and devouring.

His personal imp took up a hammer and beat against the inside of his skull. He winced.

But today was the day of Puccini's execution. No matter how terrible he felt, he was going to see it.

"Paolo," he cried. Where was Paolo? The servant should have been here to wake him, bring him food and clean clothes. The man was worthless.

Pulling on yesterday's stained cioppa, he stumbled down the steps to the kitchen. With his declining income, he'd let go nearly all of the staff. His manservant, Paolo, was now also his cook.

Again, he called the servant's name but received no answer. He grabbed a hunk of bread from the pantry, drank a cup of water, and walked to the entryway. But the bread was hard to swallow. And by the time he arrived at the door, he was breathing heavily. Why did he feel so awful? He put a hand to his forehead. Was it warm? No, he was imagining it.

Stumbling down the steps, he crossed Piazza dei Rossi, still wet from last night's downpour. Clouds raced across the sky, and a breeze swept by him. But not enough to cool his face.

He took a side street and entered the Piazza della Signoria.

Mobbing the execution site was a crowd far larger than had attended the duomo ceremony two days ago. From a huge mound of sticks and logs rose the single post where they'd soon tie Puccini. The monks' words echoed again in his head.

Flames, Dario Rossi. I've seen you . . . in the flames.

He shuddered. Today, it was Puccini, not he, who would face the flames.

At the front of the gathering stood Simona Mancini. She and the multitude beside her were gazing toward the town hall, waiting for the prisoner to emerge.

When the jailer turned the key in the lock, Amadeo's heart leaped inside his chest. How slowly the night had passed. Unable to sleep, he'd paced his cell, occasionally looked down through the high window onto the moon-washed rooftops. He'd tried to think of something else, but always he returned to this moment.

Now, less than an hour remained of his time on earth.

Grim-faced, Luigi creaked open the cell door. "It's time, signore."

Amadeo tried to cheer him up with a smile, but it fell flat. Slowly, he rose from the straw mattress. He followed the guard onto the spiral steps. It was cool this morning, and dew from the open windows spaced every twenty feet made the steps slick. Where an opening revealed the harbor to the west, he paused to savor a last view.

Clouds raced their shadows over a cerulean sea dotted with white-caps. Far out in the bay, a single ship sailed with full canvas, heading for port. What cargo did it carry? What manner of persons and what was their business here today?

He swallowed. What he wouldn't give to trade places with whoever rode that ship, facing another day of life, perhaps soon to be reunited with a daughter or a wife. Tonight, maybe that traveler would eat in a taverna, sampling the best food, drinking the richest wine Colpena's chefs could offer. Would the man fall into his bed this night, satisfied that he'd lived the best day possible? Did he realize how precious life was?

Amadeo drank in the scene of the white-capped ocean, the clouds, the ship, the fresh sea breezes. Only God could create such a painting.

A day from now, where he was going, would he remember any of this?

"Come, signore," Luigi called back up the steps. "We mustn't dawdle."

Amadeo nodded and continued on, his feet echoing down the stone stairwell. They reached the first floor and a waiting contingent of four Church guards.

"We'll take him from here," said the leader.

"I'm sorry for this." Luigi opened his hands. "You were my favorite prisoner."

"Thank you, Luigi." This time, Amadeo's smile succeeded.

Two Church guards—dressed in brass breastplates and feathered hats and bearing swords in jewel-studded halberds—gripped his arms and ushered him out the door. At the top steps, they paused.

The piazza below was crowded to overflowing. He recognized many peasants whom he'd helped with loans. Also present were workers from the duomo, many of whom were supposed to have gone to their villages months ago. Most of the masters were also here—Vittorio Rivera, Bernardo Pugliesi, Damiano De Luca, Umberto Sabbatini. He recognized some of the Thirty and most of the Signoria. When work on the cathedral was winding down last April, barely a third of the workforce had remained in the city. Had the duomo workers returned only to see his trial and execution?

He lifted his glance to the great jumble of sticks and logs rising opposite the fountain. But they'd laid too much wood on that pile. It was said that, when an executioner built such a stack with too many logs, it burned hotter and slower on the outside, and the fire's heat took longer to reach the prisoner in the center. This caused a slower, more agonizing death. And with last night's rain, today's fire would burn even slower.

"Give me strength, Lord." He drew a deep breath. "Sustain me in the moments to come."

When the people saw him, a great murmur, like a storm rippling the waters of a quiet pond, spread through the throng.

Near the burn pile, Bishop Ferata stood on the dais in his green robes with red-garbed Cardinal Gonzaga. Behind the churchmen, four more guards stood to attention on the platform.

Amadeo's escort tightened their grip on his arms. They dragged him roughly down the town hall steps. As they approached the mass of townsfolk, a path opened. Looking from side to side and clutching their sword hilts, the guards hesitated, glanced warily at the crowd.

"Go in," said the tall leader to his fellows.

The group entered the throng. But immediately, bodies shoved in ahead and behind. They were trapped.

"Let us through." The leader's hand reached for his sword hilt.

But his fingers never touched the weapon. Bodies pressed close. Many hands gripped his arms and held them tight. All four guards were blocked in, frozen in position.

"By order of the Church," shouted Ferata from the dais, "let them through."

But the people paid him no mind and merely crowded in closer.

Gonzaga waved to one soldier on the platform. The man put a horn to his lips and blew.

Moments later, a contingent of the city guard, perhaps forty strong, marched from a side street off Via Santa Croce, their feet stomping the cobbles in unison. Bearing lances and shields, they headed for the entrapped guards and Amadeo. After a brief scuffle, their lances parted the crowd. Facing outthrust spears and shields, the unarmed peasants, merchants, and duomo laborers had no choice but to stand aside.

The soldiers then escorted Amadeo to the burn pile. Two guards dragged him onto the jumbled mass of logs and twigs toward the top. A branch scraped a gash on his leg, and he winced. But that was nothing compared with the pain to come.

When they reached the stake, his heart was beating so fast, he feared he would pass out. No escaping this now. His legs were like lard, barely able to keep him upright.

"Dear Lord, sustain me," he whispered.

The guard leader bound him with ropes to the stake—first his chest, then his legs, then his arms and hands. When the soldier offered Amadeo a blindfold, he shook his head. He would face the end of his life with open eyes.

The guards below fanned out in a circle. A ring of lances now surrounded the pile and the churchmen's dais. For all its good intentions, the crowd wouldn't be able to help him now.

Below, one soldier held a flaming torch. He looked to the dais for instruction.

Gonzaga tried to speak, but his voice would not carry.

Ferata took over. "Do you have any last words, Amadeo Puccini?"

He glanced at the two churchmen. "I forgive you, Bishop Ferata, and you, Cardinal Gonzaga. And I declare, here and now, that everything I have done was for the love of my Lord and my Savior, Christ Jesus."

Ferata stared, speechless, at him.

Gonzaga finally found his voice. "Burn him!"

The soldier lowered his flame to the pile.

WHEN THE SOLDIER THRUST HIS torch into the wet kindling, Dario spun away from the scene. He could watch no longer. As fast as his wobbly legs could carry him, he crossed the piazza. No doubt about it. Last night's binge had left him weak and feverish. Today was the culmination of his revenge on Puccini. But his desire for revenge, like a crow bloated on carrion, had staggered away. Besides, he was too sick to enjoy much of anything.

His heart pounding wildly, he raised a hand to his forehead. It was on fire.

Was it because of the hangover? Or the inner turmoil he'd felt ever since the trial?

Or something worse?

Behind him, the crowd roared, but their anger was too late to help Puccini. At first, when the people had stopped the Church guards from reaching the burn pile, Dario wondered if there would even be an execution today. But when Gonzaga's surprise appeared—his conscripted city guards—Puccini's death was a foregone conclusion.

Ahead rose the steps to his palazzo. He climbed but, halfway up, had to stop to catch his breath and again at the top. His neck, armpits, and groin ached. Laying a hand on his neck, he felt a lump.

"N–no!" he cried to no one in particular. Feeling lightheaded, he pushed through the door into an empty palazzo. "Paolo!" he shouted. "I need you."

No answer. The man was worthless.

Dario staggered into the kitchen and turned the corner. In the same spot where he'd found Grazziano's dead body lay—Paolo. Startled, Dario gasped.

The chest was still, the cheeks pale and lifeless. And the eyes stared, unmoving, at the ceiling.

"Paolo?"

No answer.

Kneeling, he grazed shaking fingers over the man's forehead—cold.

He yanked his hand away.

Then he saw the buboes on the man's neck. Bulging, bold, and bloody.

Paolo had died of the plague.

His hand flew to his own neck where he felt the outline of a large swelling. His heart racing faster than his feet, he bounded up the steps. At the top, he staggered, saw spots before his eyes. He fell to his knees and frantically sucked in air, fearing that, at any moment, he would pass out.

Was the monk's prophecy coming true?

After catching his breath, he lurched to the mirror and tore off his shirt.

There, on both sides of his neck, was the proof.

Buboes. In the act of ripping off his shirt, he'd broken one open. It was bleeding.

The room swirled about him.

No doubt about it now. He had the plague.

Tottering toward the bed and breathing heavily, he fell face forward onto the blankets.

Finally, he rolled over and, with dimming vision, tried to focus on the canopy above. His heart was beating so fast, he feared it would burst.

"God." His voice was a weak croak. "Why did you bring me . . . to this?"

But all that returned to him was the silence of the tomb.

Amadeo stared at the flames licking the pile on his left. The wood was wet and slow to burn, but growing hotter with each passing second. "Dear Lord Jesus," he whispered, "help me."

The fire's heat bored deep beneath his skin, almost to the bone. Despite the wet wood, the flames now leapt from branch to branch, gathering strength. But the guard had lit only one side of the pile. That would only prolong his agony.

And had the man dropped his only torch into the flames? Sì, with one arm shielding his face, he tried to approach the pile but, shaking his head, quickly backed away.

The heat was already searing Amadeo's cheeks, his forehead. Only moments now before it would burn his skin.

Competing with the crackling of the logs rose shouts of anger from the crowd. They had surrounded Gonzaga and Ferata on the dais and their ring of soldiers.

Amadeo tore his gaze from the fire, the crowd, and his accusers. He looked to the sky. A handful of swallows dove and soared, sending shrieks over the piazza. Too early in the day for swallows. He closed his eyes. How much longer would he be able to take in the details of this world before pain blotted out everything else?

A sudden roar, as from some monstrous lion, issued from the people's throats. He opened his eyes.

Two riders, one on a black gelding, the second on a spotted mare, drove into the mass of bodies. The crowd parted and made a path.

It was Callisto. The second was Bonifacio, the baker—the man whom Amadeo had freed from debtor's prison so long ago.

Where had they come from? What was Callisto shouting?

The flames on his left now swirled and twisted into a torrid, angry column. Not much time left.

The crowd quieted, and the gonfaloniere's voice rose even above the roaring blaze. "Release this man at once! I have orders from Pope Leo X himself."

Amadeo's heart pounded faster. Did he dare hope?

But the guards didn't move.

"Guards, stand down!" shouted Callisto. "I am the gonfaloniere, and I order you to stand down."

The soldiers backed away. Yet the raging yellow column was now so close to the stake, no one dared climb up to save him.

Amadeo closed his eyes against the inferno and turned his face to the right. In spite of Callisto's efforts, was it already too late? Any moment now, his clothes and his hair would catch fire.

When he opened his eyes again, someone was climbing halfway up the logs on his right.

It was Bonifacio, the baker. Now an old man like himself, he was clambering over the jumbled logs. The man stopped before him, breathing heavily. Where twigs had cut his arms, he bled. He pulled out a knife and began sawing at Amadeo's bonds.

"Thank you," whispered Amadeo.

"For what you've done for me, capomaestro"—Bonifacio took a deep breath—"I would even give my own life."

The knife broke through the ropes around Amadeo's chest and head. Then Bonifacio began working on Amadeo's legs.

Even as the flames licked his tunic, the ropes dropped around him. Both men scrambled over the logs.

As Amadeo reached the cobbles, he looked back. Flames were circling the post where he'd just been. He knelt to the cool stone and whispered thanks to God.

Before he'd finished, many hands drew him to his feet. The crowd bore him on their shoulders and marched him around the square. "Capomaestro!" they shouted. "Capomaestro! Capomaestro!"

Then the people brought him back and lowered him to the ground beside Callisto.

Standing before the dais, the gonfaloniere waved a piece of paper. "I hold in my hands a papal bull from Leo X." His voice thundered up at the churchmen. "It pardons Amadeo Puccini of all charges arising from the Inquisition of Ulisse Rua. The bull also strips Rua of all authority to conduct further trials." Callisto faced the cardinal. "As for you, Cardinal Gonzaga—the pope is recalling you to Rome at once, where you must answer for bringing the Spanish terror onto Italian soil. Leo wants an accounting for what has occurred here and in other cities."

As Gonzaga's mouth opened in disbelief, the crowd roared its approval. Again, they hoisted Amadeo high, marched him once more around the square, then set him down beside Callisto and Bonifacio.

Smiling, Callisto seized Amadeo and hugged him.

"How can I ever thank you, my friend?" Amadeo felt his eyes moisten.

"It was mostly Bonifacio's doing." Callisto's voice rose to be heard above the shouting throng. "After I told Leo what was going on, he was unhappy that Gonzaga had begun inquisitions without his approval. Still, he was unsure about the pardon. Then Bonifacio fell to his knees before the pontiff and related everything you did for the people. No one could stop that outpouring of emotion, that gushing of thanks for everything you did for your workers and so many others. That's what convinced the pope to pardon you."

Amadeo took the baker's hands, lifted them to his mouth, and kissed them.

When he was released, Bonifacio bowed and stepped back.

But now Simona pushed through the crowd to him, her hands covering her mouth as if in disbelief. Tears of happiness ran down one cheek. She looked into his eyes and he into hers.

Pulling her close, he hugged her. Then he pressed his lips to hers, and a surge of joy swelled his heart. Only moments ago, he was a man expecting to enter the afterlife. Now he was in a different kind of Heaven.

From a few paces away came the blaring of a horn, the beating of a drum, accompanied by the crowd resuming its chant. "Capomaestro! Capomaestro! Capomaestro!"

When they parted, Simona grabbed his hands and stood at arm's length. "Now that you're free and the duomo is finished"—an impish grin like the first time they met brightened her face—"you have a promise to keep."

He shrugged his shoulders, feigning ignorance. "Did I make some kind of promise?"

Smiling, she slapped him on the arm.

"Oh, that promise." He winked at Callisto standing behind them. "Something about marriage, wasn't it?"

When they kissed again, the crowd exploded in celebration.

EPILOGUE

~ JUNE 1521 ~

Simona approached the brass plaque on the duomo's floor, knelt, and placed at its foot a wreath of crocuses, dahlia, and cyclamen. Beside her stood white-haired Skender holding a second wreath. A few paces back with her head bowed waited Skender's wife, Maria. From the campanile outside came the tolling of bells. The echoes bounced off the high walls, the ceiling far above, resounding in the cavernous space.

When the echoes died to silence, she read the familiar words out loud:

Amadeo Puccini
Capomaestro. Beloved Husband. True Friend of God.
Above all others, Colpena honors you.
24 January 1443 – 30 December 1520.

Still on her knees, she touched her lips to the cold brass marker and tried to still the tears that often came when she visited his grave. Amadeo had won many battles in his life. It was only last winter's coughing sickness he couldn't defeat.

Skender helped her to her feet. "A good epitaph, I think."

"He never wanted a crypt in his own duomo. But the people would have nothing else."

"I hear they revered him as a saint."

She nodded. "He helped so many. We never knew the extent of it." Walking a few feet to the next marker, she laid her second wreath, then read its all-too-familiar words:

Callisto Mancini.
Merchant. Devoted Husband. Cherished Father.
Gonfaloniere of the Signoria of Colpena.
May you rest in the same peace you brought to others.
3 March 1450 – 11 November 1514.

Skender helped her rise, but she couldn't take her glance off the plaque.

"He was a good man, your father. Tell me about that day in the piazza when he saved Amadeo. I wish I could have been there to see it."

She faced him. "He rode in on a black charger, returning from a secret visit to the pope. A baker whom Amadeo had freed from debtor's prison rode in beside him. Bonifacio was his name, and—"

"Bonifacio!" Skender's eyes brightened. "I remember him."

"Sì, Bonifacio insisted on going with Father to Rome to plead for him. They saved my husband's life. After the trial, Father refused to tell anyone why he left, saying it was personal business. At the time, I was so angry with him. I didn't understand why he wouldn't stay to help Amadeo. Before Giovanni de' Medici became pope that February, they'd met at official banquets and had even gone riding together. Father kept his trip secret, fearing that, if Gonzaga found out, he'd hasten Amadeo's execution. But he said it was only when Bonifacio got down on his knees that the pope relented."

"What a sight it must have been to see them ride in that day."

"Before he came"—she shuddered—"I expected Amadeo to die. Before my father arrived, you wouldn't have wanted to be there."

She led him past more plaques—Dario Rossi, Basilio Bramante, Enzio Borroni. All taken in the months of September and October of 1513.

"In Pisa that year," said Skender, "the plague skipped us."

"Before it ended, it took three hundred here in Colpena. Every ten years or so, it returns. Perhaps one day, it will stop altogether. Father escaped it but died the next year. His heart, we think. But come, I never tire of seeing Amadeo's frescoes."

Their feet echoing across the marble, they walked to the center of the vast cathedral. Light from the morning sun burst through the starburst stained-glass window high above the chancel, casting brilliant colors over Michelangelo's statue of *Christ Rising*.

She raised her eyes to the three frescoes beyond that had caused so much trouble.

The first depicted Christ's birth. The second showed him preaching to the crowds during the Sermon on the Mount. And the last was Christ on the cross, with the sky darkening, the centurion fearful, Mary weeping, and the Apostles kneeling.

Bishop Ferata, now an old man, hobbled over. "They seem to belong there, don't they?"

"They do, bishop." She smiled. "And these haven't blackened, have they?"

"No. It was as if God himself wanted them here. We should have listened to your husband."

In the year following the events in the piazza, an unusual black mold had spread across the surfaces of all three frescoes of Mary. Cardinal Gonzaga had ordered the plaster scraped off and the scenes repainted.

But a year later, the mold returned even worse than before.

Finally, after mold destroyed the third repainting, and after Gonzaga had died of a stroke, Bishop Ferata commissioned Amadeo himself to paint the frescoes according to his original plan.

Today, Amadeo's scenes of Christ were as bright, alive, and inspiring as the day he finished them five years ago.

"I'll leave you to your prayers." Ferata shuffled across the floor toward the Chapel of Martyrs, where a sputtering candle dripped wax onto the floor.

"I wish I could have returned sooner." Skender waved toward the funeral plaques. "I miss him."

"As do I. But I have no regrets. We had a good life together at Fair Fields before we moved to Florence."

"That's when I lost track of you. I returned to Colpena once on business, but had no time to stop in Fair Fields."

"At that point, he'd given up being capomaestro, saying he was too old to climb the high scaffolding anymore. Instead, he painted scenes in Florence's town hall, in Santa Maria Novella, and in other churches. He also did portraits. And these frescoes."

"But now you're living here in Colpena?"

"It's where I grew up. We kept my father's palazzo, and the renters have recently moved out. My father was a rich man, Skender." She gazed at the gold trim on his velvet cloak. "You haven't done too badly yourself."

He smiled. "Skender, the rich merchant. Who would have thought?"

Bishop Ferata returned to their side. "It does me good to see you again, Simona Mancini. And you, too, Skender."

"I've decided to stay in the city. So you'll be seeing more of me."

He smiled. "Your presence in the Cattedrale della Beata San Maria will only bring joy and light to our body."

"But, bishop"—she whirled to face him—"none of the people ever call the duomo by that name. Didn't you know?"

"They don't?" His brows creased.

"No. Even after all these years, the only name for this duomo I've ever heard on the people's lips is the Cattedrale del Figlio sul Mare."

Behind the bishop, a wide smile spread across Skender's face.

Simona couldn't help but smile back.

AUTHOR'S NOTES

What part of this novel, the reader might ask, is fiction and what part fact? Here are a few notes on that subject.

Colpena

For some months, I was in a quandary about where to locate the fictional city of Colpena. The location had to be near Florence. It also had to be unoccupied for a span of about three hundred years, as I didn't want to distort anyone's cherished local history—or at least much of it.

In June 2018, on my two-week research trip through Italy, I considered Grosetto and Tarquinia. But after sitting in a hotel room in Tarquinia, I knew Colpena didn't belong there. Besides, it wasn't in Tuscany. An internet search led me to a promontory of land several miles north. The next morning, I checked out of my hotel and drove about an hour to Ansedonia.

Built upon the ruins of an ancient Etruscan town and then a Roman settlement called Cosa, Ansedonia is a beautiful headlands sticking out into the ocean. Surrounded by the blue waters of the Tyrrhenian Sea, with the island of Monte Argentario to the north, it's really one big hill. Hundreds of expensive vacation villas now line its slopes, hiding behind gated drives, swallowed by lush vegetation. Its major attraction for the traveler is the ruins of Cosa, called "the flagship of American archaeology in Italy."

I parked and walked up the dusty road past the ancient Roman walls. At the top, I paid admittance to the museum and ruins. Archaeological excavations have been going on at Cosa since 1948, with students from Florida State University now digging there. On my one-day visit, I was fortunate to be able to interview three of those students and the director of the site, gleaning what information I could.

From them I learned that:

- Montemerano was the nearest quarry, but the Romans had depleted it.

- There are abundant forests nearby, enough to build a duomo.
- In the thirteenth through fifteenth century, the place held no significant settlements.
- All the earlier Cosa settlements relied on cisterns for their water; access to water was always a problem in Cosa.

In my exploration of the ruins, I was also impressed by the incessant droning of the cicadas, by the swallows, and by the beauty of this seaside headlands.

After the Sienese destroyed an earlier outpost around 1300—a true event—my fictional history has Dario Rossi's great-grandfather establishing the first Florentine settlement. To build the city of Colpena, my fictional settlers long ago scavenged the Roman ruins for building material. Thus, the ruins of ancient Cosa now being excavated don't factor into this story.

I also chose to enlarge the headland's diameter by about a mile, giving Colpena a bit of a flatter top, with more room for palazzos and a duomo. Colpena's walls also encompass the entire promontory, not just the top of the hill, as was the case with Cosa.

Otherwise, the geography, flora, fauna, and surrounding environs are the same.

For more information on the current Cosa dig and pictures of the excavation site and promontory, see: http://www.cosaexcavations.org

The culture and political structure of Colpena mirror that of Florence, its founding city and greatest ally. Both have a ruling Signoria, a gonfaloniere, and a council of influential merchants—for Colpena, it's the Council of Thirty—with whom they confer. At the peak of its power in the fifteenth century, Florence is able to protect Colpena from designs by its archrival, Siena.

Florence

All the major events in this book that occur in Florence and Tuscany are true to history, including:

- Lorenzo de' Medici's wedding celebration
- The Carrara marble quarry, another site well worth the visit

- Lorenzo's sculpture garden in San Marco and the bottega run by Bertoldo di Giovanni
- The details of the assassination attempt on Lorenzo's life, supported by Pope Sixtus IV
- The subsequent chaos that spread throughout Tuscany
- The war with Naples, backed by Sixtus, a contentious and warring pope
- Lorenzo's brave solo trip to King Ferrante of Naples, where he secured peace
- The unfortunate sacking and pillage of Volterra by Lorenzo's condottiere
- Savonarola's rise and fall
- The death of Lorenzo and the brief rule of his ill-fated son, Piero
- The French army's invasion of Italy, its capture of Colle, and its wintering in Siena

Lorenzo de' Medici

I have tried to portray Lorenzo's complicated nature as historians have painted him. This founder of the Renaissance would often swing from deep reflection to wild abandon. One moment he'd be discussing poetry and life with the great artists of the day, while in the next, he was attending orgies. My reading of Lorenzo de' Medici's dichotomous and contradictory nature actually helped crystallize this novel's plot. I also found that historians are not in agreement on many details of the events of his life.

The Inquisition

In this story, Emilio Gonzaga was a fictional cardinal imported from Spain because of his brother's marriage to Italian nobility. Thus, he would have closely followed the Spanish Inquisition that started in his homeland around 1478 and intensified around 1502. The Italian Inquisition didn't actually begin until a hundred years later in the second half of the sixteenth century. In this novel, Gonzaga only brings a preview of the Church's reign of terror into Italy before the arrival of the real thing. The Inquisition is one of the most egregious examples of how far sinful mankind and the medieval Church strayed from the teachings of Christ and the Apostles.

Alum

The Papal States did have an alum mine at Tolfa, and it did not peter out as it does in this story. Here, the papal mine declines just in time to allow Dario Rossi's acquisition of his own mine, providing Colpena with a rich income source for many years. Please forgive this minor rewriting of history for the sake of plot. The alum discovered near Volterra and the subsequent disaster that Lorenzo's condottiere inflicted on that town after it surrendered is true.

Who Was Fictional?

- All of the builders, artists, and workers on Colpena's duomo, with the obvious exception of Michelangelo
- Baron Calabrese and his castle
- Basilio Bramante—In this story, he's the fictional half-brother of the real Donato Bramante of Urbino, who was eventually commissioned to finish St. Peter's Basilica in Rome. Basilio shares Donato's character in that both never seemed to finish their work. Due to Donato's shoddy work and with no end to the construction in sight, Michelangelo eventually replaced him as the capomaestro in charge of building St. Peter's Basilica.

On The Bachelorhood Of Renaissance Artists

Until the epilogue, Amadeo Puccini holds fast to his vow of celibacy and bachelorhood. Bachelorhood, but not celibacy, was, indeed, typical for the artists and architects of the period.

Although he had occasional affairs with women, Michelangelo's first love was to his sculpture and his work. Poliziano, the one-time cleric turned Renaissance poet and friend of Lorenzo de' Medici, was also a bachelor. We see this same tendency toward the unattached life for: the Renaissance philosopher Pico dell Mirandola; Filippo Brunelleschi, the architect of the great dome of the cathedral of Santa Maria del Fiore in Florence; Donatello, the Renaissance sculptor who created the first, freestanding bronze statue since ancient Rome; and Donato Bramante, builder of several churches and the architect whose work on St. Peter's Basilica in Rome Michelangelo finally took over and finished. The quintessential Renaissance man, Leon Battista Alberti, was also a bachelor.

So devoted to their art were these men that they had little room for permanent attachments and so chose bachelorhood. But unlike Amadeo, most had frequent sexual liaisons. And in the often hedonistic atmosphere that was Florence in the fifteenth century, some of their affairs were not confined to women. Thus did Savonarola rail against the wanton, unrestrained sexual lifestyles of the day.

On Cathedrals and the Idea for This Book

After my second two-week trip to Italy, I have now visited cathedrals and churches in Rome, Venice, Florence, Orvieto, Luca, Pisa, Siena, and Montepulciano. I never ceased to be amazed by these wonders of ancient architecture that became the main centers for medieval art, architecture, politics, commerce, and religion. Although a Protestant, I attended mass in the Pisan and Sienese duomos, where every seat was taken—half with tourists like myself. I've visited other Italian churches and cathedrals—all great physical monuments to God—that were filled with a bare handful of parishioners on a Sunday.

Seeing Siena's cathedral on my first trip to Italy with my wife in 2015 is what gave me the idea for this story. Although of Gothic design, Siena's is possibly the most beautiful cathedral in Italy.

While visiting that duomo, I read something like this: "The cathedral builder must be a man of exceptional piety and righteousness."

That, dear readers, is the phrase that sparked the idea for the novel that I wrote three years later, proving that you just never know what's going to happen when you travel.

MARK'S BOOKS

Christian Fiction:
The Bonfires Of Beltane: Following St. Patrick Across Ancient, Celtic Ireland
The Medallion: An Epic Quest In A.D. 486
The Slaves Of Autumn: A Tale Of Stolen Love In Ancient, Celtic Ireland

General Market Fiction:
Death Of The Master Builder: Love, Envy, and The Struggle To Raise The Greatest Cathedral Of The Italian Renaissance

Days of the Apocalypse, A Series of Christian End-Times Thrillers:
Book 1, *The Day They Vanished* (coming soon)

To learn about Mark's other books, including his young
adult fantasy, please visit:
www.MarkFisherAuthor.com

GLOSSARY

- Apse—A semicircular recess covered with a hemispherical vault or half a dome. An apse usually terminates the building above the chancel. Other apses may exist elsewhere in the building.
- Arcades—The narrow aisles in a cathedral formed by the columns on either side of the nave and the transepts.
- Bardiglio [Bar-DEE-lee-oh]—A medium-hard, gray or blue marble, often streaked.
- Bays—Small enclosures along the sides of the arcades often devoted to frescoes, paintings of biblical events, or saints.
- Beretta—A soft cap like a beret worn by men.
- Bottega [Bo-TAY-gah]—A group of artisans, regularly assembling in a studio, who follow a particular master artisan, sculptor, painter, or craftsman. Or the studio where they meet.
- Calze [CALL-tze]—Long stockings worn by men.
- Campanile—A bell tower.
- Capomaestro—Master builder.
- Chancel—The space around the altar, including the choir and sanctuary.
- Cioppa [chee-OP-pah]—A man's overcoat with a lining different in color from the outer fabric.
- Clerestory—A window-lined row on the top level of a cathedral's walls to let in light and sometimes air.
- Contadino—(contadini, *pl.*) A peasant, farmworker, or farmer.
- Duomo—Italian for "cathedral".
- Gamurra—A long gown worn by Italian women.
- Giornea—For men, this was a closely fitted, pleated overcoat with wide, puffy sleeves, sometimes with brocade. For women, the giornea was a belted dress, tight at the waist, pleated, reaching to the ground and covering the feet.
- Gonfaloniere [Gon-fall-OHN-ee-AYR-ay]—The elected leader of the Signoria.

- Nave—The central aisle and usually the longest part of a church or cathedral, where the congregation sits.
- Padrone [Pa-DRON-Ay]—Patron.
- Palazzo—A palace.
- Pediment—A triangular gable at the top of the façade or sidewall that rests on the columns.
- Piazza—A town square.
- Piazzetta—A small town square.
- Pilaster—A rectangular column partially projecting from the wall for decoration, not support.
- Primero—A Renaissance card game.
- Quintana––The small narrow spaces that separated houses, once required by law to prevent fires.
- Scalpellini—Stonecutters.
- Signore [See-NYOR-ay]—(signiori, *pl*) "Sir"
- Signorina [See-nyor-EE-na]—"Miss"
- Signora [See-NYOR-ah]—"Missus"
- Signoria [See-NYOR-ee-ah]—The ruling council of Colpena, with seven sitting members chosen by the Signoria itself from the wealthiest, most powerful merchants and businessmen of the city.
- Stinche—Florence's prison.
- Transept—The transverse parts of a church or duomo that lie across the nave to form a traditional cross-shaped building.
- Woad—Yellow-flowered plant of the cabbage family and the source of a blue dye.